INTENT
TO HARM

Books by Jonnie Jacobs

Kali O'Brien Novels of Legal Suspense

SHADOW OF DOUBT
EVIDENCE OF GUILT
MOTION TO DISMISS
WITNESS FOR THE DEFENSE
COLD JUSTICE
INTENT TO HARM

The Kate Austen Mysteries

MURDER AMONG NEIGHBORS
MURDER AMONG FRIENDS
MURDER AMONG US
MURDER AMONG STRANGERS

Published by Kensington Publishing Corporation

INTENT
TO HARM

JONNIE JACOBS

KENSINGTON BOOKS
http://www.kensingtonbooks.com

KENSINGTON BOOKS are published by

Kensington Publishing Corp.
850 Third Avenue
New York, NY 10022

Library of Congress Card Catalogue Number: 2003103718
ISBN 1-57566-829-7

First Printing: October 2003
10 9 8 7 6 5 4 3 2 1

Printed in the United States of America

INTENT
TO HARM

CHAPTER 1

The blue Toyota turned off Highway 89 along the western shore of Lake Tahoe and into Ponderosa Pines Park. The driver, a round-shouldered woman in her late fifties, clenched the steering wheel tightly with both hands. She drove slowly down the narrow entrance road to the small, wooded parking lot, then turned and just as slowly retraced her path to the highway.

She hadn't been to the area in several years and she'd worried the spot where she'd set the meeting might no longer be functional. She was relieved to find that despite minor changes in the layout of rest rooms and picnic tables, the camping area was basically unchanged. The parking lot was exactly where it had been and easily accessible by the route she'd described.

The meeting wasn't for another hour yet. Time enough to tweak her story if she wanted to. She'd intentionally left the photo at home, but now she wondered if it might not have been better to start there. It wasn't that she was tempted to alter the facts, such as they were. It was really more a question of just how much to divulge.

No matter what, she didn't want to make things worse.

For any of them.

She eased the car across the highway and into a pullout near the lake. She could wait out the hour there surrounded by the beauty of the Sierra. Not that the majestic mountains and glistening lake would quiet the churning inside her. She took a deep breath, then another, fighting the nervousness. But she'd been nervous for weeks now. The fingernails bitten to the quick were proof of that.

She'd taken precautions. She could only hope they were enough. For today, she was simply Betty. No ID, a borrowed car. She'd even considered wearing a wig before deciding that was going a bit far. Even if the lawyer didn't want to help, or couldn't, it stretched the imagination to think she'd make an effort to track Betty down.

Still, there was a lot at stake. And a lot she didn't understand. She worried that once she started asking questions, there'd be no turning back. She'd lose everything.

She thought again of the photo. The way her heart had raced and her skin had gone clammy when she'd stumbled across it while looking through a magazine at Gail's several weeks ago.

Why hadn't she simply left well enough alone?

It wasn't too late, she reminded herself. She could head home and forget she'd ever made the appointment.

Except, it really was too late. You couldn't forget what you knew.

Across the highway in the forest behind the park's central lot, a burly man in a heavy denim jacket was also waiting. Turning back never crossed his mind. This was a job like any other. Only it paid better.

The man pulled the hat low over his forehead and slipped the binoculars back into his pack. He took out his gun and checked the clip, then slipped it into his waistband. He hoped they'd be out in the open where he could pick up the conversation easily. But he was prepared in case they weren't.

The air was cool, especially in the shade where he'd positioned himself behind a cluster of pines. He'd been there an hour already and his muscles were getting stiff. He rolled his shoulders, stretched his legs, flexed his fingers. It felt good to move. He needed to be quick and limber when the time came.

He checked his watch. An hour to go.

CHAPTER 2

Seated in her cousin's kitchen overlooking the lake, Kali sipped her coffee and offered silent thanks for the phone call that had prompted her trip to Tahoe on such a glorious day.

The May sky was clear, the water smooth as glass. Although the surrounding mountains were still marbled with snow, here at lake level only sparse patches remained. Aspen shimmered with newly minted green, flowers lifted their heads hopefully toward the sun, and the Truckee River swelled with spring melt. Perhaps best of all, the area was blessedly uncongested. With the hordes of winter skiers long gone (although a handful of diehards continued to hit the one open lift at Squaw Valley) and the bustle of summer vacationers holding off until school was out in June, the timing couldn't have been better.

If only she knew what the meeting was about. But the woman who'd called had been amazingly tight-lipped. She'd fill Kali in when they met, she explained.

"More coffee?" Helen asked. She was older than Kali by five years, with dark hair and fair skin. She'd been a beauty when they were younger and was still a striking woman.

"Just a touch." Kali held out her mug while Helen poured. "Thanks."

"I'm so glad you told me you were coming. It's been over a year since you were last here."

"Two years ago this Fourth of July, I think. Tyler had just gotten braces." Despite the exchange of cards at Christmas and the more frequent, if sporadic, communication by E-mail, neither of them had managed a visit since then. But when her mysterious new client had requested they meet at a location not far from Helen's Tahoe City home, Kali had seized the opportunity to spend some time catching up.

"So what time is this appointment of yours?" Helen asked. "You'll be back for dinner, won't you?"

"Absolutely. We'll eat out. My treat."

"Don't be silly. I'm looking forward to cooking for an appreciative audience for a change."

"Your son doesn't like your cooking?"

Helen laughed. "He likes it fine as long as it's meat, and the only vegetable I serve is potato. When do you think you'll be back?"

"I'm meeting her at four. I can't imagine I'll be more than an hour."

"Who is it? Or can't you say?"

"I don't know," Kali said truthfully.

Client confidentiality would have prevented Kali from saying even if she'd known, but she didn't. The woman had given only her first name, Betty.

Helen frowned. "How can you represent someone if you don't know who she is?"

"It's complicated." And highly unusual. "She wouldn't even say what it was about."

"Yet you came all the way up here to meet her?"

"I know it doesn't make much sense. But there was something in her manner, an urgency I had trouble ignoring. Besides, she's paying for my time and I can't afford to say no to a potential client right now."

Kali had recently returned to private practice following a special assignment with the District Attorney's office. She'd been planning on sharing an office and a single employee with an old law school classmate, Nina Barrett. But between chronic illness and a new baby, Nina had decided that the demands of a career were too great. Kali had taken over Nina's office lease, a few of her clients, and sole responsibility for their associate, Jared Takahashi-Jackson. Kali wasn't in any position to be picky about the work she took on.

"Still, it seems strange she'd call someone from out of the area," Helen said.

"I think she did that intentionally. She seemed nervous about contacting an attorney. Nervous that she might be found out, I mean."

"What do you mean, 'found out?' Like an ugly divorce?"

"Maybe." Although Kali's sense was that it was something different. The woman had questioned Kali intensely about confidentiality and attorney–client privilege, then insisted on sending a retainer before their meeting so privilege would attach. She'd sent five thousand dollars, twice the amount Kali had asked for, and she'd sent it in the form of a non-traceable money order.

"Well, you'll know soon enough," Helen said.

Just then, a short, Hispanic-looking woman appeared at the kitchen doorway. "So sorry to bother you, Mrs. Helen. But the vacuum, she is making a funny noise."

"Doesn't surprise me," Helen replied. "Tyler has decided it's easier to vacuum the hamster's cage than empty it." She turned to Kali. "Maria is Ramon's mother. You remember Ramon, don't you? He's the one who rescued Tyler when he hit his head jumping into the lake."

Kali nodded. An afternoon of summer fun five years ago that had spun to near tragedy. She had no trouble remembering the blood, the seemingly lifeless form of a boy too long under water, the confusion of the emergency room. Her memory of Ramon was vaguer. Thin and quiet, as she recalled, and quite a bit older than Tyler.

"Pleased to meet you," she said to Maria.

"Kali is my cousin," Helen explained to her housekeeper. "A famous attorney from the Bay Area."

Kali rolled her eyes. Notorious in some circles, perhaps. But hardly famous.

Maria smiled. "Like on TV, no? I watch about lawyers."

Helen pushed back her chair and addressed Kali. "Sorry about this. I'll only be a minute."

"I need to get going anyway. But count me in for dinner. I'll call if I'm going to be later than six."

In her eleven years as an attorney, Kali had met with clients in some unusual spots. Jail, of course, and everything from hospitals to hot tubs, but she couldn't recall a time she'd done an initial client interview in a park. Ponderosa Pines, popular for camping in summer and cross-country skiing in winter, was largely deserted during the off seasons. Kali could only assume that was why the mysterious Betty had chosen it as the place for their meeting.

Kali allowed herself extra time for the drive in case the directions hadn't been as clear as they seemed, but she found the spot easily. Though there was plenty of traffic on the highway, she'd passed no one since turning into the park. And hers was the only car in the lot. A shiver of trepidation ran down Kali's spine. Should she have insisted on a meeting place that was less isolated?

Well, there was nothing she could do about that now. She checked her purse for pepper spray. The can was still there, right next to her cell phone. And if Betty looked at all threatening, Kali would drive off without getting out of the car. The woman certainly hadn't *sounded* threatening.

Fifteen minutes to kill. Kali turned the radio on to a soft rock station out of Reno, one of the few stations she was able to pick up in the mountains. Then she leaned back and let her mind dwell on the possible reasons for Betty's secrecy.

Divorce, as Helen had suggested. Especially if there were tricky child custody issues involved. But Kali thought it was more likely a criminal matter. She couldn't decide, however, if it was her client who was in trouble, or if the woman was worried about someone else. When Kali had tried pressing her, Betty had mumbled something about having faith, then hung up abruptly.

Well, she'd know what it was about soon enough now. The prospect of a new case, especially one that had potential of being intricate and challenging, pleased her.

Kali watched as two squirrels chased each other around the base of a pine tree then scampered off into the woods. Kali liked the out-of-doors, far better, in truth, than she liked cities and crowds. On any other occasion, she'd be basking in the tranquillity of the setting. Today, she was acutely aware of the tension in her shoulders and chest. And inside her head, which felt as though it might burst for all the whirling.

As the radio switched from music to news at the top of the hour, Kali heard the crunch of tires on gravel. She turned to see a blue Toyota with a bent rear bumper pull into the lot and park in the row of spaces behind her. A woman got out of the driver's side, then leaned in again to retrieve a sweater, which she slipped on. She appeared to be in her early sixties, stocky, and heavily grayed. More grandmotherly than guilty. Although Kali knew criminal behavior defied stereotypes, she felt the tension ease.

The woman looked toward Kali, shielding her eyes with her hands. Kali stepped out of her car and started across the parking lot.

"You must be Betty."

The woman nodded.

Kali put out her hand. "I'm Kali O'Brien."

"Thank you for meeting me here. I know it must have seemed like a strange request." She was soft-spoken and her voice quavered slightly.

"Somewhat unusual, I admit. But I'm always happy for a reason to come to Tahoe. I'm curious, though, why you called me rather than a local attorney."

The woman fingered the top button of her sweater. "I wanted to be . . . discreet, I guess. I mean, after I explain everything, and depending on what you tell me, well . . . Our conversation today may be the end of it."

It wasn't really an answer, but Kali understood. The woman didn't want whatever story she was going to tell getting back to the wrong people. Nor did she want Kali connecting it with her true identity, which was why she'd given Kali only a first name and no contact information. And that was how things would remain unless today's conversation presented options the woman was comfortable with.

"I saw your name in the paper," Betty added. "It was that horrible thing a couple of months ago with the Bayside Strangler."

Whatever Betty wanted to see her about, Kali hoped it was nothing like the Strangler case. "Why don't we sit over there, at one of the picnic tables in the sun," she suggested, trying to sound reassuring. "You can tell me what's on your mind and we'll take it from there."

"I feel better already, just meeting you." Betty offered a fleeting smile but avoided making eye contact. "I hope you can help."

"I hope I can, too."

Hands in her sweater pockets, Betty moved toward the picnic area. "I'm not sure where to begin."

"Wherever you'd like."

In the woods behind them, Kali heard the snap of a branch followed by two soft cracks. As she turned toward the sound, she felt a rush of air, as if a bird had brushed against her skin.

She heard Betty suck in her breath sharply and then groan. Kali spun around in time to see the woman slump to the ground. Betty's mouth was open, as if literally caught speechless, and her eyes were wide with fright. A red stain was already spreading across her chest.

Kali froze in numbed horror.

For a moment, there was no sound anywhere. Even nature seemed to be holding her breath. The birds were quiet, the air still. She dropped to her knees to check on her companion.

Another crack broke the silence.

She felt a stab of heat at her left shoulder and gripped the spot with her hand. It felt warm and sticky. When she pulled her hand free, she saw blood.

When her brain engaged again, Kali found herself huddled behind the blue Toyota, gripping her cell phone tightly in her bloodied hand. Let there be a signal, she prayed. Please let there be a signal.

Fingers trembling, she punched in 9-1-1. With one ear she listened for the approach of footsteps; with the other she waited for the call to connect. Her shoulder burned with fiery heat but the rest of her was ice-cold.

Wind whistled through the trees. A crow squawked overhead. From her spot behind the car, all Kali could see of Betty was her feet. One of her black loafers had come loose at the heel and Kali was overcome with the irrational urge to set it right. For a while, she half thought she'd crawled to Betty and straightened the shoe.

The phone gave off a spurt of static. "Hello," Kali said. "Can you hear me?"

More static.

She felt as though the ground beneath her were spinning. She closed her eyes. It only made things worse.

"Please. Please. We need help."

Her whole body throbbed. The pain started in her shoulder and radiated down her arm, across her back and chest. She could feel it all the way down to her toes. So hot, so gripping it threatened to consume her.

"Is anyone *there*?" In her head, her words rang desperate and shrill. But to her ear, the volume was so soft she couldn't be sure she'd spoken out loud.

Another shot rang out.

Kali tried squeezing herself beneath the car, but found it impossible. Every movement sent another piercing stab of pain through her body.

She heard the crunch of boots on pavement. Caught a glimpse of movement out of the corner of her eye.

"You might as well come out, bitch. You can't hide."

The sun slipped behind a cloud and the day darkened. Kali squinted, looked up. The sky was clear and cloudless.

Why was everything suddenly so pale?

When she glanced again at Betty's feet, it was like looking through the wrong end of binoculars. They were small, and very, very far away. Growing smaller and farther all the time.

The boots again. Closer.

Crunch. Pause. *Crunch.*

Somewhere in the distance, the hum of an engine.

The ground beneath her began to spin. Kali closed her eyes and pressed her forehead against the metal of the car door, focusing all of her attention on the spot where her flesh connected with solid reality.

"Ponderosa Pines," she whispered into the phone. "A shooting. He's going to kill me."

The phone slid from her hand. Kali couldn't remember whether she'd spoken her final plea aloud, or only imagined it.

CHAPTER 3

It was one hell of a hangover, Kali thought. Until she opened her eyes a crack and looked up into a sea of faces and flashing red lights. Consciousness rolled through her.

The park. Betty. The man with the gun.

She tried to sit up but there was a strap across her chest holding her down.

"Where's Betty?" The words slurred.

She was surrounded by people in blue. The one hovering closest, to whom she'd addressed her comment, was a paramedic, she decided. Either that or a Boy Scout. He looked about thirteen. He ignored her and slipped an IV needle smoothly into her inner arm.

"I'm o-k-kay," Kali insisted. Her throat was so dry it hurt to talk. "I just need to rest."

"You've been shot, lady."

A young woman, also in blue, was poking at Kali's shoulder. It felt like she was scrubbing it with gravel.

"I have to call my c-cousin," Kali said, forcing the words through lips that refused to cooperate. "She's expecting me . . ."

"You can call from the hospital," the baby-faced young man replied.

"I told you, I don't need—"

The female paramedic put pressure on Kali's arm. A crushing crescendo of pain overtook her. Spots danced before her eyes. Suddenly, a hospital didn't seem like such a bad idea.

Kali's body was shaking, even though she felt hot. She took a deep breath and tried to keep her mind focused. "What about B-Betty? Is she . . . okay?"

A different face moved into view. Older and sterner, though not unkind. His shirt was a different blue, with a deputy's badge. "The other woman who was shot, you know her?"

Kali didn't have the energy to explain. She opted for short and easy. "Yes."

"You say her name is Betty?"

Kali nodded, though she was shivering so badly she wasn't sure the deputy would notice.

"Last name?"

"S-s-sorry."

"Do you know where she lives?"

Kali shook her head.

The deputy gave her a funny look. "Not much of a friend, was she?"

"I didn't s-s-say she was a fr-fr-friend." Kali closed her eyes. It took too much effort to keep them open.

"How did you happen to—"

The female paramedic cut him off. "Her blood pressure is dropping. You'll have to save the questions for later."

The sounds around her became one, covering her like a blanket. Voices, sirens, the slamming of doors. And then a flurry of new voices. But they, too, faded.

Kali woke with a start. The room was unfamiliar. Beige walls, Formica-topped table, a curtained divider. The window next to her bed was pitch black. She closed her eyes and opened them again. Helen was seated beside her, thumbing through a magazine. For a moment Kali was confused.

She had foggy memories of a parade of uniforms. First the dark blue, insignia-emblazoned shirts of paramedics and law enforcement. Then the crisp whites and rumpled greens of hospital personnel. All of them efficient and focused. She'd been dimly aware of being transported here—wherever she was—but pain and shivering had so consumed her, she hadn't been fully aware.

Now the pain was mostly gone. As was the shivering and shaking. She felt spent, as though she'd been dragged through a knothole, but by and large comfortable.

Helen raised her eyes. "Kali? You're awake?" She put the magazine down and stood beside the bed, taking Kali's good hand in her own. "Thank God, you're okay. How are you feeling?"

Kali tried to speak. Her mouth felt as dry as cotton. She licked her lips, which didn't help much, and croaked, "Okay."

She tried reaching for the pitcher of water on the bedside table, and found she couldn't move her left arm. What's more, sharp pain raised its ugly head the moment she tried.

"Let me do that," Helen said. She poured water into a glass, peeled back the paper from a straw, and held it to Kali's lips.

The water was tepid but tasted better than anything she could remember.

"I expect you *should* feel okay, given the painkillers they have you on." Helen set the glass back on the bedside table. "Let me know when you're ready for more."

Kali murmured her thanks. Slowly, her head was clearing.

"They want to keep you here overnight, which is actually a good thing because they'll probably send you home with nothing but a prescription for Vicodin. Right now you need something stronger."

Helen barely paused for a breath. "Not that I meant home, home. But home away as opposed to the hospital. You'll stay with us, of course, until you're well." She patted Kali's hand, then squeezed it gently and didn't let go. "We don't get many gunshot wounds around here, but they seem to know what they're doing. Though of course, if you'd feel better calling your own doctor—"

"Helen, would you stop babbling?" Kali managed a smile. This was something of a standing joke between them. When Helen was nervous, she talked. That was the circumstance when Kali was most quiet.

"Sorry, it's just that . . ." Helen bit her lower lip. "I've been so worried about you. I get a phone call out of the blue. I'm expecting it to be you apologizing for being late for dinner, and instead it's the sheriff asking if I know you. Then he tells me you've been shot. Nothing about how you're doing, whether you'll live . . ." She reached for a tissue and wiped her eyes.

"How'd he get your name?" Kali asked.

"You apparently told him. Over and over."

"Made a nuisance of myself, did I?"

Helen blew her nose and smiled. "Let's just say you got your point across." She was silent a moment. "He asked me about the other woman, too."

"Betty?" Kali was afraid to ask.

Helen hesitated. "She died, Kali. She was already gone when the ambulance got there."

The weight of Helen's words landed like lead on Kali's chest. She felt her eyes tear up.

"I'm so sorry, Kali."

"It's not like I really knew her or anything, but . . ."

"But you were there," Helen pointed out. "You saw it. You could have been killed, too."

Suddenly the pall of fear pushed aside everything else. "He didn't hit anything vital, did he?" Kali wiggled her toes to make sure they were still there, visually checked the form of her body under the bedcovers.

"Just your shoulder. Another few inches though . . ."

Kali remembered stepping forward and dropping to her knees just as the bullet grazed her shoulder. Had those few inches of lucky movement saved her life?

"What happened out there anyway?" Helen asked.

"I'm not sure. I'd just introduced myself to Betty. We were still in the parking lot. Then all of a sudden there were shots, only I didn't realize at the time that's what they were."

"The deputy has been itching to talk to you. And he's been pressing me for what I knew. I told him you were an attorney, meeting the other woman but that you didn't know her. I hope that was okay. He was persistent."

"That's fine." Kali saw no reason not to cooperate fully.

As if on cue, a broad-faced man dressed in official blue stepped into the room.

Helen nodded. "Good evening, Deputy Bauman."

"Hello, Mrs. Gibson. And hello to you, too, Ms. O'Brien. I'm glad to see you're doing so well." He was close to fifty, with close-cropped hair and finely wrinkled skin. Attractive in an outdoorsy way. He had the serious, almost grim look of so many people in law enforcement, but his eyes were kind.

"You up to answering a few questions?" he asked.

Kali suspected the questions would come whether she was up to it or not.

In fact, Bauman didn't wait for her response before plunging ahead. "I understand you're an attorney from the Bay Area. It was a client you were with at the park, right?"

"Right."

"And yet you don't know anything about her?" Here his voice took on an overtone of skepticism.

"Only that her name was Betty. No last name. She was a new client. Prospective client, actually."

"Address or phone number?"

"Neither, I'm afraid. She sent a retainer in the form of a money order. The envelope was postmarked Truckee. That's all I know."

"You'd talked with her before today?"

"Only briefly."

Bauman stroked his jaw. "What did she need with an attorney?"

"She didn't say. All I know is that she was extremely interested in confidentiality. She kept asking about attorney–client privilege. But she never told me a thing. Have you contacted her family?"

"We don't even know who she is. She wasn't carrying any identification, and the car is registered in Nevada. We'll sort it out eventually, but I was hoping you'd be able to help." He regarded her for a moment, as though giving her the chance to reconsider. "Kind of unusual calling a Bay Area attorney and asking you to drive all the way up here without telling you what it's all about."

"Yes, it is."

"That didn't raise any questions in your mind?"

"It raised lots of questions, which is part of the reason I came. Believe me, Deputy Bauman, if I knew more, I'd tell you."

He frowned, pulling his bushy eyebrows tight into a single line across his forehead. "Why don't you tell me what you *do* know, starting with what happened this afternoon."

The chain of events had already blurred in Kali's mind but she described them as best she could. She felt cold fear descend anew as she stirred the memories.

"Did you see anyone?" Bauman asked.

"No, I—wait. I didn't actually notice anyone, but I vaguely re-call seeing a flash of movement in the woods."

"Movement?"

"My impression was of someone big. Tall and broad. And heavy boots." She remembered the crunch of shoes on gravel.

"Could you identify him if you saw him again?"

"No. I'm not even sure I saw anyone. It could just be my imag-ination playing tricks. I didn't remember until you asked."

Bauman rocked forward on his toes. "Do you have any idea who the killer might be?"

"Why would I?"

"Ex-husband, jealous boyfriend, angry client. Is there anyone like that in your life?"

"No, not at all." The question had taken her by surprise. He didn't think that she was the target, did he?

Bauman hesitated a moment, as if he was about to speak, then apparently changed his mind. He pulled a business card from his pocket and started to hand it to Kali, then set it on the bedside table instead. "I'll be back tomorrow to take a formal statement. In the meantime, you think of anything else, give me a call right away."

Kali nodded. She was already probing her mind for clues.

"You were damn lucky today," Bauman said. "You want to see that it stays that way. I suspect he'd have finished you off, too, if someone else hadn't driven up just then."

"Who was it?"

"A man from the sanitation department. Conditions permit-ting, the park opens for camping on Memorial Day."

"Did he get a glimpse of the killer?"

"Afraid not."

The deputy had no sooner left than Helen reached for her jacket. "I'd better let you get some sleep. I'll come back in the morning and stay until they release you."

"Thanks, Helen."

Helen leaned over and pressed her cheek against Kali's fore-head. "You take care, now."

It was only when Helen had gone and the nurse had again checked her over, and Kali was alone in a darkened room with even darker thoughts, that the full impact of all that had happened hit her. Her client had been killed. Kali, herself, had been shot. But for the grace of whatever god was on duty that afternoon, she might also have been killed. And now Bauman had raised the specter of a killer who'd been after her all along. Might still be after her.

Despite a heavy dose of medication, it took her a long time to fall asleep.

Helen showed up the next morning as Kali was poking at her breakfast tray. Even in her state of drug-induced complacency, she found the food unappealing. A scoop of lumpy scrambled eggs, toast made of thin, barely browned, white bread, orange-flavored sugar water masquerading as orange juice, a bowl of prunes, and coffee so vile even the smell was off-putting. The prunes were the best of the lot.

"Help yourself," Kali offered.

Helen laughed. "No thanks. Eat up, though. Deputy Bauman is on his way. I saw him downstairs."

"I don't know anything more than I knew yesterday."

The deputy arrived only minutes behind Helen. "How are you feeling this morning?"

"Pretty good, all things considered." She was alive. That counted for a lot.

"The name Trudy Barber mean anything to you?" he asked.

"Afraid not."

"How about Elizabeth Arnold?"

Kali shook her head. "Why? Who are they?"

"Elizabeth Arnold was your client. She went by Betty most of the time. A neighbor reported her missing last night and confirmed the identity this morning. Ms. Barber owns the car Mrs. Arnold was driving. They're friends, and apparently Mrs. Arnold sometimes borrows the car, though she usually asks first."

"This time she didn't?"

"Nope. Ms. Barber got off work, went to get into her car, and discovered it was gone. I guess Mrs. Arnold wasn't figuring on getting shot and thought she'd be back before her friend noticed."

Her client had a last name. And friends. "What do you know about her?" Kali asked.

"Lives in Reno. According to her friend she was the office manager at a cabinet shop there."

"Family?"

"A husband with Alzheimer's. He's in a care facility. No children. Haven't found any other family yet. We were hoping the name might mean something to you."

"I wish I could help."

Deputy Bauman hitched a thumb under his belt. "Who else besides your cousin here knew you were meeting a client at Ponderosa Pines?"

"The attorney I work with. I may have mentioned it to a few friends in passing. Certainly they knew I was coming to Tahoe for a few days." Kali's eyes narrowed. "Why are you asking? You don't really think the shooter was after *me*, do you?"

"I have no idea who he was after. But you're an attorney. I did some checking on you, you've handled some high-profile criminal cases. Seems to me there might be people out there you've managed to tick off big time."

"No," Kali said, "I really don't think that's it." But inside, she felt less certain.

"Just a thought. Mrs. Arnold doesn't appear to have any obvious enemies."

"It could have been random."

Deputy Bauman shook his head. "Doesn't strike me as likely, given the location."

It didn't strike Kali as likely, either, once she thought about it. What did stand out in her mind was the way Betty Arnold had made sure their meeting was shrouded in secrecy. Her client might not have obvious enemies, but the not so obvious ones were another matter.

CHAPTER 4

Sid Mertz hobbled from the elevator to the door of his penthouse apartment, making his way slowly with the awkward gait of a man unused to using a cane. He hated the damn thing. Hated using it. Hated how helpless it made him feel. Hated the way it was a constant reminder of his own vulnerability.

And his own stupidity.

To have survived as many treacherous, adrenaline-filled moments as he had only to be felled by his own stairway seemed the height of irony. And Sid was not a man who appreciated irony.

At least the cane was better than the wheelchair they'd tried to saddle him with. A hit man in a wheelchair. Now that took the cake.

He unlocked the apartment door and pushed it open just as the phone started ringing. Dropping the day's mail onto the nearest chair, he propelled himself forward so fast he was forced to grab hold of the doorjamb next to the phone to keep from falling on his face.

He yanked the receiver from the phone. "Hello?"

Silence.

"Hello?" Sid said again, more loudly. It had to be Hans. After the cryptic message the dumb lout had left yesterday afternoon, there'd been nothing further. This, despite Sid's repeated instructions to get in touch immediately.

"Who's there?" Sid demanded.

"Good day, is this Mr. Sidney Mertz? How are you today, sir? I'm with Pacific Fi—"

Sid slammed the phone into the cradle. Damn telemarketers.

The name was a dead giveaway, even if the false cheeriness hadn't been. Nobody called him by his given name but his mother and strangers who wanted to sell him something.

Damn Hans, too. The directions had been clear enough. Follow the women if necessary. But get the information and report back. The sooner the better. It didn't take a genius to understand something as simple as that.

Which was a good thing since Hans was anything but a genius. That was his strength as far as Sid was concerned—Hans didn't have brains enough to ask questions—but it was also a risk.

If it hadn't been for his busted leg, Sid would have handled the job himself. A job like this, it was more than just important. It was vital to his future. He couldn't use any of the regulars, either, or word might get back to Mr. D. Hans had been the best choice available, but not necessarily a *good* choice.

Sid poured himself a double Jack Daniel's and eased his weary bones onto the black leather sofa. It was lambskin, soft and welcoming. He might not be living in the grand manner he'd once hoped for—he rented an apartment rather than owning a house, he bought his clothes off the rack rather than having them custom tailored, and he only rarely treated himself to a hand-rolled Montecristo—but his life was a damn sight better than it might have been. The apartment had two bedrooms plus a den, a roomy living area with a high ceiling that made the place feel larger than it was. The main room looked out over the Bay Bridge, which was right there practically under his nose, and the towers of the Golden Gate Bridge peeked above the fog from the windows in the kitchen. The Financial District, where he worked, was only a short walk away.

His neighbors were professionals mostly. Quiet and busy with their own lives. Just the sort of environment Sid liked.

Sid considered himself a professional, too. An ex-marine, he'd long ago turned his talents for covert work into something the private sector would pay for. He had a small but dependable clientele for whom he provided executive security. The big guys, major banks and corporations, had their own internal security departments, but there were plenty of smaller companies, ranging from dot-coms to law firms, that relied on independent consultants.

Trouble was, even though the work was steady, it was monotonous. Like filling in as a lab tech when you'd been trained as a surgeon. And the money was strictly small potatoes. That's why Sid did jobs for Mr. D on the side. Mr. D was Sid's road to a comfortable life. Eleven years now. They were practically like family. Sid intended to hold onto his piece of the dream, no matter what it took.

He swirled the whiskey and inhaled the pungent aroma before taking a sip. For the first time, Sid allowed himself to wonder if something had gone wrong yesterday afternoon. If Hans had been picked up, Sid would have heard about it, wouldn't he? And if the women had met somewhere else? No, Sid had listened to the tape of the call himself. Ponderosa Pines Park. The main parking lot. The directions were clear.

He was stewing over the possibilities when the buzzer sounded. Sid pulled himself upright and limped to the intercom.

"Yes?"

"Mr. Mertz?" The voice was Hans's.

"Who else would it be in my apartment?"

"Just making sure. You said you wanted to see me when I got back into town."

When he got back into town. Like the trip to Tahoe had been a leisurely vacation instead of a time-sensitive job. And what about the phone call Hans was supposed to make?

That wasn't a discussion to have over the intercom, however.

Sid pressed the button to unlock the main floor entrance, then returned to his spot on the sofa and took another swig of Jack Daniel's. A few minutes later there was a knock on the apartment door.

"It's open," Sid bellowed.

Hans, wearing his usual insipid sneer, stepped inside and sprawled in the leather armchair as if he owned the place. His denim jacket was stained and his jeans looked like they hadn't been washed in weeks. But because of his youth—Hans hadn't yet turned thirty—and fair Aryan coloring, the look said *fashion statement* rather than *bum.*

"What took you so long?" Sid said.

Hans responded with a dazed expression, broken by a sheepish smile. "Sorry, I, uh, took a short detour into Reno."

"Reno!"

"Yeah, last night. Seeing as how I was so close, seemed a shame not to. I didn't think you'd care much if I came back yesterday or today."

Sid bit back an urge the throttle the guy. "So what happened?"

Hans gave him the thumbs-up. "Came out a couple hundred bucks ahead."

"I was asking about the job you were sent to do, dimwit, *not* your luck at the tables."

Hans stretched out a leg and started to drop it onto the coffee table until Sid barked at him. Instead, he crossed it over his knee.

"I killed her," Hans said, squaring his shoulders and leaning back in the chair. "Perfect hit."

"Killed who?"

"That Arnold woman."

"You killed her already?" Sid hadn't expected things to go so quickly. Maybe he'd underestimated Hans. "You must have gotten some good stuff, then."

"I wasn't so lucky with the lawyer, though. There was another car pulled into the park right about then. I could hear the engine rumbling closer. I thought it best to hightail it out of there. I didn't figure you'd want me sticking around just to finish her off."

"How'd you manage it so fast? Did Arnold give her the details right away?"

"Nah, she hardly said anything."

"Did she have it on her, then?"

Hans tugged on his jeans near the crotch. "I didn't get that far."

"You didn't get that . . ." Sid felt a tremor deep inside his gut. "What do you mean, you didn't get that far?"

"I didn't get the exact information you were after."

"But enough? You got enough, right?"

Hans angled his neck sideways. "She was meeting that lawyer, just like you said."

"But what did they say?"

"Not much." Hans stifled a yawn. "I could use a little of whatever you're drinking. It was a long drive home."

Sid ignored the request. "Did you follow them?"

"No. Just shot her right there in the park. Wasn't no one around."

"Jesus Christ, Hans. What the fuck did you think you were

doing?" Sid could feel the blood pounding in his temples. He should never have used a moron like Hans for something this important. "What were the instructions I gave you? Listen. Learn. Follow."

"You said we'd have to kill her eventually."

"But not right away. That was the whole point. How am I supposed to know where to—" He stopped himself before he said too much. It was safer if Hans didn't know. "Why did you shoot her so soon?"

"She looked up. I think she spotted me."

"So what? She didn't know you! I can't believe you were so . . . so stupid. It was information I was after. I thought I made that clear."

"But you wanted her dead, too."

"Not until I had some information!" Sid raked a hand through the bristles of his balding head. This was about as bad an outcome as could be imagined. Hans had made a total jumble of his carefully crafted plan. "You just better hope that lawyer has the specifics. She's alive, isn't she?"

"Yeah, I called the hospital to check. Figured you'd ask me that." Hans grinned, proud of his own cleverness.

Sid pulled himself from the sofa. "Get out, you dimwit. Get out of my sight." He was so angry he raised his cane and swung it.

Hans ducked out of the way. "When do I get the rest of the money?"

"Get out of here before I beat the living shit out of you."

Hans stood by the door, glaring at him coldly. "The deal was half before, half after the job was done. That's what we agreed on."

"But the job I asked for wasn't done!" Sid swung the cane again, catching Hans in the legs. "I gave you explicit instructions. I even—"

"I want the money by the end of the week." Hans didn't bother shutting the door on his way out.

Sid crumpled onto the sofa and downed the rest of his drink in quick swallows, then poured himself another. A double.

Betty Arnold was dead. What the hell was he going to do now?

* * *

At nine o'clock, Detective Gary Bauman was ready to call it a night. He'd been on the case for over twenty-four hours, and in that period of time had managed maybe three hours sleep, cat-napping at his desk. He hadn't been home at all. If nothing else, he needed a shower and a change of clothes.

He was cleaning off his desk getting ready to leave the station when the phone rang.

"Hey, Gary. It's Skip." Skip Hogland, Bauman's ex-brother-in-law and childhood friend, was a reporter for the local paper. It was undoubtedly the latter connection that prompted the late-night call.

"I figured you might still be there," Skip said. "You're getting too old to pull those long shifts, man."

"Forty-eight isn't that old." Though on nights like this, it felt it. "Anyway, I was just leaving."

"Good thing I caught you then. How about a beer before you head home?"

Beer sounded good. Bed sounded better. "I'm beat, Skip. Half dead myself."

"Have you eaten yet?"

"Not since lunch. I thought I'd stop by McDonald's and pick up a burger on my way."

"Tell you what. I'll pick up burgers and beer. Meet you at your place in twenty minutes. How's that sound?"

"You're wasting your time if you're after information about the shootings. The press release this afternoon about covered every-thing we know."

"You think I'm calling to *use* our friendship?" Skip managed to sound outraged.

Bauman knew damn well that was why Skip was calling, but it didn't really matter. There wasn't any inside scoop to be had. And it *would* be nice to have someone else pick up dinner. "Twenty minutes," he said. "And bring me a large order of fries."

Skip opened two bottles of Sierra Nevada and set them on the kitchen table. Bauman had already unwrapped his burger and taken a bite. He was hungrier than he'd thought. He washed it down with a long drink of beer.

"I talked to Betty Arnold's boss," Skip said, "and to one of her neighbors. They're totally blown away. According to them, she led a simple, uneventful life. Didn't gamble, didn't drink. They can't imagine her being gunned down."

Same story the deputies had picked up. "What did you do, spend the day shadowing our guys?"

Skip grinned. "Close enough. So what do you think? The killer was after the attorney?"

Bauman shrugged, then he crumpled the paper burger wrapper and tossed it into the open trash can next to the fridge.

"Come on, Gary. What'd'ya think?"

"Are we off the record here?"

"Any way you want it."

"Off the record. As of now, yes, that would be my guess. But I have nothing to back it up." He paused for another sip of beer. "There are also problems with that scenario."

"Like what?"

Bauman dunked a french fry in ketchup and stuck it in his mouth. "Like why'd he shoot Betty Arnold? And why go for her first?"

"Maybe she was standing between him and the attorney."

"Why'd he shoot her here instead of back in the Bay Area?"

"He lives here?" Skip frowned. "Okay, I see what you mean. If he lives here, what's his beef with her? And how'd he know she was here, anyway?"

Bauman nibbled a fry. There were too many unknowns to come up with an hypothesis at this point. But Betty Arnold seemed such an unlikely target for murder, it had to be the attorney.

He eyed Skip's burger, as yet untouched. "You going to eat?"

"Nah, I'm not really hungry. You want it?"

"Thanks."

"How about that guy who called it in?" Skip asked. "Could he tell you anything?"

"Just that he saw the Arnold woman on the ground, got out of the car to help her, and then saw the attorney. Says his first thought was that they'd shot each other. He didn't see any other cars except the two that belonged to the women."

"That possible?"

"That the attorney killed Arnold? I doubt it. There were no guns found."

"What about other evidence at the scene?"

Skip was pressing for information, but Bauman was used to that. They'd more or less worked out acceptable parameters over the years.

"Nothing except for shoe prints. The ground's pretty wet this time of year so we were able to get an impression. Probably a man's judging from the size. But it's not clear enough to do much good."

"What have you got on the weapon?"

"Nine millimeter. We've got forensics taking a look to see if we can narrow down possible makes. That's not going to help us catch the guy, though."

"No, I guess not. But it might help you build a case down the road."

If they ever got that far. With no witnesses, no leads, no obvious motive, the odds were against it. And an unsolved murder, particularly one that piqued public interest, was bound to be used as ammunition by those in the county who considered the Tahoe division of the Sheriff's Department to be second rate. *Down the road* was the least of Bauman's worries right now.

"You think you'll find this guy?" Skip asked.

"I sure as hell hope so." Bauman drained the last of his beer. He wanted another, thought he probably shouldn't, then opted for a second bottle anyway. "You want more beer?"

"Sure. Thanks."

"Off the record," Bauman said, returning from the fridge, "and I mean really off the record, I've got my eye on the commander's job when Jennings retires next year. An unsolved homicide won't help. In fact, it would probably be a bullet through the heart, so to speak. I don't intend to let that happen if I can help it."

"The commander's job. Hey, that would be great. You've put in time just about everywhere in the system. You'd be perfect."

Bauman laughed at the display of enthusiasm. He could see Skip's eyes getting bigger already at the thought of having access to someone at the top. "Too bad you're not the one making the decision."

"It'll work out," Skip assured him. "I feel it in my bones."

"Well, damn if that isn't reassuring."

"Who have you got working with you on this?"

"I've been authorized to call on deputies as needed. Kim Wong has been assigned specifically to the case."

Skip grinned. "Cutest ass in the whole department. How'd you manage that?"

"It wasn't my doing."

Nor was Bauman entirely comfortable with Kim's assignment to the case. As a cop, she was first-rate. It was the personal stuff he worried about.

But there were some things he didn't talk about, even off the record.

CHAPTER 5

Irene Thompson glanced at the door, as she did every time a customer came into the coffee shop. It had become such a habit that she was hardly aware she was doing it. But she knew she could never let down her guard.

Her life depended on it.

"Hey, Irene. When you get a minute, I could use some more coffee. And a piece of that apple pie, too."

"Sure thing, Mr. Abbott."

She delivered the egg salad sandwich order to table seven, then picked up the pie and the coffeepot for Mort Abbott, who at age seventy-six lived largely on the two meals a day he regularly ate at Elma's.

"You into all that E-mail and computer stuff?" he asked when she poured his coffee.

"Some. Why?"

"My son's after me to get a computer. Says it's a great way to stay in touch, especially with my grandkids. He's offering to buy me one."

"So what are you waiting for?"

"I don't see how typing an E-mail is any easier than writing a note or picking up the phone. He insists that it is, though. Particularly with the kids."

Irene thought about her boyfriend Elliot's son, Patrick. Only nine years old and already more comfortable at the computer than she'd ever be. "It doesn't make sense, but I think somehow it's true. Kids seem to be wired for it or something."

"They'd be wired for writing if their parents made them do it."

Abbott poured creamer into his coffee. "How'd Patrick do in the finals?"

"He toppled his opponent when he got 'papilionaceous' right."

Abbott laughed. "Would have tripped me up. What's it mean?"

"Shaped like a butterfly. But he didn't have to know the meaning, just how to spell it."

"It's still mighty impressive."

"It sure is." Irene, who was a terrible speller herself, had been so proud for Patrick she could have burst. But looking back, she wished now she'd never gone to the meet.

Come on, Irene, you should be in the picture, too.

But I'm not family, Patrick.

I want you in the picture. Please.

Patrick walked with a limp and wore glasses so thick they slid down his nose. A serious boy who rarely smiled. And there he was grinning from ear to ear. How could she refuse him?

Still, she should have known better. Should have known that someone might recognize her.

"You don't think I'm too old to learn?" Mr. Abbott asked.

Irene had been lost in thought. "Learn what?"

"The computer."

"Absolutely not, Mr. Abbott. Once you get started, you'll be hooked." She wasn't sure why she was sounding so upbeat, but it seemed to be what he wanted.

"I don't know, I still haven't figured how to use the danged VCR my son gave me."

"I'll tell you what. Once you get your computer, I'll see if I can persuade Patrick to give you a demo."

"Guess that's an offer I can't refuse." He grinned at her, then tackled his pie.

Elliot called just before her shift ended. "I'm making chicken and dumplings for dinner. Can I tempt you?"

"You know I'm trying to lose a few pounds."

He upped the ante. "Patrick is spending the night at a friend's. We'd have the house to ourselves."

"Well . . ." She thought of Elliot's soft gray eyes and the way he had of looking at her. "I guess I don't *have* to eat the dumplings."

"I won't even make them. In fact, I only thought of chicken and dumplings because you liked them so much before. You want grilled tofu instead?"

The words were light, but Irene heard the earnestness behind them, like a kid eager to please. It wasn't anything new, but it scared her a little. "Elliot, I'm thinking that maybe we—"

He cut her off. "Stop right there, Irene. Whenever you get that tone in your voice, I know what's coming. I love you and I'm not going to let you go until you look me in the eye and say that it's over."

Could she do that, she wondered. Certainly not with any conviction.

Sweet, shy, Elliot. Tall and lanky, with hollow cheeks and a long nose. He wasn't the sort of man who caught your eye in a roomful of people. Or anywhere. A veterinarian and widower for eight years, he was far more comfortable with animals than with humans. People who'd known him when his wife was alive said he was quiet then, too, but less withdrawn. Her death, and the responsibility of raising a child alone, weighed on him.

Irene had taken up with Elliot for all the wrong reasons. Selfish reasons. She'd been lonely and broke. And afraid to go anywhere near the Las Vegas strip where the tourists gathered for fear of running into someone she knew. She'd begun dating Elliot to relieve the boredom of endless nights at home alone.

He'd fallen in love with her anyway, and then she with him. Love was a powerful thing. Now she worried that it might also be dangerous. Especially for Elliot and Patrick.

"I'll expect you around six?" he asked.

She took a deep breath. The woman had never phoned again except for that one time, so maybe everything would work out, after all. Irene couldn't even say for sure that it had been Betty who'd called.

"I'll be there," Irene said. "And you'd better not serve grilled tofu."

CHAPTER 6

Although she'd never have admitted it out loud, Kali was enjoying being pampered. Having lived on her own for so many years, she couldn't remember the last time anyone had fussed over her the way Helen was. Helen brought her coffee and snacks, made special comfort meals, fetched tissues or books when Kali needed them, reminded her to take her medicine, and even fluffed her pillows, which was something Kali thought happened only in books. This morning, after driving Tyler to school, Helen had helped Kali wash and blow-dry her hair, giving it more bounce than Kali ever managed on her own.

And she was stubborn as a mule whenever Kali talked about returning home, as she'd done again just now.

"Don't be silly," Helen said. "You're in no shape to be alone. And you certainly aren't ready to go back to work yet."

Kali had called Jared from the hospital and again this morning. He assured her he could handle things and told her to take as much time as she needed. Nonetheless, Kali worried. It was *her* practice, her name on the office lease. And while she was fortunate there was nothing that needed her immediate attention, there *was* work to be done.

"I can't stay here forever," Kali said.

Helen smiled. "Why not? Since I've just about given up on finding another husband, having a roommate isn't such a bad idea."

"You haven't found a husband because you don't let any guy stick around long enough to broach the subject."

"Look who's talking. How are things with you and that cop, anyway?"

"Bryce? Things are . . . on hold, I guess. We're seeing each other again but it's a little like walking on eggshells." A breach of trust was hard to repair. Maybe impossible.

"But you like him enough to want to make it work?"

Did she? Sometimes the answer was a definite yes. Other times Kali worried that she was leading with her heart, something that had cost her dearly in the past. Bryce was a little too brash, lived a little too close to the edge for her comfort. But there was definitely an attraction there. At one time, that would have been enough. Lately though, she'd begun to think in terms of the future. Of stability, marriage, even children.

"For now, yeah."

Helen gave her a thumbs-up.

"Getting shot may have been good for the relationship," Kali added. "Bryce sounded very protective when I told him what had happened."

"I should hope so!" Helen straightened the stack of magazines on the coffee table. "Anyway, I didn't say anything about your staying forever. Only until you've healed a bit."

So Kali spent another day drifting in and out of sleep, masking the pain in her shoulder with Vicodin, and lazily gazing out at the ever-changing reflection of clouds on the lake.

And trying to keep her mind from exploring the ragged terrain of her own fear. Someone had tried to kill her. Was he biding time, waiting to finish the job? And if it was Betty he'd been after, why?

She'd learned nothing more about the crime, or her mysterious client, since leaving the hospital. And what she'd known then was precious little.

By Wednesday morning, the weight of so many unanswered questions was driving her nuts. She cut her medication in half and called Detective Bauman to ask about progress with the investigation.

"We have a possible witness," he told her. "Someone who saw a truck leaving the park by a back road around the time we logged in the 9-1-1 call."

A lucky break. "Did he get a look at the license plate?"

"It was a she, actually. A jogger. The truck almost ran her down. She got a general description of the vehicle but no plate. Still, it might lead us somewhere."

"How about the victim?" Kali asked. "Anything more on her?"

"Her neighbors and coworkers say she was well-liked and friendly. No enemies, angry lovers, or fortune-seeking relatives that any of them knew about."

"She was wealthy?"

"That was just a hypothetical. In fact, Betty Arnold and her husband seemed to have been living pretty much month-to-month on his Social Security and her paycheck until they inherited some money last year. Most of that went for the nursing home he's in now. He has Alzheimer's."

Had Betty contacted her about a health care issue? It seemed odd that someone of limited financial means would seek out a private attorney when less costly options were available. And why the concern for privacy?

"What about other family members?" Kali asked.

"The nursing home lists a brother, her husband's brother that is, in Atlanta. We're still trying to reach him."

"Will he be the conservator for Mr. Arnold, then?" Kali was thinking of the retainer, most of which would be returned to her client's estate. Too bad she'd been counting on it to get through the month.

"I couldn't say, but it seems likely." Bauman cleared his throat. "Have you given any more thought to who in your life might have reason to want you dead?"

As if she could have *not* thought about it. She'd mentally gone through the cases she'd tried recently, including her special assignment with the District Attorney's office, and had come up empty-handed.

Her personal life was equally void of possibilities. No hearts she'd broken lately. Not even close—except for Bryce. And she doubted she'd affected his heart so much as assaulted his ego. No enemies, either. She might not have many close friends, but by the same token there was no one she could think of who would be angry or jealous or eager for revenge.

"Nobody comes to mind," she replied.

"You're still convinced the killer was after your client, and not you?"

"Not convinced, no." When she looked at the options logically, it made the most sense. Logic was good for only so much, however. It couldn't quiet the terrifying dreams, the flashes of panic, the unsettling compulsion to constantly look over her shoulder.

Had the killer been after her or Betty? She'd never have a moment's peace until she knew.

"Do you think you'll find him?" Kali asked.

"We're certainly trying. That's why anything you can tell us—"

"I've told you everything I know! You can't possibly think I'm holding back, can you?"

"You tell me, Ms. O'Brien. Are you?"

When Kali got off the phone, she returned to the armchair where she'd spent most of the last three days. She tried to interest herself in the book Helen had given her, but now that her mind was no longer glazed over with drugs, the questions rattling inside her took on a new sharpness.

Helen called to her. "I'm going to make some coffee. Would you like a cup?"

"No, thanks." Kali pulled herself to her feet and shuffled into the kitchen. If she moved wrong, her shoulder exploded in pain, but as long as she kept it largely immobile, she was okay.

"Is there a bus that goes from here to Reno?" she asked.

Helen squinted. "Probably. Why?"

"I might go there this afternoon."

"By bus? Are you crazy?"

Now that Kali was on her feet, she was thinking the same thing. But from the protective comfort of the armchair, it had seemed a workable solution.

"Why do you want to go to Reno?" Helen asked.

"I was thinking of talking to Betty Arnold's neighbors and maybe some of her coworkers."

"I'm sure the cops have already done that."

"They have. But we're not necessarily looking for the same things."

Helen looked puzzled. "You both want to know who killed her, right?"

Kali nodded, leaned against the doorjamb. "But it also bothers me that I know so little about her. She was my client, after all, and she wanted my counsel about something important enough that she wouldn't tell me what until we met."

"Important to her doesn't necessarily mean it's *important*. I mean it's probably not something you need to worry yourself about now."

"Maybe it's just a matter of having been there when she was killed," Kali said. And knowing that she herself might be next. "All I know is that I've got questions and my mind won't let go of them. It's like having a loose tooth—you can tell yourself to ignore it but you can't."

Helen put down the kettle she was filling. "There's no way you can manage an investigation on a bus, Kali. Even if you were up to the long ride, which you clearly aren't." She dried her hands on a towel. "If you're determined to do this, I'll drive you. Just let me change my shoes."

Betty Arnold had lived on the northern edge of town, in a large trailer park set behind a pink concrete wall. Two lava rock pillars marked the entrance. A row of scraggly oleanders lined the main drive, and pots of flowers perched on porch steps at a few of the individual trailers, but most of the development's landscaping consisted of Astroturf and asphalt.

Helen found the correct address and stopped the car. "I'm going to park over there in the shade," she said. "I brought a book to read, so take your time."

The Arnolds' trailer was one of the ones with flowers. Two pots of bright yellow pansies. There was also a wreath of twisted grape vines woven with green ribbon hanging on the door.

Kali was hoping it was the sort of community where the residents knew one another. All she needed was one person in whom Betty Arnold had confided.

First trying the trailer to the left, Kali rang the bell twice, then knocked. When no one answered, she tried the trailer to the right. This time the door opened even before she had a chance to ring.

The woman who answered looked to be in her sixties. Though she was trim and able-bodied, she had the heavily wrinkled face of a lifelong smoker.

Kali introduced herself. "I'm interested in Betty Arnold. Did you know her?"

The woman nodded. "We were neighbors. We also played bridge together." She paused, sizing Kali up with her eyes. "Are you a reporter?"

"An attorney. I was with her when she was shot."

"It was you?" Her eyes went to Kali's arm and the sling that held it. "I'm Trudy Barber. What can I do for you?"

Barber. "You're the friend whose car she borrowed."

"That's right. But it was fine by me. We had an understanding." She frowned. "Though I wasn't so happy when the police impounded it for evidence."

"Do they still have it?"

"No, I got it back yesterday." Trudy Barber stepped back. "Come in, why don't you."

Kali followed her inside and sat in one of the two armchairs the living room offered. It wasn't particularly comfortable, but that might have been because Kali's bandaged arm kept her from sitting squarely in the chair. The room was thick with the stench of cigarette smoke.

"Didn't Betty have a car of her own?" Kali asked.

"Of course she did. It would be hard living way out here without one. But it sometimes had problems. When that happened, she'd borrow mine if I didn't need it. 'Course usually she asked me first."

"But not this time?"

"No. When I got off work Friday—I work three days a week at the Kmart—my car was gone and Betty's was parked in its place, key in the ignition. It struck me as odd at the time. Why would she take mine without asking? And her car was running just fine. I still don't know why she did it."

She'd borrowed Trudy's car, Kali suspected, not because her own was acting up but because she wanted to further protect her identity. But why the secrecy?

"What was Betty like?" Kali asked.

"Quiet, reserved. It's so unfair that someone like her, without an enemy in the world, would end up murdered." Trudy Barber reached for a pack of Salem Lights. "It's the senselessness of it that angers me most."

Kali nodded, tried not to breathe until the puff of smoke had cleared. "It would be nice if bad guys would stick to killing other bad guys." Of course *bad guy* was an ever amorphous concept, which was part of the reason there were murders and wars to begin with. "Do you know of anyone Betty had a run-in with recently?"

Trudy shook her head. "Betty wasn't like that. She'd let someone walk all over her rather than cause a fuss."

"Was she upset about anything? Or worried?"

Trudy frowned, thinking about the question before answering. "She seemed a little jumpy the last couple of weeks, but I assumed it was because of Carl, her husband. She always worried about him."

"He's in a nursing home now, isn't he?"

"As of December. He was already in the early stages of Alzheimer's when they moved here a couple of years ago, but this last year was a real downward spiral for him. It got to the point where Betty couldn't care for him, no matter how much she wanted to."

Kali leaned back in an effort to escape a new plume of smoke. "It must have been hard for her, both the caring for him and then putting him in a home."

"I'm sure it was, but she never complained. Not seriously. We'd do our share of commiserating over a cup of coffee, but bottom line was, Betty was grounded. She didn't see any point in bellyaching about what couldn't be changed."

"Was she happy with the care Carl was getting at the nursing home?" This was, conceivably, an area where an attorney might prove helpful. But why choose an out-of-state attorney? Worry that word might get back to the director of the home?

"She was quite pleased, in fact," Trudy said. "Betty and Carl hadn't been able to save much over the years, and she didn't see how she'd ever be able to afford decent care on Social Security and Medicare. That's part of the reason she held off so long putting him in a home. Then she inherited from her sister, and that allowed her to place Carl in a privately funded home. It's here in town, called Pinewood Manor."

Not a health care issue, after all, Kali thought. "Did Betty mention anything to you about needing an attorney?"

Trudy Barber's eyes narrowed. "You were Betty's attorney? The newspaper listed your name and occupation, but it wasn't clear to me what your connection to Betty was."

"She was looking for someone to represent her. She never told me why, though."

Trudy rubbed her chin. "Drawing up a will maybe? Except I know they got all that done when they learned Carl was sick."

Kali shifted positions. Her arm was beginning to throb again. And her head hurt from the cigarette smoke. "Did Betty have family? Other close friends?"

"The only family I ever heard her mention was Carl's brother. And the sister I mentioned who died. She was killed in an airplane crash. As for friends . . . there was our bridge group, of course. And people she worked with, although I don't believe she was close to any of them. She had friends from California, too. She and Carl lived near Sacramento before they moved here."

A cuckoo clock above the television sounded the hour. Trudy said, "I was on my way next door to feed Betty's cat when you arrived. Do you want to come along? I don't suppose you're in the market for a cat, are you? This one's very friendly, but she's so old she doesn't do much aside from sleep."

"I don't think my dog would take well to sharing her house with a new anything, much less a cat."

Trudy rose from her chair. "I'd take her myself but my granddaughter's allergic to them. Not that I'm much of a cat lover anyway, but I used to take over when Betty and Carl were away. I guess the poor thing will have to be put to sleep eventually."

"There's no one else in the neighborhood who might take her?"

"Not that I've found so far. I'll keep asking."

Kali stood. The movement sent a jolt of pain through her shoulder. Payback for cutting the dose of Vicodin. She gritted her teeth. Outside, she saw Helen look up from her book and then, seeing that Trudy and Kali were headed to the Arnolds', return to her reading.

Trudy opened the metal screen door, fit the key into the lock and opened the front door. A large gray cat sauntered from across the living room to meet them. Kali bent to pet it, but stopped short when her shoulder protested. The cat looked at her disdainfully, then pranced to the kitchen.

"Did the Arnolds go away a lot?" Kali asked.

"Not a lot, no, but they did take short trips now and then before Carl got real bad." Trudy headed into the kitchen and Kali followed.

It was a narrow galley kitchen with dark wood cabinets and almond-colored Formica. A microwave and coffeemaker took up most of the counter space next to the stove. A glass container of M&Ms was on the sill above the sink.

"When Carl got worse," Trudy continued, "it was hard for Betty to manage so they rarely went anywhere. After he went to the nursing home she'd occasionally go away for a couple of days, usually to visit an old friend in Sacramento. She said she felt bad about leaving him."

Kali pulled the bottle of Vicodin from her purse, shook out two pills, and washed them down with a handful of water from the kitchen faucet. "For my shoulder," Kali explained.

"Must hurt like the dickens. I'm surprised you're not home in bed."

"I was. Getting out helps to get my mind off it. And I wanted to learn more about Betty."

Trudy opened the cupboard and took out a can of cat food. "In fact," she added, turning to face Kali, "the friend in Sacramento was the last trip Betty took. Only a couple of weeks ago, I believe. She'd planned to be gone the whole weekend and came home after only one night. She seemed anxious and upset. Said she was worried about Carl. I told her he was in good hands and her being here wasn't going to change anything."

While Trudy was scooping out cat food and refilling the water bowl, Kali looked around the trailer. It was a single-wide—one main room divided into living and dining areas, a kitchen ell, and two small bedrooms. One had a bed, the other had been converted into a den, with a television and two easy chairs. As Kali peered into the bedroom, the photos on the dresser caught her eye. There were three of them, all in silver frames. The largest was a wedding picture, which Kali took to be of Betty and her husband. Next to it was a more recent snapshot of the two of them seated outdoors on a bench. Another photo showed what looked like mother and daughter at the daughter's graduation. The older woman bore a strong family resemblance to Betty and almost had to be the now deceased sister.

Kali called to Trudy. "Did Betty's sister have children?"

"Just one. A daughter. She died long before Carl and Betty moved here."

Kali turned away from the photos. "Mind if I open a few drawers?"

"I don't see what the problem would be. You were her attorney. Don't think you'll find anything though. The cops beat you to it."

That was no surprise, but Kali wanted to see things for herself. She was hoping to find some thread that might suggest why Betty Arnold had been interested in meeting with her.

Kali made quick work of the dresser, finding only neatly folded underwear and sweaters, then moved back into the kitchen. She started with the calendar. Their fated appointment was noted simply as 4:00. No name, no place. The weeks before and after were bare save for a dentist appointment and a brunch. Kali leafed through bills, then turned her attention to an address book. The listings were sparse—hairdresser, pharmacy, some doctors, and a few individual names. She found her own phone number, interestingly enough, only on a scrap of paper tucked into the back of the book.

Kali called to Trudy. "You wouldn't happen to know the name of Betty's friend in Sacramento, would you?"

"Her first name was Gail. I don't recall the last name."

Kali flipped through the pages again, found a listing for Gail Lombardi in Sacramento, and copied it onto a piece of paper.

"Find anything helpful?" Trudy asked.

"Not really. I thought I might call the friend from Sacramento, though."

"Good idea," Trudy said. "She and Betty had been friends for years."

The cat had finished her meal and come to sniff Kali's shoes. Kali managed to dip to one side enough to give her a pat. She thanked Trudy for her help, left her card in case something else came to mind, and returned to Helen's Cherokee.

Helen tossed her book into the backseat. "Ready to go?"

"Actually, I was hoping you had time for one more stop." Kali could feel the medicine beginning to kick in. While the throbbing in her arm was now less intense, the downside was that her head once again felt like it was wrapped in cotton. "I'm glad you're driving, Helen. I really appreciate this."

"Good. That you appreciate it, I mean. I don't get appreciated very often." She grinned. "Where to next?"

"A nursing home, Pinewood Manor. It's supposedly not far from here."

"Betty's husband?"

"It's a long shot, but maybe he's not so far gone he'll know what was going on."

Kali used her cell phone to call information, then got the address and directions by calling the facility itself. She closed her eyes and rested while Helen drove.

Ten minutes later, they parked in the lot of a sprawling mission-style building that was far more inviting than the trailer park they'd just left.

"Looks more like a resort than a nursing home," Helen said.

"You want to come check it out?"

Helen laughed. "Maybe not *that* much like a resort. I think I'll stay in the car."

Inside, the decor was soft peach and green. The entry was carpeted, the walls were hung with floral prints, and the staff was friendly. As nursing homes went, it was one of the nicest Kali had seen. But it was still a nursing home. Like every one she'd ever visited, it smelled of sickness and old age.

She explained that she was here to see Carl Arnold, and a Filipino nurse escorted her down the hallway to his room. It was a private room, unlike most they had passed along the way, and Kali could see that Betty had added many personal touches, including a copy of the wedding photo she had seen earlier at the Arnolds' trailer.

Carl Arnold was in a wheelchair by the window, a dark plaid blanket covering his legs. He was a thin man with wisps of pure white hair.

"He doesn't recognize anyone," the nurse told her. "Even his wife. It's a blessing, I guess. He won't know she's gone."

Kali touched his hand. "Mr. Arnold? I'm Kali O'Brien. How are you doing today?"

"The dog ate it."

"The dog ate what, Mr. Arnold?"

"Whatever you were asking about." His voice faded off and he closed his eyes.

"Is he ever lucid?" Kali asked the nurse.

"I'm afraid not. Betty tried. She'd tell him stories from their past, show him photographs. It was like talking to a tree."

"What will happen to him now that she's dead?"

"In terms of care, you mean? He'll probably stay here. Betty set up a trust fund to cover the costs. Lots of our patients have arrangements like that."

Paid for with the money she'd inherited from her sister. Kali found herself wishing she'd had a chance to know Betty. She seemed to have been a generous woman.

The nurse opened the closet and took out a blue tote bag. "This was Betty's. She left it here so she'd have something to occupy her while she visited. Can I give it to you? I don't know what else to do with it."

"Sure." Kali looked inside. A mystery novel, a couple of magazines and newspapers, and some knitting. She could give it to Deputy Bauman or whichever attorney was handling Betty's estate, though it would probably end up in the trash.

"I'm sorry about what happened to her," the nurse said. "She was a nice woman, and devoted to her husband. It's not easy loving someone with advanced Alzheimer's but you could see she wasn't simply going through the motions. She put his well-being above all else."

Kali observed carefully on her way out—the staff, the patients, the general feel of the place. She hadn't picked up on anything that was likely to have alarmed her client.

So why had Betty needed an attorney?

CHAPTER 7

Sid made the call from a pay phone, just in case. "I've got your money."

"I thought you'd see it my way." Hans's response was capped with a snicker that grated on Sid like fingernails on a chalkboard. Dumb and arrogant. How had he chosen so poorly?

"And another job for you," Sid added. "Tonight. Can you make it?"

"How much?"

"Two thousand."

Hans considered. "Three."

"What! It's a piece-of-cake assignment."

"You want me it's going to cost you three."

Yeah, Sid wanted him all right. "Okay, three. I'm driving. I'll pick you up at six."

Hans yakked during the entire drive north. Sid tried playing a CD of The Eagles, and when that didn't shut him up, he switched to a talk radio show. Finally, Sid just tuned Hans out.

When they finally pulled off the main road, Hans seemed to take notice of rolling hills and surrounding open space for the first time. "Where are we going?"

"You don't need to know."

"So what's the job? I need some direction here."

"Just do what I say and everything will be fine. You got your gun?"

"Yeah."

"Any other weapons?"

"No. You didn't tell me to bring anything else." Hans sounded irritated.

"Just asking. The gun is fine."

They passed a cabin.

"Who lives here?" Hans asked.

"A friend of mine."

"It's in the middle of fucking nowhere."

"Yeah. He likes his privacy."

"I'll say."

Half a mile farther in, Sid pulled to a stop by an old barn. "Let me take a look at your gun," he said.

Hans pulled it from his shoulder holster and handed it to Sid. "I got it from a friend who picked it up during a burglary. No way to trace it to me. Solid action, high-capacity magazine. Hadn't even been fired when I got it."

Sid gripped the gun in his hand. It didn't feel as comfortable as his own.

"Pretty nice, huh?"

"Yeah. Nice." Sid slid the safety off and opened the car door.

"Hey, where are you—"

Sid pointed the gun back at Hans. "Get out."

Hans scrambled out of the door.

"Hands on top of your head."

"Hey, whatever it is . . . The money, is that it? I can be reasonable. I'm sure we can—"

Sid aimed first for the right knee.

Deputy Kim Wong pulled the patrol car into the gift shop parking lot and turned off the engine. Then she reread the dispatch report on the witness to make sure she had all the pertinent information. Bobbie Manes, jogging on Friday afternoon, had reported seeing a white truck in the vicinity of Ponderosa Pines Park around four. The driver had screeched onto the highway from a road just north of the park, almost running her down. A bare-bones report, but Kim had learned early on that witness interviews were far more productive when she was prepared.

Kim had been with the Placer County Sheriff's Department for four of the six years she'd been a cop, but she'd been assigned to the Tahoe Substation only last November. She hadn't been particularly happy about the move. Not that she didn't love the Tahoe area—in fact, the lure of the outdoors and the beauty of the mountains was what had prompted her move from the Los Angeles PD to the sheriff's office in the first place. That and a widowed father who refused to leave the tiny house near Gold Run where he and Kim's mother had lived for most of the thirty-four years of their marriage.

What dampened her enthusiasm for the new assignment was the fear that it would be a dead end in terms of her career. And that she'd been transferred there for that very reason.

It wasn't that the department was overtly sexist, except maybe for Dub Smalley. In fact, most of the guys were pretty decent. Kim had worked with her share of arrogant, macho cops in L.A., and even Dub was easier to get along with than them.

But Kim was one of the few women in the department and the only one at her level. She was also not quite five-three in her stocking feet, younger than many, though not as young as she looked, and Chinese. The men paid lip service to gender equality, then patted themselves on the back for being so open-minded. When push came to shove, however, equality went out the window. Not only was there a glass ceiling, but glass walls, too. Kim was well enough liked, but she never lost sight of the fact that she was an outsider in a close-knit group of brothers.

Now it looked as though she might get a chance to make her mark. Because Dub was busy working a string of residential burglaries, she'd drawn the Elizabeth Arnold homicide. Not as lead detective, of course, though she hoped that day would come, but as the deputy assigned to work the investigation. She'd report directly to Gary Bauman, which was a problem of a different nature, but at least she'd be actively involved in the case. In moments of wild fantasy, she had visions of solving the case herself. Wouldn't that just show them.

Kim radioed her location to dispatch, then entered the gift shop where Bobbie Manes worked. There was only one saleswoman present, a tall, slender woman with frosted hair. She appeared to be in her forties, older than Kim was expecting. Kim silently chastised herself for assuming a jogger had to be young.

Manes was with a customer so Kim waited until she'd finished, biding her time by looking around the store. The merchandise was heavily into country rustic. Lots of pinecones, deer antlers, lamp shades stenciled with animal and nature scenes. None of it was Kim's style. She liked clean and sleek.

The customer left, and Kim turned. "Ms. Manes?"

The woman nodded.

"I'm Kim Wong, with the Placer County Sheriff's office."

"You're a police . . . a regular member of the department?" The woman's voice rang with surprise. "You look so young."

"Deputy sergeant," Kim said, squaring her shoulders and lifting her chin. She waited long enough for emphasis, then moved on. It bugged her when people didn't take her seriously. "You called in a report about seeing a truck leaving Ponderosa Pines Park on Friday afternoon."

"Yes. I was jogging and he about ran me over. He was driving fast, barely slowed at the stop sign. Then I heard about those women who got shot and I thought, well, maybe there's some connection." She paused for just a moment. "And it's Mrs., not Ms."

"I'll make note of it." At one time, Kim would have apologized. Then she'd started watching the men in the department. There were subtle ways of maintaining control in an interview, and not backpedaling was one of them. "Do you know what time you saw this truck?" she asked.

"Around four. I told that to the woman when I called."

"How close to four, do you think?"

"I don't know, maybe ten minutes either way." She straightened the edge of a patchwork quilt that was on display. "I was home by four-thirty so it had to be after four when I saw the truck. Four-ten, four-fifteen, something like that."

The timing was right anyway. And Kim had been right to press the question. It was amazing how often people really did know more than their first response indicated. "Did you see anyone else in the park?" she asked.

"Just the truck."

"Can you describe it?"

"White. Old."

"What make?"

"How should I know?" Her tone dripped with disdain.

"What kind of truck? Big? Small?"

"It was a truck," Bobbie Manes said with impatience. "A pickup truck. Beyond that, I can't say." She waved her hand though the air as though the very topic were beneath her.

"How about the driver?"

"Male. But I didn't see enough to give you a description."

Kim scribbled in her notebook, a sort of shorthand only she was able to read. She'd transcribe it when she wrote her report. "Did you get a look at the license plate?"

"I had my mind on more important things," Bobbie Manes declared haughtily, "like not getting run over." She paused. "I'm pretty sure there was a 'three' in it, though."

"Beginning or end of the sequence?"

"I haven't the foggiest."

"How about decals, bumper stickers, that sort of thing?"

Bobbie Manes thought a moment. "There may have been something on the back bumper. In fact, I'm pretty sure there was."

"A bumper sticker?"

"A decal."

At the risk of further irritating the woman, Kim pressed for details about the description of the truck. "Was it one of those little pickups? Or a big one, maybe with double back wheels?"

"I told you," Bobbie Manes snapped, "I don't remember anything more about it."

Kim nodded, saying nothing.

"It was a full-size pickup, like a work truck," Bobbie Manes said after a moment. "It was a little dinged up, too, like it was used for hauling or something. There were spots of rust, I think. Along the side."

Kim kept her smile to herself. She didn't think Bobbie Manes even realized she'd elaborated on the description she'd given earlier.

Back in the cruiser, Kim called Jean at the station and asked her to check for plates with a number three in them. White pickup trucks.

"There's going to be a lot of them."

"I know, but I'm counting on the fact that it's local." Not a sure bet, by any means, but a place to start.

"It's still going to be a long list."

"I can deal with it."

Next, she put in a call to the attorney who'd been wounded in the shooting. Gary Bauman had taken a preliminary statement, but Kim wanted to talk with the woman herself. No one picked up, so she left a message.

A work truck, Bobbie Manes had said. A little dinged. Most of the trucks around the area were driven by locals. The vacationers came in station wagons and SUVs, or high-end cars like Audis and BMWs. And the locals who drove trucks did so because they used the trucks in their jobs. She thought of cruising the north end of the lake, especially the sites where there was new construction. She decided it would be a waste of time, then did it anyway.

Lots of trucks, many of them white. Most of them a little dinged. A surprising number with the number three on their plates. But not a single one exactly matched the description Bobbie Manes had given.

When Kim got back to the station, Jean handed her a list. "The names you asked for. A hundred and seven white pickup trucks with the number three in the license."

"Thanks." It wasn't as bad as she'd expected.

"That's for Placer County. There're ninety-eight in Nevada County."

Kim knew she'd have to check both. The county line bisected the valley at this end of the lake.

"Even more if we include El Dorado and Sierra counties." Jean grinned. "I told you there'd be a lot of them."

Kim went to her desk and scanned the printout for Placer and Nevada counties, mentally sorting the list by location. It would take only a couple of hours to get through the names closest to the lake, but the chances were slim that she'd find anyone home in the afternoon. She'd have to do it this evening, instead.

She called Bauman to let him know what she'd found.

"Let's hope the truck is significant," he said. "I'd like to take a look at the list. Maybe some of the names will ring a bell with me."

"That would be good."

"I'll be in Tahoe Vista the rest of the day. You want to meet at Blackberries?"

"I'm on my way."

* * *

Gary Bauman was already seated when she arrived. He was at a booth in the back. A group of women sat at one of the heavily distressed wood tables near the window. The place was otherwise deserted.

He'd ordered coffee and a piece of chocolate cake. He signaled to the waitress as soon as Kim sat down. "Tea, right?"

She nodded.

"Do you want something to eat?"

"No thanks." She could use his help in looking over the names but she wanted to keep the personal stuff simple. Even cake seemed to complicate things.

"Sorry I didn't wait for you. I was starved."

Bauman was an attractive man. Lean and muscular at an age where he could easily have started putting on weight. His eyes were a bright, almost turquoise, blue. It was those eyes that had gotten her in trouble.

"That's okay," she told him.

The waitress brought the tea.

"You're not dieting, I hope," he said when they were alone again. "You haven't got an ounce of fat on you as it is."

"I'm not hungry, is all." Her eyes were lowered but she could feel him looking at her.

"Kim, I wish—"

She raised her eyes and gave him a steely glare. She did not want to go there. If she could do her job without ever seeing him or talking to him, she'd be happy.

"You wanted to see the list of names?" Kim asked.

A beat of silence. "Right."

She slid it across the table, then turned her attention to her tea. But her mind was back on that cold December night when she'd acted like such a fool. She still hadn't stopped kicking herself.

He looked up from his reading. "Two of these names you can pretty much eliminate as suspects," he said. "Stu Mosley is pastor of the Methodist church and Aaron Blanchard works security at Squaw."

"That doesn't mean they weren't at the park Friday afternoon."

"No, it doesn't." Bauman slid his finger down the list. "At the other end of the spectrum, there are a couple of names here I'd pay close attention to."

Kim sipped her tea and waited for him to continue. The water was lukewarm and tasted like it had been heated in a coffeepot.

"Ramon Escobar and Brent Hopkins. Ramon works construction. Brent is a bartender."

Construction fit with what Bobbie Manes had told her. "Are they friends?"

"Not that I know of. Brent's had a few run-ins with the law for knocking his wife around, and at least one arrest for drunk and disorderly. Ramon's name comes up wherever there's trouble. One of those guys who thinks nothing's ever his fault."

"I'll keep that in mind. Thanks."

"You going to talk to them?"

"Talk to them, check to see if either one has rust spots on his truck and a decal on the rear fender. I'm also going to talk with the attorney who was hit." Kim watched Bauman take the last bite of cake. It looked good. She wished now she'd ordered some herself. "Anything new turn up on the victim or the attorney?"

"Nothing on Betty Arnold. She seems to have led a quiet life. Nothing specific on Kali O'Brien either, but she's been involved in some high-profile murder cases the last few years, even one involving a serial killer."

"But all of them were in the Bay Area, weren't they?"

"Most recently, yes. Before that she was in Silver Creek. She insists there's nobody with a grudge against her, and people I talked to on her home turf agree."

"If he wasn't after one of the women, we're back to dealing with some random nutcase."

Bauman frowned. "It doesn't feel right."

"What do you mean?" Kim pushed her cup aside. Why was it so hard for restaurants to make decent tea?

"An arm's-length crime is unusual when you're dealing with a psychopath. They get their kicks from having things up close and dirty. Unless you're talking gang violence, and that's not a problem we have here. Yet, anyway."

"Maybe he'll start bragging to his friends about what he did. I'll ask around."

"We're covered. I've assigned a couple of guys to bar duty.

They're going to spend evenings at the places popular with locals and see what they pick up."

Guys. That figured. "Not a woman's job, huh?"

Bauman studied her. "You have your hands full, Kim. And truth is, if guys are going to gossip they'll be more likely to do so with another guy." He rubbed his cheek. "How are things going for you in the department?"

"Fine."

"You're doing a good job. I wouldn't have allowed you on this investigation if that wasn't so."

What the hell did that mean? She was supposed to feel reassured that she hadn't slept her way into the opportunity?

"Thank you," she said coolly. "I take the responsibility of the job seriously."

A smile flickered across Bauman's face. "I know you do."

After he left, Kim stopped by the ladies' room. Damn Gary Bauman anyway. It would certainly be easier for her if he was a total prick. Of course if that were the case, she wouldn't be in this pickle to begin with. It wasn't like she was desperate for male attention.

She was just getting back into her cruiser when the radio squawked.

It was Jean. "I've got something you might be interested in," she said. "An accident report involving the car Betty Arnold was driving the day she was killed. It was only a fender bender, but according to a witness, both parties were pretty agitated."

"Do you have a description of the other car?"

"White pickup." Jean's tone was triumphant. "The license matches one that was on that list I gave you. Ramon Escobar."

"Thanks." Kim was grateful there was no one around to see the way she was grinning. She was going to break this case.

Elma rang up the bill for table six and handed Irene the change on a tray. It came with two mints and two individually wrapped toothpicks. Irene thought the toothpicks were tacky but so far she'd failed to convince Elma of that.

"I wish you'd come with me," Elma urged. "It should be fun. Sure the heck beats another night of watching the boob tube."

"The what?"

"The boob tube. The idiot box. You know, TV. You're probably too young to have heard it called that."

Elma was only ten years older than Irene, but their backgrounds and upbringing were so different it sometimes seemed they were from different generations entirely.

"What is a psychic festival anyway?" Irene asked after she'd delivered the change to her table. Business at the cafe was slow that afternoon and it felt good not to be racing around for a change.

"Got me. The neighbor who gave me the tickets is a little strange, to tell you the truth. The impression I got was that it's like a country fair only instead of tossing rings onto soda bottles, you get your palm read."

"That's not really my kind of thing."

"You think it's mine?" Elma snorted. "But the tickets didn't cost me anything. Besides, aren't you the one who's always telling me I need to broaden my horizons?"

"I meant in terms of meeting new people," Irene said. Elma's husband of twenty-some years had moved out last spring and taken up with his secretary.

"So maybe I'll meet some dashing young warlock." Elma tossed her head of overly permed hair with a dramatic gesture, then turned serious. "Please, I really can't stand another night alone."

Irene relented. "Okay. Let's just hope he's a *rich* warlock on top of everything else."

"Amen to that. It'll be good for you, too, Irene. You've been jumpy as a puppet on a string these few weeks." Elma paused, popping one of the mints into her mouth. "Something bothering you?"

"Everything's fine."

Elma was quiet while she sucked on the candy, but her expression spoke volumes. "Elliot's a good man," she said finally. "You could do a lot worse."

He was a good man. And that was the problem. Irene cursed herself again for getting involved with him.

"There's nothing wrong," she said again.

Maybe, just maybe, the past was behind her.

If only she knew for sure whether the caller had been Betty.

Irene had played their brief conversation over many times in her mind. But the call had caught her off guard, had so confounded her, that she wasn't sure she'd really recognized the voice.

Maybe there was a way to tell, though. "I'm going to take my break," she announced.

"Sounds good to me. The place is dead right now."

Irene grabbed a handful of change from her purse and went to use the pay phone at the gas station next door. She dialed the number from memory, her hands shaking.

No longer in service, the recorded voice told her. And there was no new number.

She put the receiver back on the hook. A thin film of perspiration glazed her forehead. She could feel her heart racing. The disappointment was almost worse than the buildup.

And then she remembered Reno. Betty and Carl had talked about retiring there. Irene dropped more coins in the slot and called information.

"A listing for a Carl or a Betty Arnold, please."

"I have a Carl and Elizabeth," the operator told her. "Would that be it?"

"Yes, thank you."

She didn't have a pen so she repeated the number aloud to herself while she dropped more coins into the phone. And then she held her breath, praying silently that Betty would answer and not Carl.

What she got was the answering machine. *We're unable to come to the phone right now. Please leave a message and we'll get back to you. Have a great day.*

Irene slouched against the side of the phone booth. Her legs felt weak. It was the voice of her caller. No doubt about it.

How had Betty found her? It had to be that damned photograph.

And if Betty knew, who else did?

The old fear was again burning in Irene's chest. The past wasn't behind her, after all.

CHAPTER 8

Because Kali and Helen didn't get back from Reno until after four, and then Helen needed to drive Tyler to baseball practice, take-out pizza was the dinner of choice. By the time they finished eating and cleaned up afterward, it was almost nine. The long day had taken a toll on Kali's energy.

She was in Tyler's room ostensibly learning the ins and outs of his favorite computer game, but in truth she was too tired, and probably too old, to understand half of what he was saying. Tyler was in the midst of explaining how a right-click over a warrior's head sometimes gave you super powers, but only if you'd passed into level B, when Kali became aware of voices downstairs. Someone—a woman—was speaking in a rapid, agitated tone, punctuated with outbursts of weeping. Helen's voice, though softer, had an urgency to it that made Kali take note.

"It sounds like your mother has company," Kali said.

Tyler listened a moment, then went back to his game. "It's just Maria."

"The housekeeper?"

"Yeah."

"What do you suppose she's doing here at night?"

He shrugged. "My mom helps her with stuff sometimes. Like taxes and history."

"History?"

"She's taking classes to be a citizen."

The wailing grew louder.

"You know, Tyler, I think I've absorbed about all of this game

I'm going to be able to in one sitting. I'm not a quick learner the way you are."

He gave her a smile of encouragement. "You'll get better. It's really not as confusing as it sounds."

"Can we continue tomorrow?"

"Sure."

In the hallway, Kali hesitated. She didn't want to barge in on a private conversation, but there was clearly something amiss. She couldn't simply ignore that.

Helen settled the matter by appearing at the bottom of the stairway.

"Kali, I was just coming to find you." Her voice was strained. "It's about Ramon."

"What about him?" Kali asked, descending the stairs as she spoke.

"The police want to talk to him about the murder of Betty Arnold."

"About the . . ." It took a minute for Kali to grasp her meaning. "They think he knows something?"

Helen brushed the hair from her face, a gesture of nervousness. "They think he might have killed her."

And tried to kill me, Kali added silently. A wave of anger swept over her. She didn't care who he was or that he'd saved Tyler from drowning, she wasn't feeling particularly sympathetic. In fact, she was relieved the cops had a suspect so quickly.

"They came to the house with a search warrant," Helen explained.

"Ramon's house?"

"Maria's house. He lives with her."

"What did Ramon say?"

Helen was rubbing her arms as though she were cold. "He wasn't home. He hasn't been home all day. Maria doesn't know where he is. She hasn't seen him since he left for work this morning."

Kali and Helen were standing at the foot of the stairs. Through the open doorway, Kali could see Maria's plump form seated at the kitchen table. Her dark head was bowed and her mouth moved silently, as if she were praying.

Helen touched Kali's shoulder. "He couldn't have done it. I've known Ramon for years. It doesn't fit."

"How old is Ramon?" He'd been a young teenager that summer he'd pulled Tyler from the lake.

"Twenty. He's a good kid."

No longer a kid, Kali thought. "Why do the cops want to talk to him, then?"

"He's had a few run-ins with the law," Helen conceded.

"Like what?"

"Nothing serious. A shoplifting charge when he was still a minor, drug possession, that sort of thing. He gets a little carried away sometimes, but his heart is good, Kali. You can tell that about a person."

Kali thought otherwise. She'd been fooled too many times, but she didn't press the point. "Why do they want to talk to him about the murder? Did they—"

Maria caught sight of them and started weeping again. "Please, what I do now? I so scared. Ramon no hurt anybody."

Kali could feel her pulse racing. Even if her throbbing shoulder hadn't been a constant reminder, she wasn't likely to forget that she'd been shot. And now the police were saying it might be Maria's son who did it. This wasn't a conversation Kali wanted to be part of. But Helen dragged her into the kitchen before she could think of a way to extricate herself.

"Did you try calling his girlfriend's house?" Helen asked Maria.

Maria nodded. "He's not there. He's not at work. Nobody see him all day." She turned to Kali, her eyes pleading. "I'm so sorry you are shot, Miss Kali, but my Ramon didn't do it. He's a good boy."

"Where does he work?" As long as Kali was going to be bombarded with information, she wanted a framework to make sense of it.

It was Helen who replied. "He works construction for a builder in the area. At the moment he's working on a project in Northstar."

"Why do the police think he's involved in the shooting?"

This time Helen looked to Maria for the answer. "They say he is angry. They say he fight with her."

"With Betty Arnold?" Kali asked. "He knew her?"

"I don' know. I don' know what they mean, he fight. Ramon is a good boy. He no kill anyone."

Helen clasped Maria's hands. "I'm sure this is a mixup of some sort. It will all work out with time."

"The police, they no understand. They no listen to me."

"You should go home, Maria, in case Ramon calls," Helen urged her from her chair. "You need to be where he can reach you."

Maria nodded but showed no sign of moving.

"Come on," Helen said. She pulled Maria to her feet, helped her into her jacket, then walked Maria to her car.

Kali filled a glass of water from the tap and drank it. She was still so exhausted she could barely hold her head up, but she felt jumpy, too. Giving the shooter a name and face brought the whole awful experience into focus again.

"I'm sorry," Helen said when she returned. "It's awkward, Maria's coming here and the police wanting to talk to Ramon."

Awkward was the least of it. "I'm surprised they have a suspect so soon." Surprised but relieved.

"They're wrong though. Ramon isn't a killer."

Or maybe Helen just didn't want to believe that he was. Ramon had saved Tyler's life, after all. That predisposed her to thinking well of him.

"The police must have their reasons," Kali pointed out. "You said they came to the house with a search warrant. They couldn't have gotten one without evidence of some sort."

Helen leaned against the counter. "The local cops are always looking for an excuse to hassle Ramon."

"For no reason whatsoever?" Kali laid on the sarcasm. She couldn't help it. Helen had never outgrown her adolescent distrust of authority.

"Like I said, he's not squeaky clean. He sold pot in high school, but just to his friends. It wasn't like he was a big-time drug dealer or anything. The real reason, though, is because the daughter of that detective who interviewed you in the hospital, Bauman—she and Ramon were tight in high school. Much to Dad's displeasure. It's over now. She's in college and Ramon has a steady girlfriend, but Bauman has never let it go."

"You think he's got his eye on Ramon simply because of that?" It was a wild accusation, even for Helen.

"I don't know, Kali. None of this makes sense."

"There's got to be more."

"Yes, I suppose so." Helen's expression was taut with anxiety. She put her head in her hands. "Oh, God. Do you suppose he really might have done it?"

Kali hoped Helen wasn't actually expecting an answer.

Helen looked up. "Did you ever return the call from that woman deputy who left a message?"

"It was too late when we got back. I thought I'd try in the morning."

"When you do, will you see what you can find out? Maybe there's an easy explanation for all this."

Kali woke the next morning at six, but she put off making the call until nine when she thought the chances of finding the deputy on duty were greater. Still, she was surprised when Kim Wong came on the line immediately.

"I'm sorry I didn't get a chance to return your call yesterday," Kali said. "I didn't get the message until late."

"If it had been urgent, I'd have said so." The deputy sounded almost snappish. "How are you feeling?"

"Pretty good, actually."

"Glad to hear it." Kali could hear the rustle of papers being shuffled in the background. "I know you gave a statement to Detective Bauman, but there are a few things I'd like to go over with you again."

"Fine." Kali was having difficulty forming a mental image of Kim Wong. From the name, Kali assumed she was Chinese. And she sounded young. Yet there was a direct quality about her manner, bordering on brusque, that didn't fit with the rest of her mental picture.

"Did you notice anyone in or around the park when you got there?" Wong asked. "Any vehicles, maybe?"

"The parking lot was completely empty. No sign of people, either."

"What about after the shooting, did you see anything then?"

"Like I told Detective Bauman, I might have seen a flash of movement but I can't be sure."

"Did Mrs. Arnold say anything to you about an auto accident she'd been in that afternoon? Or maybe an argument she'd gotten in because of it?"

Kali recalled Maria's comment about Ramon and Betty fighting. Was that what Deputy Wong was asking about? "We didn't have time to exchange more than a few sentences," Kali explained. She decided to take a flyer and see what she could learn. "I understand you've got a possible suspect already."

"Where'd you hear that?"

"It's a small town. Word gets around."

"I'll say." Deputy Wong laughed and her tone softened a bit. Kali decided the brusqueness was part of the uniform. "There *is* someone we're interested in questioning. Ramon Escobar. Do you know him?"

"Only indirectly."

"He and Mrs. Arnold apparently exchanged heated words earlier that afternoon when she stopped suddenly and he rear-ended her."

"Is there anything that actually ties him to the shooting?"

"We have a witness who saw a white pickup truck leaving a road that parallels the border of the park about the time of the shooting."

"And Ramon Escobar drives a white pickup?"

"Yep."

That gave Ramon a motive as well as possibly placing him at the scene of the crime. "Still," Kali said, "white trucks are fairly common." She'd been a defense attorney long enough that challenging evidence was second nature to her.

"Ramon missed work Friday afternoon," Deputy Wong explained. "And then yesterday, when we wanted to talk to him, we couldn't find him. He never returned from his lunch break, and he hasn't been home. What's more, a gun of the same caliber and likely make as killed Mrs. Arnold is registered in his name. We didn't find it during a search of the residence, which means he has it with him or has tossed it. But we did find extra ammo for it."

Motive, opportunity, and means. Helen's assurances aside, Kali found herself agreeing with the deputy. Ramon Escobar sounded like a viable suspect.

There was relief, and some measure of satisfaction, in knowing the killer hadn't been after her. But it was also troubling that someone so close to Helen might be the murderer.

*   *   *

As soon as Kali hung up, Helen appeared in the doorway. She'd no doubt been listening from the hallway. "What did you learn?"

Kali told her what the deputy had said.

"Around here it's no big deal to own a gun," Helen protested. "Lots of people have them."

"But Ramon's matches what they have on the murder weapon."

"I'm sure his isn't the only one registered in the area that does."

"Why did he run, then?"

"We don't know that he ran. Maybe he's hurt or something bad has happened to him."

"Not likely." Kali was finding the role of victim oddly unsettling. She was usually the one poking holes in the cops' case, trying hard to come up with the *other explanation* that raised reasonable doubt about her client's guilt. Not now. Someone, some evil, hateful, or arrogantly reckless person had shot her and killed Betty Arnold. Kali was angry. She wanted that person found and punished.

"Maybe Ramon is even home by now." Helen reached for her purse. "I promised Maria I'd stop by this morning. Will you be okay here by yourself for a bit?"

"I'll be fine. In fact, I'm thinking I'll probably head back tomorrow. It'll be a week already." Helen had been wonderful, but Kali knew she couldn't put off returning to work much longer. And she craved the familiarity of home.

"Are you sure you're up to it?"

"I feel as good as new." Kali raised her arm in a show of health, and winced. "Okay, not perfect, but I'm getting there."

"You're not leaving because of Ramon, are you? Like I'm taking his side instead of yours?"

"I feel ready to get back, is all." Not a total lie, Kali told herself. But Helen's remark hit close to the mark.

She spent the morning tidying up around the house. She did a load of laundry, then cleaned up in the kitchen. Her shoulder felt so much better that morning, she tried skipping the Vicodin altogether. By noon, however, it bothered her enough that she took two Motrin and sat down to rest. She flipped on the television and caught part of the local news. A picture of Betty Arnold was on the screen, and alongside it, one of Ramon Escobar. She wouldn't have picked him out of a crowd as the boy who'd rescued Tyler, but he did have the same dark complexion and wiry build she remembered. He was a good-looking young man, or could have been if he'd taken the scowl off his face.

The newscaster recapped the story, adding nothing to what Kali already knew. But she was only half listening. The picture of Ramon had jarred a memory, or the filament of a memory, at least. She was thinking of the flash of movement she'd seen the afternoon of the shooting. A big man. A blond man. Or was her mind playing tricks on her?

She turned off the TV, shut her eyes, and tried to concentrate. If only she could recall things more clearly. But she couldn't. And she knew from her work as a trial attorney that eyewitness testimony was notably unreliable.

Still, it bothered her that Ramon looked nothing like that fleeting image in her mind.

CHAPTER 9

Sid climbed the fence awkwardly. His bad leg slowed him down and made his footing unsure. He slipped once, gashing his hand on a loose piece of wire. Normally, he'd have been over the thing in a flash and he felt his anger rising at his own incompetence. Finally, he dropped down onto the soft earth inside the yard. A jolt of pain shot through him. He gritted his teeth until it passed.

He hated having to do damage control, but sometimes it was the only choice left. Sid had learned to focus on what needed doing and not let the "should haves" tie him in knots. Hans had fucked up big-time, but that was water under the bridge now. Sid had to look forward, come up with a new way to deal with the problem.

First step, he'd gotten rid of Hans. And not just because of the way Hans had bungled things (although Sid had to admit that watching him beg for his life had been a satisfying moment). More important was that Hans's screw-up had shown what a loose cannon the guy was. Sid worried he might shoot his mouth off, maybe unintentionally, maybe not. But either way, he'd end up dragging Sid's name in. Too much was at stake to take that chance.

Which brought him back to the issue of damage control. Hans was beyond talking—a safeguard which brought Sid a small measure of comfort—but that didn't resolve the main question about what Betty Arnold had known and whom she'd told.

Nor did it bring him any closer to getting what he was after.

That, too, was a matter of damage control.

He'd committed himself to this course eight years ago. It hadn't been a matter of choice, even then. You wanted to stay in business—hell, if you wanted to stay alive and healthy—you made sure the big man got what he wanted. One way or another.

At the time, Sid hadn't even considered coming clean. And he certainly wasn't about to do it now. So here he was all these years later, still walking the tightrope of his own lie and trying to fashion a safety net out of scraps.

The attorney posed the greatest risk. Also the best means to find what he needed. She was alive and Betty Arnold had been her client. She had to know something.

Sid needed to find out how much.

He expected she'd return to the Bay Area any day now. It was human instinct. People who were sick or injured always wanted to get home. Even when home was a dump, though that wasn't the case here. Kali O'Brien's house, in the Berkeley hills, was neither pretentious nor grand, but he could tell, just from the neighborhood, it hadn't been cheap.

He'd approached the hillside house by foot, from the rear, so what he first saw when he landed in her yard were the west-facing walls. Two floors of glass, which he knew would offer spectacular views of the San Francisco Bay.

He hobbled to the lower back door and was relieved to find that her locks were the simple, straightforward variety. No surprise, really. You'd think a lawyer would be more security conscious, but in Sid's experience, that was rarely the case. It was the big-shot businessmen—the CEOs, CFOs, chairmen of this and that, who took precautions. Sid consulted with many of them personally.

He let himself in through the back door on the lower level and went to work quickly. He didn't think anyone had seen him, but all it took was one busybody looking out the wrong window at the wrong time and he'd have a lot of explaining to do. Best to get in and out as quickly as possible.

Her computer was in the downstairs office. A good solid machine, but it was a couple of years old and not top of the line, which made his job easier. He reconfigured her firewall, loaded the software he needed to monitor her activity, then wiped the surface with a soft cloth. When he was done, he moved the computer tower back exactly where it had been, aided by indentation marks on the carpet and a line of dust at the rear.

The phones were next. One downstairs in the office, two more upstairs on the main floor—kitchen and master bedroom. Bugging them was child's play.

He kept his eye out as he went through the house. You never knew what you could learn about a person from the way they lived. He wasn't tempted to take anything—the last thing he wanted was for her to suspect someone had been inside. There wasn't much that grabbed his interest, anyway. Nice furnishings—a different league altogether than what he'd found in the Arnolds' trailer—but definitely low-tech. A sound system that had to be ten years old, and a TV with a twenty-one-inch screen that wasn't much newer. The jewelry he found was more artsy than valuable.

Sid went back to the office and turned his attention to her file cabinets. He was always amazed at the volume of peripheral stuff people accumulated, and Kali O'Brien was no exception. She had files for strength training exercises, computer columns clipped from newspapers, interior design ideas, a file for RESTAURANTS-LOCAL, as well as RESTAURANTS-OTHER.

But nothing that looked like it pertained to Betty Arnold.

He leafed through bills and bank statements, copied down her Social Security number, bank account and credit card numbers for good measure, although the information was easily available from other sources should he need them. He also scanned the contents of a folder labeled MEDICAL RECORDS just to see if it contained anything juicy. To his disappointment, it didn't. But Sid believed in making your own luck. The more dirt you collected on someone, the more likely it was some of it would prove useful.

Sid emptied the wastebasket onto a sheet of plastic he'd brought with him, and smiled when he retrieved an envelope postmarked Truckee. There was no return address, but he recognized Betty Arnold's distinctive back-slant handwriting. So she *had* sent Kali something. Less than two weeks ago, from the date of the postmark.

A sound near the front of the house sent a shot of adrenaline through Sid's system. His breath caught in his chest. He could feel his skin tingle.

The click of a latch. The soft whomp of a door shutting. Christ, she was home already.

Maybe he should just confront her, rough her up a bit and see what she knew, then get rid of her. There was a lot to be said for the direct approach.

But it sure as hell would complicate matters. An attorney and her client, both murdered. The cops were bound to start asking questions and looking for the connection. It had been a stroke of luck that they'd latched onto some local Tahoe kid as their chief suspect in the Arnold murder. Sid saw no reason to look a gift horse in the mouth.

Besides, there'd be time for roughing up later.

As he headed for the door he'd entered through, he heard her talking. Who was with her?

"Yes, Loretta's doing just fine." A short pause. "Of course she misses you." Another pause followed by a dramatic groan. "No, dogs do *not* just love anyone who feeds them, that's cats."

She was talking on the phone, he realized. And coming closer. He could hear the shuffle of her shoes on the hardwood floor in the next room. Then she stopped.

"Where did you want me to look?"

Sid hazarded a peek. She didn't look anything like the photo he'd seen. This woman was tall and flamboyant, with flaming red hair that fell to her shoulders in waves and wisps, and a chest that defied nature. He wasn't sure that she'd bear up under close scrutiny, but at thirty feet or so, she was a knockout. She was sorting through a stack of mail and papers.

"No, I don't see anything like that here. Of course, I'm sure. Honestly, Kali, if you weren't such a good friend I'd—" She laughed. "Okay, truce."

He smiled. So this wasn't the attorney herself, but a friend.

"Anything else you want me to look at while I'm here? I'd better water the primroses on the porch, too, they're looking a little droopy. Okay, see you tomorrow. Drive carefully."

The woman clicked off the phone. Sid watched her walk toward the front of the house. Her hips were firm. They swayed with the easy rhythm of a woman who didn't try to hide her feminine side. Sid liked that.

Good thing he'd just about finished here. The musky scent of the visitor's perfume lingered in the air after she'd gone, and played havoc with his concentration.

Kali was just finishing the last in a series of phone calls when Helen returned home.

"Any luck finding Ramon?" Kali asked.

Helen shook her head. "No one's seen or heard from him since yesterday morning."

"And his truck?"

"They've put a description out over the wire." Helen tossed her purse onto the kitchen chair. She seemed tired. "It doesn't look good for him. He was apparently coming back from his lunch break when the cops showed up at his job site. One of his coworkers saw his truck make a U-turn. I guess he spotted the cop cars and just took off."

Kali's doubts about whom she might have seen in the park were mollified a bit. Innocent men didn't run. "I'm sorry, Helen. I know you want to think the best of him."

"I still do. I know Ramon. He'd never shoot anyone, not in cold blood. It's just that . . . well, as I said, it doesn't look good."

She put a pot of water on for coffee. "Were you calling the office just now? I wish you weren't so set on going back tomorrow."

"I've got things that need doing. I called the office earlier. This last call was to my neighbor. I asked her to check my mail. I was hoping maybe there'd been a letter or package from Betty Arnold, mailed before she was killed."

"Why would she have sent it if she was going to see you in person?"

Kali shrugged. "You never know. It bugs me that she obviously had something important to discuss, something that demanded great secrecy, and that I haven't the foggiest idea what it was." Kali drummed the fingers of her good hand on the table. "I keep thinking it might be connected to her death."

Helen turned with a look of surprise. "You're not convinced Ramon was the killer, then?"

"How can I be convinced of anything? I don't know what evidence the cops have, or what Ramon has to say for himself. I know nothing about it at all. Besides, it doesn't matter whether *I'm* convinced or not."

"Geesh, you don't have to yell at me."

"Sorry." Kali realized her voice had risen several decibels. But she was yelling at herself as much as at Helen. Out of sheer frustration.

Her role in this investigation was that of victim and witness. Period.

Except that she had a vested interest in knowing the cops were focusing on the right man. That the killer wasn't a faceless threat still on her trail.

Helen poured water through the coffee filter. "The neighbor you were calling wasn't the neighbor you told me about, was it? The one who's . . . who was a man?"

"Technically still is as far as I know."

Helen rolled her eyes. "You get all types down there in the Bay Area, don't you?"

"That we do. Margot is actually pretty mainstream, though. I mean aside from the gender thing, she's just . . . ordinary."

Helen grinned. "*Aside from the gender thing.* That's a big aside, Kali. No wonder you're anxious to get back home. By comparison, life around here is dullsville."

"Except for an occasional murder in the park."

"Yeah." She handed Kali a cup of coffee. "By the way, did you know your client was Faith Foster's aunt?"

"Who?" The name was vaguely familiar.

"Faith Foster. Remember the young schoolteacher who disappeared about seven or eight years ago? I think it was in Palo Alto."

"Right. I thought the name was familiar. How do you know?"

"It was on the news as I was driving home. One of those human interest pieces. Betty's sister, that's Faith's mother, was one of the people killed when that plane lost a rudder outside of Denver a few years ago. That's part of what this news report was about, how tragedy lands disproportionately on some families. It's weird, don't you think?"

Kali nodded, but she was only half listening. Her mind was trying to call up the exact words Betty had used when Kali pressed her about the need for an attorney. Something about keeping faith or needing faith.

Had Betty meant Faith instead of faith?

Kali felt a chill in her spine. With nothing more to go on than instinct, Kali felt certain she was onto something.

CHAPTER 10

Kali arrived home from Tahoe a little before noon the following day, the muscle kinks from the three-hour drive compounded by the awkwardness of steering with only one good
arm. It felt wonderful to be back in her own house again, surrounded by her own things. She wanted to revel in the fact that
she was alive to enjoy them.

But questions about Faith Foster wouldn't let her rest. Kali dal-
lied only long enough to retrieve Loretta from Margot across the
street, listen to her phone messages, and thumb through the accumulated mail. Then she headed for the library, where she now sat
hunched in front of the microfiche reader, scanning old issues of
the *San Francisco Chronicle* and *San Jose Mercury News*.

She'd pulled her hair into a ponytail and wrapped it in a
scrunchie. The look was far from elegant, but it kept the hair from
falling into her eyes as she peered at the screen. The disappearance of Faith Foster had been front-page news for less than a
week before being relegated to an occasional short snippet in the
middle section of the paper. Kali remembered following the story
at the time it broke, but the details had faded from memory.

The photo accompanying the story showed a young woman
with curly brown hair and a heart-shaped face. What didn't show
up in the photo, but Kali recalled from the television coverage at
the time, was the startling seafoam green of Faith Foster's eyes
and the smattering of freckles across her nose. She'd been twenty-
three years old, several years younger than Kali had been at the
time, but their ages were close enough that her disappearance

had resonated with Kali in a way that most newsworthy crimes didn't.

Friends and coworkers spoke of Faith's levelheaded common sense, and insisted she'd never have gone off with a stranger or taken undue risks. Kali remembered thinking that her own friends would probably say something similar.

Faith was last seen on a Friday in late January leaving the upscale Stanford Shopping Center where she and a friend had gone looking for a birthday present for Faith's fiancé. She wasn't reported missing until the following Monday when she failed to show up for work. Her car was found several months later at the bottom of a rugged cliff off Highway 1 on the northern coast near Fort Bragg. Her purse and a shoe were found on nearby rocks, and the companion shoe washed up on a nearby beach not long after. As far as Kali could tell, her body had never been recovered.

Kali pushed back her chair, stood and stretched, careful to keep her left arm close to her side. She could feel tension in her lower back and neck, and her shoulder ached.

A teenage boy in baggy pants and headphones was using the microfiche machine next to hers. She could hear the music vibrate in the space between them, see it in the rhythmic bobbing of his torso. Both were playing havoc with her concentration. She looked to see if there was an empty machine. There wasn't.

If only she could remember Betty Arnold's exact words. Faith, or faith? Was Kali grasping at straws?

She sat down again and inserted another reel, checking it off on the list of citations she'd found earlier. A follow-up interview with Faith's mother and stepfather on the anniversary of her disappearance. Kali, who had no children and, until recently, no maternal yearnings, found a lump forming in her throat as she read through the article. How did people handle the grief of losing a child?

By five o'clock, Kali had read every news account she could find relating to Faith Foster's disappearance. As was so often the case, she ended up with more questions than answers.

She returned the tapes to the librarian at the desk, then stepped outside, turned on her cell phone, and called the Palo Alto police department. She left a message and headed for her car.

The thought of the hot shower awaiting her at home was like a beacon.

Pulling into her driveway twenty minutes later, Kali noticed that the front shutters were open. Movement flashed across the glass and she froze with fear.

Then she saw Bryce's car parked at the curb. A welcome sight under normal circumstances, but given her disheveled state, she was less than thrilled. Besides, what gave him the right to waltz in and make himself at home? True, she'd had fantasies about it in the past, but in her romantic visions she was always freshly showered and eager for company.

She pushed open the door. "What are you doing here?" She sounded even pricklier than she felt.

"Waiting for you." Bryce crouched near the floor as he tried to wrestle Loretta's chew toy from her mouth. It was a game the springer spaniel forced on any willing participant.

He looked up long enough to give Kali a wide smile. "I tried calling you at your cousin's and she said you'd left for home already. I knew you'd been here because Loretta was back."

She set her briefcase and purse on the floor. "How'd you get in?"

"You've got lousy locks, Kali. I've told you that before." Bryce was a cop, and while he didn't often throw that fact in her face, the locks were an ongoing point of contention.

"I had them changed not too long ago, if you'll recall."

"Changed but not improved." Bryce freed the toy from Loretta's jaws and tossed it the length of the hallway. The dog scampered after it.

"You could have called," Kali said.

"I did. Your cell phone was off." He crossed to where she was standing and gave her a gentle hug.

"I was in the library."

"How's the shoulder?"

"Don't change the subject by going all nice on me."

He touched her cheek. "Why not? I'm feeling 'all nice.' Especially now that you're back."

"Well I'm feeling sore, tired, and grumpy." And, she had to

admit, glad to see him. Though she was still slightly miffed at the way he'd made himself at home.

"I was trying to surprise you." He held up three fingers, Boy Scout's honor. "I didn't steal the silver."

"There isn't any."

"I brought stuff for margaritas," he added. "In fact, they're already mixed and in the fridge."

Okay, she conceded silently. *Maybe making himself at home wasn't all bad.*

"Also a steak," he added. "It's marinating. And a bag of charcoal in case you were out."

She relented and let go of the scowl. Bryce slipped an arm around her waist, carefully avoiding the injured shoulder. The solid warmth of his hand on her back melted whatever residual peevishness she felt.

He studied her carefully. His dark eyes, so often flat and unreadable, were soft. "How are you feeling, really?"

"I'm managing. My shoulder still throbs, but at this point it's more of a nuisance than anything."

"How about the rest of you?"

"I was telling the truth about being tired and grumpy, but otherwise I'm fine."

He shook his head. "Getting shot isn't like breaking a fingernail, Kali. You can't simply move on as though nothing happened."

Is that what he thought she was doing? Just because she hadn't turned into a quivering puddle of jelly didn't mean she was unaffected. But she didn't want to talk about it. Not yet. The nightmares, the flashes of fear that came out of nowhere and sucked the air from her lungs, the sense of dread that followed her like a shadow—they were too real still, too close to the surface. She was afraid that acknowledging them aloud would allow them the upper hand.

"My client was murdered," she told him instead. "I'm not exactly in denial about it."

Bryce started to say something, then apparently thought better of it. "Anyway, I'm glad you're home again and mostly in one piece. Let's hope it stays that way."

"Yeah, let's hope." No matter how careful she was, a determined killer would have no trouble finding a way to finish the job. It scared the hell out of her.

Bryce shoved a shock of dark hair out of his eyes. "You ready for a margarita?"

"Never readier." Kali followed him into the kitchen. He'd already salted the glasses. She could definitely get used to this sort of treatment.

She sat on one of the wicker bar stools by the counter. "Does the name Faith Foster ring a bell with you?"

"Vaguely, but I couldn't tell you why."

"She was a teacher who disappeared eight years ago."

Recognition registered in his expression. "She lived down the peninsula, right? And her stepfather was a judge. I remember now. I was with LAPD at the time. We did some background work because she'd graduated from UCLA." He took the double measuring cup of iced liquid from the refrigerator. "Why do you ask?"

"Betty Arnold was her aunt."

He drew in a breath. "Bad karma must run in the family."

"Seems that way, doesn't it? And Faith's mother, Betty's sister, was killed in a plane crash a few years ago."

Bryce winced. "That's tough." He poured the golden liquid into the salted glasses, handed her one, then raised his own in a toast. "To health and healing."

Kali lifted her glass as well. "That's an easy one. I'm already ninety percent there."

He arched an eyebrow and smiled his soft, sexy smile. "I wasn't talking only about your shoulder."

The way he said it, she knew instantly what he meant. "About us?"

"We're making progress, I think."

"I think so, too." But they were nowhere near ninety percent yet. The relationship had gotten off to such a terrible start—no, not true. It had gotten off to a good start, then she'd all but destroyed it in a moment of panic by accusing him of murder. The fact that they were even seeing each other was a positive sign. "I appreciate that you're making an effort," she told him.

Bryce grinned. "My motives are purely selfish."

"Are they, now?" she teased.

"You'd better believe it."

She'd believe it more if he wasn't so determined to let the relationship evolve at its own pace.

They moved onto the deck while Bryce set up the barbecue. He worked efficiently and smoothly, his expression intense, as it so often was when he was occupied.

"You were saying something about Faith Foster," he reminded her after a moment.

Loretta wandered outside and sat at Kali's feet, waiting for attention. Kali petted her head. "When Betty contacted me, she was vague about the reason. I pushed, and she finally said something about faith. Having faith or keeping faith or something along those lines. I thought she was simply putting me off, telling me to have faith and not be impatient. But now I'm thinking she may have been talking about her niece. Faith with a capital 'F.' "

"You mean, she wanted to talk to you about Faith Foster?"

"Right."

Bryce looked up from the grill. "It's an awfully tenuous link." Practically nonexistent, judging from his tone. But he was a skeptic by nature.

"I know it is. It's not a lot to go on but it feels important to me. Betty clearly had *some* reason for needing an attorney. She was so mysterious about everything . . . and the *faith* remark came out of left field. I remember thinking at the time that it seemed an odd response."

"You think she might have had information about her niece's disappearance?"

Kali nodded. "It's also possible that's the reason Betty was killed."

Bryce whistled softly under his breath. "That's a big leap. Though I suppose there is a certain logic to it."

Kali's gaze settled on the San Francisco skyline in the horizon. Coastal fog was spilling over the city, shrouding it in a layer of white fluff. Only the tips of the Golden Gate Bridge and the Sutro tower poked above the foggy dunes.

"Unless Betty was totally paranoid, which doesn't fit with

what I've learned about her, she must have had reason for insisting on such secrecy in our dealings."

"But Faith Foster disappeared eight years ago. If she had knowledge about what happened, why wait all this time to come forward?"

"Maybe she recently came across new information."

Bryce rubbed his chin. "In that case, why didn't she go to the police?"

"She might have been trying to protect someone." Kali thought of Betty's husband, now in an Alzheimer's facility. There was no way he'd be found competent to stand trial. Was that why Betty had decided the time had finally come to speak out?

"Or maybe," Kali continued, "the guilt about not coming forward earlier finally got to her." Then another thought struck. "It could also be that Betty Arnold was feeling guilty about being *part* of what happened to Faith."

"She wanted to turn herself in, you mean?"

"It would explain why she was so protective of her identity and why she wanted to make sure what she told me would remain confidential. I've never had a client take such extreme privacy measures before."

Bryce stirred the glowing embers. "They apparently weren't extreme enough if the killer knew where she was meeting you. Have you thought about that?"

That was one of the pieces that didn't fit. But then none of them fit neatly. "He could have followed her there. Or it could have been somebody she'd told about our meeting."

Bryce frowned, adjusted the air vents on the barbecue. "It doesn't make sense she'd tell someone after she went to such lengths to keep it quiet."

"Unless the person she told knew the whole story already." Kali shivered and buttoned her sweater. The wind blowing across the fog was cold.

"Looks like the fire's finally caught," Bryce said. "You want to move inside?" He was already heading for the door.

Kali followed gratefully. Her fingertips had turned white with the chill. "The police theory is that her killer was a man who got into an argument with her earlier that day." Kali explained the evidence against Ramon.

"Sounds like a reasonable assumption," he said when she'd finished. "I'd want to talk to the kid, too."

"It didn't seem so far off to me, either. Although Helen knows him and insists he's no killer. But all that was before I knew about Betty being Faith Foster's aunt."

"Which isn't really evidence."

"Not hard evidence, no." But it was sometimes just as helpful to weave threads of a more tenuous sort. "There's also the catch that Ramon is small and dark while the man I may have seen was big and fair."

Bryce had settled into the black-and-brown easy chair, but now he sat up straight. His face registered surprise. "You got a look at the killer?"

She shook her head, then took a sip of her drink. She was going out on a limb here and she knew she was going to sound foolish. "Not exactly. It's more an impression I have."

"An impression?"

"I can't say for sure that I saw him, but I think I did. It all happened very fast."

Bryce rolled his eyes, but the look on his face was more amused than disparaging. "You know how useless that is, right?"

"Yeah, I do." Eyewitness testimony often proved worthless, even when witnesses were certain they remembered what they'd seen.

The lesson was first brought home to her in law school. Her professor had staged a confrontation between a seeming stranger and himself that took place at the beginning of class in front of the entire room. The "stranger" had yelled wildly and threatened the professor, supposedly over a grade from last term, before grabbing papers from the podium and fleeing through a back door. Class members were then asked to describe the culprit, as if filing a witness report. The responses were all over the map, with the stranger portrayed as everything from a short, slender Hispanic in his twenties to a heavy-set, middle-aged Caucasian. He'd been, in fact, the thirty-four-year-old custodian of Greek decent they'd seen in the hallways of the school almost every day. No one in the class had recognized him out of context.

Kali was reminded of this demonstration every time she opened the paper and read about another felon who'd been convicted on eyewitness testimony and later freed when DNA evidence showed he couldn't have committed the crime.

She knew her *impression* didn't carry a lot of weight, except in her own mind. "What if I'm right, though? If I saw what I think I saw, the man with the gun couldn't have been Ramon."

Bryce scratched his cheek. "Did the cops have any suspects in Faith Foster's disappearance?"

"That's what I was doing at the library just now, reading over the newspaper accounts. They apparently questioned her family, coworkers and friends, including a fiancé. There was some speculation early on that he might have been involved, but I didn't see more mentioned so I guess they were eventually satisfied he wasn't part of it."

"Any mention of your client or her husband?"

"None that I saw." Kali leaned on the arm of the sofa and tucked a foot under her. "But we both know what makes it to the papers isn't always an accurate reflection of what's going on with an investigation."

"Even if you're right about Faith," Bryce said, "you've got an uphill battle trying to figure out what your client was up to."

"I know." But Kali didn't think she could just turn her back on the question either.

Bryce went outside to check on the fire. "Just about ready," he said when he returned. "There's still some margarita left in the fridge, you want more?"

"Not if I want to stay on my feet. What I'd really like is a shower. Do I have time?"

"Sure, I'll hold off putting the steak on."

The shower was heaven. Kali could feel some of the aches and tensions wash away along with the dust of library research. But Bryce's company held promise of even better things to come. She was in and out of the shower in less than five minutes, and into clean clothes and fresh makeup in another five. Then she took a few minutes longer to tidy the bedroom.

Just in case.

* * *

They'd moved from margaritas to wine, from serious conversation to playful flirtation, and were finishing dinner when the phone rang.

It was Helen. "How was your trip home?" she asked.

"Easy. There was hardly any traffic."

"Good. I'm not interrupting anything, am I?"

Not yet. "No, Bryce and I were just finishing dinner. He grilled a steak to welcome me home."

"He called here after you'd left." Helen hesitated. "I hate to ask this. I know you just got home and . . . and . . . everything."

Kali glanced over at Bryce, who was savoring the last drops from his wineglass and looking very relaxed. Is that what Helen had in mind by *everything*?

"Ramon called Maria," Helen continued, still sounding hesitant.

Kali sat up straighter. "Where is he?"

"He wouldn't say. He's agreed to talk to the police but he wants an attorney to go with him."

"He wants to turn himself in?"

"Not exactly. He says he had nothing to do with the murder. But he's scared, Kali. He's had experience with the police before."

Which wasn't exactly the fault of the cops. "Having an attorney is a good idea."

"Maria told him you might . . ."

"Hold it, Helen. I can't represent him."

"It has to be someone he trusts or he won't do it."

"Ramon doesn't even know me."

"He knows me, though. And you're the only attorney Maria knows. That's how she persuaded him to talk to the police in the first place."

"Maria doesn't know me either," Kali pointed out.

"Just talk to him, please? I know there's got to be a way to clear this up. And you'll be paid. Whatever your regular rate is."

"Money's not the issue."

Helen was quiet for a moment. "I thought you'd want to get to the bottom of this, Kali. To find out what really happened."

"I do—"

"Don't you want to be certain there's not someone out gunning for you?"

Helen knew how to get to her. "He can get—"

"He's willing to talk to the police if you go with him. It may be now or never. If he refuses to talk to them and they hunt him down . . . it could turn out very . . . very badly."

"That's his choice," Kali said. But the bigger picture wasn't lost on her. If Faith Foster's disappearance was at the root of all this, the cops were missing the mark with Ramon. The sooner they realized it and started looking for the real killer, the better. Particularly if the killer was still looking for her.

Or maybe Ramon *was* the killer. Either way, wasn't it better he talk to the cops than not?

"Does he know I'm one of the people he's accused of shooting?" Kali asked.

"He's not accused of anything yet. They just want to question him. But yes, he knows who you are."

"Okay, I'll talk to him. And I'll arrange a meeting with the detectives. But that's the extent of my involvement. I can't represent him if it goes farther."

"Thank you, Kali. I really appreciate this."

"I should be there by noon tomorrow. I'll try to reach the detectives before then. Ramon will be ready to talk with me?"

"Yes. He gave his word."

When she was off the phone, Bryce gave her a quizzical look. She explained.

"Sounds to me like you're sticking your toe into quicksand," he said. "Before you know it, you'll be up to your neck. Are you sure this is a good idea?"

Kali shook her head. "No, but it's expedient. I *can't* represent him in court. I'm sure it would be a violation of some sort. So it's just this one time. And I want to tell the detectives about Faith Foster anyway."

"Better that you go with him, I suppose, than some hotheaded defense attorney who'd tell him to shut his mouth and not say a word."

"Is that a backhanded compliment?" As a cop, Bryce had little regard for defense attorneys.

He grinned. "Of the highest order. Let's clean up, then I'll take off so you can get a good night's sleep."

"You're leaving?" She hoped her voice didn't betray her disappointment.

"You sound surprised."

"I am."

"We're taking it slow, remember?"

"Not too slow, I hope."

He looked at her and smiled faintly.

Genuine caution, Kali wondered, or payback for how she'd treated him? Maybe they were one and the same.

CHAPTER 11

Heading down I-80 on the eastern side of the summit the next morning, Kali took her eyes from the road long enough to take in the view of Donner Lake below. Diamonds of sunlight sparkled on the blue surface but the expanse of water was otherwise unbroken. In another couple of weeks or so the lake would be abuzz with boats and human activity, but for the time being the setting was serene.

Too bad the same couldn't be said for her mind. When she'd made this same drive a little more than a week earlier, she'd been awed by the lushness of the mountain spring. Now the echo of gunshots and the rumble of unanswered questions marred her pleasure.

As she descended farther into the valley, she checked her cell phone for signal strength, and called Helen.

"I set a meeting for two o'clock," Kali said. "Tahoe City substation. Just checking to make sure Ramon will be there."

"He'll be there, but he wants to meet with you first. He's here at my house right now."

She'd half expected he would have disappeared again. "Good. I'm almost to Highway 89. I should be at your place in half an hour."

When she'd finally tracked down Detective Bauman last night, he'd greeted her announcement with skepticism—although it was clear he wasn't about to turn his back on an offer to produce Ramon. But that was as far as it went. Bauman hadn't been forthcoming with information, nor had he seemed particularly interested in the connection between Betty Arnold and Faith Foster.

And maybe it wasn't *significant,* Kali reminded herself.

As she pulled into Helen's long driveway, Kali's stomach clenched with nervousness. Even if this meeting wasn't some sort of elaborate trap—a thought that had crossed her mind more than once—and even if Betty *had* wanted to see Kali about Faith Foster, Ramon still might be a killer.

A dark-haired male was seated at Helen's kitchen table, fingers drumming fitfully on the pine surface while his legs bounced and jangled to their own beat.

"Kali, this is Ramon. Ramon, Kali. You've met before, but it's been a while." Helen's voice was full of forced cheer.

Ramon stood up. Kali could read nervousness in his expression, yet his gaze met hers as he shook her hand. His eyes were brown and soft, almost as if he were smiling, though the rest of his face remained taut.

"There's coffee already made," Helen said pertly. "And banana bread. Help yourselves." She folded her hands, then unfolded them. "I'll be outside if you need me."

"You want something to drink?" Kali asked when they were alone.

Ramon shook his head. He was smooth-skinned and slender. Not frail so much as small-boned, with delicate, almost feminine features.

Kali poured a half cup for herself, more out of habit than any real desire for coffee. Ramon waited for Kali to sit before doing so himself. A sign of manners she didn't often see, even from men twice his age.

"I sure appreciate this," he said. "My mom says you can make the cops understand it wasn't me."

Kali shook her head. If Maria had offered assurances by way of cajoling her son to talk to the police, Kali wanted to set the record straight up front. "I can't make any promises, Ramon. I don't know what the cops know, or think they know, and I don't have any say in what they ultimately decide. All I can do is make sure your rights aren't violated, and try to keep you from shooting yourself in the foot."

He looked surprised and she realized her choice of words had been less than apt. "That's a figure of speech. It means I'll try to prevent you from saying things that will get you into more trouble."

"I know what it means." A faint smile, then he grew serious again. He ran his hands along his knees. He was dressed casually, but neatly, in jeans and a dark green T-shirt. His well-worn leather jacket was draped over the back of his chair.

"I don't have much money," he said. "Neither does my mom. How much are we going to owe you for this?"

"Nothing." Helen would want to pay her but Kali didn't want money from Helen either. It wasn't about money, it was about settling the doubts in her own mind. And because it had been Helen who asked.

"I don't want charity," Ramon insisted.

"This isn't charity. But it *is* a one-time thing. You understand that, don't you?"

He nodded. "Helen told me."

Kali sipped her coffee, studied Ramon again for a moment. "Why do you think the cops are interested in talking to you?" she asked.

"They say my truck was at the park where you and that woman were shot. That she and me had an argument earlier about an accident."

"Is that true?"

"Which part?"

"Let's start with the argument."

"Yeah, that part's right, only it was her that was all hot and bothered. She stopped suddenly in the middle of the road and I bumped her fender. Wasn't like anyone was hurt. The dent was hardly noticeable. Still, she was screaming at me like I'd done it on purpose or something. And when I tried to get her name and driver's license number, she refused. Just drove off."

Kali wrapped a hand around her coffee mug. "The woman did all the yelling, then? Not you?"

"I probably said some things back to her. I don't like being yelled at."

"So you *were* angry?"

Ramon rolled his shoulders. "Angry about the way she was treating me, sure. But not angry, *angry*, if you know what I mean."

"Not exactly. Why don't you explain."

"Not angry enough to kill her, that's for sure. I should have thanked her for not filing an accident report. Last thing I need is for my insurance to go up."

Kali couldn't tell how much of this rendition was self-serving, but the basic scenario wasn't so far-fetched. Not only was Betty Arnold driving a car she'd borrowed without permission, she wanted to keep her identity and trip to Tahoe quiet. Her reaction to being rear-ended might well have been more vehement than normal.

"What about the truck at the park?" Kali asked. "Could that have been yours?"

"No way. I wasn't anywhere near the park."

"Where were you that afternoon? Your boss said you didn't show up for work that day."

Ramon looked at the floor. "Nowhere in particular. I was just driving."

"Is that something you do often, just drive?"

"I had a lot to think about."

"Like?"

He turned slightly in his chair. "It's personal."

"The same could be said for murder."

For the first time, emotion flashed in Ramon's eyes. "If I'd killed someone, you think I'd be stupid enough to just drive around afterward?"

She'd known it to happen. "How about the rest of the weekend, how did you spend the time?"

"Hanging out with friends."

"What about your girlfriend?"

"What about her?" His tone had turned sharp.

"Did you spend time with her?"

"She was working most of the weekend. We talked on the phone."

"The cops are going to contact these people, if they haven't already. What are they going to hear about your mood?"

"What difference does it make?"

"It will show your state of mind, whether you were nervous, relaxed, worried . . . Whether you said anything that might be construed as an admission of guilt."

Ramon shrugged. "They're my friends, they're not going to talk bad about me." He was sounding impatient, restless.

"When the cops showed up at work earlier this week to talk to you, you took off. Why is that?"

"No real reason. I just panicked."

"You saw the police cars and were scared?"

"Yeah."

"Most people don't panic when they see police cars, Ramon, and they certainly don't run. Not unless they expect trouble."

"I'm not most people." Ramon pressed his knuckles against his cheeks. He took a deep breath. "I know it looks bad, but it's the truth. I was scared and I didn't think. That's all."

A response that might defy logic, but Kali had heard it often enough in her career to know there was a segment of society where running from the cops made sense. Still, Ramon hadn't helped his case any by fleeing.

"What about the gun the cops couldn't find?" she asked.

"I don't have it anymore. I lent it to a friend."

"When was this?"

"About a year ago."

Kali frowned. "Who's the friend?"

"Willie Pinkus."

"Where can I reach him?"

"He's doing time in Folsom."

Which made him a witness with the credibility of a flea. Kali sighed. "Does the name Faith Foster mean anything to you?"

Ramon shook his head. "Should it?"

"Not necessarily." She hadn't really expected that it would, but she had to ask. "Is there anything else you want to tell me?"

"I didn't shoot anyone. Not that woman, not you, not anyone." He looked her straight in the eye. "I didn't do it."

"It's cops you have to convince, not me."

"I can't go to jail, Ms. O'Brien. I got to set this right."

Kali and Ramon arrived at the station together in Kali's car. During the short drive from Helen's, Ramon had been both jumpy and silent. Kali was grateful for the latter, but his twitching only added to her own nervousness.

Kali told the man at the desk who they were. He buzzed them through security and showed them to an interview room, leaving them alone with the door closed and undoubtedly locked. The room was small and bare, with a metal-frame table and four hard, molded-plastic chairs, but it was cleaner and nicer than the interview rooms Kali was used to in the Bay Area.

Kali checked her watch and timed the wait. It was only five minutes until the door opened again. Not bad at all. She gave them points for that.

Detective Bauman arrived with a young Asian woman Kali took to be Kim Wong. Introductions confirmed that she was right.

Bauman looked at Ramon hard for a few moments, then nodded. "Hello, Ramon. Here we are again. Didn't I predict that last time?"

To his credit, Ramon didn't rise to the bait. He said, "I heard you wanted to see me."

"You heard," Bauman mimicked. "Nice of you to show up. Unlike Wednesday where you turned tail and ran the minute you saw a police car."

Kali spoke up. She was tired of the detective's innuendo. "Is Mr. Escobar a suspect in this crime?" she asked.

"No. We simply have some questions we'd like to clear up."

"Okay, then. He came in voluntarily to answer them. So why don't you get on with it."

Bauman did most of the asking while Kim Wong listened intently, hardly taking her eyes off Ramon. Kali sensed the younger detective would have liked to play a more active role, but she deferred to Bauman.

The questions they asked covered more or less the same territory Kali had explored with Ramon earlier. As Kali had predicted, they'd spoken with his friends and coworkers. The consensus seemed to be that Ramon had appeared distracted over the weekend, and a little nervous. Or maybe the detectives were simply trying to rattle him. They pushed harder than Kali had, and tried to trip Ramon up when they could, but they were never out of line.

Still, it was difficult to read their reactions.

"We'd like to take a look at your truck," Bauman said. "That okay with you?"

Ramon looked at Kali. "If you don't give them permission," she said, "they'll have to get a warrant first, but eventually they'll look at it."

"Sure, look all you want," Ramon said. "I've got nothing to hide. It's not here though, I drove in with my attorney."

They made arrangements for someone to follow Kali and Ramon to Helen's.

"And you can be sure we'll be talking to Willie Pinkus," Bauman said.

"I told you, I've got nothing to hide."

Kali turned to Bauman as they were leaving. "You haven't forgotten what I told you about Faith Foster, have you? About her disappearance maybe being a factor in Betty Arnold's murder."

"I haven't forgotten." His tone made it clear he wasn't giving it a lot of credence, however. "It strikes me," he added, "that you seem awfully interested in protecting a man who may have shot you."

"What I'm interested in is getting at the truth."

He grinned with what struck Kali as genuine good humor. "Spoken like a true defense attorney," he said.

Kim Wong closed her notebook and recapped her pen. She'd gotten ink on her finger but she didn't want to call attention to it now by trying to wipe it clean.

"What do you think?" Bauman asked.

"I don't know, it could go either way." She wanted Ramon to be their man. She'd run the plates that led them to him. His arrest would look good on her record. But she couldn't ignore the niggling of doubt in her mind.

"Ms. O'Brien thinks the man she saw in the woods was bigger than Ramon," Kim pointed out, "and that his coloring was fair."

"She wasn't sure, though. Wasn't sure she'd actually seen *anyone*, in fact. She didn't mention it at all until I pressed her for details. And now she's representing Ramon. I'd say she's not a credible witness."

"She's not representing him," Kim said. There was a part of her that didn't want to talk to Gary Bauman at all. And another part that wanted to argue with everything he said. "She made that point clear, remember? It was just today, because Ramon Escobar was willing to come talk to us."

"So she says." Bauman pressed his palms together. "Let's get our jogging witness to look at Ramon's truck and see if she can make a positive identification. Have someone talk to Pinkus about the gun, too."

"What about the stuff with Faith Foster? Shouldn't we check into that?"

"Check into what? That more than eight years after the fact, Betty Arnold might have been about to point a finger at the guilty party?" He shook his head in disbelief. "We've got a live suspect here, Kim. With a motive."

"Not much of one."

"Enough. He's got a history of flying off the handle with anger. And we've got evidence against him. We don't need to rule out all other possibilities."

"You don't like Ramon, do you?" The words were out of Kim's mouth before she'd thought about them.

Bauman raised an eyebrow at her. "Is it that obvious?"

"Probably not to most people."

He thought for a moment. "No, I don't like him. But that's not the issue here."

Kim wondered if he actually believed that.

Sid Mertz was hobbling across California Street on his way to a weekend meeting with a client in the Embarcadero Center, when his cell phone rang. It didn't actually ring, because phones rarely did these days, and Sid had set his for the least obtrusive tone he could find. A soft, melodic scale of three notes.

He checked the number, then stepped against the building to answer. He wasn't about to walk down the street broadcasting his business to the world the way some people did.

"Yeah," he said.

"Hello, Sid. How's the leg?" Mr. D had manners. Always the gentleman, even when the reason for his call might be unpleasant.

"Getting better every day," Sid replied.

"That's good. Listen, I need someone to scope out a situation for me. Strictly low impact. No fireworks, no confrontation. You up for it?"

"Sure thing."

"There'll be three crates delivered at the port of Oakland

Monday morning. Marked for delivery to K.S.T. Textiles. I want to know what happens to them."

"Can do."

"I know, Sid. That's why I count on you." There was a muffled throat clearing on the other end. "Don't know if you heard the news—Faith Foster's aunt was murdered last week outside of Tahoe City."

Sid's heart jumped. "No, I hadn't heard."

"I thought it might interest you. Six degrees of separation and all. Give me a call tomorrow. About four."

The line went dead before Sid could reply. He was sweating. How the hell did Mr. D know about Betty Arnold?

The story had been in the newspapers, Sid reminded himself. And Mr. D liked to stay on top of what was happening. Still, Sid couldn't help wonder if there was a hidden message in his remark.

That was the problem with manners and polite conversation. It was impossible to tell what was really being said.

Sid started to slip the phone back into his jacket pocket, then flipped it open again instead and dialed a buddy of his who'd retired up in the Tahoe area.

"What do you hear about that recent murder?" Sid asked when they'd dismissed with the preliminaries.

"Only that they're looking at a local kid as the shooter."

"Yeah. I heard that he and his attorney met with the cops this morning." Because of the bugs he'd placed, Sid knew about the call O'Brien had received last night. What he wanted to learn was how much she actually knew. "Think you can pick up any static for me?"

"I can give it a try. What's your interest? The victim a friend of yours?"

Sid took a minute to consider how best to answer. "We have some shared history," he said finally.

"Ah."

Sid knew the guy was thinking romance. Let him.

Sid shoved the cell phone back into his pocket and hobbled for the crosswalk, entering it as the red hand began flashing. The cars could damn well wait if necessary.

The local boy they'd picked up was the first lucky break he'd had. With Hans dead, Sid knew it would have been next to impossible for the cops to have tied the shootings back to him. Now, at least, they were no longer asking questions.

But that damned attorney was.

And Mr. D was watching.

Sid could feel the tension building in his shoulders. *First things first*, he told himself. He had to make sure the kid stayed on their radar. And he needed some answers of his own.

He'd found nothing in O'Brien's house or her office. And his search of Betty Arnold's place in that godforsaken trailer park hadn't turned up anything, either. Nothing. No photograph. No clipping. No magazine.

The stupid woman had probably already passed it to the attorney. But Sid had searched both her office and her home, and it hadn't shown up. So where the hell was it?

Sid's buddy from Tahoe called back a couple of hours later. Sid was still in his meeting, but he stepped outside to take the call when he saw who it was.

"You learn something?" Sid asked.

"Like I said, they're zeroing in on the kid. Turns out he has a gun like the one used in the shooting, though he says he loaned it to a friend. Guy who's now doing time."

"You have the name?"

"Willie Pinkus. Folsom State Prison."

Sid smiled to himself. He knew just who he needed to talk to at the prison.

CHAPTER 12

Kali was sitting at her own kitchen table, one bare foot resting on the rung of the chair next to her, sipping an afternoon cup of coffee. Loretta slept in a spot of sun by the French doors. It had been a long and exhausting couple of days, and Kali was glad to be home.

She'd spent the weekend at Helen's, intending to leave early Monday morning. But the two women had stayed up late Sunday rehashing all that had happened over a bottle of wine, and when Kali had finally gone to bed, sleep had not come easily. In the morning, she turned off the alarm, thinking to give herself another five minutes of rest. She awoke an hour and a half later to bright sunlight streaming through the bedroom window.

The late start was compounded by a three-car pileup near Auburn that brought traffic to a near standstill. As a result, the trip had taken almost five hours instead of the usual three. Five hours alone with her thoughts, playing the possibilities one against the other. And her mind still wouldn't let go.

Ramon. Betty. Faith. A flash memory of the shooter. The sudden swiftness of unanticipated death. And shadowing every image was a barely restrained fear that threatened to erupt into full blown panic. What if the killer was looking for her?

The phone rang and Kali jumped before picking it up.

"Ms. O'Brien?" The voice was male and brusque. "Detective Martin, here. Palo Alto police. You left a message inquiring about an old case."

Kali removed her foot from the chair and sat up straight, as though Martin could see her. "Yes, the Faith Foster case. She disappeared eight years ago."

He offered no acknowledgment.

"I understand the original detective has retired and the case is now yours."

"I can't say that I'm up to speed on it. Are you a relative?"

"An attorney." That usually got their attention, but not always for the better.

"What's your interest in this?" Martin asked.

She explained the events that had led to her call. "I think it's possible that Betty Arnold knew something about the crime."

"Any idea what?"

"I'm afraid not."

Martin sighed. "I'll contact the Placer County Sheriff's department," he said with an obvious lack of interest. "Ask them to get in touch once they've made an arrest."

Kali had been hoping for something a bit more proactive. "What can you tell me about the investigation into Faith's disappearance? Was anyone identified as a possible suspect?"

"I'd have to go back and look at the file."

"What about Betty Arnold? Do you know if she was living in the area at the time?"

"Again, I'd have to take a look at the file."

"Will you do that?"

A beat of silence. "I've got a full load of active cases, Ms. O'Brien, including a fresh homicide this morning. Time constraints make it impossible to follow up on every little thing. I'm sure you must realize that."

"I do. It's just that if Betty was killed because of what she knew, then there's an obvious connection between her murder and Faith's."

"Interesting, but at this point not very useful. If you come across some actual information, please give me another call." He hung up before she could respond.

What a prick. Maybe Kali hadn't given him hot, case-breaking details, but she'd thought Betty's connection to Faith Foster might at least stir the embers of interest. Wrong. Detective Martin was even less interested in what she had to say than Deputy Bauman had been.

She dumped what was left of her coffee into the sink and rinsed the cup. She called the office. Jared picked up on the first ring.

"Things still under control there?" Kali asked. She knew Jared would never admit otherwise, but from previous calls she felt reasonably certain he was on top of what needed doing. She was glad he'd decided to stay with her after Nina left rather than taking a better-paying job elsewhere.

"If you don't count the fact we've had only two people call about the secretarial position we listed," Jared said. "One of them barely spoke English and the other didn't know how to use a computer."

"We'll find someone eventually. What about the Robinson matter?"

"I got the motion filed on time. The hearing isn't for a couple of weeks. How are you doing?"

"It's up and down. I should be back in the office tomorrow."

"I'll have the beer cans and candy wrappers picked up by then."

"The what?"

"Just joking. It'll be nice to have you back. It's been kind of lonely here."

"It will be nice to *be* back." Loretta pulled herself to her feet and whimpered to go out. Kali took pity on her. "I've got to go," she told Jared. "Talk to you later."

She got the leash and the yellow plastic bag the morning *Chronicle* had come in—it was ideal for dog detail—and headed out. She checked the street for strange cars and fought the mental image of a shooter behind every bush.

When she returned, she called information and asked for the number for Leonard Sandborn, the detective who'd worked the Faith Foster case originally. She'd be damned if she would let Martin's brush-off be the end of it.

"I don't have any listing by that name," the operator told her.

No surprise. Even retired, it was a rare cop who listed his home phone number. She tried Bryce next.

"Hi. It's me."

"Hey." His voice took on a warm glow. "Where are you? Are you back home yet?"

"I got back a little while ago."

"How'd it go?"

"With Ramon? He wasn't arrested on the spot, but I don't know that he won either of the detectives over to his side, either."

"What about you?"

She sighed. "His physical appearance, his voice, none of it fits with what I remember. On the other hand, I wasn't my most observant self with bullets flying through the air and my client crumpled on the ground dying."

Bryce was quiet a moment. Then he said, "If it wasn't him . . . I worry about you, Kali."

That made two of them. But it also gave Kali a nice, fuzzy feeling to hear Bryce say so. "That's nice to know," she told him.

"That I'm worried about you?" He laughed. "Did you think I wouldn't be?"

"I don't know what you think sometimes."

The silence that followed wasn't exactly stony, but he didn't rush to tell her he adored her, either. Rather than push it, she got to the reason for her call. "I have a question for you. Is there some sort of retirement roster for police officers?"

"Each jurisdiction is probably different. What do you need?"

"A phone number for Leonard Sandborn. He was the original detective in charge of the Faith Foster case."

"Let me see what I can find out." Bryce paused for a moment and Kali could hear a scratching sound, like pen on paper. "You know what year he retired?"

"Afraid not."

"Probably doesn't matter."

Bryce called her back in less than an hour. "Sandborn lives in Pacifica," he said. "Retired three years ago." He gave her a phone number.

"Thanks. I owe you."

"I'm not going to let you forget it, either. Only I'm going to take payment in favors of a slightly more personal nature."

"You're the one who wanted to go home the other night." She'd tried to make it sound light but it came out whiny instead. She gave an apologetic laugh. "Sorry, I'm finished with my clingy female impersonation now."

"Actually," he said, sounding amused, "I kind of like it."

* * *

As soon as she'd hung up, Kali called Sandborn. He picked up in the middle of the fourth ring, just as she was preparing herself for the answering machine.

"I believe you worked on the Faith Foster case eight years ago," Kali said after she'd introduced herself. "A young teacher who disappeared."

"Not one of our successes, I'm sorry to say." His voice was deep and rich, the vowels fully rounded.

"I was hoping you could tell me something about the investigation."

"This relate to a case you're working on now?"

"I'm not sure. It's complicated, probably best explained in person." No way was she going to let Sandborn brush her off the way Martin had.

"I don't know how much help I'll be."

"I won't take much of your time," Kali said. "I can be there in about an hour. Or tomorrow if you'd rather." She wasn't fond of railroad tactics but sometimes they were necessary.

Sandborn was quiet a moment. "Sure, why not. Now's as good a time as any. You like fish?"

Fish covered a lot of territory. Kali hoped he wasn't suggesting they meet on a boat. Her sea legs were nonexistent. But with information this close at hand, she wasn't about to be difficult. "Sure."

"There's a great restaurant here in town. The Grotto. You buy me dinner and I'll tell you what I can. How's six o'clock sound?"

"Perfect." She wrote down the address and Sandborn's elaborate set of directions, then took along a map for good measure.

Dinner was not going to set her back much. Kali could tell that the minute she pulled into the restaurant's parking lot. The place looked like little more than a shack.

The inside was an improvement, though only marginally. Naturally distressed wooden tables and mismatched chairs. Fishing nets and floats covering the walls, a large stuffed swordfish behind the bar. The place had a certain charm, but it wasn't a restaurant Kali would have picked if she were the one getting a free meal.

A broad-shouldered black man got up from the bar and came toward her. "Ms. O'Brien? I'm Leonard Sandborn. I hope you didn't have any trouble finding the restaurant."

She shook his hand. "Your directions were perfect."

The waitress led them to a corner table. Sandborn ordered a second beer; Kali said she'd stick with water.

"Working, huh?"

"Driving," she said.

Sandborn smiled. He was an attractive man, with deep-set eyes and a full head of tight salt-and-pepper curls. He was meticulously dressed in wool slacks and a dark tweed blazer. A far cry from the tottering old man she'd expected.

"The clam chowder's to die for," Sandborn said. "But it's all good."

He ordered the fried fish plate, Kali the grilled salmon. They both had the chowder, as well.

"Faith Foster," Sandborn said when the waitress left them. "It's been a while since I've thought about that case."

"I know the basics from the newspaper accounts. But I don't know if there were any witnesses, leads, or solid theories about why or how she died."

"Nothing that panned out. We had our suspicions about a sex offender who'd been recently released from 'treatment.' " Sandborn twisted the word with sarcasm. "He was living in San Francisco at the time, and was later convicted of raping and strangling a nurse in the East Bay, but we were never able to tie him to Faith Foster."

"You think he might have killed her, though?"

Sandborn sipped his beer. "I honestly don't know. Her parents pressed me on that, too. I'm sure they wanted it to be him just so they'd have some sense of closure."

"I can't imagine there's ever closure in a death like that."

"Me neither. But a lot of people want to believe there will be."

"Where is he now?" Kali asked. "The sex offender you were talking about."

The waitress brought their soup. Sandborn waited until she'd left to reply. "Prison. He couldn't have had anything to do with your client's death, if that's what you're thinking."

"You read my mind." Kali tasted the chowder. Sandborn had been right, it was first-rate. Creamy but not thick with glutenous flour as so often was the case. And there were real, bite-size pieces of clams.

"The trouble with the Faith Foster case," Sandborn said, "was that we had so little to go on. No body, no witnesses, no one who saw her after she left her friend at the shopping center. We don't know if she was killed as a result of a chance encounter with a predator or if she was targeted by someone. It's even possible she drove up the coast voluntarily and simply took the turn too fast."

The lack of conviction in his voice caught Kali's attention. "But you don't think it was an accident?"

Sandborn shook his head. "We had no hard evidence one way or another, but no, I don't. Her friends all said it would be out of character. It's a four-hour drive up a winding highway, and Faith was apparently worried about driving long distances in a car she didn't consider reliable. What's more, she'd planned on joining a group of fellow teachers for an informal picnic that Sunday."

"No one called when she failed to show up?"

"They assumed she'd changed her mind or forgotten. One of the teachers tried calling her that evening but they weren't worried."

"What about people Faith knew? Any chance one of them was involved?"

"We looked at the fiancé, of course. Boyfriends, husbands, ex-whatevers, they always warrant a good hard look. But Faith's fiancé had a solid alibi. He was out of town on a business trip. We verified it." Sandborn paused, rubbed his chin. "Less than a week later he committed suicide, though."

Kali looked up, startled. She'd missed that in her search of newspaper files. Or maybe the story hadn't garnered much attention. "You think he was implicated in Faith's death?"

"There was never any evidence. No motive we could come up with, either. And people do commit suicide out of grief." Sandborn was clearly troubled by something.

"What is it?" Kali asked him.

"Nothing I can put my finger on. But I took an instant dislike to the guy. He was a bit too smooth, and at the same time, very remote. Like everything about him was an act. Suicide seemed too emotional a response for someone like him."

"Do you remember his name?"

"Andrew Major, the third. He was a lawyer," Sandborn added, as if that explained everything.

"A lawyer. No wonder you didn't like him."

Sandborn laughed. "You're wrong there. My two brothers are both lawyers."

"There was no question it was a suicide?"

"Not that I ever heard. He lived up in Foster City. Different jurisdiction."

"So you questioned him but he wasn't really a suspect. And then he killed himself?"

"That's it in a nutshell. Not enough there for us to close the case or even publicly pin a murder rap on him."

"Do you remember anything about Faith's aunt, Betty Arnold? Was she around at the time?"

He thought a minute. "I don't recall. I'm sure there must have been at least a phone interview. The file would probably say."

"The detective on the case now isn't talking."

"Who's that?"

"Someone by the last name of Martin."

Sandborn looked at her over his half-raised soupspoon. He shook his head. "No, you won't get much out of him."

"I take it that, unlike you, he's not fond of attorneys."

"He's not fond of anyone. He's a good cop, though."

The main course arrived. A mountain of food, and it was good. They ate in silence for a few minutes.

"Why'd you retire?" Kali asked finally, "if you don't mind my asking. You don't look old enough."

"It wasn't me that was so old, it was my ticker. I had a heart attack and triple bypass surgery. Damn lucky to be alive. I decided it was time to do something else with my life."

Kali noticed the heart trouble hadn't stopped him from loading up on fried food. "So what do you do with your time now?"

"I keep busy. So busy I don't know how I ever found time to work. I'm with my granddaughter a lot, and I'm working on a book."

"A thriller?"

He laughed. "That would be the thing to do, wouldn't it? No, I'm writing a children's book. Reliving all the stuff I should have enjoyed with my own kids." He speared a prawn. "What's the

Placer County sheriff's office think about all this? Are they looking into the connection between your client's murder and her
niece's?"

Kali shook her head and told him about Ramon. "They seem
to think it's a case of delayed road rage."

"The obvious is often the answer, you know. No fancy motive,
no hidden secrets—just some dumb, petty conflict most of us
would simply roll with."

Sandborn finished his meal, then checked his watch. "If you
think of anything else, give me a call. Sorry to run off, but I'm
staying with my granddaughter tonight. Her mom has a hot
date."

He stood. "For the record, I'm not happy about the divorce or
the dating. Not that my opinion counts for a hill of beans. Thanks
for the dinner."

"Thanks for taking the time to talk with me. And I bet your
opinion counts for more than you think."

He grinned. "You've clearly never met my daughter."

Tuesday afternoon, Kim Wong went to see Ramon's girlfriend,
Nadia. She found the girl behind the counter at the dry cleaners
her family operated, sorting clothes.

"Can we step outside for a moment?" Kim asked.

In the corner of the shop, a woman huddled over a large black
sewing machine looked up. She had the sharp eyes and pinched
face of someone who found little joy in life.

Nadia nodded and started around to the front of the counter.
The woman barked something in a Slavic-sounding language
Kim couldn't place. The tone was strident.

Nadia answered in English. "It's okay, Mama. It's probably
about Ramon." She looked at Kim. "Right?"

The mother shook her fist. "That boy is a bad influence. Always
trouble. We tell you, no?"

Nadia rolled her eyes and followed Kim outside to the small
gravel parking lot in front of the building. A liquor store was next
door, a furniture consignment shop beyond that. Nadia moved all
the way to the end of the lot in front of the consignment shop before turning to face Kim.

"Mothers can be so protective," Kim prompted. She thought

the casual, woman-to-woman approach might ease the conversation.

But Nadia wasn't buying into it. "That's a mother's role." She gave Kim a bored yawn.

The girl was seventeen. Kim knew that from the report of the officer who'd questioned her initially, but she looked older. She was attractive, Kim thought, but not really pretty. There was no sparkle in her eyes, no vibrance about her at all. But maybe that had to do with the circumstances of their meeting.

"I need to get back to work, so ask me what you came to ask."

"Have you talked to Ramon recently?"

"He called yesterday, but I couldn't talk."

"Couldn't? How come?"

Nadia scuffed her left shoe in the gravel. "I needed to take my little sister to get some school supplies."

Although it had been a while, Kim had been in love, herself. And she'd once been seventeen. She'd never known a trip to the store to stand in the way of conversation with a boyfriend. "He didn't call back?"

Nadia shrugged. "He must have been busy."

"So when was the last time you actually talked to Ramon?"

"Last Sunday." Nadia didn't even stop to think about the answer.

Two days after he'd allegedly shot Betty Arnold. "How'd he seem?"

"What do you mean?" For the first time since they'd come outside, Nadia looked directly at Kim.

"Was there anything bothering him? Did he seem upset or nervous?"

She shook her head. "No."

"Other friends say he seemed preoccupied and agitated. Like he was worried."

She shook her head again, more vehemently. "Not that I saw."

Kim got the feeling Nadia was deflecting questions more than answering them. She switched gears. "Is Ramon violent?"

Nadia gave her a look that Kim read as *That's a stupid question.* She tried again. "Have you ever seen him lose his temper?"

"Ramon has feelings, okay? Everyone does. He gets angry sometimes, sure. But he's not mean or violent. There's a difference."

Kim thought the difference involved a line so fine it was some-times difficult to tell when it had been crossed. "He's got a tem-per, though. Right?"

Nadia folded her arms. "If you knew Ramon," she snapped, "you'd know there was no way he killed that woman. He's al-ways helping people."

"Like the guy whose nose he broke?" Kim had reviewed his rap sheet that morning. All petty stuff but taken together it pre-sented a pattern.

Defiance flashed in Nadia's eyes. "That was different. The guy provoked him."

"And the man whose garage Ramon broke into."

"You don't know anything, do you?" Defiance turned to anger. "Ramon sold that trailer to Mr. Turner, but Turner never paid him. Ramon was just taking back what was rightfully his."

"You must care about him a great deal," Kim said gently.

Tears welled in the girl's eyes. She turned to go back inside. "I need to get to work."

She *was* pretty, Kim decided. It was the mask of sullenness that had made Kim think otherwise.

Kim was on her way to her car when her cell phone rang. It was the deputy who was following up on the gun Ramon owned.

"I talked to Willie Pinkus," he told her. "Pinkus says he bor-rowed the gun for target shooting and gave it back a couple of weeks later."

"That's not what Ramon says."

"One of them is lying, then."

And the odds were it wasn't Pinkus.

CHAPTER 13

When the phoniness of Las Vegas began to wear on her, Irene often took refuge in the library. Her local branch was modern and sleek, nothing like the cozy, slightly musty rooms of her childhood or the ivy-covered brick of her student days, but at least it contained books (though in no greater number than videos and CDs), and was blessedly free of slot machines.

Irene didn't like living in Las Vegas. In fact, she hated it. She hated the glitzy extravagances of the Strip and the exclusive gated communities of multimillion-dollar homes big enough to pass for hotels. She hated the cul-de-sacs of tacky housing developments and the sprawl of look-alike apartments and condos. Nothing about the city felt solid or grounded. But Las Vegas was booming, one of the fastest growing cities in the country. And in an area where everyone was a transplant, a newcomer could blend in without incurring so much as a curious glance. In that respect, Irene liked the city just fine.

She picked several books from the shelf of new fiction and carried them with her to the magazine section where she began leafing through the latest issue of *Cosmopolitan*.

"Irene," someone called.

She looked up as Jane Temple, the principal from Patrick's school, took a seat opposite her.

"It's good to see you again," Jane said. "I was hoping I might run into you at the state finals in Reno, but Elliot said you weren't feeling well that weekend."

"A touch of the flu, I think." That was what she'd told Elliot. In truth, she simply wasn't taking any chances. The phone call from the woman who'd sounded like Betty had jolted her from complacency.

"I'm sorry you had to miss it. Patrick's very fond of you, you know."

Irene nodded. That was another problem. She'd decided it was time to pull back. She was becoming part of a life that wasn't hers. When she had to move on, Elliot would cope somehow, but she didn't want Patrick on her conscience. He'd already lost his mother; it would be devastating for him to lose another adult he felt close to.

"The boy is amazing. Me, I can't spell a thing." Jane laughed. "I shouldn't admit to that, I suppose. A principal who can't spell worth a darn. What a role model."

"You're probably quite proficient with the dictionary, then. That's an even better role model."

"These days, it's more often the spell checker than the dictionary. But you're kind to cast it in a positive light. I had a professor in graduate school who said the same thing."

"There you go."

Jane Temple was a round-figured woman in her late forties. She had a soft voice that made Irene wonder how she'd ever survived in the classroom. When she spoke next the voice seemed even softer than usual, which was why Irene missed the first few words of what she was saying.

"Reno paper . . . about a local murder. I was wondering if you knew the details."

Irene leaned forward. "A murder?"

"It happened near Lake Tahoe, but the woman lived in Reno. I recognized the name as the same woman who was here not long ago about the spelling bee. Betty Arnold. From what she said, I thought you might know her."

Irene felt the rush of ice water through her veins. "What are you talking about?"

"Oh dear, you hadn't heard the news, had you?"

"No." The word was as much a protest as a denial. And much too harsh. "No, it's not that," Irene amended. "I mean, I hadn't heard, but I didn't know her either."

Jane gave her an odd look. "I got the impression she knew you, from some time in the past."

"The name isn't even familiar." Irene knew her tone belied her words. She couldn't decide which was worse—that Betty was dead or that Betty had been here in Las Vagas. "You say she was here about a spelling bee?"

"She interviewed me about the championship. She had a copy of the *Journal of English Education* with the photo taken when Patrick won district rounds. It was of the three of you, remember? You, Elliot, and Patrick."

Breathe, Irene told herself. But her lungs seemed frozen.

"Maybe her name wasn't Arnold when you knew her," Jane said. "It's a good argument for women not taking their husband's name."

"Do they know who killed her?"

Jane shook her head. "Not that the article mentioned. The murder had taken place a few days earlier. Along the north shore of the lake. She was shot in a park in the middle of the afternoon. The woman with her was wounded. Seems like no place is safe anymore."

Irene had trouble thinking for the hammering in her head. "What . . . why was she interviewing you?"

"She was writing an article on the demise of spelling among today's youth. The journal photo listed the school. I imagine that's how she got my name."

Irene felt faint. She worked to keep her equilibrium. "What did she say about me?"

"She wanted to know what you were doing these days, if Elliot was your husband, that sort of thing. I can't remember whether she actually *said* she knew you or not. Maybe it was just an interview technique." Jane touched Irene's arm. "In any case, I'm sorry I brought it up. I can tell you're upset."

Irene brushed the concern aside. "There's no need to apologize. I was just confused about what you were saying."

"The interview was nothing really, but then when I read in the paper that she'd been killed . . ." Jane Temple was clearly uncomfortable. She fingered her watchband, then stood. "I need to be going. You take care, Irene. I hope we see more of you at school."

As soon as the principal was out of sight, Irene left her books on the table and dashed for the ladies' room. She was shaking so badly her knees almost gave out. Her skin was clammy and she felt nauseous.

Betty had found her. Not only had she called, she'd been right here in town.

And now she was dead.

Murdered.

Irene fought back another wave of queasiness. She splashed water on her face, rinsed out her mouth, then looked at herself hard in the mirror. Fear and sorrow settled over her like a lead mantle and her eyes stung with hot tears.

When she'd managed to get control of herself again, she looked around the library to make sure Jane Temple had indeed left. Then she found an open computer and logged on to the Internet. The local Tahoe papers weren't listed, and the *Reno Gazette* on-line carried only the current day's news. So much for the power of technology. The librarian pointed her to the newspaper stacks where Irene found copies of the Reno paper.

She pulled out the last week's issues and began frantically flipping the pages. There it was. Page two of Monday's paper. Betty and another woman, an attorney, had been in a lakeshore park when shots came out of nowhere. The other woman was wounded, but had already been released from the hospital. Betty had been dead when the paramedics arrived at the scene.

Later in the week, there was another article. The police were interested in questioning a young man who'd flown into a rage when he and Betty had been in a minor traffic accident earlier on the day of the shooting.

Irene set the newspaper down. Could it be that simple? Nothing more than a coincidence. Nothing to do with Irene.

She wanted to believe that was so, but her heart was having none of it.

"You all right, miss?"

The voice startled her. Irene yelped, then blushed at her nervousness. "I'm fine, thank you."

The man was close to seventy, with a kindly face and gentle demeanor. But Irene's heart continued to race. First Betty's phone call, and now her murder. The old feelings of distrust and fear were not so far buried as Irene had thought.

You picked the wrong man to mess with.

Don't say I didn't warn you.

Tears again pricked at her eyes. There was no way she could convince herself that Betty's death was simply bad luck.

Sid listened to the tape again, then removed his headset and rubbed his temples. He'd been right to worry. That damned attorney was nosing around, asking about Faith Foster.

That didn't necessarily mean she knew anything, he reminded himself.

Not altogether true. She had to know *something*. Why the hell else would she be asking about Faith?

He couldn't simply kill her, either—not yet, anyway—although the idea was appealing. While it might fix things in the short run, it would do nothing to resolve the real problem. And following so closely on the heels of Betty Arnold's death, it would be bound to raise questions.

Besides, at the moment O'Brien was his only link to the information he'd hoped to get from Betty Arnold. He'd just have to make sure he watched the attorney closely and kept one step ahead of the game. It would require diligence and patience, but when the stakes were this high, Sid had plenty of both.

His mind flashed on the woman he'd seen checking Kali's mail for her. She was a looker. And judging from her appearance, not the shy, retiring type. Maybe she'd know what Kali was up to. At the very least, he might be able to finagle some hot sex out of the deal. She looked like a woman who didn't hold back. He felt the flush of excitement. Too bad he had to work tonight. He promised himself he'd make sure their paths crossed soon.

Sid pushed back from his desk and headed for the bathroom, where he stripped, showered, and shaved, then dressed in his Armani charcoal pinstripe. He wore a white shirt, as he always did when he was working security, and an understated maroon tie. Clients, even those as agreeable as Judge McDougall, didn't like the hired help to outshine them.

And the last thing he wanted was to piss off McDougall.

Sid arrived at the imposing house in Marin County half an hour before the first guests would be appearing. The caterers had finished most of the setup. He conferred with the man in charge to see if more deliveries were expected. They weren't. Then he found the two men he'd hired for the evening—both off-duty highway patrol officers—and went over their assignments with them. They'd worked for him before so there wasn't a lot to cover. It was actually a pretty cushy job, which is the reason he had his pick of men to choose from. Mostly it involved standing around looking alert, just in case there was trouble. Didn't happen often, but all it took was some stringer from the tabloids, or some hot-head with his own personal or political agenda trying to crash a party. That's why so many of Sid's more important clients opted to have security on hand when they entertained.

Sid was headed outside for a smoke when McDougall appeared across the room. He had a receding hairline and a mouth that was too wide for his face, but he was still an imposing figure.

"Sid."

Sid nodded and extended a hand. "Good evening, Judge."

"How's the leg?"

"A pain in the ass, if you want to know the truth. But on the mend."

"We're not expecting any trouble tonight, but you've got help?"

Sid nodded. "Two men. They've both done this sort of thing before."

"Good. It's always best to err on the side of caution."

"Absolutely."

McDougall looked around the room. Sid couldn't tell if he was checking on the preparations or trying to determine if the two of them were alone.

"My wife's sister was killed last week," McDougall said, his voice lowered. "Murdered."

"Sorry to hear that."

"It's a real shock."

Sid wasn't sure how to respond, so he mumbled something sympathetic. And hoped to hell McDougall hadn't picked up on the alarm that had to have flickered in Sid's eyes.

"She lived in Reno but she'd gone to Tahoe City for the day. That's where it happened."

"Terrible news." What in the hell was a normal response? Sid hadn't the foggiest idea.

"We weren't close," McDougall continued. "In fact, I'd only

seen Betty a couple of times since Laura's death. She and Laura talked on the phone quite a bit. The husbands though, we weren't part of it." The frown between McDougall's brows deepened. "But Lenny said she came to see me a couple of weeks ago."

Sid felt another tremor of alarm. "Odd how that sort of thing happens."

McDougall nodded. "What's really odd is she told Lenny she wanted to talk to me about Faith. I was out of town, but Lenny says you were here that day, too. I was thinking she might have said something to you."

Sid shook his head. "Nobody said a word to me. What do you think she wanted?"

"Probably something to do with the money she inherited from Laura. It would have been Faith's if she'd . . ." McDougall cleared his throat. "If she'd lived."

"Most likely that was it. Maybe she contacted your attorney instead."

McDougall nodded. "It's not important. It just seemed . . . well, as I said, odd."

And that was only the half of it, Sid thought.

CHAPTER 14

Slouching in the uncomfortable wooden chair of the police interview room, Ramon was alone with his thoughts. He'd known all along that it would come to this. Not known in his head perhaps, though maybe there too, but certainly in that hollow, fearful place deep in his belly. It was why he'd panicked when he saw the cops waiting for him at the job site last week. Forget all that crap they fed you in school about innocent until proven guilty; once the cops had their eyes on you, you were screwed.

Running only made things worse. He'd known that too. But he'd reacted instinctively. Like an animal. When a jackal appears on the knoll, the rabbit doesn't stop to analyze its options.

His attorney hadn't understood, and neither had the cops. How could they? For them, the system worked.

The door to the interview room opened. It was one of the cops who'd arrested him. The woman. Chinese. She couldn't have been much over five feet, with short dark hair and liquid brown eyes. He wondered why someone as attractive as she was would want to be a cop.

"How are you doing?" she asked.

"How do you think." Ramon rubbed his wrists. The handcuffs had chafed his skin and the harsh soap they'd made him scrub with had burned it raw.

She sat down. "It would be good if we could clear up a few things. Like the gun. Your friend Pinkus says he borrowed it, yeah, but he gave it back to you a couple of months ago."

"He's lying."

"Why would he do that?"

Ramon was asking himself the same thing. "How should I know? Maybe he thinks it will look bad for him if he's got a gun. All I know is he never gave it back."

"You weren't angry about that?"

"Sure I was. But then he got sent away. Last I heard he didn't know where it was."

Her eyes fixed on his and he turned away. He'd have preferred the other cop. It was easier to deal with a man.

"Your friends say you were jumpy and tense that weekend after the murder, like you were worried about something."

"I had stuff on my mind."

"Like?"

"It's personal."

"Ramon, listen to me." She leaned forward and her voice softened. He could see a smudge of mascara under one eye. "You're in jail facing a possible murder charge. Once we turn it over to the DA, it's out of our hands. If you tell me what happened maybe we can—"

"Don't I get a phone call? I thought that was part of the program. A phone call and the right to remain silent. Isn't that what you said before?"

The cop's eyes grew fierce. She started to say something, then she sighed instead. Her face lost its intensity and she seemed almost bored. "Sure. One call. Don't waste it."

Ramon realized he didn't know how to reach Kali O'Brien. She'd said she couldn't represent him, and he didn't think she believed him, either, but he didn't know any other attorneys. Who was he going to call? Not his mother, who would be useless and would worry herself sick. He didn't want to burden Nadia either, but in the end that's what he did.

Her tone was cool and guarded until he told her he was calling from jail, then she sounded so concerned it made his heart ache.

"Oh, Ramon. My God. Jail." He could tell she was fighting back tears.

"I need you to do some stuff for me, okay? Call my mom and let her know what happened. Tell her not to worry. I'm doing fine. But most important, call that attorney, Kali O'Brien. Helen knows how to reach her."

"How long will they keep you there?"

"I don't know."

"How can they think you killed that woman?"

He saw the detective tapping her foot. "I've got to go," he said.

"I love you," Nadia whispered. "No matter what."

Ramon turned away from the detective and cupped the phone with his hand. His voice was barely audible. "I love you, too."

The cop called for the guard to escort him from the room. "Anytime you want to talk, Ramon, I'm ready to listen." She regarded him intensely.

He didn't bother to respond.

They put him in a cell with a man who had a runny nose and a sharp, abrasive cough that sounded like it was tearing up his lungs. The guy snored loudly for most of the night, and then woke early in the morning and started talking to God.

Ramon didn't sleep a wink. He tried to concentrate on a vision of Lady Justice, like the one on the cover of his civics books senior year. But the scales she was holding kept tipping out of balance.

A bouquet of brightly colored balloons greeted Kali on her first day back at the office.

"It seemed better than flowers," Jared said, looking a bit embarrassed.

"You did this? They're beautiful. What a sweet thing to do."

He held up his hands. "Don't go getting all soft and sappy on me."

Kali smiled. "Me? Soft?" Truth was, being shot had sent her into emotional overdrive. More often it was unexplained tears, but also, as now, feeling deeply touched by little things. "In any case, thanks."

The phone rang before she'd made it through the stack of message slips and mail—including a handful of get well cards from clients—that had been on her desk awaiting her return. It was her private line, so she picked up.

"Ms. O'Brien?" The voice was female. Soft. "My name is Nadia. I'm Ramon Escobar's . . . I'm his girlfriend. I'm sorry to bother you."

"It's okay."

"He's in jail, Ms. O'Brien. He needs your help."

Kali was momentarily stunned. "They arrested him?"

"He asked me to call you."

Her head was spinning. Had they discovered new evidence? "I can't represent him," Kali explained. "I already told him so."

"He didn't shoot that woman. Ramon's not like that. You've got to believe him."

"It's not that I think he's guilty, Nadia." Though in the back of her mind she was revisiting that possibility. "It's that there are rules and—"

"One of the cops came to see me yesterday." Nadia's delivery was clipped and quick, like she had something to say and she wanted to get through it. "A woman. She said she's heard Ramon was acting strange over the weekend. Nervous. And his boss told her that Friday was the first time Ramon hadn't shown up at work without calling ahead. She made a big deal about that, like it proves he did something wrong." The words rang with indignation.

"Police look at a suspect's behavior as part of an overall picture," Kali explained. "Ramon's agitation and his absence from work support what they already know about him."

"That he's guilty, you mean."

"It appears that's their conclusion." So different from what her own had been. She'd looked into Ramon's eyes, believed his claims of innocence. Had she let her questions about Betty overshadow hard evidence?

"It's not fair," Nadia said, sounding suddenly very young. "They're twisting everything the wrong way."

"His attorney will make sure the jury hears another explanation."

"That's what he wants, an attorney. Can't you help him?"

Kali tried to explain. "There are limits on what I can do since I'm also a potential witness. The court will appoint an attorney for him. All he needs to do is ask for one."

"But he's locked up in jail," Nadia wailed. "He needs—"

There was heated conversation in the background and then Helen came on the line.

"I tried to explain to her, but she insisted on talking to you herself."

"He needs to ask for a court-appointed attorney," Kali said.

"A public defender?" Kali could imagine Helen wrinkling her nose at the words. "Can't you recommend someone? Someone good. I have money I could use, and there are others who might be willing to contribute, too."

Kali sighed. What had Bryce said about quicksand? "Let me ask around, okay?"

"I just don't want him to slip through the cracks," Helen said.

What Kali wanted was answers. While she didn't have the same blind faith in Ramon that Helen did, she needed to know that the cops had the right man. For her own peace of mind if nothing else. Once Ramon was charged, the official investigation would be closed. Anything further would come from the efforts of the defense. And public defenders, even the most dedicated ones, were notoriously limited in time and resources.

"No, none of us wants that," Kali replied.

"You're sure you can't defend him?"

"Even if I could, Helen, it would be a mistake. If Ramon is innocent, he's going to be fine." A prophecy she hoped wouldn't come back to haunt her.

By the time Kali got off the phone, the cup of coffee she'd brought to work with her was lukewarm. She dumped it out and put on the kettle in the tiny supply room that doubled as the office kitchen. When the water reached a boil, she poured it through the filter, then took her fresh cup back to her desk.

It wasn't her case, she reminded herself. She needed to let it go.

Except there was still that niggling question—what had Betty wanted to tell her about Faith Foster?

And the possibility the answer to that question just might provide a motive for murder. A motive that pointed to someone besides Ramon.

Kali had just turned back to the pile of papers needing her attention when the phone rang again. Another unfamiliar female voice, this one deep and raspy.

Gail Lombardi," the woman said. "You left a message on my answering machine. I've only just returned home."

Kali struggled to place the name.

"About Betty Arnold, you said."

Betty's friend from Sacramento. Kali remembered now. She

had gotten the woman's name and number from Betty's neighbor. "Right. Thanks for returning the call."

"What's that? I'm a little hard of hearing."

Kali raised her voice. "I said, thanks for calling back."

"I heard about Betty's murder. Are you with the police?"

"I'm an attorney she called before her death."

"You're right, a most tragic death."

Kali ignored the non-sequitur response. "I was hoping she might have said something to you about why she wanted to see an attorney."

"No, she didn't have any problem seeing. Except she wore glasses for reading."

The chances of intelligent phone conversation looked slim. "When did you and Betty last talk . . ." Kali paused. She looked at her watch. Here was someone who knew Betty. Had known her for years. If anyone had answers, it was likely to be Gail Lombardi. And Kali thought she stood a better chance of getting those answers in person than over the phone.

"I know you've just returned from a trip," Kali said, speaking as clearly as she could. "But would it be okay if I dropped by to talk with you? I won't take a lot of your time, I promise."

"I've got time. You take all you want. I hear better face-to-face, anyway."

"Around noon?" That would allow Kali to at least get her paperwork organized before heading out. And tomorrow she could really focus on catching up. "I'll bring sandwiches."

"That would be lovely."

Kali took down the address, and directions. If nothing else, she'd come away with a better understanding of Betty Arnold. And with luck, information that might provide a motive for murder.

Gail Lombardi lived in a small ranch-style house set in a maze of other small ranch-style houses. A high-voltage power line divided her property from the neighbor's to her left. In front, where you'd expect to see lawn, there was a garden of cactus and shiny white rock. Kali noticed several other houses on the street with similar landscaping schemes. Maybe the garden contractor had offered a group rate.

The door opened with a creak. "You must be Kali O'Brien. The deli bag is a dead giveaway." The woman smiled. "I'm Gail. Please come in."

Gail Lombardi was a large woman with an enormous bosom that melded with her equally sizable middle. She had several chins, and the softest, grayest eyes Kali had seen outside the illustrations of a children's book.

Kali took a seat on the deeply pillowed sofa. The living room was simply but comfortably furnished. Yellow walls, red floral print upholstery, a country landscape in oils above the fireplace.

Gail brought plates, glasses, and a pitcher of iced tea. She moved a stack of mail from the club chair and sat down, then poured tea for both of them. "It's always so nice to be home again, no matter how lovely the trip."

"Were you away on business or vacation?"

"What's that?" Gail leaned forward.

"Your trip, was it for work or pleasure?"

"A niece's wedding, which I suppose was pleasurable. There were moments, however . . ." She made a face. "But you aren't here to listen to stories about my family. I used to tell my students to stick to the point. I need to remind myself of that advice occasionally."

"What did you teach?"

"English. Junior high.

"That's a tough age from what I hear." Kali made sure to face Gail when she spoke, and to enunciate clearly. It seemed to help.

"They're certainly spirited. Now, what can I tell you about Betty?"

"The neighbor who gave me your name said you and Betty were old friends."

"We grew up together. Had a crush on the same boy in high school. He didn't give either one of us a second glance, which probably helped us stay friends." Gail reached for the bag of sandwiches and chips.

"Take your pick," Kali said. "One's turkey and one's tuna." She waited while Gail unwrapped the turkey sandwich and opened a packet of chips. "When did you last see her?"

"She came for a visit about a month ago. But I've talked to her since then. In fact, she called just before I left to go east for my niece's wedding. That would have been a couple of days before she was killed."

"Can you remember what she said?"

"Cheese?" Gail looked at the sandwich. "I don't think so."

Gail Lombardi's hearing wasn't perfect, even face-to-face. "What did Betty say when she called?"

"Nothing out of the ordinary. But she sounded a little . . . I was going to say strange, but that's not really right. Worried, maybe."

"About what?"

Gail shook her head. "I asked her and she said everything was fine. She said the same thing last time she came to visit, but then she left after one night even though she'd planned on staying longer. She wouldn't tell me what that was about, either."

"Something upset her?"

"I wondered about that. We'd gone out to dinner the night before and had a good time, though she felt bad enjoying herself when her husband was in a nursing home. I know she worried about him and felt guilty that he was there. But it's a good home, not one of those horrible, institutional places."

Gail paused, then picked up her thread of thought. "Anyway, the next morning we were sitting thinking we might take in a movie, and the next thing I knew, Betty was saying she had to get home."

"Something came up in conversation, maybe?" Kali asked.

"I can't imagine what. We'd chosen a movie, then I went into the kitchen to clean up and Betty stayed in the living room looking through some old magazines. She came in about half an hour later, clearly agitated, and announced that she had to go home."

"She didn't explain?"

"She said she was worried about Carl, but I think that was just an excuse. I mean, why all of a sudden? And then she asked if she could take an issue of the magazine she was reading. Like she was in such a hurry she couldn't stay to finish it."

"And she left, just like that?"

Gail nodded.

Kali wasn't hungry. She'd taken a few small bites of her sandwich out of politeness and now she set it aside. "Did Betty ever say anything to you about contacting an attorney?"

"A what?"

"Did she mention contacting a lawyer."

"Not recently, no. She and Carl had their wills done up, oh, maybe five, six years ago. I remember how relieved she was to have it taken care of while he was still competent enough to sign the thing."

"Did she happen to mention Faith Foster?"

Gail looked startled. "Why? Has there been a new development?"

"Not that I'm aware of, but Betty may have mentioned the name when she called me to set the appointment."

"She was hiring you about Faith?" Gail looked perplexed.

"At the time, it didn't register. I thought she was making a comment about faith, as in confidence. But now I think she might have been referring to her niece."

Gail sat back. "Oh, my."

"What?"

"It's just . . . The last time we talked, before I went east, Betty asked me if I thought the police would get in touch with family if they had new evidence. Do you think that's why she wanted to talk to you?"

"Possibly." Kali felt a tingle of excitement. If Betty had access to incriminating information, it would certainly provide a motive for murder. "Did Betty say why she was asking about new evidence?"

"No. It was more a hypothetical question. At least, that's what I thought at the time."

"Were Betty and Faith close?" Kali asked.

"In some ways, closer than Faith and her mother."

"There were problems between mother and daughter?"

"Not anything more than with most kids. It's just that Betty adored Faith, and Laura . . . Laura adored life. Betty was always the serious one. Quiet, careful, methodical. Laura was . . . not exactly flighty, but someone who seemed to land on her feet through no effort of her own."

Kali knew the type. She had a sister just like her. "Did the family have any theories about what happened to Faith?"

Gail hesitated. "There was some talk early on about the fiancé."

"I thought he was out of town at the time."

"He was. But he committed suicide not long after. Laura saw that as a sign of guilty remorse."

Or maybe a mother's need to hold someone responsible for her loss. "What would be his motive?"

"I'm not sure they ever came up with anything specific. It could have been the threat of a broken engagement, jealousy . . . we read about cases like that in the papers all the time. And Faith had recently signed up for a self-defense class. She'd said she wanted to protect herself against hotheaded men. Betty thought it was a joke. But after what happened . . ." Gail shrugged.

Interesting, but it didn't bring Kali any closer to understanding what Betty had known that might have led to her murder.

If, in fact, it had. The police had already made an arrest. Was she chasing after something that existed only in her own mind?

In Sid's business, contacts were important. And Sid prided himself on maintaining a wide network of people he could call on in confidence. If he didn't already know someone suited for a particular task, it never took more than a phone call or two to come up with a name.

Unfortunately, most of his contacts—especially when it came to legal matters—had ties to Mr. D, and in this instance it was crucial that Mr. D be kept out of the loop.

Sid scrolled through the database of names he kept on his computer. Names of people who owed him or who would love nothing more than to have Sid owe them. A whole unwritten ledger of accounts. It was like money in the bank. Finally, he reached for the phone and called Patsy.

"Hey, Sid, honey. Long time, no see." Her voice had a nasal quality to it that Sid found irritating. "You calling to take me out to dinner?"

"Maybe, Patsy. Depends on what you've got for me."

"What kind of odds are you looking for?"

"Not that kind of 'got.' I need to find a lawyer. Placer County, criminal defense work. Someone whose ethics are in mothballs. It'll be easy money if he doesn't care about winning."

She giggled. "You're going to pay him not to work? Kind of like farm subsidies."

"Something like that, yeah."

"And all I get is dinner?" The last word was a protracted whine.

"Dinner anywhere you'd like—New York, New Orleans, Montreal."

"Paris?"

What the heck. Sid was either going to pull this off and walk away with a secure future, or he was dead. A weekend in Paris was cheap by comparison. "Sure, if you want Paris, Paris it'll be."

He only wished Patsy looked like that neighbor he'd seen at the O'Brien woman's house. He'd done some snooping in her mailbox and learned her name, Margot Lerner. And that she lived alone. He also knew she received the Victoria's Secret catalog, had a Macy's charge card, saw a doctor with offices in San Francisco, and owned several dogs. Sid wasn't fond of dogs, but he figured he could fake it for a bit. He was going to make sure their paths crossed soon.

"That's a promise?" Patsy's grating voice broke his reverie.

"It's a promise."

"Okay, lemme think." She hummed softly to herself. "I got it. Robert Lamont. He's your man. Let me give you his number."

Sid memorized the number as she read it off. A simple slip of paper in the wrong hands could ruin everything.

CHAPTER 15

Irene slipped into the brown suede jacket that had been a Christmas gift from Elliot and hugged it close across her chest. The day had been pleasant, but with the late afternoon sun now low in the sky, the temperature was dropping quickly.

Patrick was in the outfield, staring off dreamily into space.

"Keep your eye on the ball," Elliot yelled.

Patrick looked their way. His face broke into a grin when he saw Irene. He waved at her.

"It's good of you to come to his game," Elliot said, slipping his arm around her shoulder. "It's not the most exciting baseball in the world. Half the time I wonder if they even know what game they're playing."

"I enjoy it."

"Watch out, your nose is starting to grow."

Instinctively, Irene put her hand to her face, then realized he'd been teasing. She gave him a soft jab with her elbow. "I do enjoy it."

"You're a cheap date, I'll give you that."

It wasn't the game that appealed to Irene—Elliot was right, baseball played by a third-string team of nine-year-olds was something like watching grass grow. What she loved was being part of Elliot's and Patrick's lives. A Norman Rockwell moment of feeling normal again.

But now that Betty had been murdered . . . well, that changed everything. Irene again felt a swell of fear. Normal was nothing but an illusion. She'd been naive to think otherwise.

She turned to Elliot, trying to appear offhand. "Has anyone asked about me lately?"

"All the time." He grinned. "My mother wants to know when we're going to get married, Ruth keeps asking when you're going to come by the clinic again, and Patrick must mention your name half a dozen times a day."

Marriage was a word that had crept into their conversations more and more over the last few months. Elliot was pushing for it and Irene resisted. Not out of any qualms about Elliot. He was as kind and loving a man as she could ever hope to find. And that was precisely the reason she couldn't marry him. He trusted her. Patrick trusted her. Neither of them deserved the kind of trouble she might bring.

"I meant like someone we don't know," Irene explained. She was incapable right then of echoing Elliot's teasing. "Someone from out of town, maybe in connection with that story that ran about Patrick's spelling victory."

Elliot frowned. The bushy eyebrows met over his nose. "Not that I can recall. Why?"

"Nothing really. I ran into Jane Temple at the library yesterday afternoon. She mentioned something about a woman who'd interviewed her."

"About you?"

"About Patrick. But she'd seen the photo of the three of us after Patrick's victory at district rounds . . ." Irene let the thought trail off with a shrug, as though it were of no consequence. But she could feel her heart pounding in her chest. Betty had seen the photo, and through it, traced her to Las Vegas. Called her at home. Had she told anyone that she'd learned Irene's whereabouts?

"He's got a birthday coming up next month," Elliot said.

Irene pulled her thoughts back to the present. "I know. June twentieth."

"School will be out by then. I thought we might take a trip to California. Spend some time at Disneyland, then head to San Francisco. He's dying to visit Alcatraz, of all things." Elliot paused. "If you could come too, it would make the trip really special for him. For both of us."

"I . . . I don't think . . . I'm not sure I . . . that I can get time off."

She couldn't go anywhere near the Bay Area. That would be asking for trouble.

"Sure you can," Elliot said. "It's over a month away still. I'll tell Elma she doesn't have a choice." Elma was Irene's boss and Elliot's cousin, which was how they'd met in the first place.

"Don't you dare say a word to her," Irene snapped.

Elliot looked surprised at the intensity of her response. He held up his hands in surrender. "Okay. I won't. I was only joking anyway."

"Sorry, it's just that I want my autonomy at work."

"I have no intention of interfering. I promise." He crossed his heart and gave her a self-effacing smile. "You'll ask her yourself though, won't you? We'll be gone less than a week."

Irene slipped her arm around Elliot's waist. "I'll see what I can do."

She longed to bury herself in Elliot's arms and tell him everything. But she couldn't. For his sake as much as hers. Besides, there was nothing Elliot could do. Nothing any of them could do.

"You know I love you," he said.

"I do know that."

"And?" The smile was half playful, half worried.

"And I love you, too."

Imagine losing what you love most. Don't say I didn't warn you.

Irene swallowed hard against the sour taste that rose into her throat. To think she'd once imagined the words an idle threat.

She felt suddenly woozy. She needed to get away. "Tell Patrick he's an awesome outfielder."

"Can't you tell him yourself?" Elliot sounded perplexed.

"Sorry, I have to go."

"I thought we were all going out for pizza afterward."

She was already reaching for her car keys.

"Is everything okay?"

"I have a headache. I'll give you a call tomorrow." She kissed him quickly on the cheek and left.

By the time she arrived at her apartment building she really did have a headache. It was like a band of pulsating hot metal across her forehead. And with each pulse came an unwelcome memory.

The sudden appearance of the man in a ski mask. The nauseating ether burning her throat as she struggled to defend herself. The terror of facing her own death. The grief and guilt over Andrew.

And now, Betty.

Would Elliot be next?

Irene was fumbling with her keys when a woman she didn't recognize exited the building and held the door open for her. Irene mumbled thanks as she stepped into the lobby. Pretty paltry security, but she'd known that when she'd taken the place. Buildings with security guards were few and far between, and out of her price range in any case. Besides, some poorly paid security guard couldn't offer the kind of protection she needed.

She took two Motrin, splashed cold water on her face, then looked at herself in the bathroom mirror. She'd never liked her hair short, and the blond color didn't suit her at all. She still hadn't gotten used to it. That Elliot could look her in the eye and tell her she was beautiful was a testimonial to the power of love. Irene had been toying with the idea of letting her hair grow long again and going back to her natural chestnut color.

But that was before Betty had called.

Irene had been stupid to even consider letting down her defenses. What had she been thinking, anyway—that Blake would have more pressing matters on his mind? That he would have developed a conscience?

But to kill Betty—would he really go that far? Irene gripped the edge of the counter. Why not? She'd never imagined he'd go after Andrew, either.

She turned away from the mirror. Away from Andrew. Away from visions of the wedding plans they'd made, the life they'd envisioned together.

But the memory followed her.

Andrew and Elliot. How was it possible to love two such different men?

Andrew, with his fair complexion, his preppy good looks, and unrelenting self-assurance. A go-getter attorney who'd set his sights on the brass ring and never doubted for a minute he'd get it. Sooner rather than later.

Elliot's coloring was dark—hair, eyes, even his skin tone, though it was mostly the heavy whiskers and dark hair on his arms that made it appear that way. With his long, thin face and angular body, he wasn't someone whose looks melted hearts. And he was painfully shy in unfamiliar situations.

The two men she'd loved in her life. One thing they had in common, however. She caused trouble for both of them.

Kali had woken up that morning with the thought that she needed to get in touch with Faith's stepfather. He might have some idea why Betty had called her. Even if he didn't, he deserved to know that it had likely concerned Faith. He was, as far as she knew, Faith's closest relative. But calling Judge McDougall was not something one did lightly.

She'd met him once, years ago at a bar function, though she didn't expect he would remember her. Formerly a prominent member of the San Francisco district attorney's office, he was now a respected federal court judge with a reputation for running a tight courtroom. His name had come up recently in conjunction with an appointment to the appeals court. She wasn't sure he'd even agree to talk to her.

She called the main number for the federal court, and after weaving her way through the automated answering system, was finally transferred to a human who put her through to a secretary. Kali left a message asking Judge McDougall to call her. Then she got to work reviewing a deposition in a landlord–tenant matter.

She'd thought returning to work would help take her mind off the phantom killer she imagined around every corner. It hadn't. Yesterday, driving home from meeting with Gail Lombardi, she'd twice thought someone was following her. Both times the car had eventually passed her and she'd felt foolish for being so jumpy. Even here in her own office, she found herself listening for new sounds and unexpected footsteps.

If the killer actually wanted her dead, wouldn't he have tried something before now? Though she took comfort in the thought, it wasn't enough to put her mind at rest.

Some time later, Jared knocked on the open door of Kali's office. By the time she motioned for him to come in, he was already draping his lank frame across one of the armchairs she kept for visitors.

"Will you have time to look over a pleading I drafted?"

"Sure. Get me the file when you have a chance."

"It's already on your desk," Jared said with a self-satisfied grin.

"You're so efficient."

"Damn right. Remember it at bonus time."

"Bonus? Count yourself lucky your paycheck doesn't bounce."

"That bad, huh?"

Kali was saved from having to respond by the ringing of the phone. Jared picked it up. "I'll see if she's free," he said. He put the line on hold and turned to Kali. "It's your cousin Helen. You want to talk to her or shall I take a message?"

Kali motioned for the phone. "Hi. What's up?"

"You can relax," Helen said. "I'm not calling to badger you about Ramon."

"That's good because it wouldn't make any difference."

"You're off the hook. Ramon has an attorney."

"Already?" Kali was surprised. "Defendants don't generally get assigned an attorney until they're arraigned."

"This guy wasn't assigned, he came forward on his own. He's private. Some kind of pro bono thing."

Pro bono defense? Kali figured he must be eager for the publicity of a newsworthy murder trial. "Do you know his name? I should let him know about the possible Faith Foster connection."

"I've got the name somewhere." It sounded like Helen was shuffling papers. "Here it is. Robert Lamont, in Grass Valley."

Kali saw the light for the other line blinking. A few moments later Jared was at her door again. "Judge McDougall," he mouthed.

"Helen, I've got another call. Can I call you back?"

"No need, just wanted to tell you the news about Ramon. And to invite you for a feast at Wolfdales if you're willing to drive up again. I won a gift certificate in the school raffle."

"Wouldn't you rather use it on some eligible guy?"

"Yeah, if I knew any. You're at the top of my 'B' list, though. Talk to you later."

Kali punched the button to switch lines. "Judge McDougall. Thank you for returning my call so promptly."

"You said it was about my stepdaughter."

"Only indirectly." Kali explained her connection to Betty Arnold, and thus to Faith. "I was hoping you could spare a few minutes to meet with me." Now that she had him on the phone, she felt foolish for even broaching the subject with him.

He surprised her, however. "How about this evening, around six? I have a dinner engagement at seven, but I should be able to give you twenty minutes or so. My house would be easiest for me, if you don't mind driving to Corte Madera."

Kali was grateful that he'd agreed to meet with her at all. She'd have driven to Los Angeles if necessary. "I'll be there."

Kali arrived half an hour early—she'd allowed extra time for traffic and parking because the last thing she wanted was to be late. She waited in the car until six, then rang Judge McDougall's doorbell.

He answered the door himself, dressed for a black tie event. McDougall appeared to be in his late fifties, with a receding hairline and thick, bushy eyebrows. He was only slightly taller than Kali, and stocky without being fat, yet he was a distinguished-looking man.

She followed him through a large tiled foyer to a sitting area off the main living room. The furnishings were formal, a mix of traditional and Mediterranean, and a bit pretentious for Kali's tastes. Dark woods, heavy fabrics, and not an article out of place.

"Can I get you something to drink?"

"No, thanks."

She sat on a burgundy velveteen love seat. McDougall remained standing, one arm resting on the back of a mahogany-colored club chair. His manner was cordial, but Kali sensed an underlying intensity that no doubt worked to his advantage on the bench.

"You have news about Faith?"

"Not exactly," Kali said. "But I thought you would be interested in knowing that Betty Arnold might have had information about your stepdaughter's death."

He looked stunned. "Information? Like what?"

Kali elaborated on what she'd told him earlier over the phone.

"That's it?"

Kali nodded.

McDougall rubbed the bridge of his nose. "What could Betty have known?"

"I was hoping you might have some ideas."

"But you aren't even certain that's what she wanted to see you about."

"Not certain, no."

The laugh lines around McDougall's eyes etched character into a face that was still surprisingly youthful. Now, they creased in puzzlement. He shook his head. "More likely she contacted you about a different matter entirely. Or maybe if it's related to Faith, it has something to do with money she inherited from my wife."

"But Betty was so secretive about our meeting. There had to be more to it. She never told you she was meeting with me?"

"I haven't spoken to her in almost a year." McDougall seemed lost in thought. "She came by the house a couple of weeks ago, though. I wasn't here." He paused. "She apparently said something to my caretaker about Faith."

Kali felt her heart skip a beat. "What did Betty say?"

"It was just a passing reference. But now in light of what you've told me . . ." McDougall took a seat in one of the two matching club chairs. His brow furrowed. "That she came by at all was strange."

"Strange how?"

"Unusual. My wife and her sister got along well, but Betty and I . . ." He spread his hands. "It wasn't that we *didn't* get along, merely that there was really no connection. Since the marriage was a second one for both my wife and me, and Faith by then was living on her own, well, we sort of kept the family stuff separate." He looked at Kali. "Betty didn't say anything to you about coming to see me?"

"No. But we never had much of an actual conversation."

The intensity in McDougall's expression softened. "We're in the same boat, I guess. Neither one of us knows what she wanted."

"I think whatever it was, it may have gotten her killed."

McDougall raised an eyebrow. "You said they'd arrested someone."

"That doesn't mean they have the right man." Kali took a breath, let it out slowly. "Could Betty have had anything to do with what happened to Faith?"

"Betty? She adored Faith."

"What about her husband Carl?"

McDougall frowned. "I doubt it. Anyway, I'm convinced it was Faith's fiancé who killed her. Andrew Major. He committed suicide only a couple of days later."

"I thought the police had ruled him out."

"He was supposedly out of town at the time she disappeared, but there was no one who could give him an actual alibi." McDougall's eyes narrowed. "He was a snot-nose kid, if you'll pardon my saying so."

"But they were engaged. Why would he kill her?"

"Come now, Ms. O'Brien. You seem like an intelligent woman. This can't be the first time you've heard of a man killing the woman he was involved with?"

"Of course not." It happened far too often, in fact. But surely the police would know that, too. "Might Betty have discovered evidence about Andrew Major's guilt?"

McDougall's expression registered surprise. He'd clearly not thought of that possibility. "Did she say anything about that?"

Kali shook her head. "Where are Faith's effects? Things like journals and letters. Maybe Betty came across something that shed light on the crime."

"We gave most of her things away, gradually, over time. My wife saved some mementos and such, and I haven't had the heart to throw them out. But there's nothing there that sheds light on Faith's death. We went through everything with a fine-tooth comb."

McDougall's fingers traced the curve of piping on the chair's arm. "Besides, it's . . . Betty had a good heart, but she was a simple woman. I can't imagine she'd have come across anything significant. Especially eight years after the fact. If her wanting to meet with you was in any way connected to Faith, it had to have been in relation to Laura's estate. The money would have been Faith's if she'd lived."

"But the estate was settled, wasn't it?"

"That doesn't mean Betty didn't have questions." He checked his watch and stood. "I'm sorry to have to cut this short . . ."

Kali took the hint. "Thank you for seeing me. I hope you weren't thinking I had hard information."

"After all these years I no longer expect that." A flicker of emotion crossed his face. Sadness, but something else too. "Do keep me posted if you learn anything."

"Of course." But Kali was beginning to wonder if she was grasping at straws. She wasn't even certain Betty had meant Faith rather than faith. And if she *had* been referring to her niece, it was a big jump to think she knew something about what had happened. McDougall's explanation of the inheritance made sense.

But why, then, had Betty been so secretive?

CHAPTER 16

Irene's purse was heavy with the weight of loose coins. She'd collected what she could from her dresser and the glass dish by the telephone where she dumped spare change, then decided she didn't have enough. It might take a couple of dollars simply to get beyond hold. So she'd gone to the grocery and exchanged a five-dollar bill for quarters.

Now all she needed was enough nerve to make the call.

She checked her watch. Over an hour still before she had to be at work. She'd been half hoping there wasn't time. But there clearly was.

Her hands were perspiring. She rubbed them against her pant legs. Just do it, she told herself, and opened the car door. The phone booth in front of the mini mart was empty. Customers came and went, but no one showed any interest in the phone.

Irene dropped in her quarters and called. She'd debated between the police and the attorney, settling finally on the attorney. The attorney was a woman, for one thing, and Irene felt more comfortable with that. She was also someone Betty had apparently trusted, perhaps even confided in. And it was probably safer, Irene decided, to avoid talking to the cops.

The first time she tried, she misdialed so she had to hang up and start over again. The second time the call went through.

A male voice answered. "Law offices. How can I help you?"

"Kali O'Brien, please."

"Whom shall I say is calling?"

"She doesn't know me," Irene said.

"May I tell Ms. O'Brien what this is in regard to, then?"

A black sedan pulled into the spot at the end of row where Irene was parked. The windows were tinted so she couldn't see inside. It's nothing, she told herself. Las Vegas was full of black sedans with tinted windows. Still, her pulse was racing.

"Ma'am, are you there? May I tell Ms. O'Brien—"

"The Arnold murder." Irene was surprised to find herself whispering.

An instant of silence and then he said, "Just a moment and I'll transfer you."

A recorded voice came on the phone and Irene deposited more quarters. She glanced at the sedan. No one got out.

It couldn't be him. There was no way he could have known she was going to make this call. Only a very slim chance he even knew she was in Las Vegas.

"Hello? This is Kali O'Brien."

Irene licked her lips. "You were Betty Arnold's attorney?"

"Yes, I was. Do you know something about her murder?"

"Did she happen to mention her nie—" Irene stopped short. The sedan sported California plates.

She hung up the phone abruptly. Her envelope of coins tumbled onto the ground. Irene didn't stop to pick them up. She dashed to her car, got in, and locked the doors. She was pulling out of the parking lot when she saw an older woman get out of the backseat of the sedan. The woman spoke briefly to the driver, then went into the phone booth Irene had just vacated.

"Jared, come in here. Quickly!" Kali was still holding the receiver, afraid to do anything that might interfere with their ability to trace the call.

"What is it?"

She pointed at the phone. "Is there a way to find out who that caller was or where she was calling from?"

"Depends. I checked caller ID the minute she said what she was calling about, but it was an 'unavailable' message."

Which meant either a blocked or out-of-area number. That wasn't unusual. In Kali's experience, most callers opted for blocked numbers.

"We can try star-sixty-nine and see what happens," Jared suggested. He took the phone from Kali's hand, clicked for a new connection and punched in the two-digit code. After a moment, he shook his head and dropped the receiver back into the cradle. "Must be outside the local calling area."

"Damn." Kali was short of breath, as if she'd just run up several flights of stairs. She was sure the woman had been ready to ask about Faith Foster.

Why had the caller hung up mid-sentence? Had someone grabbed the phone away from her? Or maybe she was afraid of being overheard.

"What did she tell you?" Kali asked.

"Nothing. She never even gave me her name. When I asked what she was calling about, she said 'the Arnold murder.' That's when I quickly transferred the call to you. What happened?"

Kali recounted the conversation, which had been short enough she could give it to him almost word for word. "I guess all we can do now is hope she calls back."

Kali let her head roll back against the chair for support. It wasn't yet noon and already she felt like she'd put in a full day. Some of it was the lingering discomfort in her shoulder. But mostly, she thought, it was the discomfort in her mind. Faith Foster's name kept popping up in connection with Betty Arnold, but she was never able to find the common thread.

"Speaking of calls," Kali said, "I haven't gotten one from an attorney in Grass Valley, have I? A Robert Lamont."

"Not one that I've taken. But Ben Potter called."

"I thought the family had finally worked things out." Potter was the attorney for one of four grown children duking it out over a share of their late father's estate. Kali found their collective behavior a strong argument for dying poor.

Jared shrugged. "Also Bryce Keating. He just called a few minutes ago. I'd have had him hold except I thought you might be a while."

"If the mystery woman calls back, interrupt me. No matter what."

As soon as Jared left, Kali returned Bryce's call. As always, she experienced a tingle of anticipation at hearing his voice.

"Hey," he said, in a tone that softened as soon as he knew it was her. "That was a quick meeting."

"More like a short call."

"I hate to do this, but I've got to cancel our plans for Saturday." They'd intended to drive to Napa for lunch and a little wine tasting. Kali had been hoping the day would roll into evening, and well beyond. It was about time. Taking things slowly was Bryce's plan not hers. It sounded fine in theory but as a practical matter it left much to be desired.

"A fresh homicide?"

"All the time but that's not the reason. I'm filling in for one of the guys whose father just passed away. The funeral is this weekend in the east."

"That's too bad." She felt selfish thinking about herself under the circumstances but her disappointment was so great she could almost taste it. "I was looking forward to our excursion."

"I was, too. More than you can imagine." He was quiet a moment. "It's not like I have a choice in the matter."

"I know." It was part of the territory of being a cop. And of dating a cop. But that didn't make it any easier. "So maybe the following weekend?"

"You're being so reasonable about this."

"I try."

Bryce laughed. "I guess I should be relieved that you understand, but a tiny bit of hysterics might be good for my ego. You know, like what will you do without me all weekend?"

"Settle for being relieved. You saw what happened when I got hysterical." It had just about destroyed their relationship.

"Right." The playful tone was gone. "Call you as soon as I have some time."

Ramon was lying on the upper bunk in his cell, staring at the water stain on the ceiling. It was right above his bed and he wondered if the roof leaked when it rained. He hoped he wouldn't still be here next winter to find out. He hated being locked up. The idea of spending the rest of his life behind bars was so terrifying, he worked hard to keep his mind from going there. Instead, he made an effort to focus on counting backwards from one hundred or reciting a string of Hail Marys in both English and Spanish, anything to keep from thinking about what his future might hold.

Ave Maria, llena de gracia. Hail Mary, full of grace. The Lord is . . .

With a heavy sigh, he gave up. Even the Lord couldn't still the terror gnawing away inside him.

He'd spent the night in jail once before, when he was eighteen, after being picked up for fighting. But he'd known then that he'd be out the next day, facing only a fine and the disappointment in his mother's eyes. Besides, the jail in Tahoe City was practically in his own neighborhood. Here at the county seat in Auburn, he felt like he was in a different world.

He heard the guard approach. "Escobar, you've got a visitor."

Ramon rose carefully. There was enough clearance between the bed and the ceiling that he could sit up straight, but the space was so tight he always felt as though he were going to whack his head.

"Me?"

"You're Escobar, ain't you?"

His mother had visited yesterday. She wouldn't come two days in a row. Maybe it was his attorney, at long last. Ramon had been waiting for a chance to talk with him.

Ramon slid down from his bunk, ran his hands through his hair, then held them out to be cuffed. He looked around as the guard snapped the cold metal around his wrists.

The visiting room was a long, narrow space divided in half by a counter and Plexiglas shield. Prisoners on one side, visitors on the other.

He spotted Nadia immediately. She was already seated, looking nervous. The scarf covering her head was light blue, like the sky in summer. Even from halfway across the room he could see the smoky eyes and the fringe of dark lashes.

Ramon almost turned back. He didn't want her to see him like this, in these ugly orange clothes, herded into position like a caged animal. But if he walked away, she'd think he was angry. Besides, his need to see her was too great.

He sat down, took a breath, and raised his eyes to hers. She smiled and Ramon felt something catch in his chest, as though a rubber band inside him had snapped.

Nadia leaned forward. "How are you?"

"Okay."

She bit her bottom lip.

"It's not so bad, really. I get food and exercise, and the guards treat us decently."

"How is it . . . being with the other prisoners?"

He knew what she was asking. She'd seen the same movies he had. "They're mostly hard-luck guys," Ramon said, wanting to reassure her. "In for petty crimes, nothing violent."

That would change if he went to prison. Ramon hoped it wouldn't come to that.

"How long will they keep you here?"

"I don't know. Maybe until the trial." *The trial.* His trial. Ramon got a sick feeling in his stomach thinking about it. It was funny how easy it was to toss that word around until it was your own future in question.

"What does your lawyer say?"

"I've only talked with him once, by phone. The arraignment is set for Monday. I'll have a chance to find out more then."

"Monday? You have to wait that long?"

Ramon nodded. "My attorney couldn't get here before then. I signed a waiver okaying the delay. He says that's routine."

Nadia brought her hand to her cheek then lowered it again to her lap. "When do you tell them you're innocent?"

"At the arraignment. But it doesn't matter, it's just a formality. The only time it makes a difference is if you plead guilty. Then they can do away with the trial." Ramon had learned a lot in his few days in jail. "How about you? How are you doing?"

"I worry about you."

He wished he could touch her. The smooth skin of her face, the warmth of her neck. Just one simple touch.

She lowered her eyes. "I'm going ahead with it."

He felt the slap of her words. "I thought you didn't have enough money."

"I sold the ring my grandmother left me."

It was his fault. All of this. Only he'd done nothing wrong. "When?"

"Next week. I made the appointment yesterday."

"Nadia, please. Don't." Ramon could feel the sting of tears. For himself, for Nadia, for the child who would never be born. "Give it time, Nadia."

"I *can't* give it time. Don't you know anything?"

"Just another month. Maybe I'll be out of here by then and we—"

"No!" Her tone was so vehement the old woman sitting to her left looked over sharply. Nadia lowered her voice. "We've been over this, Ramon. It has nothing to do with your being in jail."

But it did. If the cops hadn't suspected him of killing that woman in the park, he would have had time to convince Nadia to keep the baby. To marry him. He was certain he could have changed her mind. Now, he was shut out. Nadia wasn't even listening to him.

"Think of our life together," he said. "Our future. We'll be haunted by the memory of this . . . this—"

She cut him off. "What kind of future would we have starting out with a baby?"

"We'd be a family." Hadn't Nadia always said that's what she wanted?

"I'd have to give up my plans for school. My family would disown me."

"I could take on another job. We'd manage somehow."

She looked at him, her dark eyes intense with emotion. Ramon couldn't tell if it was anger or sorrow or despair. Or maybe something entirely different.

"You're in jail, remember? What am I supposed to do about that?"

"Maybe there's a way to get a quick trial. I'll ask the attorney. And I'll work as many jobs as it takes. You can still go to school."

Nadia's eyes were wet with unshed tears. "Ramon, you are a dreamer. You live by what you wish for rather than what is."

"I don't—"

She didn't let him finish. "I want you to tell your attorney about the baby. That way he'll understand why you were acting so strange the weekend of the murder. The cop I talked to made a big deal about that. How you seemed distracted, drove around, missed work. They need to understand it had nothing to do with killing that woman."

"If I tell him, it will come out at the trial. Your family will find out."

She nodded slowly. "They might, but it's the only way you can make the cops understand."

"But—"

"I don't want you to go to prison."

She'd used her family as an argument for the abortion—they'd disown her if they found out she was pregnant. But now she was willing to risk it in order to help him. The injustice of facing trial for a crime he didn't commit was staggering.

Kali couldn't stand the idea of staying home Saturday pining for the day she might have had with Bryce. Instead, she called Margot. An altogether different experience, but it was better than spending the day feeling sorry for herself.

They drove north to Point Reyes, all the way out to the lighthouse at the tip of Drake's Bay. They walked along the beach, enjoying the sunshine and fresh salt air. The wind, which was often so strong it whipped the sand into your face, today was a gentle breeze.

Kali watched a young boy and his father digging in the sand. She'd been noticing kids recently. It was funny how that happened, how grocery stores and city streets seemed suddenly brimming with parents and children. And how seeing them caused a little tug in her heart that it never had before.

She reminded herself that it wasn't a choice she faced. Not yet. Not for quite a while the way things were going. Before long, she'd be too old, in any case.

From Point Reyes, they headed east along back roads to Sonoma. The rolling hills were lush and green thanks to the winter rains, and dotted with grazing cows and old oaks. It was always amazing to find such an open, bucolic landscape so close to home. Even the little towns tucked away along less traveled roads were of a different era.

In Sonoma they stopped for a late lunch at a restaurant on the plaza, then ambled through the shops. Kali bought some cheese and a handblown glass vase. Margot fell in love with a small nightstand she found at one of the antique shops. They hauled their purchases back to the car and Kali opened the trunk.

Margot began rearranging things to make room for her nightstand. "What's this?" she asked, reaching for a blue bag. "When did you take up knitting?"

"Oh, rats. It's not mine. It belonged to Betty Arnold. It was in her husband's room at the nursing home." Kali kicked herself for not remembering she had it. She should have left it with Helen rather than putting it in her trunk. "The home didn't know what to do with it and asked me if I'd take it. I guess I need to get in touch with the attorney handling her estate."

"You think anyone's going to care? It's not worth anything. Just some knitting and old reading material." Margot pulled out a magazine. "*Journal of English Education.* Your client was a teacher?"

Kali shook her head. "A bookkeeper in a cabinet shop." She took the magazine from Margot and noted it had been sent to Gail Lombardi in Sacramento. No doubt the magazine Betty had asked to borrow on her last visit.

It fell open to an earmarked page, which was an article about teaching spelling, and a snapshot fell out—a copy of the graduation photo Kali had seen on Betty's dresser.

"Anyone you recognize?" Margot asked.

"The older woman is Betty's sister. The younger one is the woman's daughter. Faith Foster. She disappeared eight years ago."

"Disappeared?"

"Most likely abducted and murdered."

"How terrible." Margot was quiet a moment. "Why did Betty have her picture in the magazine?"

"Maybe she wanted to show it to her husband to help him remember. The nurse at the home said Betty sometimes tried to jar his memory with photos and stories about their life together."

Still, it was interesting that Betty had wanted to see Kali about Faith, and here was her photo.

She was about to close the magazine again when her eye caught the picture accompanying the article. It showed a young boy, a spelling champion. A man and woman stood beside him.

And the woman looked a lot like Faith Foster.

Kali held the snapshot next to the photo and studied them. The hair was different and the woman in the magazine was older, but the resemblance was unmistakable. Both women had the same heart-shaped face, delicate bone structure, and deep green eyes.

The tag line under the picture listed only the name of the boy, Patrick DeVries.

"What is it?" Margot asked.

Kali showed her the photos. "Do these look like the same person to you?"

"This one's blond, but yeah, could be. Either that or sisters."

But Faith didn't have a sister. And Betty had said she wanted to talk to Kali about Faith. She knew now what had happened. Betty had seen the magazine photo and come to the same conclusion Kali had.

Faith Foster was alive.

CHAPTER 17

Kali had no memory of the drive home from Sonoma, even though she'd been at the wheel. She must have driven safely and held up her end of the conversation, at least marginally, or Margot would have called her on it. But her mind had been on the journal photograph of the woman who might be Faith Foster.

And on the phone call she'd received at the office the other day. Had it been someone else who knew Faith was alive? Possibly even Faith herself?

Now that she'd dropped Margot off at home and taken Loretta for a quick evening walk, Kali tried to sort her thoughts.

Assume that Betty Arnold had discovered her niece was still alive. Why hadn't she simply gone to the police with the information?

Betty had ended up with money from her sister's estate, Kali remembered. Money originally designated for Faith. She'd used that money to secure Carl's future in the nursing home. Perhaps Betty was concerned about what would happen if Faith turned up alive.

Or had she known all along? Maybe Betty was part of whatever caused Faith's disappearance.

Kali poured herself a glass of wine and began making a salad, which would pass for dinner. After the big lunch she didn't really need even that. It gave her something to do, though, while she twisted her way through the maze of questions.

It all came back to Faith. Why was she in hiding? Whatever her reason, it had been compelling enough to keep her from contacting her parents.

Or had it? Thinking back to her conversation with Lowell McDougall, Kali recalled he'd steered her away from inquiring further into Faith's disappearance. Was that because he knew she was alive?

Kali sliced pear and avocado into the salad, then added chopped pecans. She had no idea what she was dealing with, or how to proceed, but she knew she couldn't simply let it be. She could bring the information to the attention of the police, who might not listen. Or care. If Faith was alive, they no longer had a missing persons case on their books.

Besides, what, really, did she have?

Kali brought Betty's education journal to the table and reread the article while she nibbled at her salad. The caption under the photo listed the boy's name but nothing to further identify him. She could feel the frustration boiling in her veins. Then she noted a short blurb at the end of the article about the Las Vegas school system. Was that it?

Kali called Las Vegas information and asked for a listing for Patrick DeVries. A long shot, but a lot of kids these days had their own phones.

Not Patrick.

"Can you give me the number for all the DeVrieses listed?" Kali asked. She was grateful the boy wasn't Patrick Jones.

"There are seven with that spelling," the operator told her.

"That's fine."

"We're limited to three numbers per call."

Oh, for God's sake. "Give me the first three, then." Kali knew she sounded huffy. She felt huffy.

She tried all three numbers and struck out. There was no Patrick living in any of the households.

Kali was about to try information again when she thought to try the Internet, which was where, she now realized, she should have started. She poured herself another glass of wine and sat down in front of the computer. A search for Patrick DeVries brought up several unrelated sites, but one, the archives of a local Las Vegas paper, contained a piece about a spelling championship that had been won by Patrick DeVries of Kingston Middle School. It also gave his father's name: Elliot DeVries.

Hallelujah. Kali retrieved the phone number from the Internet, too, determined not to give the phone company any more of her business than was necessary.

Her heart was racing as she placed the call.

"Mr. DeVries, I'm a freelance writer doing a piece on children's successes. I happened to read about your son Patrick's recent spelling victory." It sounded lame to her own ears, but she was hoping the spritely and deliberate enthusiasm of her delivery would carry her through.

"Yes?" It was the wary, what-is-she-trying-to-sell-me-now tone of someone annoyed by frequent telemarketers. Kali didn't blame him.

"Well, actually, I'm most interested in the mother's point of view." She pushed on, hoping to win him over with cheerfulness. "Might I talk with your wife?"

"I'm afraid not."

He was, Kali decided, a man of few words. "If this is a bad time, I could call back at her convenience."

"She passed away," he explained.

"Oh." Kali was momentarily stunned into silence. Her first thought was that Faith had died since the photo was taken. It wasn't something she'd considered before now, but there was a certain logic to it. Betty and Faith, both killed by the hand of a common enemy.

She gathered her composure. "I'm sorry. I saw a photograph of your son with you and a woman, and I assumed . . ." She stumbled in genuine confusion. "But maybe it was your sister or—"

"Who is this again?" Elliot asked.

She gave Margot's name because it was the first thing to come to mind, then used her sister's last name. Her own name had been in the news along with Betty Arnold's. The last thing she wanted was to scare Faith off.

"And you're with what magazine?"

"I'm freelance. I'm gearing the piece toward *Good Housekeeping*, but there are a lot of markets where it might find a home."

"Give me your number and I'll try to get back to you."

Kali gave her home number. It was unlisted so he couldn't trace her, and the message on her answering machine didn't identify her. Not that he was likely to call back.

* * *

Kim Wong ate an early dinner with her father in the tiny kitchen where he ate every meal now that his wife was gone. He was seventy years old, and though he'd never picked up a pot until her mother died, he now insisted on doing all the cooking himself. He made food from Kim's childhood that no longer really appealed to her. She'd become too Anglo, just as her parents had feared. She liked pasta and hamburgers, pizza and tacos, and she preferred the Chinese food at Jade Garden to home-cooked. Although she would never have hinted as much to her father.

After dinner, Kim cleaned up the dishes and listened to the family stories. He'd told them so often over the years, she could recite them as well as he could. He always acted like he was telling her something she didn't already know.

She left early, explaining that she had to work.

"How come you work at night?" her father asked.

"That's when trouble happens."

"Why you want trouble? What wrong with you be teacher? Or play piano?"

"I'm a cop, Papa. I like what I do." Kim wasn't on duty tonight, and rather than stamping out trouble, she was trying to find it. But she spared her father a full explanation.

Bauman had put a couple of deputies, men of course, on bar patrol. But Kim had worked with them. They stood out in a crowd as cops even when they weren't in uniform. Kim thought she had a distinct advantage when it came to being undercover.

Tonight she started at Jimmy's, which Ramon's girlfriend had said was one of his hangouts. Kim bought herself a beer and headed for the pool table at the back. She'd learned to play pool in college when she should have been learning economic theory and statistical analysis. Pool was more useful in her current position anyway. It was sometimes a great entree to information.

Half an hour later, disappointed that tonight there'd been no information to be had, she made her final shot, dropping the eight ball right where she wanted it. She'd noticed a pale-complected man with a thick mustache standing off to the side. He'd been watching her for the last twenty minutes.

When the game broke up, he meandered closer. "You're good."

"I owe it to a wasted youth."

"Looks to me like you're still young."

"It's all relative, I guess." Kim didn't figure the stranger to be any older than she was, but then he probably thought she was barely twenty-one.

"You want another beer?" he asked.

She wasn't interested in picking up a guy, and certainly not this guy, who looked like an anemic walrus. But she was thirsty, and the longer she stuck around the more chance she had to observe and listen.

"Okay. I got to tell you, though, my social schedule is full."

"Hey, that's fine with me. I'm just here looking for my brother. My name's Otto."

"Kim."

"Pleased to make your acquaintance, Kim." From his tone, she could tell he was trying to be funny. "You come here often?"

"Every now and then. What's with your brother?"

"That's what we'd like to know. Me and my mom, that is."

They were at the bar and Otto ordered them each a beer. Then he pulled a snapshot from his wallet. It showed a blond, broad-shouldered man with narrow eyes. He had a scar running down one cheek.

"That's my brother Hans," Otto said. "Does he look familiar?"

Kim shook her head. "Why?"

"We haven't seen him for a couple of weeks. His landlady says she hasn't seen him either."

Kim found herself in cop mode. "Which side of the state line does he live on, California or Nevada?"

"He's from South San Francisco."

It was an unexpected answer. She'd been thinking Reno, Truckee, maybe one of the small towns bordering the lake. "Why are you looking for him up here?"

"This receipt was on his dresser." Otto showed her a bar bill from Jimmy's. "Along with a slip for a big cash deposit two days earlier. It's clear Hans came up here to Tahoe and then made it back home, but now his truck is missing and so is he. I've already checked his haunts in the Bay Area."

"So you're retracing his steps?"

"Yeah. For what it's worth."

"Did you ask the bartender?"

"He hasn't seen him either."

Kim looked at the receipt more closely. It was hard to make out in the dark light, so she leaned to the left, closer to one of the hurricane lamps. The receipt showed a purchase at two o'clock in the afternoon.

"Your brother was here during the day," Kim noted. "You'd have better luck checking back then. It's a different crowd."

Otto grinned at her. "You're a smart lady."

"So I've been told." She'd been smart enough to check the date as well. Otto's brother had been here the afternoon of Betty Arnold's murder. She wasn't smart enough to know if that was significant.

"Where does your bother work?" she asked.

"Most recently, at a lumberyard in the east bay. That's the other thing, he hasn't shown up at work either. He's an adult. Not much of one, by most accounts. But legally, he can come and go as he wants. Still, two weeks . . ."

"Have you reported him missing?"

"Not yet." Otto gulped his beer. "Hans is a screw-up. He could be anywhere. I wouldn't be looking for him at all except my mother's worried sick. We want to know he's okay but we don't want to cause trouble for him, if you know what I mean."

"Why don't you give me a way to reach you in case I hear something," Kim said.

She looked up to see Gary Bauman standing at the door. He was with a woman and they were moving to a nearby table.

"That would be great." Otto wrote his phone number on a slip of paper.

Kim felt herself flush. She was sure Bauman had seen her talking to this loser of a stranger. Ostensibly exchanging phone numbers. She wanted out of there.

"Thanks for the beer," she said. "And don't forget to check with the afternoon bartender."

Otto nodded. "I hope I hear from you."

She took the roundabout way to the exit so she didn't have to pass Bauman and his date.

The soft tread of rubber-soled shoes on hardwood sent Irene's heart hammering. Then she saw the flicker of light.

He was looking for her, methodically checking the room with each sweep of the flashlight.

She was trapped. Barely concealed in a corner alcove, no way out except across that open expanse and the sweeping light.

She'd been a fool to think she'd ever be safe.

Irene's throat was dry. She was having trouble breathing. What little air she managed to suck into her lungs seemed thin and flat.

She heard whimpering, and ventured a peek into the blackness.

He had Patrick! Holding a tattooed hand over the poor kid's mouth, half pushing, half kicking him as they made their way closer.

Patrick was supposed to be spending the night with his grandmother. Had the man with the tattoo killed her, too? Irene fought back tears. So many people dead, all because of her. Was there no end to the man's thirst for revenge?

He'd warned her, hadn't he?

You picked the wrong man to mess with. Don't say I didn't warn you.

He was in front of her now, so close she could feel the heat of his body. A dark shape, thick and broad. His face featureless. Only the serpent tattoo, illuminated by the backglow of the flashlight, was visible. It was even uglier than she remembered.

He reached for her. Her throat constricted as she tried to scream. No sound came out at all. She tried again, harder, and managed a feeble squeak.

He grabbed her by the shoulder and started shaking her.

"Irene, wake up, you're having a bad dream."

Her eyes flew open. Elliot. She gasped for air and her lungs filled easily. But her heart continued to pound.

Elliot stroked her brow. "What is it, honey?"

Irene took in more air. It felt good to breathe. Her skin and hair were damp, her body flushed. "A nightmare. I . . . I thought there was someone in the room."

He smoothed the hair away from her face. "There's no one here. Everything's fine."

And then she remembered. She jerked to her elbow. "What about Patrick?"

"He's spending the weekend with my mom, remember?" Elliot traced a line along her cheekbone. "So we could have some *grown-up time.*" They worked at being discreet. Irene didn't sleep at Elliot's house if Patrick was home.

She rolled toward Elliot, slipped an arm around his solid, familiar form, and pressed her forehead against his chest. He stroked her back.

"You want to tell me about it?"

"I don't remember much," she lied. "Just that I was being chased."

"That's an awful feeling." Elliot's hand slid over her upper chest. "Gosh, I can feel your heart still pounding. It must have been a doozy of a nightmare."

Irene tried to make light of it. "Guess I drank too much wine with dinner or something."

"Can I get you some water?"

"I'll get it. I need to pee anyway."

She got up and went to the bathroom, splashed water on her face, and rinsed her mouth. Steadying herself by holding onto the tile counter, she took long, deep breaths. The dream had no doubt been triggered by the phone call Elliot told her about. A reporter who'd seen that damn photograph and recognized her. Traced her here.

Just like Betty had.

Irene felt her chest constricting again, this time for real. What was she going to do? How many deaths was she going to be responsible for?

"You okay?" Elliot called.

"Yeah. I'll be back to bed in a minute."

She closed her eyes and gripped the counter hard. She didn't have a choice. It was time to move on.

When she got into bed, Elliot curled his body around her, spoonlike. She brought his fingers to her mouth and kissed them. "I love you," she said.

"Too bad it takes a nightmare to get you to volunteer that." He kissed the nape of her neck. "I love you, too."

Irene kept his hand pressed against her cheek, even after he'd fallen asleep again. She felt cold and hollow. The terror of her dream had faded somewhat, but in its place was the anguish of inconsolable sorrow.

Tears wet her pillow. It wasn't fair.

Another wave of grief washed over her as she remembered her mother's stock response: Whoever said life was fair?

CHAPTER 18

Monday morning Kali met with Judy Martin, a client who had metastatic breast cancer. A grim situation made worse by the fact that she was a widow with three young children and no extended family. As Judy awaited her death and struggled to find the energy to get through each day, she was also attempting to place her children for adoption. The younger two had found a home. And now it looked like they'd also finally found a family for the eldest, a boy of ten.

Kali's involvement in the Harper adoption a year earlier—a case that made headlines because of the celebrity status of the principals and the homicide that followed—had brought her a number of adoption cases. Usually, she enjoyed them because the parties were working together for something positive. Judy's case was heartbreakingly different.

Kali was in a grumpy mood when the meeting ended. There was a lot to be said for tax law, she decided. It was hard to get emotionally involved with depreciation and capital gains.

The phone rang and she let Jared pick it up. A moment later he buzzed her. "Judge McDougall on line two. You want to take it?"

"Thanks." She picked up her phone. "Hello, Judge."

"I've been thinking about our conversation the other evening," McDougall said, without preamble.

"I hope I didn't upset you."

"It *is* upsetting. How could it not be? Betty comes to see me about Faith, then she's murdered. Now you tell me she mentioned Faith when she hired you." McDougall's tone was heated.

More heated than when they'd talked face-to-face last week. He paused for a breath. "But none of that is your fault. I'm sorry."

"I understand."

"I doubt you do, but that's beside the point." He paused, and Kali wondered if he'd called simply to vent his frustration. He finally continued. "There seems to be a number of . . . well, loose ends, I suppose. That bothers me."

"I can understand how it might." Though loose ends weren't in the same category as losing a stepdaughter.

"I'd like to retain you to keep an eye on them."

"To retain me to . . ." She wasn't sure she followed.

"To keep me informed. About the trial, for one thing. You seem to think this man the police have arrested for Betty's murder might be innocent. I'd like to know who really killed her and why. I owe my late wife that much." He paused. "And of course, if Betty learned something about Faith's murder, I want to know that, too."

"You've given up any hope that she's still alive, then?"

"Years ago." He paused, then spoke again as though a new thought had come to him. "Why do you ask? Did Betty say something that makes you think she might be?"

Kali wondered if she should mention the photo, then decided to wait until she knew for sure it was Faith. "No. As I said before, Betty told me almost nothing."

"And yet the fact that she came to see both of us, ostensibly about Faith, must mean something. That's why I'd like you to look into this for me."

"Wouldn't you be better off hiring a private investigator?" Kali asked.

"You're already familiar with what happened. And, truth is, I find a lawyer's eye is better for this sort of thing."

Kali wasn't in a position to turn down paid work, but Betty had been her client. While she couldn't imagine there would be a conflict of interest at this point, her head was filled with so many possible scenarios she wasn't sure. "Let me think about it, okay?"

McDougall seemed surprised. "All right. If you aren't interested I'm going to have to find someone else, so I'd appreciate it if you'd let me know soon."

Kali chewed on her knuckle for a moment when she got off the phone, then she pushed back her chair and went next door to see Jared. Their law offices occupied the top floor of an old Victorian, and while their individual offices were approximately the same size, hers had the better exposure and the bay window. Not that any of it mattered to Jared. Most of the time he kept his blinds drawn so that the room had a snug, denlike feel that gave Kali claustrophobia. She preferred sunlight and a view of the street.

"How'd it go in court this morning?" she asked, sitting down in one of the two visitor's chairs. Jared was representing his cousin's neighbor's son on a drunk-and-disorderly charge.

"Pretty good. Probation and a stern lecture."

"Great."

Jared nodded. "I just wish the client was a more likable guy."

"You can't have everything."

"Not if I expect to make a living at this, I guess. What did McDougall want?"

"Basically, for me to keep him in the loop."

"Pooling of information. Makes sense."

"Problem is, what I know about Betty Arnold and Faith is more speculation than real information. Can I run something by you?"

Kali told him about the education journal she'd found in Betty's knitting bag and the photo of the woman who looked like Faith Foster.

He whistled softly. "So she might not be dead, after all."

"That's the short of it, yeah. But why is she pretending to be?"

Jared rubbed his jaw. "There are so many possible permutations, it's hard to know where to start."

"That much I figured out on my own."

"Mind like a steel trap, boss." Jared grinned. Then he started counting off on his fingers. "Reasons why Faith might be hiding. How about an abusive boyfriend?"

"She was engaged at the time of her disappearance. To a lawyer."

"That's reason enough to run."

"Well, she can't still be running from him. He committed suicide shortly after she disappeared." Kali began mentally piecing together a scenario in which Faith had killed him, as well. "For what it's worth though, McDougall suspects the boyfriend might have had something to do with her disappearance."

"How about she's running because of something criminal?"

"Like?"

"Geez, use your imagination." Jared rolled his pen between his palms. "It could be she was embezzling money."

"She was an eighth-grade teacher."

"Extortion then. Or blackmail. Kiddie porn. Or maybe she was dealing drugs."

"But it makes no sense to run and hide unless you're being investigated," Kali said. "Nothing like that has come up."

"Maybe it's a fellow criminal she's hiding from. She could have double-crossed a partner or something." Jared leaned forward. He was clearly having fun playing with the possibilities. "Sweet teacher on the surface, but it was her secret life that got her into trouble."

Kali tapped her foot on the carpet, thinking. "According to Betty's friend in Sacramento, Faith had signed up for a self-defense class not long before she disappeared. Her aunt worried that she might have feared trouble."

"See, the clues are there once you start looking."

"It's really not much of a clue." Though it did make Kali wonder what Faith might have gotten herself messed up in.

"How about amnesia?"

"With all the publicity surrounding her disappearance? Unlikely."

"Whatever the reason," Jared said, "it's possible Faith is involved in Betty Arnold's death. Betty wanted to consult you about Faith, right? And she clearly didn't want anyone to know she was talking to you. Looks to me like Betty might have had reason to be afraid of Faith, and that's why she took the precautions she did."

Kali had considered the same possibility herself. "The only problem is, the two of them were supposedly quite close."

"Supposedly is a key word here. Plus, that was years ago when Faith was young. If Betty was going to turn her in—"

"Turn her in for what?" Kali asked.

"Well, now, that's where we were just a minute ago. Something criminal."

"Wouldn't Betty go to the police?"

"Not if she was blackmailing Faith."

"In that case, what would she want with a lawyer?"

Jared held up his hands. "You're no fun!" He grew suddenly serious. "One thing to keep in mind—whoever killed Betty tried to kill you, too."

"I haven't lost sight of that fact."

"Seems to me you've got to get to the bottom of this, for your own peace of mind if nothing else. And a big step in that direction would be finding Faith, assuming she's really alive."

"Go to Las Vegas, you mean?"

"Don't tell me you haven't considered it."

She'd considered the idea and rejected it several times. But Jared had a point. She didn't want to live the rest of her life worried that someone would step from the bushes and kill her.

Jared folded his arms on the desk. "I say go for it. I'll cover the office."

Kali spent the next hour clearing her schedule, then booked a flight to Las Vegas for the following morning. First order of business was to find out whether or not Faith was alive. Second was to hope she wasn't gunning for Kali.

Irene waited until Elliot left for work before getting out of bed. She pretended to be asleep and he no doubt thought she needed her rest after the fitful night. She listened to the sounds of his morning routine—shower, electric toothbrush, razor, the creak of the closet door, the rattle of loose change in his pant pocket. She wanted them branded in memory, something to draw on during the lonely times ahead.

When he leaned down to lightly kiss her good-bye, it was all she could do to keep from throwing her arms around him. She rolled onto her back and opened one eye just a little.

"Have a good day," she said.

"You, too. I'll call you later."

Good-bye, Elliot. I love you.

As soon as he was gone, she was out of bed. She slipped on her clothes without showering. She started to write Elliot a note, then decided it would be better to mail it so he wouldn't know right away that she'd left. It would give her a couple of days' leeway.

Back at her own apartment she took a quick shower, then packed a suitcase and removed the roll of hundred-dollar bills she kept in the toe of her old sneakers. She couldn't leave Elma up a creek by simply not showing up for work, so she called and said she had a family emergency and would be gone indefinitely. She'd only worked three days in this pay period, and she'd have to forfeit that. She stopped by the bank and closed out her account, then drove to the airport, parked her car in the long-term lot. From there she took a shuttle to the bus depot, where she bought a ticket to Phoenix.

Once again, she was on the run.

Nice digs, Sid thought, taking in the CEO's mahogany-paneled walls and expansive windows. He wouldn't mind having an office like this. Northrop had it made. Too bad he was an asshole. But then, so were a lot of the people Sid worked for. You didn't move up in the corporate world by being kind and compassionate.

It was getting close to five o'clock and Sid was anxious to be out of there. They were in Northrop's oversize, twenty-fifth-floor office with Rich Rudd, head of personnel, discussing their options for dealing with an employee who'd been submitting false expense reports. The employee was also the sister of one of the company's major customers, which was what made the situation particularly sticky.

None of this involved Sid. He'd done his part in verifying what the woman was up to. But Northrop and Rudd continued to deliberate as though Sid weren't in the room, so he sank back into the soft leather chair and occupied himself with his own internal dialogue.

He was gnawing on the call that had come into O'Brien's office the other day, a woman who implied she knew about Faith Foster. That worried him. He wondered if the attorney had been able to trace the call. Probably not, or she'd have attempted to contact the woman. And what was with that stuff last night about spelling bees? Could it have anything to do with Faith?

On top of everything, now McDougall wanted to hire Kali to keep an eye on things. What was that about? Sid knew McDougall. The judge didn't waste energy in idle curiosity. And forget that "owe it to his late wife" crap. McDougall didn't operate out of sentiment. No, he had his own reasons for being interested in Faith Foster. And that worried Sid even more.

As far as he'd been able to determine, Betty Arnold hadn't told the O'Brien woman anything of substance. That was good. Maybe it would all blow over, yet.

If only it weren't for the damn photo Betty had talked about. Some stupid magazine she'd borrowed from a friend.

It was lucky Sid had been doing a routine security check at McDougall's the day Betty had come by. Luckier still that McDougall *hadn't* been home. Sid cringed inwardly thinking about how close he'd come. If only Betty had been willing to tell him *which* magazine.

Well, he'd taken care of Betty. All he had to do now was find Faith and finish the job. McDougall would never be the wiser.

CHAPTER 19

Sid paused the tape of Kali's telephone conversations while he freshened his drink. He grabbed a handful of tortilla chips while he was at it. Even listening to them at high speed, it was tedious work. Tedious but necessary.

Returning to his chair, he slipped the headset on again and pressed play. Someone inquiring about a secretarial position. A billing question. A call from a client about having some document notarized. And then he caught the name of the next caller, Margot. Kali O'Brien's sexy neighbor. Sid smiled and slowed the speed of the tape. He'd fantasized about her so often, he wanted to savor the sound of her voice.

"Can you watch Loretta for a day or two?" O'Brien asked. "I have to go out of town on business."

"Sure. Happy to. I might not be home until late tonight, though. I've got a . . . sort of a date."

Sid's jaw clenched. He hadn't even actually met Margot and already he was jealous.

"A date? That ought to be interesting. Does he know?"

"Hardly. I'm not quite sure how to finesse the issue, either. Any suggestions?"

"I hate to break it to you, Margot, but I don't think there's any easy way to tell a man who's interested in you that you're not really a woman but a guy."

Sid choked. The whiskey in his mouth flew out in a fine spray. *Margot was a guy?*

"But I'm not," Margot said. "I mean maybe technically, but—"

"Technically is the part he's going to care about."

Margot sighed. "Ah, shit. I know you're right, it's just . . . I mean, until I get the surgery, where does that leave me?"

Sid hit the pause button again. Christ, Margot was a . . . well not a fag, but a man who got off on men. She . . . he didn't even have the right plumbing! So what if she dressed like a woman, walked like a woman, curved like a woman . . . when it came down to the nitty gritty, she wasn't. Sid shuddered. If he hadn't been so preoccupied with other matters, it could have been him tonight instead of the poor, unsuspecting slob she was meeting. He felt nauseated thinking about it. A fine sweat broke out on his forehead and he wiped it away with his sleeve before going back to the tape.

"Never mind answering," Margot said. "I *know* where it leaves me. Where are you headed on your trip?"

"Las Vegas. Remember that photo I showed you of Betty's niece? I think I've found her."

Sid's heart skipped a beat. He forgot all about Margot.

Kali O'Brien had found the photo. And Faith.

Ramon had been hoping he'd have a chance to meet his attorney before the arraignment, but that hadn't happened. It wasn't until he was in the holding cell at the courthouse on the morning of his hearing that he actually set eyes on the man. Robert Lamont was a heavyset man in his fifties with a puffy face and thinning hair. His suit was worn and shiny through the butt, and could have used a good pressing. Ramon's heart sank at the sight of him.

Lamont dropped his briefcase at his feet and took a seat on the hard wooden bench next to Ramon.

"Don't you worry about today," he said, his Texas drawl more pronounced than it had been over the phone. "Today's just a formality. Not anything going to happen today that we have any say over."

"What about bail?" Ramon asked. He had to get out of there. Maybe there was still time to talk some sense into Nadia's head.

"What about it?"

"Does that happen today?"

"I don't think you're going to get bail, son."

"But I didn't—"

Lamont cut him off. "Doesn't matter. It's not going to happen."

"We're going to ask for it, aren't we?" There was something about the attorney's attitude that rubbed Ramon the wrong way, even if the guy *was* taking his case for free.

"Sure, we can ask." Lamont was rummaging through his briefcase.

"What else happens today?"

"The judge will read the charges against you and ask if you understand them. Just say 'yes.' "

"Even if I don't?"

"That's what I'm here for." Lamont's smile barely made it to the corners of his mouth. "You'll have to enter a plea, too. We might want to think about a guilty plea. I could probably get a sentence that—"

"But I didn't kill her!"

Lamont seemed surprised by Ramon's vehemence. "Okay, okay. We can go with not guilty for now and change it later."

"I'm not going to change it. Why would I want to plead guilty to something I didn't do?"

"There's trade-offs, son. Sometimes it's easier to do your time, knowing you'll be out while you're still young enough to enjoy life."

Ramon was getting a bad, bad feeling about this. He felt bile rise in his throat. "Look, Mr. Lamont, I didn't kill anyone. I'm not going to say that I did. Not now, not ever."

The attorney nodded.

"Maybe you should ask me about my side of things," Ramon said. "You know, so you've got the full story."

"That'll come later. Let's take this one step at a time."

The deputy appeared and escorted Ramon into court, where he sat in the jury box along with a dozen others whose cases were scheduled to be heard.

The room was bustling with men, and a few women, carrying briefcases and whispering back and forth. Attorneys, Ramon decided, then realized they weren't all attorneys. Some were defendants like himself, only they weren't being held in jail. They wore street clothes instead of an orange jumpsuit and their hair was neat and trimmed.

The judge heard their cases first. It wasn't until after the lunch break that Ramon's case was called. Ramon said, "not guilty" when the judge asked how he wanted to plead. Other than that, he might well have been invisible. The prosecutor, the judge, and his attorney carried on like he wasn't even there. The whole thing was over in less than ten minutes.

Lamont gripped his shoulder as they shuffled to the side to make room for the next case. "Wait till we see what they've got. Then we'll know better where we stand."

Ramon wanted to tell him it wasn't *we*, it was him. He was the one in jail. "Can we talk about my defense now?"

The attorney checked his watch. "I'm running late. And like I said, it's premature. I'll be in touch."

Kim Wong was at her desk finishing up paperwork when Gary Bauman caught her attention through the open doorway and beckoned her into his office. She'd managed to avoid him all morning but she could hardly ignore him now. She hoped he wouldn't say anything about seeing her at Jimmy's the other night.

He was on the phone so she stopped in the open doorway. He put his hand over the receiver. "Got a minute? The assistant DA on the Betty Arnold case is on the line. I thought you might want to sit in on the call."

Kim nodded and dropped into the closest of the two empty chairs. "Who's handling it?"

"Murphy." Bauman put the phone on speaker mode.

"Hi, Kim." Danny Murphy had a high-pitched nasal voice that always struck Kim as unlawyerly, but she'd testified for him in the past and found his courtroom presence impressive.

"Hi. How'd the arraignment go?"

"Judge denied bail. No surprise there. Escobar entered a plea of not guilty, which wasn't much of a surprise either, except I'd been led to believe there was some chance he might be looking for a plea bargain. I'll need you to testify at the prelim. If you've got time, I'd like to go over a few things now while they're fresh in my mind."

"Sure."

"The gun he says he loaned his friend Pinkus, still no sign of it?"

"Nope."

"And Pinkus says he gave it back to Escobar? Any chance Pinkus will make a credible witness?"

Kim looked to Bauman. "We haven't talked to him directly," Bauman explained. "You know he's doing time?"

"Yeah. It would be good if there was someone else who could verify that the gun was back in Escobar's control. You think you can check on that, Kim?"

"Will do."

"I'll reinterview the witness to the argument between Escobar and Arnold myself. Your reports are thorough enough that I won't need to do much but make contact with most of the witnesses." There was the shuffling of papers on Murphy's end. "Let me make sure I have this straight. Escobar didn't show up for work on Friday, the day of the murder, and that was out of character for him. He did work Monday and Tuesday morning. Then when he was returning from lunch on Tuesday, he apparently saw cops at the job site and fled. One of his coworkers can testify that he saw Escobar's truck coming back from lunch and then taking off again?"

"Right," Bauman said. "And it wasn't simply a coworker, it was the foreman."

"What about the other woman, the attorney who was wounded? Will she be able to give us anything in the way of useful testimony?"

"Probably just the opposite," Bauman said. "In retrospect she thinks she *may* have seen the shooter, and he doesn't fit Escobar's description. She was passed out when the paramedics got there, though, and in a highly confused state when she made the call, so we didn't put a lot of weight in what she said. Also, turns out Escobar's mother works for the woman's cousin. I'm sure she doesn't mean to let that color her thinking—she's an attorney, after all—but it must."

Kim knew the *attorney* comment was a friendly jab, and Murphy responded with a laugh. "Believe it or not, most of us *are* human."

Kim leaned forward slightly so the machine would better pick up her voice. "There's an added complication," she said. "The attorney, Kali O'Brien, believes Betty Arnold wanted to consult with her about a long-missing niece. She thinks Arnold may have had information and it was that information that got her killed."

"Does she have any evidence to that effect?"

"Not that I'm aware of." Kim dropped her gaze so that she wasn't looking at Bauman. She knew he wasn't going to be happy about what she said next. "It might bear looking into, though. Turns out there was a man visiting here in the area the afternoon of the murder. He had a beer at Jimmy's around two o'clock. And now he's disappeared. His brother was in town looking for him."

"Any connection to Arnold or the niece?"

"Not that I know of. He's apparently got a record, though."

"You still think Ramon Escobar is the right man?"

Bauman spoke up. "Absolutely."

Kim bit her lip. He was her supervisor, after all. She could hardly make an issue of it.

"I appreciate the heads-up, Kim. But I doubt the defense will raise the issue. Escobar's attorney isn't known for his brilliant mind or his hard work. And he's taking the case pro bono."

"Who is it?"

"Bob Lamont. Do you know him?"

"I used to hear his name now and then when I was working out of Auburn," Kim said.

Lamont had been a criminal defense attorney in the Bay Area at one time. Small time, mostly drug-related crimes, but with enough connections that he was moderately successful. The way she'd heard it, he got a little too close to his clients and developed a drug habit of his own. He'd ended up in Grass Valley long before her time. He practiced enough law that his name was familiar to her, but she couldn't recall a single case where he'd been the attorney of record.

"What you say about his reputation is pretty much what I hear, too," she added.

"Why's he taking the Escobar case pro bono?" Bauman asked.

"Beats me," Murphy said. "But it makes me wonder if maybe Escobar has connections we don't know about."

"What kind of connections?"

"The wrong kind. Any dirt we can dig up on a defendant helps."

Kim jotted notes to herself, aware they'd moved into a new

phase of the case. They were no longer looking for a killer; they were looking for a conviction. She often thought of it as the polishing phase, like the final rewrite of a paper. Everything tight and smooth.

So this time, why did she feel like she was chiseling the thing out of stone?

CHAPTER 20

Kali pulled the rental car to the side of the road and spread open the Las Vegas map she'd brought with her. Two maps, actually. Las Vegas had grown into a sprawling megalopolis in the years since she'd come here as a child to visit family. In picking a city where it would be easy to remain anonymous, Faith Foster had chosen well. But anonymous was not the same as invisible, and Kali was already closer to finding Faith than she had been three hours earlier.

She'd flown into Las Vegas that morning and driven straight to the address listed in the phone book for Elliot DeVries. The house was at the end of a cul-de-sac in a quiet neighborhood of modest Mediterranean-style homes. There was no answer when she rang the bell. Not surprising at noon on a weekday. She'd struck up a conversation with an older gentleman next door who was out watering the narrow row of flowers along his driveway. The man, she learned, was a retired machinist whose wife had recently passed away. He was hungry for company, and more helpful than she'd dared hope for.

No, Elliot didn't have a wife though he did have a girlfriend, a nice woman by the name of Irene Thompson. And yes, that was her in the photograph with Elliot and his son, Patrick. Irene didn't live with them, though she was there a lot. She had her own place in the western part of the city. Worked as a waitress someplace on Sahara Avenue near the freeway. He couldn't recall the name right off. Not one of the chains. A woman's name, he thought, but he could be wrong.

Kali had expected it would take her longer to eke out such information piecemeal, so now she was ahead of the game. Assuming she could find the restaurant. She'd already struck out trying to find a home phone number for Irene Thompson.

She slid her finger down the coordinates listed in the index and located Sahara Avenue on the map. It ran the width of the city, and while Elliot's neighbor had told her the restaurant was near the freeway, he hadn't said which freeway and she hadn't thought to ask.

Starting to the west, Kali took the street in four-block segments, going up one side and down the other. It wasn't easy keeping her eyes on the road while at the same time looking out for a restaurant that might have a woman's name. She passed up a Wendy's since it was a chain. She was on her third set of four-block segments when she spotted Elma's Diner on the other side of the street. She looped around and pulled into the lot. It was a place to start, if nothing else.

Inside, Kali scanned the faces of the waitresses. There were three women and none of them at all resembled Faith. She hadn't really expected it would be that easy, but she felt the tug of disappointment nonetheless.

The restaurant had a homey feel—wooden booths along two walls, red gingham valances, an open soda fountain—but Kali noticed there were also two slot machines by the door. The minimum, she supposed, for any public place in Nevada.

The menu offered a number of appealing choices. She was tempted by the avocado-bacon burger but ordered iced tea and a small salad instead. Since this might be the first of many stops, she wanted to pace herself.

"Is Irene around?" Kali asked conversationally when the waitress brought her salad. The woman wore her hair in a ponytail and sported a name tag that identified her as Georgia.

"She won't be in today," Georgia replied.

Bingo. Kali had struck gold with the first place she'd tried. She bit back a smile. "What days does Irene work?"

"It varies. She would have been here now but she's taking some time off. Something about a family emergency."

"An emergency?" Alarm bells sounded in Kali's head. Something to do with Betty's murder? "Did she say what had happened? Or where she'd be?"

"All I know is that we've got to cover Irene's shifts for a while. It's good for me. I can use the extra money. But some of the other girls have families. They aren't so flexible."

"Do you know how to reach her?"

"No. She sounded rushed when she called. Didn't even ask about pay she has coming."

"I'll check with Elliot and see if he knows." Kali dropped the name casually, as though both he and Irene were people she knew well. "You wouldn't happen to have his work number, would you?"

"Not handy. It'll be in the phone book, though."

Kali nodded as she tore open a packet of artificial sweetener. Silently she cursed herself for being so pleased with what she'd learned about Faith she'd neglected to push the neighbor for information about Elliot.

"I'm so bad with things like that," Kali said. "I can't remember the name of the place where he works."

"Red Rock Veterinary Clinic."

"Right. Red Rock." Kali butted her forehead with her palm. "My brain is like a sieve."

The waitress smiled. "You aren't the only one, honey. And it gets worse the older you get."

Kali knew the minute she walked through the clinic entrance that speaking to Elliot DeVries at work was going to be difficult. He was the only vet in the practice, and the waiting room was filled to capacity. Dogs, cats, birds, guinea pigs—and their owners. In some cases, whole families of owners.

Kali approached the reception desk. The phone was ringing and the message lights were blinking frantically, indicating calls already on hold. The client in line ahead of Kali was talking on her cell phone while writing a check. The middle-aged woman behind the desk seemed to take the chaos in stride.

"I was hoping to have a quick word with Dr. DeVries," Kali said, when it was her turn. She had to raise her voice to be heard above the din of barking and squawking from the waiting area. At least there were no slot machines adding to the hubbub.

"Do you have an appointment?"

"No, it's personal."

The woman narrowed her eyes.

"About Irene," Kali added.

The receptionist's face registered alarm. "Has something happened? Is she hurt?"

"I really should talk to the doctor," Kali said, handing over one of her business cards.

The receptionist glanced at the card, then showed Kali into the doctor's office. One of the few perks of being an attorney was that it sometimes got people's attention.

"I'll tell him you're here, but I can't promise how quickly he'll be able to get to you. This is an unusually busy day."

"I'm sorry to be adding to the confusion."

"If it's about Irene . . . well, I'm sure the doctor will want to talk with you."

While she waited, Kali tried to discern what she could of Elliot DeVries from the trappings of his office. She saw from the diplomas on his wall that he was a graduate of UC Davis, as well as its veterinarian school. Half a dozen framed award and special recognition certificates also hung on the wall. And a big, hand-drawn poster from the third-grade class at Hawthorne Elementary thanking Dr. DeVries for coming to talk to their class.

The only photo in the office was of a young boy—the same boy she'd seen in the photo accompanying the article. Elliot's son Patrick.

Five minutes later, Elliot DeVries pushed open the door to his office. She recognized him from the photo. Early forties, she'd guess. Tall and thin, with an angular face and a mop of thick black hair. His appearance struck Kali as something of a cross between the stereotypical computer nerd and Abe Lincoln.

"My receptionist said you wanted to see me about Irene?"

Kali nodded, and said a silent prayer that Elliot wasn't connected with whatever trouble Faith was involved in. "I'm an attorney. I need to speak to her about her aunt."

Elliot looked perplexed. "Why did you come here, then, instead of going to see Irene?"

"I was hoping you could tell me how to reach her."

Bewilderment gave way to suspicion. "How'd you find me?"

Kali decided to come clean. She showed him the article and the photo. "I didn't know how to find Irene, but the article gave your son's name and I tracked you that way."

His face registered understanding. "It was you who called the other night asking to speak to Irene. You said you were a writer."

"Not my finest moment," Kali admitted. "I wasn't sure I had the correct number and it seemed easier than getting into a long explanation."

He picked up a clay paperweight that looked as though it had been a grade school craft project. "You still haven't given me an explanation, long *or* short."

"It's complicated. And some of it's confidential." She wished she had a better sense of whether to trust Elliot or not. "Her aunt was my client."

"She doesn't have an aunt," Elliot said. "She has no family at all. She was raised in foster homes."

Kali showed him the photograph of Faith and her mother she'd found in Betty's blue bag. "This picture was taken about eight or nine years ago. It's Irene, isn't it?"

Elliot looked uncomfortable. "So what? The other woman could be anyone."

There was a strong resemblance between the two women, and Elliot had to have seen it. "Is that her?" Kali asked again.

"Looks like Irene. Her hair's different, and she's a bit heavier now. But I—"

"She didn't show up for work today," Kali said. "She called in asking for some time off. Something about a family emergency."

A shadow crossed Elliot's face. More confusion than doubt.

There was a knock on the door. The receptionist poked her head in. "Sorry to disturb you, Doctor, but Mrs. Gunther says she can only wait another ten minutes."

"Okay, tell her I'm on my way." He turned to Kali. "Look, lady. I don't know what you're trying to pull here. I don't even know for sure that you're an attorney."

"You can check with the California Bar Association."

He dismissed the suggestion. "I've got a full schedule, as you may have been able to tell from the state of my waiting room. I haven't got time for this. If you want to give me your number, I'll pass the message along to Irene. About her aunt, you say?"

"Right. She died recently."

"I'll let Irene know. Good day, Ms. . . ." He looked at the card. "Ms. O'Brien." He held the door open and all put pushed her from his office.

Kali hadn't particularly wanted to stay on the Strip, but that's where the best deals were. The large sums dropped by gambling guests presumably more than made up for the reasonable room rates. Kali wasn't much of a gambler, but she bought five dollars' worth of quarters anyway. *When in Rome,* she reminded herself . . . *or in this case, Las Vegas.* She played the slots in the hotel lounge— it was quieter and less smoke-filled than the casino proper—until her money was gone. Then she bought a glass of wine, dropped her quarter's change into a different machine, and won ten dollars. Maybe she had a knack for gambling, after all.

Pocketing her winnings, she took her wine to a table outside. The patio area opened onto the lobby as well as the lounge, and as she looked in that direction she caught sight of a man she'd seen on the plane that morning. He had close-cropped gray hair and walked with a cane. He'd bought a newspaper and was now thumbing through it.

With all that had happened, she couldn't help but feel an initial stab of suspicion, though she knew it was unwarranted. There'd been a whole group of older tourists on the plane coming in, no doubt headed for the nightlife of the Strip. It wouldn't be unusual to run into one of them.

Kali gave fleeting thought to taking in one of the shows herself, but she was in no mood for play. In fact, she was feeling down-right grumpy. To have made such progress in locating Faith, and then have it fizzle into nothing. She could have predicted the trip would be a waste.

Kali thought about what she *did* know. She had no proof that Faith Foster and Irene Thompson were the same woman, but the fact that Elliot thought they might be was enough. At least for now. And it appeared that Faith was involved with a man who knew nothing of her past. Or professed to know nothing.

Kali moved inside to the hotel's restaurant and ordered din-ner—grilled chicken breast with string beans and roasted potatoes. And another glass of wine. The chicken arrived smothered in cream sauce. Kali was scraping it to the side with her knife when her cell phone rang. For once, she was grateful for the noise of the slot machines. Not a single person at the neighboring tables so much as glanced her way.

"Ms. O'Brien, this is Elliot DeVries, Irene's . . . friend."

Kali set down her knife and reached into her purse for a pen. "Right. Have you spoken with her?"

"I think I was a little short with you today."

"That's okay, I understand I got you at a bad time."

"I was wondering if we could meet and talk. Tonight if that works."

Kali's pulse was racing. Was this a trick? No way was she meeting him in some isolated, out-of-the-way spot. But she did want to talk to him. "Tonight's fine," she said cautiously.

"Are you at a hotel in town? I could be there in about an hour."

She gave him the name of the hotel.

"I'll meet you in the front lobby."

A very public place. Kali felt marginally reassured.

"Tell me again what your connection with Irene is," Elliot said. They'd found the lobby awkward for conversation and were now seated at a small table in the corner of the bar. Because she wanted a clear head, Kali had switched to sparkling water with lime. Elliot had ordered a beer.

"Her aunt, Betty Arnold, was my client," Kali explained. "Does the name mean anything to you?"

He ignored her question. "I called the bar association, like you said."

"And?"

He rubbed his jaw. "Do you have a photo ID?"

Kali showed him her driver's license.

"Okay, so you're really an attorney." Elliot studied her for a moment, then took a long swallow of beer. "You want to tell me what this is really about?"

"It's about my needing to speak to Irene."

"Because of her aunt."

Kali nodded.

"Was that her aunt in the photo you showed me?"

"No, that was her mother. She died in a plane crash a couple of years ago."

"What about her father?"

"To the best of my knowledge, he took off when she was a baby. Her mother remarried when Irene was in college so she has a stepfather, though I don't think they're close."

"And the aunt, where does she fit into all this?"

"She was murdered almost three weeks ago. I was there when it happened." She looked hard at Elliot, trying to gauge his reaction. She still wasn't sure if she should trust him.

"What happened? Who killed her?"

"The police don't know yet who did it, but they've got some leads." Kali could feel a knot forming in her stomach at the memory of that afternoon. "It was the first time I'd met the aunt. She wanted to consult with me about Fai . . . about Irene."

He looked at Kali with a puzzled expression. "About Irene? Why?"

"We never got that far. Someone shot her before she had a chance to explain."

"Jesus. This whole thing is . . . it doesn't make sense." Elliot gripped his beer in both hands. His thin face scrunched in thought.

"How well do you know Irene?"

"Well enough to want to marry her." He gave a sardonic laugh. "But if what you say is true, I'm a little short on specifics. She told me she was an orphan."

"I'm sorry."

He nodded. The muscle in his jaw jumped.

"Have you known her long?"

"We met three years ago. Her boss at the diner is my cousin. We've been serious for about a year. Though truth is, I'm more serious than Irene, I think."

"Do you happen to know where she was two weeks ago last Friday?"

"She works Fridays. Why?"

"And she was at work that Friday two weeks ago?"

Elliot frowned. "Let's see, that would have been . . . right. I picked her up after work and we went to a movie."

"You're sure?"

"Yeah. My son was at a sleep-over. He's a great kid, but we try to take advantage of those moments he's not around."

That meant Faith wasn't directly involved in Betty's death. Too bad. Although Kali had warmed to what she knew of the woman, she couldn't help thinking how much easier it would be to have found a direct link to the shooter.

Elliot leaned forward across the table. "Look, I need to know what's going on. After you left my office today, I called Irene at work. You were right. She wasn't there. She'd told them she needed some time off. I went by her apartment, too. Her clothes are gone; her car is gone. It isn't like Irene to take off without telling me."

So she *had* skipped out. Kali's own disappointment was hard to swallow. "Any idea where she might be?"

"If I had an idea," he said, his voice rising in anger, "I certainly wouldn't be sitting here talking to you. Now are you going to tell me what's going on or not?"

Kali hesitated.

"It's your fault she left," he said.

"My fault?"

"Your call. When I told her about it she freaked out. You're part of the problem, lady. If you want my help, you're going to have to level with me."

And she did need his help. Elliot was probably her best chance of ever locating Faith. And his reactions to everything she'd said seemed genuine. Kali crossed her arms on the table. "Her real name is Faith Foster. Does that ring a bell?"

"No. Should it?"

"She was a junior high teacher from the Bay Area who disappeared eight years ago. She went shopping with a friend one afternoon and has never been seen since. Her car was found some months later on a coastal cliff. Everyone assumed she was dead, either an accident or, more likely, foul play. Her aunt, my client, apparently came across a photo of her taken after your son won the spelling bee."

Elliot had the dazed look of a man who'd taken a blow to the head. "Is that why the aunt contacted you?"

"I'm sure that's part of it. Initially, when I assumed Faith was dead, I thought she might have contacted me because she knew who killed Faith, or maybe was part of it herself."

"And now?" Elliot asked.

"I don't know whether Betty Arnold knew all along that Faith was alive or just recently discovered it. She ended up with the inheritance Faith's mother left to Faith, so she was in sort of a fix either way."

"Irene would have inherited money?"

Kali nodded. "Not a fortune, but a good amount."

Elliot raked a hand through his hair. His face showed strain. "I'd say you were nuts if your story didn't explain so many things."

"Like what?"

"Irene is smart, and obviously educated. I could never understand why she wanted to stay working in that diner, scrimping by on so little money. And she'd let things drop sometimes that didn't fit with growing up in foster homes. She speaks fluent French, knows about ballet and opera and rules of etiquette. I remember one time we were talking about Florence and she made reference to standing on the Ponte Vecchio. Little things like that." He flopped back in his seat. "Jesus, it's like I've been wearing blinders."

Kali tried to imagine how it must feel to discover that someone you loved was living a lie. She found that despite her initial wariness, she'd warmed to Elliot, and she felt bad being the one to shake his world. "I don't have any idea *why* Faith let people assume she was dead. She obviously didn't want to be found, but beyond that . . ."

"There's so much that makes sense now," he continued. "She's been worried lately that people are asking about her. You, most recently. And earlier, some woman who spoke to the principal of my son's school. She'd apparently seen the same photo you did."

"Betty Arnold, maybe."

Elliot nodded. Recognition flashed in his eyes. "You know, I was at Irene's house about a month ago when she got a call that upset her. I could tell from her voice and the way her face went white. Literally. She told the caller she couldn't talk right then. She wouldn't tell me what it was about. I assumed it was some other guy, which didn't make me happy. But it could have been the aunt. Irene was jumpy and distracted for the rest of the evening."

"She never said anything more about the call?"

He shook his head. "I tried to press her a few times. I was kind of upset thinking there might be another guy. She told me it was a bill collector, but I knew she was lying. And she seemed different after that night."

"Different how?"

"It was subtle. I'm probably the only one who noticed. She was more distant, like her mind was elsewhere. She didn't laugh as much. And she was jumpy as hell."

"Maybe it *was* a bill collector."

"No, Irene is frugal. She's strictly a cash kind of gal."

The waitress appeared to ask if they wanted refills. They both declined. Kali reached for the bill, but Elliot beat her to it.

"Did she ever talk about guys from her past?" Kali asked.

"Not by name. I knew there'd been some, but I wasn't particularly eager to hear the details." Elliot seemed to be lost in thought for a moment. "Only name that ever came up was Blake. I don't even know if that's a first name or last."

"What did she say about him?"

"She called out his name a couple of times in her sleep. One time I asked her the next morning if he was an old boyfriend and she started shaking. It was an odd reaction because she had to know I was just teasing her."

"Blake? Not Andrew Major?"

"Who's he?"

"An old boyfriend. Fiancé, in fact. He committed suicide not long after Faith disappeared."

"Jesus." Elliot looked at Kali. "You think that has something to do with why she's hiding? Maybe she doesn't know he died."

"Could be, I guess." Kali recalled Faith had taken a self-defense class. But if Andrew Major were abusive, wouldn't someone have known? "Do you have the key to her apartment?" Kali asked.

"Yeah. And she has the key to my house."

"Would you be willing to let me look around?"

"For what?"

"For anything that might help us figure out what's going on."

Elliot sucked on his cheek. "Guess I'm going to have to trust you at some point. I need to get back home tonight, though. My son's alone. How about tomorrow, early morning?"

"Fine."

Elliot gave her the address. "Meet you there at seven A.M."

Sid hailed the waitress and ordered another scotch. He hadn't heard everything—the large fern that hid him from Kali's view had also muffled much of the conversation. But he'd heard enough to know that Faith had been living here under an assumed name and was again on the run. This time he was going to make sure he followed her.

On her way out, the attorney passed by Sid's table. She smiled at him. "We were on the same plane coming out."

Sid returned the smile. "Small world, isn't it?"

Still smiling, he watched her leave the restaurant. It was nice that she'd done so much of the work.

Now it was his turn. He'd check Faith's apartment tonight and then hit the airport. He needed to find her before the attorney did.

CHAPTER 21

Kali met Elliot the next morning at the entrance to Irene's apartment building. It was a four-story, boxlike building with a dirty gray-white stucco exterior. Three scrawny palm trees stood sentry near the front walkway.

Elliot looked tired. His shoulders drooped and his thin face seemed even more gaunt than it had the evening before. He opened the lobby door and held it for her. "Although I have a key, I'm hardly ever here," he explained. "She's more often at my house."

Kali could understand why on the basis of aesthetics alone. The inside walls were covered in the same stained stucco as the outside. The glass doors leading from the lobby to a concrete patio and small pool in back were layered with greasy handprints, and the brown carpet in the hallways badly needed cleaning.

They took the elevator to the third floor and exited into a closed corridor that smelled of cooked cabbage and tobacco.

Elliot unlocked the apartment door. "I couldn't sleep at all last night. I kept thinking about everything you told me. I'm still having trouble making sense of it. And I'm worried sick about Irene."

"Any more thoughts about where she might have gone?"

"None. I checked with a few of her friends. She didn't say a word to anyone."

Kali looked around the apartment quickly. It was tiny and sparsely furnished, though she could tell that Irene had tried to make the best of what she had. Colorful accent pillows brightened the beige twill couch and chair in the main room, and a vase of paper flowers sat in the center of a small maple dining table that was pushed against the wall. The only bedroom contained a double bed and pine dresser.

"Does she have a computer?" Kali asked. "It might tell us something about what's going on."

Elliot shook his head. "She'd use mine sometimes. I don't think there's anything on it that's going to give us a clue, but I'll check when I get home." He picked up a framed photograph of himself and Irene from the dresser. "This was taken only three months ago. On Valentine's Day. It was the second time I proposed to her."

"The second time?"

He offered a bittersweet smile and set the photo down again. "She never actually said no either time, but she didn't say yes, either."

"Maybe because of all this other stuff," Kali offered. She hadn't the faintest idea what Irene felt toward Elliot, but his feelings for her might as well have been etched on his forehead. She looked around the room. "What else is missing besides her clothes?"

"Nothing that I notice right off. That photo is a favorite of hers and it's still here." Again, his voice filled with emotion. "The sketch of persimmons in the other room meant a lot to her, too. One of her customers did it for her as a Christmas present." Elliot sat on the bed, elbows on his knees. "Maybe there really *was* a family emergency."

"She doesn't have any family," Kali reminded him. "None but her stepfather, and I just spoke with him two days ago."

"She must have *some* family."

"I don't think they're the reason she left town."

"No, I guess not."

Kali picked up Irene's telephone and hit redial. A recording for the time. Next, she listened to messages on the answering machine. Two from Elliot and one from a woman named Elma.

"That's Irene's boss," Elliot explained. "My cousin. She's one of the people I talked to last night."

Kali hit fast forward, then listened again, hoping to pick up older messages that hadn't been taped over or erased. Nothing.

Same result when she rewound the tape to the beginning. Irene had been thorough in covering up any loose ends that might provide a lead to her whereabouts.

"Does she have an address book?" Kali asked.

Elliot nodded. He reached over, opened the drawer to her bedside table, and poked around inside. "It's not here. She must have taken it with her."

Yet she presumably wanted to remain anonymous. "Why don't you look under the mattress," Kali suggested, "and in the corners of drawers, places she might have used for safekeeping. Maybe we'll find something that points us in the right direction."

"I don't know . . . none of this feels right." But Elliot slid off the bed and ran his hand under the mattress.

Kali tackled the bathroom. She opened drawers in the vanity, now for the most part empty. Then she looked into the cabinet under the sink. Drano, toilet paper, a bottle of Woolite, and an open carton of Tampax. She was about to leave when she remembered one of her favored hiding places from her teens. She reached for the box of tampons.

Inside was a newspaper article from last October about a conference on aging being held in Las Vegas. The keynote speaker was a dermatologist by the name of Edward Blake.

Kali called to Elliot. "What was the man's name you said Irene mumbled in her sleep a couple of times?"

"Blake. Why?"

She carried the clipping to the bedroom and showed it to Elliot. "Does this mean anything to you?"

He read it through then shook his head. "You think this Blake is someone Irene was involved with? He looks a lot older."

Kali could sense vibrations of male competitiveness. "She might know him without being romantically involved. He's from Palo Alto. That's where Faith was living before she disappeared."

"She wouldn't tear out the article and keep it unless he meant something to her." Elliot shifted from one foot to the other.

"Tell me again about Irene's calling out his name in her sleep."

"It only happened twice. Twice that I knew of, anyway. Once a couple of weeks ago. The other time was two nights ago, the night you called and said you were writing an article."

"The night before she decided to leave town," Kali pointed out. "You think she's with *him*?"

The man's jealousy was clouding his thinking. "More likely, he's got something to do with why she's been living under an assumed identity. And why she took off again."

Elliot turned on his heel. "Either way, there's nothing here that's going to help us find her. Besides," he added bitterly, "if she'd wanted me to know where she was, she'd have told me. Let's get out of here."

As they were leaving, an older woman in a Hawaiian print shirt emerged from the door across the hall.

"Good morning, Elliot. You looking for Irene?"

"You know where she is?" he asked, his face brightening with hope.

"No. She said she was going away for a while." The woman hesitated before continuing. "She left a letter for you. I was supposed to mail it today, but since you're here now I might as well give it to you. Hold on a minute."

She ducked into her apartment and returned with a sealed envelope, which she handed to Elliot.

He grabbed it eagerly, walked away a few steps, turning his back before opening it. It took only a few seconds for him to read the note, then he passed it to Kali. He had the look of a man who'd had the air knocked out of him.

The note was short, written in a neat, round cursive on plain white paper.

> *Dear Elliot,*
>
> *I have to leave, for your sake and Patrick's as much as my own. I wish I could explain but that would only make things worse. Something happened years ago. It wasn't anything bad—in fact at the time I thought it was the right thing to do—but it continues to cause me trouble. And in time, it might cause you and Patrick trouble. Please know that this has nothing to do with you or my feelings for you. I love you with all my heart.*
>
> *Irene*

"Is it bad news?" the neighbor woman asked.

"She's left," Elliot said, his voice barely above a whisper. "Gone. Forever."

Kali put a hand on his arm. "You don't know that. It could—"

Elliot shook his head, twisted away from Kali's touch. "I need to leave. I . . . I need to be alone. Please."

He didn't even wait for the elevator but pushed open the door to the stairs instead.

Sid's search of the apartment had netted him nothing but a current photo of Faith and an address book with a handful of entries, all local. No one he'd contacted had any idea where she'd gone. The only really helpful thing was the paperwork on her car. Armed with the model and license number, it had taken him less than an hour driving through the rows of parked cars at the airport to find it.

She'd parked in a highly visible spot at the end of a row, which made him suspicious right off. But it was the map of Los Angeles and the Southwest Airlines brochure on the car's dash that convinced him she hadn't really flown anywhere. No way in hell she'd be that careless. Still, he needed to be thorough. Back at the hotel, he powered up his laptop, logged on, and called up a program he'd used in the past to gain entry to the airline's reservation system. No Faith Foster and no Irene Thompson. Not proof positive, but close.

Sid was exhausted. He'd gotten only a couple hours' sleep, and that had been tortured. He pulled the rental car into a Denny's and got himself a cup of coffee and a meal of scrambled eggs, bacon, and hash browns. He was getting too old for this. He wondered if it wouldn't be simpler to kidnap the kid. Or break enough of her boyfriend's bones to put him in intensive care. She'd come running then, no question about it.

The more he thought about it, the more he liked the idea. Why chase all around the country trying to track her down when he could more easily lure her into his trap?

He'd wait to see what Kali O'Brien did first, but it eased his mind to know that he had a fallback. All he had to do was set the bait and Faith would be his.

*　*　*

The afternoon sun was relentless. It beat down on Irene through the window of the bus, which was already hot and stuffy. She was thirsty and she'd have liked to brush her teeth. Not to mention take a shower. Roughly forty-eight hours since leaving home and she felt like she'd been on the road for months.

She'd left her car at the airport with a Southwest schedule and a map of Los Angeles on the dash. She hoped the car would throw them off track. Even if the ploy didn't work, it was better than parking her car at the bus depot or leaving a trail by having a cab pick her up at the apartment.

Personal discomfort aside, the bus was a good idea. Low-profile and anonymous. It was unlikely anyone would notice her, even less likely they'd remember her after the fact. And the array of possible destinations was almost limitless. How could they guess where she was headed when she didn't know herself?

In her more rational moments, Irene found it hard to believe that Blake would send his minions searching the highways for her, but she'd clearly underestimated him in the past. She didn't want to make that mistake again.

Imagine losing what you love most.

Don't say I didn't warn you.

You picked the wrong man to mess with.

She knew that now. Eight years ago, he'd sent the man with the serpent tattoo to kill her. Why should it be any different now?

Irene closed her eyes against the sun's glare. She was trying not to think about Elliot, but it was like trying not to think about food when you were hungry. It simply couldn't be done. The more she tried to edit him out of her consciousness, the bigger role he played.

By now he'd have probably figured out she'd left town. He'd certainly have called and would wonder why she didn't call back. He'd probably have tried the restaurant, too. He'd know right away that "family emergency" was a pretense. Would he think she was angry with him? That she didn't care about him? At least he'd understand better once he got her letter.

The bus pulled off the highway and stopped at a rest station. Irene hurried to beat the lines to the rest room and whisked past the mirror without recognizing her own reflection. That was a good sign, she thought. She was no longer Irene but Ayasha, a name she'd taken from a former student. The heavy cotton scarf was pulled low over her forehead and knotted under her chin. She'd dyed her hair black and darkened her brows. There wasn't a trace of makeup on her face.

Irene emerged from the building just as a couple with a little boy pulled up in their car. The boy was crying. The father yanked the boy by his arm toward the men's room. "Stop acting like a baby or I'll beat the shit out of you," the father snarled. The boy tried to run to his mother, who turned her back on him and walked away while lighting up a cigarette. "You want dinner tonight," she said, "you'd better do what your daddy tells you."

Irene cringed. She felt sadness for the little boy, anger at the parents. And a great longing for Elliot and Patrick. One of the things that had first attracted her to Elliot was his obvious love for his son. She thought about calling his home number. He'd be at work now so she could safely listen to the sound of his voice on the answering machine.

But Elliot was no longer part of her life. The sooner she put it all behind her, the better it would be.

Back on the bus, Irene closed her eyes and slept, waking only when the bus pulled into the station in Wichita, Kansas, about eight that evening. Her stomach told her she was hungry, though the idea of food held no appeal.

She checked the schedule. The next bus wouldn't leave for several hours. It was headed south toward Dallas. That seemed as good a destination as any. But when she tried to book herself on it, the station agent shook his head.

"The bus broke down coming here," he said. "You want to go to Dallas, you'll have to wait until tomorrow evening."

"The next bus anywhere, then. When's it leave?"

He gave her a peculiar look. "Only one out of here tonight is the one you came in on. It heads back to Albuquerque in about an hour."

Her heart was racing. She didn't want to go back the way she'd come. "There's nothing else until morning?" She cringed inwardly at the desperation in her voice.

"Afraid not."

She wasn't happy about spending the night at the bus station. It smelled of fried grease and sweat. The floor was grimy and flecked with wads of chewed gum, and the walls were marred by graffiti.

Irene found an empty, relatively clean, bench and sat down, sliding her suitcase underneath. She gripped her purse in her lap and pulled her coat around her. She felt like a homeless person.

She *was* a homeless person. Tears pricked at her eyes.

Sometime later a drunk staggered to the bench opposite hers and dropped himself onto it. He looked at her and smiled without warmth. He had the same build as the man from eight years ago.

She looked at his hand. No tattoo.

But he could have had it removed.

Just to trick her? Oh, God. She was losing her mind.

"Not exactly the Ritz-Carlton, is it?" he said.

She ignored him.

"You're a long way from home."

Irene jerked to face him. "How do you know where home is?"

His smile gave her the creeps. She took her suitcase and went into the rest room where he couldn't follow her. Pushing her suitcase against the wall, she saw that her luggage had a big "Las Vegas" tag on it. How stupid. She ripped it from the handle and tossed it into the trash. She waited half an hour, then went back to her bench.

The man was gone.

This time she lay down, using her purse as a pillow and her coat as a blanket. She didn't think she'd sleep. Didn't want to sleep, in fact. She closed her eyes just so she wouldn't have to look at her surroundings.

The cold, hard metal of his gun pressed against her back. She could feel it through the thin cotton of her blouse. It terrified her. What was flesh against the power of a bullet?

"Walk," he'd told her, shoving her forward. In the dark, she was barely able to find her way. She tripped once on the uneven ground and he yanked her angrily to her feet.

"You cooperate and I'll make it easy on you. But you give me any trouble, so help me, you'll pay for it."

The raw night wind tore through her. Her shoulder ached where he'd slammed her against the car. Her ribs were bruised. There was no hope. They were miles from the road, miles from any sign of other people. The blinding terror that had consumed her initially was gone now, and in its place, a resigned sorrow so sharp it was almost unbearable. She tried not to think about the things he might do to her, the pain he might inflict. He was going to kill her, she knew that. She only wanted it to be as quick and painless as possible.

She'd gotten only a brief glance at him. He wore a ski mask but she could tell that he had a short, muscular build and a small, black serpent tattoo on his left hand. It wasn't Blake, but then she hadn't expected he'd do his own dirty work. Trouble was, she hadn't really expected he'd follow through on his threats.

Tree limbs creaked and groaned overhead. The night was dark, the moon only a tiny sliver. It gave off just enough light that she could see the clouds passing in front of the stars. A gust of wind packing dirt and leaves broadsided them. She closed her eyes and covered her face with her hands.

A branch cracked somewhere to her left. Then another.

A shot rang out. Her right leg buckled under her. Pain exploded inside her.

"You're dead," he said. "Now or later. Your choice."

Irene sat bolt upright, her heart thumping wildly in her chest. The memory of that night brought a film of perspiration to her skin. Yet she felt cold. She shivered and huddled inside her jacket.

The bus station was quiet. A few other stranded travelers slept, as she had, on hard wooden benches. In the far corner, two men, boys really, played a card game. They never looked her way.

Irene's mouth was dry. She again took her belongings into the rest room with her, splashed water on her face, and rinsed her mouth.

What if she simply contacted the authorities and told them everything?

No, she'd tried that once and look what had happened.

Besides, she had no proof.

Maybe she should just let him find her. Blake wanted her dead. It was clear he wasn't going to give up. Wouldn't it be better just to get it over with? If she continued running, he was going to keep killing people. People she cared about. First Andrew, now Betty.

Killing people close to her. Irene's heart froze. She'd thought she was protecting Elliot and Patrick by leaving. Might she have put them in danger instead?

Irene hurried to the ticket window. The light was on inside but there was no one there. She knocked. A few minutes later an older black man appeared.

"Is there a place with Internet access anywhere close?" she asked.

"Internet?"

"Right." Airports and shopping centers had kiosks, but apparently not bus terminals. "How about a copy store? Something open twenty-four hours a day."

He shook his head. "Couldn't say about that. Sorry."

She tried the phone book and found a listing for a store on Jefferson. Since the bus station was on Washington, she figured there was a good chance she was close. She got directions from the ticket agent, stored her suitcase in a locker, and walked eleven blocks to the copy store. Then she waited for two hours until it opened at seven.

It took her only ten minutes to find the E-mail address for Betty's attorney, open a Yahoo account for herself, and send a message.

CHAPTER 22

Kali called Jared from the Las Vegas airport. The phone bank was right next to a row of slot machines and she had to put her hand over her ear to hear.

"I'll be back this afternoon," she told him, "but I was hoping you'd be able to do a little Internet research for me in the interim."

"On Faith Foster?"

"Only indirectly. If you have time, see what you can find on Edward Blake. He's a doctor in Palo Alto."

"Anything in particular you're looking for?"

If only. "I won't know it until I see it, I'm afraid. And maybe not even then." Without some background on Blake she didn't even know where to start. "Anything happening on your end I should know about?"

"Nothing that can't wait. Judge McDougall called about an hour ago, wants you to call him as soon as you get a chance."

"I'll try to reach him from here. Give me his number, will you?"

Jared read off the number. "Have a good flight."

The only thing good about it would be the fact that it was short. Kali was a nervous flyer, something Jared with his youthful sense of invulnerability couldn't understand.

She wished she hadn't forgotten to recharge her cell phone since it would have been preferable to call McDougall from a quiet corner. But maybe he'd mistake the whir of the slot machines for traffic. She could only hope no one won a jackpot during the call.

"Thanks for returning my call so promptly," McDougall said. "I was wondering if you'd learned anything further about Betty's murder or her reason for contacting you."

"Not specifically," Kali said. She'd decided not to complicate matters by actually working for McDougall, but she felt he had a right to know at least some of what she'd learned. "It looks like Betty came across a photograph of someone who looks a lot like Faith. A recent photograph."

"What do you mean, recent? Faith was murdered eight years ago."

"She disappeared eight years ago," Kali pointed out. "Everyone assumed she was dead."

"You're saying she's alive? But why—"

"I don't *know* that she's alive." It was only Kali's assumption that Irene was really Faith Foster. An assumption supported by evidence, but an assumption all the same. "I think she might be, though. And I think Betty reached the same conclusion."

"That's . . . that's absurd! How could Faith be alive? Why wouldn't she get in touch with us?"

"I don't know. I don't know if Betty had the answers, either."

There was a protracted silence on the other end. Finally, McDougall spoke. "Well this is a . . . an interesting bit of information. I'd like to see the photo."

"I'll make a copy and put it in the mail to you. You might be able to say for sure whether or not it's Faith."

"Jesus," he mumbled. "Not dead."

"How involved were you in Faith's day-to-day life at the time she disappeared?"

"Hardly at all. She and her mother spoke a couple of times a month, but I only saw her at major holidays, if then. She was already in college by the time her mother and I married, don't forget."

"Does the name Edward Blake mean anything to you?"

"No. Should it?"

"Not necessarily." Kali could hear her flight being called over the loudspeaker. "I'm afraid I have to go. I've got a plane to catch."

"Thanks for getting back to me. And have a safe flight."

Safe. He understood the perils of flying better than Jared did.

* * *

Kali landed in Oakland and headed directly to the office, where Jared greeted her with thirty minutes of what he insisted on calling show-and-tell.

"The big picture wasn't all that difficult to piece together," he told her when they were seated at his desk in front of the computer. "Blake is fifty-nine and a graduate of Boston University School of Medicine. Since 1990 he's headed up a clinic in Palo Alto specializing in cosmetic dermatology. Here, take a look."

Jared clicked his computer mouse and the clinic's Web page flashed on the screen. It was a slick testimonial to the wonders of laser resurfacing, botox treatments, and chemical peels in warding off wrinkles and the ravages of age. Judging from Blake's photo, he practiced what he preached. He looked younger than his years, with a full head of hair, carefully styled, and a face that was smooth and firm, if a little too lacking in character for Kali's tastes.

"From what I've read, there's a big market for this stuff," Kali said. She wondered if Faith could have been a patient. She was only twenty-three when she disappeared, hardly an age when most women worried about looking old.

"Blake is also something of a celebrity," Jared added, "at least locally. I found several articles about him and an archived radio interview. He's a polished speaker. I bookmarked it if you want to listen to it later."

"Thanks."

"He's twice married. Two daughters from his first marriage, late teens and early twenties. A young son with his current wife. They live on Southwood in the Crescent Park area."

"The posh part of Palo Alto."

Jared nodded. "His house is assessed at close to three mil. From appearances anyway, he's the picture of success."

So what was his connection with Faith Foster? A romantic liaison? It struck Kali as unlikely in light of Faith's engagement to Andrew Major, but one never knew.

"I don't suppose you were able to get a home phone number for Blake, were you?"

"Sorry. It's unlisted."

"Not surprising." She stood. "Good job, Jared."

Back at her own desk, Kali tried calling Blake's office and couldn't get past the receptionist. She left her name and number, feeling certain she'd never hear from him, then turned her attention to reviewing interrogatories in a wrongful termination matter.

She was finding it difficult to focus on routine work. The bullet that had torn through her flesh had done minimal physical damage and she was recovering nicely, but the wound in her shoulder was in many ways the least of it. She'd begun looking at life as she hadn't before. What was important; what wasn't? Where did she want to be—emotionally, psychologically, spiritually—in the years to come? These weren't questions Kali was used to thinking about. Or wanted to think about, even. But they were there and they popped up when she least wanted them to.

On top of that, her mind wouldn't let go of Edward Blake. Finally, at four o'clock, she decided to make the trip down the Peninsula to see if she couldn't corner him in person. She fought the traffic on 880 south to the Dumbarton Bridge and crossed the southern tip of the bay into Palo Alto. She was waiting outside the clinic's carefully landscaped entrance when Blake emerged at quarter after five that evening. Pretty cushy hours for someone who raked in money the way he appeared to.

"Dr. Blake?"

He looked surprised, but recovered quickly. "Reporter or process server?"

"Attorney. I'd like a moment of your time, but it has nothing to do with any legal action against you."

Sunlight glinted in Blake's silver hair, which was thinning at the crown. The Web site photo had been flattering. Up close, he appeared older. "If it's about expert witness testimony, you need to talk to Perry at Outside Medical in San Francisco. They handle—"

"It's not that. I wanted to ask you about Faith Foster." Kali waited for a reaction. None was forthcoming but she thought his eyes narrowed slightly. "Does the name mean anything to you?" she asked after a moment.

Blake shook his head and began moving toward the parking lot.

Kali followed. "She was local. Disappeared eight years ago."

"I might have read about it."

"Was she a patient of yours?"

"Not that I recall. What's this about?"

"I'm doing some follow-up work on her disappearance."

"Sorry I can't help." Blake picked up his pace. He wove through a row of cars—mostly BMWs, Mercedes, and Lexuses.

"She appeared to know you," Kali said, trotting after him.

Blake stopped, turned. "What makes you say that?"

"She mentioned your name to a friend."

"In what context?"

Kali went out on a limb. "As someone she knew."

"I don't wish to appear vain," Blake said, pulling a key from his pocket, "but there are many people who know me by reputation. I don't know *them*, however."

"What about Andrew Major?" Kali asked.

"Did he disappear, too?" Blake's tone was terse.

"He killed himself."

"I don't know what any of this has to do with me, and I don't have time to play your games. I advise you to find someone else to hassle." He got into a sporty red Corvette and pulled out of the lot with a squeal of tires.

Kali got into her own car and tapped the steering wheel with her fingers. Had she really expected Blake would come through with answers? Still, the encounter left her feeling at loose ends. Maybe she needed to approach the question from a different angle.

Andrew Major had been an attorney with Clifford and Krebs, one of the specialty firms that had scored big during the heyday of Silicon Valley growth. If they were like most firms, they'd been forced to lay off attorneys in recent years, but during Major's tenure, the rigor of long days and high billable hours would have paid off big-time in salary, bonus and, best of all, stock in client companies. A veritable lawyers' gold rush.

Kali pulled into a gas station, found a phone book, and looked up the firm's address. Even in today's weaker economic climate, she was betting most attorneys put in longer hours than Dr. Blake.

The firm was located in a sleek two-story professional building off El Camino. The offices were tastefully decorated in soft grays and greens. Pleasant but not showy or elaborate. Kali approached the receptionist, a young woman with pink cheeks and clear plastic braces on her teeth.

She smiled as Kali approached. "Can I help you?"

Kali introduced herself. "Were you by any chance working here eight years ago?" Not likely, she realized as soon as the words were out of her mouth. The woman would have been in junior high at the time. "I guess the better question is, who could I speak to who *was* here then?"

"Well, there's Marsha. That's Mr. Denton's secretary. Or Mr. Denton himself. He's been with the firm since it started. Marsha oversees the day-to-day running of the office. There're other attorneys too, but I'm not sure how long they've been with the firm."

"Could I speak with Marsha?" *Better to start with the secretary,* Kali thought. No intrusion on billable time, and she might be able to give Kali a better picture of Andrew Major. Staff was privy to gossip that never made it past the heavy wooden doors of attorneys' private offices.

"I'll see if she's available. This is regarding . . . ?"

"Someone who used to work here," Kali replied, handing over her business card.

"Just a moment." The receptionist spoke into the telephone so quietly that Kali wasn't able to hear what she said. But a moment later, a slim woman in her late forties came down the hallway.

"I'm Marsha Nix, how can I help you?" Her hair was a cap of sleek silver, which coordinated perfectly with the silver ear hoops and chunky bracelets.

Kali introduced herself. "I'm an attorney working on a case involving the fiancée of a former employee here." The explanation seemed sufficiently vague to allow maneuvering room down the road. "The employee's name was Andrew Major."

Marsha's expression registered surprise. "You must be talking about Faith Foster. Has there been a new development in the case?"

"I'm just following up on some loose ends for the family."

"You know that Andrew committed suicide?"

Kali nodded.

"It was terrible what happened. To both of them."

"You knew Faith?"

"I'd met her, but no, I didn't really know her." Marsha Nix led the way to an empty conference room off the main lobby. It was smaller than the imposing, glass-enclosed room that had caught Kali's eye as she walked in the door. She sat at the head of the table. "What is it I can help you with?"

"Let me start with an off-the-wall question first. Are you aware of any connection between Andrew Major and the dermatologist, Edward Blake?"

"Blake? The guy with the radio commercials? *Don't let your face betray you.* 'The lunch-hour face-lift,' he calls it. Doesn't seem to me the kind of thing Andrew would do."

"Could Blake have been a client?"

"I doubt it. Andrew worked almost exclusively for Mr. Denton. They handled public offerings and financial matters. Certainly nothing having to do with medical malpractice."

"Maybe they handled a business matter for Dr. Blake?"

Marsha Nix fingered the heavy silver bracelet on her wrist. "It's possible, I suppose. Though I don't recall him being a client."

Kali knew she'd been reaching pretty far afield. She decided to forget about Blake for the moment. "What was Andrew Major like?" she asked instead.

"Full of himself," Marsha Nix replied with a laugh. "Like all our young attorneys at that time. Those were the golden years of dot-com boom and our firm's specialty is, or was, high-tech. But Andrew was as bright as a whip, and likable enough once you got past the posturing. They all had dreams of making it big—fast track to partnership, a lucrative practice, million-dollar mansions. With Andrew it was more than a dream, though. He took personal success as a matter of course. Went out and ordered himself a custom-built Cobra replica, in fact, only a couple of weeks before he killed himself."

Kali sat back in her chair. It was a soft leather that fit her back perfectly. "How did people he worked with react to his suicide?"

"We were all saddened by it." Marsha Nix seemed almost insulted and Kali realized she'd misunderstood the question.

"I meant, was it a surprise? Had he been having problems before Faith's disappearance?"

Marsha hesitated before answering. "He wouldn't have shared them with anyone here if he had."

"Keeping up appearances?"

"That, and he didn't have many friends in the firm. People who admired him, yes, but no one he was close to."

Kali nodded. In her experience, lawyers on the fast track often took a me-versus-them posture that didn't allow room for friendships. "How did he handle Faith's disappearance?"

"He was distraught, as would be expected." She paused. "It was *more* than I expected, actually. He was usually so controlled."

"He was out of town when she went missing?"

"Right. He'd been on a business trip with Denton and another associate. Closing a deal in Portland. The police apparently contacted him there when she was first reported missing."

"Andrew Major was a suspect?"

"As I recall, there was some talk to that effect initially, but it never went anywhere. They were mostly calling for information—do you know where she might have gone, that sort of thing. By the time he got back, though, the police were already thinking there might have been foul play involved. Andrew was beside himself. He came into work the first day he was back, but you could tell just from looking at him, he wasn't going to be able to concentrate. I liked him better for it. I never thought Andrew cared much about anyone but himself."

"How did he kill himself?" Kali knew the basics from talking to Sandborn, but his was the official, detective's perspective and she thought Marsha Nix might be able to add to it.

"He shot himself. Mr. Denton told him to take some time off and we all thought that's what he'd done. Wasn't until later in the week that a hiker found his car parked up in the hills. He'd apparently been dead for a couple of days."

"Wasn't there still hope Faith might be alive?" Maybe Kali's knowledge that she *was* alive was coloring her thinking, but it struck her that Andrew Major had given up awfully soon.

"Sure there was hope, but we all more or less suspected the worst. And Andrew was upset. I doubt he was thinking logically." Marsha paused. "There was also evidence he'd been drinking heavily before he killed himself. I'm guessing that contributed to it. Sometimes drowning your sorrows in liquor only makes them seem worse."

"True." Kali's own father had been proof enough of that.

Kali wondered why Faith hadn't spared her fiancé, of all people, the anguish of thinking her dead. The note she'd left Elliot referenced a wrong she'd committed, something that seemed right at the time. Was she feeling the responsibility for Andrew's death? And what could have been so terrible that she had to fake her own?

"Did Andrew have family in the area?" Kali asked.

"No, his parents were back East."

"And no one at the firm he was close to?"

"Nancy Baylor and Andrew were hired at the same time so they offered each other support, especially in the beginning. And I think her being a woman made her seem somehow less like a competitor."

"Male trumps female?"

Marsha Nix smiled. "Something like that, yes."

"Is she still with the firm?"

"She's with Marshall and Mulvaney now. In Pleasanton."

Kali wondered if Nancy had been squeezed out as the ranks narrowed toward partnership. Probably so. She'd been only half joking with her trump comment. Of course, Andrew Major was dead and Nancy was alive. Bottom line was, life trumped death.

Kali thanked Marsha Nix and left, stopping at the first phone booth she saw to again check a listing. This time for Faith's roommate, whose name Kali had learned from the newspaper accounts of Faith's disappearance. The woman was probably married by now with a different last name, assuming she still lived in the area at all.

To Kali's surprise, however, Lana Seger was listed. Kali called, expecting to get a machine, and was again surprised when a woman's voice answered.

"Lana?"

"Speaking."

"My name's Kali O'Brien. I'm—"

"Take me off your call list. I'm not interested."

"No, wait. I'm not selling anything, I'm an attorney working on some new developments in Faith Foster's disappearance."

A moment of silence on the other end. "I don't know anything I haven't already told the police," Lana said finally. "And that wasn't much. I wasn't even home the weekend she disappeared."

"My interest is more of a general nature. For example, how would you characterize Faith's relationship with Andrew Major?"

"They were engaged."

"Even people who are engaged sometimes have troubles. Was theirs a good match?"

"We were roommates, not friends." Lana's voice was wrapped in indifference.

"Does the name Dr. Edward Blake sound familiar?"

"Yeah, he's that 'look younger, feel better' doctor. Wants us all to look like Ken and Barbie, even when we're seventy."

"Any connection you know of between him and Faith?"

"Only through his daughter."

Kali felt a surge of excitement. "His daughter was a friend of Faith's?"

"She was one of Faith's students. Though I suppose in a way they were friends, too. Faith was young and enthusiastic. It was only her second year teaching. She wanted to make a difference in every kid's life." Lana sounded cynical. "She'd have the kids call her at home, have groups of them over for pizza dinners and stuff."

"So Blake's daughter came over for dinner?"

"Yeah. I remember her in particular 'cuz she had an eating disorder. She'd gorge herself on food then go into the bathroom and throw up. Totally disgusting. I guess that's what happens when you've got a dad who thinks external beauty is all that counts."

"Anything else you remember about the daughter or Dr. Blake?"

"Nope. For the most part, I stayed away when Faith had those dinners. Hanging out with a bunch of obnoxious teenagers wasn't my idea of a good time. Why are you interested in Dr. Blake anyway? Is he a suspect in Faith's murder?"

"No, nothing like that." Hardly a lie, since Faith wasn't dead. "Was she into anything dangerous before she disappeared?"

"You mean like drugs and prostitution? That's what the police asked me. As if. Faith was more like a missionary. Minus the religion."

"So she didn't seem upset or worried about anything?" Kali was still having trouble fathoming what might be behind Faith's disappearing act.

"Faith was always worried about something. But like I said, we weren't really friends." There was a blipping sound on the line. "I've got another call. Have to go."

Kali heaved a discouraged sigh. She'd finally managed to find the connection between Faith and Dr. Blake, only to learn it wasn't much of a connection after all.

But then why would Faith hide the newspaper article about him? Maybe because part of her missed her old life?

Okay, the news clipping Kali could deal with. But what about Faith's calling out Blake's name in her sleep? There had to be more to it than a hankering to keep in touch with the past.

And none of that explained why she'd let everyone believe she was dead.

Kali started the car. She was sick of the whole tangled mess. And except for Elliot, she seemed to be the only person who cared about getting at the truth.

Suddenly she felt the need for human companionship. Bryce's companionship. She hadn't talked to him since he'd called to break their date last weekend. It surprised her to discover how much she missed him. That she would lust after him when he was right before her eyes was a given. But this quiet longing to be with him, to find comfort in having him near, that was something she hadn't counted on.

She pulled out her cell phone again and called him. She wasn't sure she'd actually reach him, and when she did, she felt a little flutter of pleasure.

"If you can wait till eight to eat, I'll buy you dinner," she said.

"You after more information?"

His tone was light, but the words cut. "What I want is your fine company."

"I'm not very good company right now. I'm tired and I'm working a stakeout later tonight."

"Even your grumpy company would be nice."

Bryce hesitated, then relented. "Guess that's an offer I can't refuse."

"Wow, you know how to make a girl feel special."

He laughed. "There's no one in the world I'd rather have dinner with. Is that better?"

"Much." She only wished she knew if it was the truth. "How about Zachary's?"

"See you there."

Kali was waiting outside the restaurant when Bryce showed up at eight o'clock on the dot. He did look tired, but very attractive in a rumpled sort of way. His hair was still damp from a recent shower and his neck bore a shaving nick. He slid an arm around her waist and kissed her lightly on the cheek.

"Good idea you had. I've missed you."

"I've been around."

He smiled. "No you haven't. I called. A couple of times."

"You didn't leave a message."

"No, I didn't. Were you back up at Tahoe?"

"Las Vegas." She gave him a short rundown of what she'd learned. "But I don't want to talk business tonight."

They shared a deep-dish spinach pizza and a salad along with easy conversation. After dinner they walked along College Avenue, peering in windows of the shops. Bryce took her hand, a simple but surprisingly intimate gesture that spoke of comfort and familiarity more than romance. Kali breathed in the night air, which was sweet with the scent of star jasmine, and felt herself relax.

"You never talk much about old boyfriends," Bryce said.

The statement came out of the blue and caught her by surprise. "What makes you think I have any?"

He came close to smiling. "Were any of them serious?"

"In varying degrees. But they're all history now." She turned and tapped his chest playfully. "You, on other hand, don't have to talk about your love life. It's pretty much public knowledge throughout the department." That wasn't entirely true. Bryce had a reputation as a playboy, but details were in short supply. He also had an ex-wife, and even less was known about her.

"It's not the same," he said.

"Not the same how?"

"Just isn't." He seemed to regret having raised the issue.

"Do I detect a double standard here?"

Bryce shuffled uncomfortably. "Rumors are like snowballs, they have a tendency to grow."

"Meaning?"

"Meaning, don't believe everything you hear."

"Oh? How much of it should I believe?"

He stopped and looked at her hard, dropping her hand. "It wasn't so long ago you were ready to write me off as a murderer, don't forget. That hurt, Kali. It still does."

"Bryce, I'm so—"

"That's what's real. Not all this stupid gossip about what woman I might have dated sometime in the past."

"I was scared. And at the time, the evidence fit. If I could go back and erase what happened, I would. It bothers me as much as it bothers you."

"I doubt that." He stuck his hands in his pockets and started walking again. "It's . . . I don't know, maybe my problem as much as yours. I don't let myself care about people easily. I care about you."

His words made her skin tingle. "And I care about you. A great deal."

"That's why we're going slow. I *want* this to be different."

"Me, too." But Kali sometimes wondered if that was possible.

Bryce figured prominently, and most pleasantly, in her dreams that night. She bounced into work the next morning full of good cheer and whipped out the revisions to a lengthy commercial lease. It wasn't until mid-morning, armed with her second cup of coffee, that she found time to check her E-mail.

There among the annoying ads for Viagra and instant wealth was a message with a subject line that brought her world back into cold relief.

Information about the murder of Betty Arnold.

CHAPTER 23

K ali felt a rush of adrenaline. The message came from a Yahoo
account identified by a seemingly random mix of letters and
numbers. If Betty Arnold's name hadn't jumped out at her, she
would have sent it straight to the trash bin.

Kali clicked on the message and read it twice. Once very
quickly, then a second time with great care.

> *I know who killed Betty Arnold. It's because of me, be-
> cause of something that happened in my past. She wasn't the
> first and I'm afraid there will be more murders if I don't stop
> it. I'm contacting you because I don't know where else to
> turn and I guess Betty trusted you. But I don't want to place
> you in danger. I know this must seem odd, but it is not a joke.
> Let me know if you are willing to help. Please don't tell any-
> one about this message. You may be putting yourself at risk if
> you do.*

The E-mail was unsigned, but Kali felt certain it was from
Faith, or Irene as she called herself now. The wording was similar
to her note to Elliot and the rest of it fit, as well.

Kali was wary. But charged with excitement, too.

She wrote back immediately, first typing out a long and cumber-
some message filled with questions and some of her own discov-
eries. She deleted it and instead sent a short note.

Faith, is that you?

She stared at the machine for a full five minutes, willing an instant response, but none arrived. Kali stretched, closed out of the

mail program, then opened it again. How the hell was she going to bring herself to do anything for the remainder of the day but wait for another message?

The ringing of the telephone startled her. She experienced a momentary flash of hope that the caller would be Faith. Instead, it was Helen.

"Have I got you at a bad time?" Helen asked.

"No, a good time, in fact." Anything to keep her mind from the computer screen.

"Ramon's arraignment was Tuesday."

"How'd it go?"

"They denied him bail." She sounded angry.

"That's not unusual in cases like this, Helen."

"I know. It's just that his attorney did nothing."

"There's not a lot he could have done," Kali explained. "Even the most eloquent and reasoned argument wouldn't have been likely to change the outcome."

"Well, it certainly wasn't either of those. Lamont is urging Ramon to take some kind of plea bargain. Ramon won't hear of it, and part of me agrees with him. I mean, if he's innocent, why should he agree to *any* time in prison? On the other hand, if it's a short sentence . . . and there's a possibility he could be paroled early . . . isn't that better than risking spending the rest of his life behind bars?"

Not an uncommon conundrum. It was why the majority of cases were disposed of without a trial. Given that most defendants were guilty, it wasn't such a bad system. But for those who weren't, the choice was tough. At what price did they maintain innocent?

"Did Lamont offer any specifics?" Kali asked.

"Not that I'm aware of. You should have seen this guy, Kali. He looked more someone you'd see sitting on a park bench feeding the pigeons than an attorney. His suit was wrinkled and there was a yellow spot on his shirt."

"I know it's hard to have much confidence in someone like that, but believe it or not, there are some dynamite attorneys who have no fashion sense."

"It's more than that," Helen explained. "He seemed totally uninterested in Ramon's case. Like he was just going through the motions."

Kali was reminded that Lamont had yet to return her phone call. Calls plural, in fact. She'd left a second message thinking the first might not have reached him. Now more than ever, though, it was important that he know about the Faith Foster connection.

"It's early in the process," Kali said. "He might be waiting for the preliminary hearing to get a feel for the state's case."

"There's not going to be one. He said it wasn't necessary."

"What?" Sometimes it made sense to waive the preliminary hearing. When the prosecution case was strong, for example, and the defense feared a hearing would cement testimony of prosecution witnesses. But it wasn't a strategy that made sense in this instance. "Did he say *why* it wasn't necessary?"

"Just that it wouldn't do any good."

It seemed to Kali this was precisely the sort of situation where a prelim was most useful. The defense would be in a much better position to weigh the odds and make a decision about a plea bargain once the prosecution had outlined its case.

Unless, maybe, Lamont knew something she didn't.

She tried to reassure Helen. "The legal system can be frustrating, but most of the time it works." Still, Kali made a note to reach Lamont, whatever it took.

When she got off the phone, she checked her E-mail again. Nothing new but an invitation to join hot teenage girls and their barnyard animals. She deleted the message, pulled out a will she was drafting, and got to work.

Sid poured himself a cup of coffee, leaned closer to his desk, and read the two E-mails a second time. The joys of being a computer snoop. He'd been scanning Kali's E-mail on a daily basis with little result, and now it looked as though his perseverance had paid off. When he'd connected with her computer just now his eyes lighted immediately on the message about Betty Arnold. And he was pleased by Kali's reply. She'd come to the same conclusion he had. The message was from Faith.

After eight years of chasing dead ends looking for her, she'd come to him. It was almost too good to be true.

Still logged into Kali's account, Sid sent a second message to the Yahoo address.

> *On second thought, it would be best if we could meet. Name a time and place.*

He signed Kali's name.

Now all he had to do was wait. He was hoping Faith would pick some out-of-the-way place like Betty had, but if it was public, he could handle it. All he had to do was follow her. She'd gotten away from him once. A major mistake on his part. Now, he was about to correct it.

Kim eased the cruiser though a gap in the orange construction cones on North Lake Boulevard, parked and got out. She approached a group of three men standing near a backhoe.

"I'm looking for Craig Conrad," she told them.

They pointed to the sandy-haired flagman at the intersection. Kim walked over to talk to him and noted the alarm in his expression when he saw she was headed his way. The uniform sometimes had that effect on people.

He relaxed just as quickly once he realized she was there to talk about Ramon. "How's he doing?" Craig was Mr. Congenial now that he knew he wasn't on the hot seat himself.

Kim shrugged. She was hardly the person to ask. "Being in jail isn't anyone's idea of fun. I wanted to ask you about the gun Ramon owned."

That look of alarm again. "Why me?"

"It's my understanding that you and Ramon did some target shooting." Nadia had put it a little less politely. She clearly didn't share their interest in guns.

Craig turned his construction sign from stop to slow and waved the traffic through. "Yeah, we'd sometimes try to hit a few cans. It's not like we were running around waving them at people, or anything. We're both real careful. And the guns are registered."

"When was the last time the two of you took target practice?"

"About a month ago, I guess. Why?"

Kim could tell that Craig was wary, afraid that she was going to trip him up on some incriminating slip of the tongue. She let him worry. "What'd Ramon use, do you remember?"

"Use?"

"What kind of gun."

"He used mine. He let a friend borrow his last fall and he never got it back."

Kim tensed. "You know the friend's name?"

"Willie Pinkus. The guy's doing time now—nothing violent, if that's what you're after. But Ramon figured his gun was gone for good."

"You're sure Ramon didn't have it?"

"He wouldn't have bothered with mine if he had his."

Kim had talked with three other friends of Ramon's. They didn't know anything about the gun but they all agreed Pinkus was scum. The consensus was that he'd probably sold the gun for drug money, and that Ramon was stupid to have loaned it to him in the first place. Now here was Craig, certain that Ramon hadn't had the gun a month before the murder.

It wasn't what the DA had been hoping for. He'd asked Kim to follow up on the gun hoping she would turn up a witness for the state. Someone who would testify that Ramon *did* have possession of his gun.

The question she faced now was what to do with the information. Exculpatory evidence was supposed to be made available to the defendant. But it was rarely handed over on a silver platter.

She could go to Bauman and let him decide how to handle it. Kim was certain he'd simply mention the interview to the DA. There'd be no written report, no notation in the file. Nothing for Lamont to get his hands on. Craig's statement would help Ramon's defense, but his attorney would have to dig for it himself, which wasn't likely to happen.

On the other hand, normal procedure called for her to write up a report. A report that would become part of the official file and eventually find its way to the defense. Maybe that was a good thing. Kim didn't want to admit it, but she was beginning to think they'd arrested the wrong man.

Bauman had pushed for the arrest, whether out of his personal dislike of Ramon Escobar or because of pressure from above for a quick resolution—or maybe even because he found the evidence convincing. But Kim wasn't in any position to point the finger. She'd wanted the arrest, too. She'd seen it as an opportunity to shine, a toehold on her climb up the ladder of rank. Now, it left a bad taste in her mouth.

She was back in the office typing up her report when she got a call.

"This is Otto, from Jimmy's the other night. Remember me?"

"You were looking for your brother, right?" And Gary Bauman had seen her talking to him like some cheap bar pickup.

"Right. I took your advice and went back to talk to the afternoon bartender. He recognized Hans as having been there."

"You knew that from the receipt."

"Yeah, but I didn't know why he was there."

"The bartender was able to help?"

"Not really. He said Hans was quiet. No small talk about where he was from or what he was doing in the area. The bartender, he's a real talker himself and I got the impression my brother basically told him to stuff it."

"Maybe he just wanted peace and quiet. Could be that's why he's taken off now, too."

"I don't think so. It's looking worse. I got a call from the Oakland cops."

"Your brother's in trouble?"

"His truck was involved in a high-speed chase. Turns out it was stolen by some punk kids. They claim they found it unlocked, parked in the warehouse district of Emeryville."

Worse was right. "You must be worried."

"Hans and trouble go hand-in-hand. I've gotten used to it. But our mother hasn't. She's the one who wanted me to call you. I mean, I sort of wanted to call you too, but not because of Hans." He waited a beat, and when she said nothing, he continued. "Mom was thinking maybe there's a tie-in between Tahoe City and one of the companies housed around where his truck was found."

"How so?"

"It isn't like Hans to go off to the middle of nowhere without a reason." He paused, seemed to realize he'd just insulted her home turf, and started backpedaling. "Not that Tahoe City is nowhere, but it's a bit quiet for—"

"That's okay, you don't have to explain." Despite the name, it wasn't citylike at all. Summers and weekends during the ski season, the main road was one big traffic jam, but the rest of the time it *was* quiet. That's what people came for. Outdoor recreation was the big draw. There wasn't a lot else.

"Anyway," Otto said, "let me give you the names of the industries around where his car was found."

He read off six names, none of which Kim recognized. Except for LB Printing, she didn't even have a clue what type of businesses they were.

"Sorry," she said. "Nothing sounds familiar. If they did business around this part of Tahoe, I'd know about them."

"Thanks, anyway. I know it was a long shot. It's just that so many things don't add up. The trip to Tahoe, the fact that Hans normally never left his truck unlocked. It wasn't much, lots of dings and scratches, and it was so dirty half the time it looked beige instead of white, but Hans treated it like his baby."

Kim felt a buzzing inside her head. There were lots of white trucks, she reminded herself. Lots of dirty, dinged white trucks. But Hans had been in the area the day of the murder. And he had a record. Coming on top of what she'd just learned about Ramon Escobar's gun, she couldn't put the coincidence aside.

"What kind of truck does your brother drive?"

"A Dodge pickup. Nineteen ninety-six."

"You know the license number?"

"Not off the top of my head."

"Any decals or bumper stickers?"

"As I recall, there's something on the back fender, but I couldn't say what."

"I know this sounds weird," Kim said, "but could I get a photo of it?"

"Of the truck?" He was clearly perplexed.

"Yeah. Side and back views."

"Sure, if it will help find Hans."

"I can't promise you that." And if it did, the outcome would not be what Otto hoped.

"You want me to mail it? It would be quicker if I E-mail it."

"E-mail's good." She gave him her address at work. "And the license number if you can find it."

"As soon as you hear anything, you'll let me know?"

"Absolutely."

It probably meant nothing, Kim told herself again. But the buzzing in her head had grown to a loud roar.

CHAPTER 24

A hot shower was the first order of business, Irene decided when she stepped off the bus Saturday afternoon. After traveling all night and most of yesterday, she felt grimy and stiff. She hadn't slept much either, dozing a little here and there, always waking with a start and a racing heart.

Had she made a mistake contacting Betty's attorney? She was already having second thoughts. What could the attorney do, anyway? For that matter, what could anyone do?

But Irene was tired of running and hiding. Tired of fearing for people she cared about. Not to mention herself. If Kali O'Brien couldn't help, or wouldn't help, Irene would try the police again. And if all else failed, she'd turn herself over to Blake. Once she was dead, he'd have no reason to hurt anyone else.

Irene dragged her suitcase over to the pay phone near the entrance of the bus station and looked in the yellow pages for a reasonably priced motel. She was only a couple of hours from the Bay Area, but she'd decided to stop in Sacramento to clean up and plan the next step. She needed to check her E-mail, too.

She found a Budget Inn which, according to the big city map on the wall, wasn't far. She called, confirmed that they had a vacancy, and headed off on foot. The blocks were longer than they appeared to be on the map, and the roads were noisy. What's more, there were whole stretches where the sidewalk was swallowed up by parking lots and driveways. By the time she arrived at the motel half an hour later, Irene had added a fresh layer of sweat and grime to her sticky skin.

The man behind the desk gave her a wary look when she paid

with cash, but handed her a room key and said that he hoped she would enjoy her stay. She'd assured him she would. With the luxury of a bed and a bath, how could she *not*?

A hot shower and change of clothes worked wonders, not only for her appearance but her mood as well. She washed her hair too, but only had the patience to dry it partially before heading back to the Kinko's she'd passed on her way to the motel.

There was a flurry of activity at the copy machines and at the paper cutting station, but only one of the four computers was in use. Irene signed in at the desk, then sat down at the computer closest to the wall and logged on to her new account.

Two new messages, both from Kali O'Brien. Irene read them in chronological order, then sat back and mentally tried to slow her racing pulse. Kali had guessed her true identity, which wasn't really much of a surprise. Irene should probably have made it clear up front but she was so used to concealing her name and anything about her past that being totally up front hadn't crossed her mind. Kali's knowing was a good thing, she decided. That was one less thing she had to explain.

The suggestion they meet was what gave her pause. It made sense from Kali's point of view. She must have a list of questions a mile long. And for all she knew, Irene could be a flake. But the idea of exposing herself that way made Irene nervous.

And what if she couldn't make Kali believe her? Irene had planned on writing it all out. That way she could make sure she got it right. Telling her story in person, she was likely to get flustered or frightened, and leave something out.

But Irene was determined to see this through. If a face-to-face meeting was what it took, so be it. She put her hands on the keyboard, thought about what to say. Finally, she started typing.

> *You obviously know part of the story. I don't know how much Betty told you. You must have questions, too. I guess that's why we should meet.*

She tried to think of a meeting place. Public was better than private. Betty had tried for someplace private and look what happened to her.

Irene felt the chill of fear anew. She was crazy to announce where she was going to be. Who knew what resources Blake had? No place would be safe.

Irene looked around the store. All these people, free to come and go, to live their lives without looking over their shoulders. Isn't that what she wanted?

If actually meeting the attorney was what it took . . . But it had to be someplace convenient and very public. She remembered one of her favorite haunts from college. Her fingers flew across the keyboard.

> *Jack London Square in Oakland, Sunday at two, in front of the marina. Wear a red scarf and carry a Sue Grafton novel.*

It felt silly, like a cloak-and-dagger movie, but she needed a way to recognize Kali O'Brien. And Irene didn't want to give away her own identity.

She read over what she'd written, then added another sentence.

> *Be careful you aren't followed.*

She took a breath and hit send. It was done.

Kim shuffled the photos Otto had sent her of his brother's truck. He'd gone overboard and sent six in all, from varying perspectives. She'd printed them out at home because her own printer was better than the one at the station. The images were remarkably clear. The rear view showed some kind of decal on the left bumper, and the side view revealed a spot on the door that could have been rust. She'd already confirmed that there was a number three in the license.

She pulled the photo of Ramon's truck from the case file. His was a Ford rather than a Dodge and it looked smaller. Also older, although Kim didn't know enough about trucks to say for sure.

The question was, would Bobbie Manes have noted enough detail about the truck she saw leaving the park to tell the difference? Kim called the gift shop to make sure Manes was at work, then slipped the photos into a large manila envelope and decided to find out.

The door chime sounded as Kim entered the shop. It was empty of customers. Bobbie Manes looked up from the pinecone lamp she was dusting.

"I have a couple of quick questions," Kim told her.

"I already told you everything I remembered."

Kim nodded, showed her two of the photos. "Do either of these look like the truck you saw?"

Bobbie Manes looked at them a moment. "Yeah."

"Which one?"

"Both."

"But they're different," Kim said. "Different trucks."

Bobbie looked more closely. "I guess so, now that you mention it."

Kim pulled out two more photos. "These are from a different angle," she said. "You can see that the tailgate is different, and the brake lights. One is much wider than the other."

"Yeah, I see that. But I couldn't tell you which one I saw. It might not have been either one."

Any halfway competent defense attorney would be able to make mincemeat out of her testimony. That would be good for Ramon but it didn't help Kim.

"Sorry," Bobbie Manes said. "I'm just not into cars."

Kim returned to the station where she called the Oakland police department to see what she could find out about Hans Vogel. According to his brother, Hans was a magnet for trouble. Kim wanted to know what kind of trouble, and what the official word was on his status as a missing person. She reached Detective Bryce Keating.

"His truck was involved in a drag race that got the attention of one of our officers," Keating said. "A couple of teenage boys took it for a joyride. Said they found it in an industrial part of Emeryville. The guy's brother called a couple of days ago and says he's missing."

"Has there been any activity on his bank account?"

"No, but I'm not sure it means much. The history shows fairly sporadic transactions. I'm guessing he dealt mostly in cash. But that's were it gets interesting. He made a couple of big cash deposits recently. All just under the reporting limit."

"Drugs?"

"It's as good a guess as any. He's no choirboy. Did time for armed robbery and assault. Got out two and a half years ago. What's your interest in him?"

"He made a trip up here a couple of days before he vanished. His brother finds that strange. He says Hans wouldn't drive 'to the middle of nowhere' just for the heck of it."

"Tahoe's the middle of nowhere?"

"In some circles, apparently so." Kim hesitated. "It just so happens he was here the day we had a homicide."

"The Betty Arnold shooting?"

Kim was surprised he'd made the connection. "Did it get a lot of coverage in the Bay Area?"

"Some, not a lot. I know the attorney who was wounded in the shooting."

Of course he would. Kali O'Brien had recently been with the Oakland DA's office. Kim hadn't really stopped to think about that before now. "She was lucky," Kim said.

"I know."

There was something almost proprietary about his tone. Kim wondered how well the attorney and Keating knew each other. "Ms. O'Brien doesn't seem to think the guy we arrested did it."

"Are you sure he did?"

"We made the arrest, didn't we?"

"That's not what I asked." Keating didn't press the issue. Kim sensed the question was rhetorical anyway. "You want me to call you if anything breaks?" he asked.

"Please."

She'd barely hung up when Bauman rang through. "Have you got a minute? I'd like to see you." There was a vein of ice to his voice.

A minute later, Kim hesitated at his door. "Come in," he said, leafing through papers on his desk. He waited until she was seated to look up. "What's the meaning of this?" He held out a file.

"The meaning of what?" But she knew.

"Your report on interviews with Escobar's friends about his

gun. Don't you realize it will wind up in the hands of the defense?"

Enemy hands. As though they were locked in battle. "It's evidence. Isn't the exchange of information what discovery is about?"

"To the extent the defense has enough information to prepare its case, yes. But it doesn't mean we have to do their work for them."

"The information is relevant, though. If Ramon Escobar never got his gun back from Pinkus, he couldn't have had it the afternoon Betty Arnold was killed."

"That's stuff they should go after on their own."

"Except you know that's not likely to happen. Not unless Ramon could afford some high-priced attorney who would bend over backwards to make sure he was acquitted."

Bauman folded his hands. "That's not our problem."

"It is if we arrested an innocent man."

"That's a question for the jury. Juries aren't afraid to tell the cops they made a mistake. It happens all the time, even when it shouldn't. You know that as well as I do."

"But that's the point," Kim insisted. "The jury can't decide without hearing all the evidence."

Bauman leaned back in his chair, rubbed his temples, looked at her hard. His eyes narrowed but the anger she expected to see there was missing. "Is this about what happened between us last winter?"

And what was that, Kim wanted to know. *What, exactly*, had *happened?* The humiliation of having to ask was more than she could endure. Besides, if she was upset with anyone, it was herself. "It's not *about* anything," Kim said. "I'm just doing my job. You interview someone, you write up a report. It was the District Attorney who asked me to check on the gun, don't forget."

Bauman shook his head. "I've seen the other side of you, Kim. I know you're not always such a tight ass."

She was wondering how she'd ever found him attractive enough to end up in bed with him.

CHAPTER 25

Sid buttoned his jacket against the wind and pulled his cap low so that it partially concealed his face. He strolled along the waterfront, trying to orient himself. He rarely ventured across the bay into Oakland unless he was working security at some client function. And those usually took place in the upscale sections of the city, either at a country club or at one of the large private homes in the hills. He'd been to Jack London Square only once before, maybe ten years earlier when Syntrak, a genetics company he'd sometimes worked for, was holding a director's dinner at a restaurant there. Sid couldn't remember the name of the place, but it was built on stilts out over the water, exposed on three sides. The boats continually making their way up and down the estuary had made Sid nervous as hell. It wouldn't be hard for one of them to intentionally smash into the pilings or set off an explosive from underneath. He'd have thought a company cautious enough to hire guards would also take security into account when booking a restaurant. Apparently not. Syntrak had since gone belly up, probably from the same lack of planning and foresight Sid had encountered.

Jack London Square wasn't a square at all, but a strip of shops and restaurants along the estuary. On Sundays, Sid had discovered, it was also home to the local farmers' market. The entire walkway was lined with canopied stalls offering vegetables, fruits, flowers, nuts, jams, even candles and jewelry. And it was teeming with people. No way was he going to be able to nab Faith in this crowd. He'd have to follow her and wait for the right moment.

What a relief it was going to be to finish this. Eight years was a long time to wait for the other shoe to drop.

He easily found the spot Faith had given for the meeting—a stretch of marina where the pleasure boats were docked. They looked like toys, bobbing against the backdrop of cargo ships farther out. It was less crowded here than at the hub of the market. That would work in Sid's favor. He'd be able to keep an eye on Faith without getting too close.

He had arrived early to allow time to get the lay of the land, and now he had half an hour still to kill. He wandered into the bookstore, bought a copy of *Road and Track* and a cup of coffee. As he left the store, he passed a kiosk selling kettle corn, and bought a small bag of that, as well. Then he settled himself on a bench where he had a clear view of the central plaza and the marina beyond.

At ten minutes before noon, Sid spotted Kali O'Brien walking toward the plaza from the direction of Broadway. She was wearing dark slacks and a leather jacket, and had a red scarf draped around her neck, just as Faith had instructed. And she was carrying a book.

She stopped in the middle of the plaza, looked around, walked over to the railing by the boats and stood there for a few moments. On several occasions, as a lone woman neared, Kali would smile expectantly and try to make eye contact. Even from as far away as he was sitting, Sid could tell that none of the women was Faith. He wasn't sure he'd actually be able to recognize her, but it was easy to tell who wasn't her.

Kali checked her watch, hugged the book to her chest, cover out. Sid chuckled. She was so obedient.

He turned the pages of his magazine, not reading the words, not looking at the photos even. He kept Kali in his peripheral vision and glanced up every once in a while to reorient himself.

It was during one of these casual, visual sweeps that he spotted Faith. She'd reached for a sample slice of peach being handed out at one of the stalls. She was a bit heavier than last time he'd seen her, and had gone to great lengths to disguise her appearance, but it was Faith. He was certain of that.

She'd been watching Kali, and finally, as she swallowed the last bite of peach, Faith joined a small group of people headed in Kali's direction.

Sid could feel the muscles in his right hand twitch. If only he could finish her off right now and be done with it. But impatience was what had tripped him up before. He wasn't going to make the same mistake twice.

Kali brushed the hair out of her eyes. She wanted to go to the rest room but didn't dare leave her spot by the railing. It was just nervousness, she told herself. She'd allowed herself only one cup of morning coffee for this very reason.

People passed in front of her, some strolling leisurely, simply enjoying the day, others determinedly lugging sacks of produce and other purchases. Each time a lone woman approached, Kali felt herself tense expectantly. So far, they'd all walked past without so much as glancing in her direction.

Kali had received the response to her E-mail message last night. She'd been checking the computer constantly, fearing she'd blown it by using Faith's real name. But that seemed not to be the case. Assuming Faith actually showed up today.

Of course she would. She'd been the one to suggest the meeting, after all.

Kali had been careful to take a circuitous route here, keeping an eye on her rearview mirror. She was certain she wasn't followed. After parking, she'd walked through a couple of stores on her way to the spot Faith suggested for their meeting. While part of her wondered if Faith wasn't being paranoid, she wasn't about to forget that Betty was dead and she herself had been shot. Better to err on the side of caution, she'd decided.

She hadn't ruled out the possibility that Faith was setting some sort of trap, either. Kali had been relieved that they weren't meeting in some isolated spot.

"Did anyone follow you here?"

Startled, Kali turned to look at the speaker. A woman had separated herself from a group of women pushing baby strollers, and now stood to Kali's left with her back to the railing. She had short hair, the sort of inky black that came from dye. She was slight of build with a heart-shaped face. Her eyes were concealed by dark glasses. "Faith?"

"Were you careful about being followed?" the woman asked again.

"Yes."

"Good." Faith sighed. She tapped her foot. "I used to come here when I was a student at UC. It wasn't as built up then." She gazed out over the plaza, then back to Kali. "So what now?"

"Maybe we can get a cup of coffee or something and you can tell me what's going on."

Faith smiled self-consciously. "You make it sound so simple."

"Believe me, I know that's not the case. How about over there?" Kali pointed to the tables outside the bookstore. "Or would you rather try one of the restaurants?"

"No, sitting outside would be nice. And coffee's fine. I'm not really hungry."

They started toward the bookstore.

"Why did Betty hire you?" Faith asked. "Did she tell you she'd found me?"

"She didn't tell me anything. But she had an education journal with your photo in it, and I sort of put two and two together. That's all—"

There was a commotion at the bench they were nearing. A black lab was gobbling up popcorn that had spilled onto the bench and the ground beneath. A man was angrily blotting coffee from his lap. He had a large wet spot going down one leg. The dog's owner, a tall, slender, black woman with a head full of tiny braids, was apologizing profusely. Her child, on roller blades, was sprawled at the man's feet, crying.

"Dahirna, are you okay?" The woman pulled the girl to her feet and brushed her off. She turned back to the man. "I'm so sorry. I don't know what happened, she was looking at the boats—"

"Why don't you teach your damn kid to watch where she's going? Look at what she's done!"

"I'm so, so sorry. Can I—"

"You people think you can get away with anything."

The woman stepped back as though she'd been slapped. "*I beg your pardon!*"

Kali turned to say something to Faith, and saw that her face was drained of color. Faith gasped and reversed direction abruptly, pushing her way through a crowd of onlookers. Her pace was quick and determined.

"Wait," Kali called. "What's the matter?" She shuffled to catch up.

"That man."

Glancing over her shoulder, she saw the man still trying to extricate himself from a confrontation with the black woman. He finally shoved her aside and started walking in their direction.

Faith looked back, then broke into a trot, threading her way through the crowd and coming perilously close to knocking over a table of strawberries. Kali darted after her. She was huffing by the time they reached the ferry slip and Faith finally slowed. They both looked back.

"Do you see him?" Faith asked.

"The man with the coffee? No." But with so many people it was hard to be certain he wasn't there.

"I warned you about being followed!"

"I wasn't," Kali insisted. "Who is he, anyway?"

Faith's eyes narrowed. "Maybe he didn't have to follow you because you *told* him where I'd be."

"Why would I—"

"How should I know? How do I know I can trust you?"

Kali was tired of playing games. She wanted answers. "You were the one who contacted *me*, don't forget."

Faith grabbed Kali's forearm. "There, near the flagpole. Isn't that him?" As she spoke, she jerked back out of his line of vision, pulling Kali with her.

They were standing outside a toy store. Faith slipped inside and moved quickly to the back of the shop. Kali followed.

"Who is he?" Kali asked again.

"I don't know. I'm not even certain it's the same man, but it sounds like him."

"Who?"

"The man who's after me."

That much Kali could have guessed. "But who is he? What's he want?"

"He wants to kill me," Faith said. Her voice was wound tight, her upper body shaking.

Kali was confused. The man on the bench looked nothing like the man she'd glimpsed at Ponderosa Pines Park.

"Why does he want to kill you?"

"He's—" Faith sucked in her breath, averted her face. "There he is again."

The man appeared in front of the shop, craning his neck, scanning the crowds. His red-and-gold 49ers cap was pulled low on his forehead so Kali couldn't get a good look at his face. But he didn't appear threatening. He was fiftyish, conservatively dressed in dark chinos and a windbreaker. She'd noticed him walking with a slight limp earlier, when he was moving fast, but he showed no sign now of favoring either leg.

Faith cowered in the corner of the shop behind a large stuffed bear. Picking up on her fear, Kali pressed herself against the wall.

The man's gaze swept the shop window. Faith uttered a tiny cry and Kali's own heart skipped a beat. For a moment it seemed he had to be looking straight at them. Then his head swiveled again. Finally, he turned away and walked on. Either the glare had prevented him from seeing them or he hadn't been following them, after all.

"He's probably waiting for us to come out," Faith whispered.

"Or he might be looking for his wife who was shopping while he rested," Kali pointed out. But he *had* followed them, hadn't he?

"Did you notice if there was a tattoo on his hand?" Faith asked.

"No, why? Does your man have a tattoo?" Kali hoped she didn't sound as patronizing as she thought she did.

Faith nodded. "A serpent kind of thing, here." She touched the soft skin of her right hand between her thumb and index finger.

"Wouldn't you recognize him?"

"He was wearing a mask before."

The saleswoman approached. She'd been watching them out of the corner of her eye while helping another customer. "Can I help you ladies find something?"

"No thanks," Kali said. "We're just—"

Faith interrupted. "Do you have a back door?"

"A back—"

"A back way out."

The saleswoman eyed them warily. "No, just the door you came in through."

"So what now?" Kali addressed the question to Faith. "We can't very well stay here forever."

"Is something wrong? Shall I call the police?" The saleswoman had already begun backing away, toward the register.

Kali looked toward Faith.

"It won't do any good," Faith said. "It would only get his attention."

The saleswoman would probably call the police in any case if they stayed much longer. For all she knew, it was the police they were running *from*.

"I'm parked in the Clay Street garage," Kali said. She walked to the front of the store and looked out the shop window. "I don't see him anywhere. Let's get to my car and we can figure out what to do from there."

Faith hesitated. She looked around the store once more as though she were hoping a secret door might magically appear. Finally, she took a deep breath and nodded. "Doesn't look like we have a lot of options."

They moved quickly and silently across the open courtyard toward Clay. A ferry boat had docked and was loading passengers. There were lots of people milling about but Kali saw no one with a 49ers hat and dark chinos.

"I know he's here somewhere," Faith muttered.

"If you were so worried about being followed, why did you suggest the meeting?"

Faith slowed and gave her a funny look. "I didn't suggest it, you did."

"What are you talking about?"

Faith pulled some papers from her pocketbook and shoved them at Kali. "There. All your messages."

Kali examined the three printed E-mail messages. She recognized the first as one she'd sent, and the third as a confirmation of time and place. The second was the message suggesting they meet. It was also from her account. But she'd never seen it before.

She felt a wave of queasiness. He had to have hacked into her account. And God knew what else.

At that moment she spotted the man. He hadn't seen them yet, but it was only a matter of time. He was moving through the crowd, searching for someone.

For them.

"There," she told Faith. "That's him, isn't it?"

"Where is—" Faith stopped mid-sentence just as the man looked their way. He turned quickly, but Kali knew he'd spotted them.

Her chest was so tight she could barely breath.

"Shit," Faith muttered. "We'll never make it to your car."

They started off again, moving quickly. The man was keeping pace with them, but not trying to narrow the gap. Not here where there were so many people. As long as they stayed in a crowd, Kali thought, they were probably safe.

The ferry whistle blew.

Faith nodded in the direction of the dock. "Let's run for it."

She took off at a healthy sprint, pushing her way past the ticket taker and up the gangplank just as it was being rolled away from the boat. Kali was right behind her.

"Ladies, you'll have to wait for the next—"

Faith made a flying leap onto the boat. Without stopping to think, Kali leaped also. The boat lurched and she fell forward into the cabin. She'd made it!

The boat's engine churned, and after a moment, they began to move away from the dock.

CHAPTER 26

Faith's hammering heart didn't begin to slow until she was on shore in San Francisco. She still felt jumpy and on edge.

On the boat, she and Kali had spoken very little. Even if they'd been inclined to talk, the throngs of people, whipping wind, and engine noise would have made conversation difficult. Faith had positioned herself along the outside rail near an emergency floatation device with the thought that jumping would be a means of escape if the man had followed them aboard. Kali, too, had seemed to keep a watchful eye on the faces about them.

Once in San Francisco, they'd found a hole-in-the-wall restaurant near the Ferry Building where they'd disembarked. Kali had suggested they take a cab back to Oakland, but Faith wanted to say her piece and be gone. She'd decided that contacting Kali had been a mistake. What Faith needed was a bodyguard, not a lawyer.

She looked around the restaurant at the handful of customers. There was no one who even faintly resembled the man with the tattoo. She cupped the mug of coffee in both hands. It was steaming hot and she was chilled to the bone—not from the bracing ride across the bay, but from dread.

"You sure he didn't get on the boat?" she asked Kali again.

"We haven't seen him."

"But he wasn't on the dock, either." Not that it probably mattered. He'd found her once; he'd find her again.

"You want to tell me what's going on?" Kali said. Faith detected impatience in her tone, and maybe fear as well.

They were sitting kitty-corner, both facing the door. The restaurant wasn't crowded—the hour was post-lunch and pre-dinner for most people—and that made it easier to keep track of anyone who came in. Faith noticed that Kali's gaze angled toward the entrance as often as her own did.

"Where do you want me to start?" Faith asked.

She wondered if she was being foolish trusting Kali, about whom she knew very little. Then again, she didn't know where else to turn. And Kali had seemed genuinely surprised—and upset—to discover there'd been a second E-mail. Still, Faith wasn't about to let down her guard.

Kali sipped her coffee. "Anywhere you'd like."

Faith thought she should probably start at the beginning, though she was no longer sure where that was. Or maybe she should start with Betty, since that's how Kali had become involved initially.

"You said he was trying to kill you," Kali prompted. She no longer sounded quite so impatient.

"He is. I'm pretty sure he killed Betty, too. And my fiancé. Former fiancé."

Surprise registered in Kali's expression. "Andrew Major? I thought he committed suicide."

"No way." Faith shook her head. "Andrew was murdered." There'd never been any doubt in her mind about that.

"Why kill *him*?"

"To get at me."

Kali smiled faintly. Faith could tell she had trouble believing that.

"A man you don't know," Kali said, "but think is the man we saw today, killed Andrew and Betty simply to 'get at' you?"

The way Kali said it, it did sound far-fetched. But Faith knew it wasn't. "Not the man today. I mean, he probably did the killing, but he works for someone else. A doctor by the name of Blake."

Kali set her cup on the table so hard she sloshed coffee over the sides. Faith could tell from her expression the name was familiar. More than familiar. Was she a patient of his? A personal friend? These were complications Faith hadn't considered.

"You know him?"

Kali seemed to hesitate. "I've heard of him."

"What does that mean?"

"I've heard the name. Radio commercials, ads, you know."

"He does radio commercials now?" The guy was probably famous. Nobody would believe her.

Kali nodded.

Faith shifted uncomfortably. Okay, so maybe he did commercials, but that didn't explain Kali's reaction to the name. Her face had registered something different than simple recognition. Faith shook her head. "There's more to it than that."

Another smile, this time with no hint of condescension. "You're perceptive," Kali said. "You had a newspaper clipping about a conference where Blake was giving the keynote address. It was hidden in a box of tampons under your sink."

Faith rocked back. "You were in my apartment?"

Kali licked her lips. "I went to Las Vegas to find you, but you'd already left."

"That doesn't give you the right to snoop around my apartment."

"Elliot let me in. We were looking for anything that might tell us where you'd gone."

"He had no right!"

"He loves you, Faith."

"That's none of your—"

Kali's eyes narrowed. "You've been living a lie. You let your parents think you were dead. You pretended to Elliot to be someone you're not."

"It was for their own good."

"Your aunt was murdered, and someone tried to kill me. You seem to have no problem spinning a web of deceit, then you have the gall to take affront when anyone questions it."

Faith felt the slap of Kali's words. "You think I'm happy that people got killed because of me? You think I liked living a lie? It wasn't easy not telling Elliot who I was. I had no choice."

"Isn't that why we're here?" Kali said gently. "To see if we can untangle some of that web."

Tears sprang to Faith's eyes. Anger, sadness, worry. Her love for Elliot. Her longing to be free of Blake. The outrage faded. It felt good to share her troubles with someone. Faith wiped her eyes and nodded.

"Now, why don't you tell me why Dr. Blake wants you dead."

"Because he's angry about what I did. He accused me of ruining his life."

"How?"

So many times had Faith relived the sequence of events in her mind and wondered what she might have done differently, that it felt strange to recount them aloud. "I had his daughter, Jessie, in one of my classes," she explained.

"When you were living in Palo Alto?"

"Right. Eighth grade English, fourth period." Faith could see the classroom as clearly as though she'd been there that morning. "Jessie told me her father was . . . that he'd been having sex with her. It had been going on for years. She was worried because he was starting to show the same kind of interest in her younger sister."

"My God, that's awful."

Faith nodded. "At first she didn't come right out and say that in so many words."

Jessie had been dropping hints ever since she'd written a book report dealing with the same subject, but Faith had been slow to pick up on her student's plea for help. Maybe she hadn't wanted to. Definitely she hadn't wanted to. Nothing in her training or experience had prepared her for that. There was a part of her, too, that wondered if Jessie was telling the truth.

"When it got to the point where she was practically hitting me over the head with what she wasn't saying, I finally asked her if that was what was going on."

"That he was abusing her?" Kali asked.

"Right, though I don't think either of us ever used that term. She told me how he touched her, how he'd come into her bed in the middle of the night and rub against her . . . stuff like that."

Even then, Faith had been unsure about how much to believe. Jessie had a flair for the dramatic. A thin wisp of a girl, she drew attention to herself in ways that were off-putting. As a result, she was often on the barbed end of snippy comments from her classmates. But Jessie could give as good as she got. Maybe she didn't exactly hold her own, but it wasn't for lack of trying.

"I talked to Andrew about it," Faith continued, "about what I should do. Legally, teachers have to report suspected abuse. But I thought maybe Jessie was telling tales simply for the shock value.

Or maybe to get my sympathy. And her father seemed like a nice man. He came to all the parent conferences and to back-to-school night. He was an important man. A doctor."

Kali nodded. "But in the end, you filed a report." It wasn't even a question.

"I did, eventually. But before I could do anything Dr. Blake came to see me. Jessie had apparently told him about our conversation, probably in a taunting way when she was angry at him. I know I used to do the same thing with my stepdad. Not that he abused me or anything, but I knew how to push his buttons."

The waitress appeared and refilled both coffee cups. Faith thought she'd probably drunk enough, but the cup gave her something to hold on to. "The other times Blake had been to school, he'd been really nice. But that day he was different. I stayed late to work on the yearbook. Most of the other teachers had already gone home when he showed up at my door. There was nothing overtly threatening in what he said. I later decided my perceptions were colored by the late hour and the things Jessie had told me about him. But at the time, I felt frightened."

"What did he say?"

"That Jessie had told him she'd lied to me just to see what would happen. That she'd been under the care of a therapist because she was a pathological liar. That he hoped I wouldn't get in the middle of this, and that I should leave it to the professionals."

Kali's lower lip puckered with concern. "Did you believe him?"

"His words made sense. I knew Jessie was given to exaggeration. But there was something there I couldn't put my finger on. His eyes were cold. It was like they bore right through me. And his expression was so tight, like skin over stone. I told myself it was a serious subject, so of course he wouldn't be smiling like he usually did. More than anything specific though, it was creepy. Then he stopped at the classroom door on his way out. He said something about being able to count on my good judgment, and then . . ." Faith shuddered, remembering the words. "He said, 'Imagine losing what you love most.' "

"He was threatening you?"

"I told myself I was being silly, but yes, I felt uneasy." More than uneasy, she'd felt as though the hand of death had brushed her cheek. "That was a Friday. On Monday, Jessie didn't come to class, but she came to see me after school. She said her father was trying to buy her off."

"Get her to recant, you mean?"

Faith nodded. "That's what it sounded like to me. That evening when I was out jogging a man came up behind me and grabbed me by the throat."

"Dr. Blake?"

"I'm not sure."

"The man we saw today?"

"I don't know. Maybe. He said something about life being sweet and that I should tell my little friend to stop playing games. And then he said, 'Imagine losing what you love most.' It was virtually the same thing Dr. Blake told me when he came to visit. The man squeezed my throat, cutting off my air. I thought he was going to kill me. Then he said, 'You picked the wrong man to mess with. Don't say I didn't warn you.' "

"Did you go to the police?"

Faith nodded. It was the first thing she'd done. "They weren't interested. I couldn't identify the man, I wasn't harmed. He hadn't said anything that convinced them the attack had anything to do with Dr. Blake."

Kali frowned. "But you were sure it did?"

"The words were nearly the same. When Jessie came to school the next day, I saw that she had cuts all along both forearms. I knew, instinctively, that she'd cut herself. On purpose. I went straight to the principal and reported what I suspected about the abuse. To make a long story short, Children's Protective Services got involved and Jessie was removed from the home while they investigated. I think that's when Dr. Blake decided to have me killed."

"Murder is a big step. Why would he take such a risk?"

"His whole life was at stake," Faith said. "His job, his reputation, his family. Blake was a powerful man, the kind who probably doesn't mind stepping on others to get ahead."

"Then who is the man we saw today?"

"I'm pretty sure he's the one who tried to kill me." The man who'd been haunting both her dreams and waking hours for the last eight years. And now, at last, she'd gotten a better look at his face. "He broke into my house a couple of days after Jessie was removed from her family. I'd just come in from shopping and my arms were full. He was already there. It all happened so fast. I remember his hand on my mouth and then a hot, acrid smell that must have been ether or something. When I came to, my lungs burned, my head hurt, and my throat was dry. It was night. I was in the back of my car with my hands tied. He parked along at the end of a long dirt road, and then we walked. He had a gun and he kept poking me in the back with it. I never saw his face because he was wearing a ski mask, but I saw the tattoo on his hand when he was driving, and I remember the voice."

"He didn't kill you, though?"

Faith could feel the adrenaline in her veins just thinking about that night. Her palms were sweaty and her breathing constricted. "I was lucky. It was really windy, like it gets right before a storm. The air was filled with dust and debris. I could feel grit stinging my legs and face. Then suddenly there was this big cracking sound practically right overhead. A huge tree limb fell right where I'd been standing. At the sound, I'd stepped to the side without thinking, and I tumbled off an embankment I hadn't even known was there. It was a long fall, and afterward I hurt like hell, but at the time I was too scared to notice. He fired shots in my direction, but I managed to scramble behind a boulder. Then I felt dirt raining down on me from the hill above. I knew he was coming after me.

"There was a streambed at the bottom of the ravine and I hobbled along it as best I could, trying to get away. I expected that any minute he'd reach out and grab me. Or shoot me." Faith would never forget the terror of waiting in pitch blackness for a bullet to hit. "The last thing he screamed at me was that I was dead one way or the other. That he would hunt me down, and when he found me, he'd make me pray for a bullet to end my misery."

Kali's face was pale. She rubbed her shoulder as she looked toward the doorway.

"I'm so sorry to have dragged you into this," Faith told her. "I should never have contacted you."

Kali shook her head. "I was looking for you, too, don't forget." She picked up her cup, then set it down again without taking a drink. "But to just disappear like you did and let your family think you'd been killed . . . or did you tell them? Did your mother and stepfather know you were still alive?"

"No, I couldn't contact them. I was too afraid. It wasn't just what he said about hunting me down." Faith's chest was so tight she could barely breathe. She forced herself to inhale deeply. "I finally managed to free my hands. I wandered for a couple of days. I think I probably passed out for a good stretch of time, too. But eventually I stumbled onto a road and got a ride into town. Such as it was. A tiny store with one gas pump in the middle of nowhere. But it had a phone. I called Andrew and a stranger answered. He told me that Andrew was dead, that he'd committed suicide the day before." She swallowed hard. "But I knew it wasn't suicide."

"Why?"

"Andrew would never kill himself. He was too much in love with life, with himself, and all that he was going to accomplish. I knew he'd been murdered as a warning."

A deep furrow formed between Kali's eyes. "What did you do?"

"I had money in my jacket pocket. A lot of it. I'd been shopping for a present for Andrew and I was planning to pay cash because I didn't want him to see the credit card bill. So I simply disappeared. I didn't see any other way."

In the years since, Faith had wondered what would have happened if she'd gone to the police. She always came back to the same answer. She'd be dead. There was no way to tie the would-be killer to Blake and she had no description of the man himself. He'd sworn to finish her off, and he'd killed Andrew to show her he was serious.

"So you built a new life for yourself?" Kali asked.

Faith nodded. "At first, it was really hard. I missed my family and Andrew. And I felt horribly guilty about his death. I thought about letting my mother know I was alive, but I worried she'd inadvertently let it slip and word would get out. Then I met Elliot and . . . I still missed my family but I had a life too, as Irene. About a month ago, I got a call from someone who called me Faith. It sounded like Betty but I thought no, that can't be. How would she know who I was or where to find me? Then I learned that she'd been asking about me at Patrick's school. She'd seen a photo of me that was taken when Patrick won a spelling bee. And I found out she'd been murdered."

"So you took off again?"

"I knew then that he was still after me. And people I care about." Faith ran her finger along the base of her coffee cup. "Now I've put you in danger too."

From the look on her face, Faith knew that the fact hadn't been lost on Kali.

CHAPTER 27

Sid slapped his palm on the car's horn and pushed, venting his anger and frustration at the world as well as the stupid cow behind the wheel of the Suburban in front of him. *Visualize whirled peas,* indeed. What kind of idiot bumper sticker was that?

"How about, visualize using your turn signal, bitch." He raised his middle finger as he swerved past.

The afternoon had been a disaster. A total, fucking disaster. Not only had he lost Faith again, he'd drawn attention to himself. He was sure the two women had spotted him.

But so what? There was no way Faith could have recognized him. He'd been careful eight years ago to make sure she never saw his face. Maybe it was just skittishness that sent them flying onto the ferry. Still, today was only the tip of the iceberg. If he didn't put a cork in things soon, Sid was as good as dead, himself.

Sid blared his horn again, this time at the mother and kid in the crosswalk up ahead. He reined in the urge to mow them down just for the heck of it.

But he wasn't going to let himself be sidetracked. The pressing need was to get rid of Faith. And Kali O'Brien too, for good measure. And he'd better do it soon, before the shit hit the fan.

His cell phone rang as he was pulling onto the freeway. He punched the receive button. "Yeah."

"Hello, Sid." Mr. D's voice was smooth as silk.

Sid's stomach clenched. Mr. D never called simply to chat. "Hello, sir."

"How's the leg, better?"

"Good as new."

"Glad to hear it. You know, Sid, you've been with me a lot of years."

"Close to twelve."

"We've got a relationship built on trust, right?"

"Right."

"So how come I'm hearing rumors that a certain young lady's come back from the grave?"

The back of Sid's neck felt hot and clammy. "Rumors?"

"You know how that goes. Word gets around." He paused and his voice dropped a few levels. "I thought that was all taken care of a long time ago."

"It was. Something you're hearing isn't right."

"Is that so?"

Sid's hands were damp with perspiration. "There's no need to worry, sir. It's under control."

A beat of silence. "Funny that you seem to know exactly who I'm talking about."

Sid felt like he'd been slammed in the gut with a baseball bat.

"You've got me between a rock and a hard place here, Sid. The client's always right. Isn't that how it goes?"

"Maybe all he's got is rumor, too."

"You know, Sid, my mama, may God rest her soul, used to tell me, 'You make a mess, you clean it up. If you're smart, you'll clean it up so well I don't ever know you made it.'"

"Wise woman, your mama."

"Yeah, but she had *real* sharp eyes. It wasn't easy to put one over on her. You take care now, Sid." The phone disconnected.

Sid's mind was racing as fast as his heart. He was going to whack Faith next chance he got, no matter what. And he'd make sure that happened soon.

The blast of an air horn jolted him from his thoughts. He'd started to drift into the next lane where a large tractor-trailer was barreling past. That would be one way out, all right. Crushed out of his misery.

But he wasn't out of options yet.

Kali crossed her arms and hugged herself. She was cold despite having turned the car heater on during the drive home from

San Francisco. Cold and frightened. She was glad she'd been able to reach Bryce right away. He and Randy, the police technician Bryce had called on for help, were now giving her house a careful check.

Randy whistled and ran a hand through his wavy red hair. "Yep, just what I thought." He tapped a few more keys, bringing up on Kali's computer screen a string of DOS commands.

At least that's what she assumed they were. Either that or some other form of computer hieroglyphics. The young tech, however, seemed quite pleased with what he saw.

"This guy not only had access to your E-mail account," Randy said, "he's been recording every keystroke you make. He knows your passwords and other sensitive data. I'd change it all right away if I were you."

"But she has a firewall," Bryce pointed out.

"A firewall is only as good as the rules it's programmed with. Your guy's manipulated those to allow himself access to everything on Kali's computer."

Kali felt ill. Violated and frightened and angry all at once. Coming on top of a harrowing afternoon, it hit her especially hard. She gripped the back of a chair to steady herself.

She'd called Bryce from her car on the way home, feeling a tad foolish, but drained enough that she didn't care. After a preliminary walk-through, he'd called Randy, and together they'd searched her house and computer looking for bugs. Kali had watched with growing unease as their search paid off. Her phone was bugged, her computer was bugged, and odds were, they'd find the same in her office when they checked there.

"He's gone to a lot of trouble," Bryce said.

Randy nodded, typed in another line of code, then rebooted the machine. "That should take care of it." He pushed back from the desk and looked at Kali. "He had to get into your house to set things up initially. You never noticed any signs of a break-in?"

Kali shook her head, though short of a broken window or smashed door, she wasn't sure she'd have noticed. "I'm ordering an alarm system first thing tomorrow morning."

"Even those won't protect you against someone who knows what he's doing, but it's a good move all the same. You want me to take a look at the office now?"

"Tomorrow will be fine," Kali told him. "I don't suppose it's worth checking for prints?"

Randy shook his head, then looked at Bryce.

"The guy's too good to have left prints," Bryce said. "Our best shot is the bug from the phone. We'll give that a dusting. I've seen it with ammunition. Guys will load their guns, and *then* put on gloves. We can sometimes gets prints from the casings. I think it's a long shot here, though."

"Thanks for doing this," Kali told Randy. "On a weekend, too."

"Happy to help. I didn't have much going on anyway. My girl-friend's away visiting her parents." He grabbed his windbreaker from the chair where he'd left it. "See you in the morning."

Bryce walked him to the door. "I appreciate this, buddy."

It was now almost seven in the evening. The long afternoon had taken its toll on Kali's nerves. "I could use some wine," she said when Bryce returned. "You want some?"

"I'd prefer a beer if you've got one."

"Sure." They moved into the kitchen. She handed him a bottle of Anchor Steam from the fridge and poured herself a glass of merlot.

Bryce draped an arm around her and drew her close. "You holding up okay?"

"A little creeped out, to tell the truth. But having you here helps."

He grinned, then kissed her. "Any time. As for the creeped-out part, you've got good reason. You're sure the guy from this after-noon was really following you two?"

Kali nodded. "Especially now that you've found the bugs."

"And you think he's somehow connected to that doctor, Blake, was it?"

"Edward Blake. You haven't seen his ads on wrinkle revenge?"

"Can't say that I have."

More proof that men and women really were from different planets. They could listen to the same radio stations, read the same newspapers and magazines, and come away having heard or read entirely different things.

"You want something to eat?" Kali asked. She wasn't really hungry but she realized she hadn't eaten all day. And Bryce probably wanted dinner. "I've got a box of macaroni and cheese, and stuff for salad."

He looked at her like she'd suggested fried worms.

"It's not too bad, especially if you add a little vermouth and pepper to the sauce."

"That so?" Bryce reached for the refrigerator door. "Mind if I have a look?"

"Go right ahead." Mildly peeved, she took her wine and sat down at the table while Bryce examined the contents of her refrigerator and cupboards. "You really want macaroni and cheese?" he asked.

"Not if you have a better idea." Maybe this planet thing wasn't foolproof. Bryce was a far better cook than she was.

"You can be in charge of the salad." He rolled up his shirt-sleeves and began slicing green onions. "So tell me again why Blake wants Faith-Irene dead."

Kali had given Bryce an abbreviated version of her afternoon when he'd first arrived. Now she went through it again in more detail. "Faith is pretty sure the guy from this afternoon is the same one who tried to kill her eight years ago. And she's sure Blake is behind it."

"But she didn't have enough to convince local cops?"

"No. It was all very . . . nebulous."

Bryce tossed chopped onion and garlic into the frying pan and put a pot of pasta water on to boil. "I'll run a check on him."

"Thanks." She was sure he wouldn't find anything tying Blake to the murders. If for no other reason, too much time had elapsed. But there would undoubtedly be some record of the abuse report.

"Maybe there's a way to nail him for Betty's murder," Kali said.

"Do you know a Deputy Wong from the Placer County sheriff's department?"

"I've met her. She's one of the detectives who arrested Ramon Escobar. Why?"

"I got a call from her yesterday. Seems a Bay Area man, Hans Vogel, was in Tahoe City the day of the murder and he's since disappeared."

"They suspect foul play?" Even if he'd been murdered, Kali had trouble seeing what that had to do with Betty's death.

"I don't know what they're thinking. But his brother was concerned enough to contact authorities—there and here. Seems Hans is drawn to trouble like a bee to honey. He's done time for robbery and aggravated assault."

So that was it. Hans as perpetrator rather than victim. It was still a leap. "Just because he's missing, though—"

Bryce shook his head. "There's more. He drives a white truck."

Kali felt a flutter in her chest. "A white pickup? Like the witness saw leaving the park?"

"Apparently so. His license plate has a three in it, too."

Kali had to tell Robert Lamont. Even a slouch of a lawyer like Lamont would see the value in having another viable suspect.

"You going to make that salad?" Bryce asked. "Or you want me to?"

"Oops." Kali pulled a head of butter lettuce and some baby romaine from the fridge, and washed it. She had pecans in the freezer, and blue cheese, if it wasn't too old. With luck she could find a pear that hadn't turned to mush.

"You think Hans was the man following us today?"

"The guy today was older than the killer, you said. And shorter."

Kali nodded. "Assuming what I remember about the killer is accurate." She finally saw where he was going. "So maybe Betty's murder had nothing to do with Faith."

"It's all supposition at this point." Bryce got himself another beer and watched her work. "Where's Faith now?" he asked.

"She wouldn't tell me where she was headed. Said she'd call me in a day or two. We parted in San Francisco."

"Too bad your friend from today doesn't know that."

"Doesn't know what?" Recognition dawned as she spoke. Her mouth went dry. "You're saying he might come here looking for her?"

"You've gotten yourself into a real tangle here, sweetheart."

Kali wasn't sure if he meant the word as an endearment or not, and at the moment, she didn't really care. The emotional roller coaster she was on right then was of an entirely different sort. Bryce was right about the tangle part.

"I hate this," she said. "All I wanted was to get my feet on the ground again in private practice. I wish I'd never even spoken to Betty Arnold."

Bryce tucked a loose strand of hair behind her left ear. "It's not good, I agree. But you can't change what's done."

"What am I supposed to do, barricade myself in my room with a shotgun?"

"For starters, it might be a good idea if I stayed the night."

"Moonlighting as a bodyguard."

He smiled. "More or less."

From the safety perspective, it was an appealing offer. From a more personal standpoint, there were problems. There'd be the whole sex thing, for one. And the subtle changes that would follow when their relationship moved on to new ground. Or more accurately, revisited old ground.

Wasn't that what she'd been looking to have happen? Kali felt a wave of conflicting emotions. It wasn't that she didn't want it; it was that she didn't want it tonight. Not with everything else on her mind and her body feeling like something from the waking dead.

"Any other night I'd be wildly enthusiastic. But I'm—"

"I could sleep on the couch, it that's what's bothering you."

It wouldn't work, and she knew it. "I'll be okay."

He looked at her for a moment, then nodded begrudgingly and stepped away.

Over dinner they talked of other things and even got in a few laughs. But Kali sensed a shift in Bryce's mood. He left not long after they'd finished eating.

Kali slept only in fits and starts, though it wasn't so much fear that kept her awake as regret at sending Bryce home. Maybe it wouldn't have been the perfect, romantic evening she'd been envisioning these last few months, but so what? She wanted to feel his arms around her and the warmth of his body close by. Why hadn't she just let the evening evolve?

She flopped onto her side and kicked her feet across the width of the bed. Cold and empty. Jesus, she was such an idiot sometimes.

* * *

She got to work early Monday morning and settled into catching up on a backlog of documents. At nine, Randy showed up and worked his magic on her office phone and computer. Both had been tapped just like the ones at her house.

"Whoa," Jared said, with a touch of awe, after Randy left. "This is serious stuff. How can you focus on Reverse Q-Tip trusts with all that's going on?"

"The client is paying me to focus on it. You too."

"Guess you mean for me to get back to work."

She smiled.

Jared attempted to click his heels and salute, but ended up almost tripping. "On my way, boss."

"Try to make it in one piece."

Bryce called later that morning. "Glad to see you survived the night."

"You waited this long to check?"

"You were the one who insisted on being so independent."

He was right, of course. But that didn't mean she wouldn't appreciate a show of concern.

"Besides, Randy told me you were in one piece." He tried to make light of it, but Kali could tell the tone was forced.

"I wasn't rejecting you, Bryce."

"Glad to hear it." He didn't sound reassured. "I'm calling with the information on Blake I promised you. His name came up during the original investigation into Faith's disappearance, but only because of what went on with his daughter. There was never any evidence linking him to Faith's abduction."

"Her story about Jessie checks out?"

"From what I can tell. Jessica Blake was removed from her parents' home when she was thirteen following a report filed with Children's Protective Services. She lived in foster care for about six months while there was an investigation into her home life. There were never any formal charges brought against Blake, in large part because Jessie refused to testify, as did the younger daughter. Dr. Blake's reputation suffered because of the adverse news coverage, but from what you say, he's made a comeback."

"My impression is that he's doing better than ever."

"Blake's wife left him during the course of the investigation and the girls eventually went to live with her. Blake remarried. Has a much younger wife now and a new baby."

"That doesn't mean he's not still seeking revenge against Faith."

"True. He wouldn't be the first guy so whacked out with hatred it twists his whole life. And he was hauled in ten years ago for punching out his medical partner. The charges were eventually dropped, but I'd say the doctor has a temper."

"Do you know if Jessie Blake is still living around here?"

"Last address shown for her is in Fremont. The younger sister and mother have moved out of state."

"Thanks." She hesitated. "It really wasn't personal last night, Bryce. I mean, not personal rejection. I just . . . I felt . . . The timing wasn't right. I needed to be alone."

He was quiet a moment. "You're good at that, you know. At building barriers."

It was on the tip of her tongue to say, "You're hardly one to talk." But what good would that do? Instead, she said, "It's an old habit I'm trying to break."

His tone softened. "I wasn't trying to give you a hard time."

"Truth is, I hardly slept because I missed you. I spent the night wishing you'd stayed."

"You should have called my cell," Bryce said after a moment. "I spent the night parked across the street just in case there was trouble."

"You didn't." Kali felt awash with guilt. She was more than an idiot.

"I did. But you're on your own today. Be careful, okay?"

"I will be." Mixed with the guilt was a warm glow. He cared.

Kali tried to put thoughts of Bryce—pleasant though they were—from her mind. But he was only part of what kept her from concentrating. Jared had been right, it was hard to keep focus on the subtleties of testamentary trusts with so many questions about Faith vying for her attention. By late afternoon she gave up trying, and called directory assistance for Fremont.

There was no listing for a Jessica Blake, but there were four J. Blakes. Kali tried the first and reached a recording for John and Karen. The second number was answered by what sounded like an elderly woman who didn't know anyone by the name of Jessica. On the third try, Kali got lucky.

"Hi, this is Jess." The voice was thin, with an overlay of attempted sexiness that fell short of its mark. "You know what to do. So go ahead, do it."

Kali was getting ready to leave a message when a woman came on the line. She sounded breathless. "Don't hang up. I forgot the machine was set for two rings." The clicks and beeps finally stopped, and the woman said, "Did you get it?"

She'd obviously been expecting someone else. "I'm calling for Jessie Blake."

"Who's this?"

"My name is Kali O'Brien. Are you Jessie?"

"What do you want?" The tone was more petulant than hostile.

"I'm calling about a former teacher of yours. Faith Foster."

"Who?"

"From eighth grade. She taught English."

"Ms. Foster? She died years ago."

"I'm doing some follow-up on—"

"Are you a cop?"

"A lawyer."

There was a moment's pause. "Working for my father?"

An interesting jump. "No, but that's part of what I wanted to talk to you about."

"I'm not going to testify, if that's what you're after."

"No, it's not that." Kali couldn't very well just come out and ask Jessie if she had information about her father's involvement in Faith's disappearance. But if she could get the girl talking about Faith, she might be able to eke out some useful details.

"I can't talk now," Jessie said. "I'm expecting a call."

"Could I come by?" Face-to-face was better than the phone anyway. People loosened up, and their body language and facial expressions often spoke louder than words.

"How much?" Jessie asked.

"Probably fifteen minutes or so."

"Not time." She sounded impatient. "How much are you willing to pay?"

The question caught Kali by surprise. Was Jessie desperate for money or simply accustomed to asking for it? Kali hadn't a clue how to answer. "Twenty dollars," she said after a moment.

"Is that all?"

"Twenty-five."

"Make it thirty-five and I'll give you the address."

CHAPTER 28

The two-story apartment house Jessie Blake called home had seen better days. Same thing with the neighborhood. It wasn't a slum, but it was a far cry from the lifestyle to which she must have been accustomed to living with her family in Palo Alto. The building, probably built in the early sixties, was a faded pink stucco with no central lobby or entrance. Kali climbed the grimy, open stairway to the second floor, found the apartment number Jessie had given her, and rang the bell.

The door opened a crack. "Who is it?"

"Kali O'Brien."

The door closed and Kali heard the sound of a chain being removed, then it opened again.

"Jessie?"

"Are you that lawyer who called?"

Kali nodded. The young woman in the doorway had none of the freshness and vitality typical of most twenty-year-olds. She was rail thin with watery eyes, sallow skin, and unkempt, straw-like hair that was more yellow than blond. The stench of marijuana and stale cigarette smoke emanating from the apartment was overpowering.

"You're going to pay me in cash, right?"

"Sure." Kali started to reach for her wallet, then thought better of it. "After we've talked."

Jessie shrugged. "Come in. The place is kind of a mess, I'm afraid."

Kind of was putting it mildly. The main living area—one room with a kitchen ell—was strewn with dirty dishes, candy wrappers, magazines, assorted articles of clothing, and a proliferation of cigarette butts. Though the furniture was shabby and none too clean, Kali noted a newish-looking television and stereo system.

Taking a seat in the chair Jessie had cleared for her, Kali decided the direct approach was best. This wasn't a woman to schmooze over a cup of tea.

"I don't know how to go about this without bringing up unpleasant memories," Kali began.

"About my father you mean?" Jessie brushed the air with her hand. She had the quick, jerky movements of someone who'd ingested a lot of caffeine. Or more likely, Kali thought, a lot of speed. "It's no big deal anymore."

How could it *not* be a big deal? What Kali had heard from other victims of abuse is that it was *always* a big deal. You moved beyond it maybe, but the betrayal never went away.

Jessie reached for a pack of cigarettes and lit one, tossing the burnt match onto the tabletop next to her. "Ms. Foster was the one who caused all the trouble," she said.

It wasn't the reaction Kali expected. "Didn't you and Ms. Foster get along?"

"Yeah. Until she told the whole world my business. My dad was pissed, my mom was pissed. Even my sister was mad at me, 'cuz I broke up our happy little home." Mockery weighted the last part of the sentence. "It only made things worse. I got this marine sergeant social worker who sent me to live in some fucking shelter for kids nobody wanted. I fit right in."

"What about your mother?" Kali asked. "How did she react?"

"She took an overdose of sleeping pills." Jessie blew out a long stream of cigarette smoke, her gaze fixed on Kali's. Then she crossed her legs and looked away. "Eventually, she moved out and divorced my father. But she always blamed me. She was living a pretty good life until I blew it apart by squealing." More punctuation by sarcasm.

"You don't honestly believe what happened is your fault, do you?"

There was a flicker of something in the young woman's expression, a sliver-moment when the hardened mask dropped and Kali found herself looking into the eyes of a child close to tears. Then Jessie shrugged. She tugged at the sleeves of her shirt and tossed her head. "It doesn't matter. Besides, that's not why you're here."

"In a way, it is."

"How so? You said you were looking into what happened to Ms. Foster."

Kali ignored her question. "Do you think Ms. Foster shouldn't have spoken up for you?"

Jessie picked at the cuticle on her thumb. "She meant well, I guess."

"I should think you'd have been grateful someone cared."

The eyes hardened. Her pupils were like pinpricks. "Yeah, well, you weren't there."

Kali sat back. "You're right." Affection and allegiance in families were complicated matters, especially in situations like Jessie's. "You did confide in Ms. Foster," Kali pointed out.

"I was a kid, for God's sake. Who knows what I was thinking."

"What's your relationship with your father like now?"

"Cordial." A note of wariness had crept into Jessie's voice.

"Do you see him often?"

"Hardly at all, but we get along okay."

How did you get along with someone who'd so abominably abused your trust?

"He helps me out sometimes," Jessie added, rising to his defense. "When I'm short of money."

Buying absolution, no doubt. And maybe silence. "That's good of him," Kali said out loud. "Were you aware he threatened Ms. Foster?"

Jessie had been about to take another drag on her cigarette. She lowered her hand instead. "Threatened her how?"

"Told her not to go to the authorities, and then when Ms. Foster did, he wanted her to use her influence to persuade you not to testify."

"Doesn't surprise me. He threatens everyone who gets in his way."

"You didn't know then?"

"I was at the shelter. I never saw him."

"Has your father mentioned Ms. Foster since?"

Jessie crushed out her cigarette in a saucer doubling as an ash-tray. "She's dead. What's he going to say about her?"

Kali was fishing. Fishing in a pond where it was likely there were no fish to be had. "He must have been secretly pleased when she disappeared."

"Probably. Even though he never got in trouble with the law, she smeared his reputation. A lot of his patients left. And his wife."

"You make it sound like he was the victim."

"He's no victim." Her mouth made a tight, thin line. She started tapping her heel on the floor.

"Do you recall any of your father's friends having a tattoo on his hand?"

"My father's friends have Armani suits and Rolex watches, not tattoos." It wasn't clear which side Jessie came down on.

Nothing Kali heard connected Blake to Faith's disappearance or Betty's death, but what she'd learned by reading between the lines added weight to Faith's story. That, in itself, was something.

Kali pulled thirty-five dollars from her wallet and handed the money to Jessie along with her business card. "If you think of any-thing else, give me a call. There may be more money in it for you."

Jessie grabbed the money and stuck it in her shirt pocket. When they were at the door, she said, "You think he might have had something to do with Ms. Foster's death, don't you?"

"Did he?"

Jessie's anemic complexion grew even paler. She pressed a knuckle against her mouth. "No, he wouldn't do anything like that."

She shook her head emphatically, but her voice betrayed sounds of doubt.

Folsom State Prison's sprawling structure was built in the late 1800s. Although updated and remodeled in the intervening years, it stood in stark contrast to the burgeoning commercial and resi-dential development that had taken hold in the surrounding area. To Kim Wong's eye, both were ugly.

She'd arranged for an afternoon meeting with Ramon's friend, Willie Pinkus, and while she waited for the guard to bring him to the prison interview area, she once again read over the statement he'd given earlier. It was so short and simple, she was hard-pressed to find anything suspicious about it. Pinkus had borrowed Ramon Escobar's gun, with Ramon's permission, used it for a couple of weeks—target shooting and taking aim at a squirrel or two during a camping trip—then he'd given it back. All of this was maybe a month or so before the convenience store robbery that sent Pinkus away.

But according to both Ramon's girlfriend Nadia and his friend Craig, not to mention Ramon himself, the gun hadn't been returned. If Ramon never got his gun back, Kim reasoned, he couldn't very well have used it to kill Betty Arnold.

Out of the corner of her eye, Kim caught movement on the other side of the glass partition. She looked up as a skinny guy in his early twenties sank into the seat across from her. With his pointy face and gray, pock-marked skin, he looked something like a hairless rat.

"You wanted to see me?" His tone was flat. Indifferent. He leaned back and looked around the room.

Kim nodded. "About the gun you borrowed from Ramon Escobar."

"I gave it back. There was some cop here not long ago asked me the same thing. I already told him."

Kim tapped the file she'd brought. "I know, I've read your statement."

"So what do you want from me?" Pinkus was still half slouched in his chair but his gaze had grown sharp. He looked directly at Kim.

"When was it that you returned the gun?"

A shrug. "I dunno. Before the whole thing went down with the robbery. I didn't have no gun then."

"Did you take it over to his house or what?"

Pinkus thought for a moment. "Yeah, his house."

"And then what?"

"I handed it to him. Said thanks for the loan. You know, just shootin' the breeze and stuff."

"Was anyone else home?"

Pinkus shifted in his chair. "I don't think so."

"What time of day was it?"

"I don't know . . . uh, late afternoon?"

"You tell me," Kim said. "I wasn't there."

"Yeah. Late afternoon."

"And you're sure you gave the gun back to him?"

"Yeah, I'd had it for a while you know, longer than I'd meant to keep it. Ramon was asking about it."

Kim looked him in the eye and took a gamble. "You're lying, Willie."

"Whatd'ya mean?" His expression flashed with anger.

"You told the deputy who was here before that Ramon came to your place to get the gun. At night."

He shrugged. "I have a lousy memory for details."

"Why lie about it, Willie? Nobody's claiming you did anything wrong with the gun."

He folded his arms and studied a spot on the ceiling.

"Who got to you, Willie? What did they promise?"

Silence.

Kim leaned forward. "You never gave the gun back, did you?"

"It's my word against Ramon's."

"Ramon's, plus two other witnesses who say you never returned it."

"You ain't got proof."

Kim sensed his uncertainty. "Whatever they promised," she said, "it had better be worth the trouble. Perjuring yourself on the witness stand is going to add years to your sentence. And now you've given the police two contradictory statements. How credible do you think that makes you seem?"

Pinkus shifted in his seat. "I got my own back to protect."

"Did someone threaten you?"

"You think I'm dumb enough to rat out? Maybe this ain't much of a life, but at least I'm still breathing with all my parts intact."

"Until the next time they need something. If you go along with a plan like that, Willie, you're going to be spending the rest of your life behind bars."

He looked at the ceiling.

Kim pushed back her chair. "You're stupider than I thought, Willie."

She was halfway to the door when he called, "Wait."

"Yeah?"

Pinkus lowered his voice. "He said all I have to do is tell them I gave Ramon his gun."

"Who told you to say that?"

"Word gets back to him, I'm dead."

"I'll try to keep that from happening."

Pinkus hesitated.

"Who was it?"

He looked over his shoulder then back, lowered his voice to a whisper. "One of the guards. Sandy-haired guy, beefy. Name's something like Haskel."

Back in her car, Kim rubbed her temples, then searched her purse for some aspirin. She'd been thinking Willie might have been pressured by one of the other inmates. That it was a guard threw her. She hated the fact that she no longer knew whom to trust.

Still, she'd gotten Willie to talk and that was good. Tripped him up by one of the oldest tricks in the book. The first deputy who'd interviewed him about the gun hadn't even thought to ask for details about time and place.

At one time she'd have felt bad about resorting to trickery and lies, but those days were long past. It was unfortunate that what she'd learned from Pinkus was the exact opposite of what the DA had hoped for.

CHAPTER 29

Faith set her cleaning supplies, neatly arranged in a new plastic bin, at the foot of the bed. She tried to decide what she was feeling after her meeting with Kali yesterday. Trepidation for sure. But relief, too. So many years bearing the weight of her fear alone, and now she'd finally told someone the truth. If nothing else, it made her feel better.

But what good would it do? The police weren't going to listen to her, even with a lawyer by her side. And Kali would hardly be able to persuade Blake to confess. It would be dangerous to even approach him.

Kali had given Faith her cell phone number and Faith had said she would get in touch in a day or two. But she wasn't certain she actually would. Maybe it was better to simply disappear again.

She'd started a new job this morning—a job that had literally fallen into her lap. She'd been riding the train back to Sacramento yesterday when the woman seated next to her dozed off momentarily and dropped her book into Faith's lap. From there, they'd gotten to talking. The woman, who had unruly, dark eyebrows, a prominent nose, and the ill-suited name of Lolita, cleaned houses with her sister, who'd just run off and married a guy she'd known only six weeks. This left Lolita short a pair of hands. By the time the train pulled into the station in Sacramento, Faith had a job. She'd be paid in cash. No questions, no records. Exactly what Faith needed.

The house this morning had been a simple bungalow they'd finished cleaning in two hours. The place they were cleaning now was larger and grander. Soft taupe walls were set off by finely detailed crown molding, and French doors opened onto a brick patio and arbor of wisteria. It was the sort of home she and Andrew once dreamed of owning, and now, as Faith dusted the dresser and straightened the white eyelet comforter cover on the four-poster bed, she couldn't help imagining herself living here with Elliot and Patrick. She could almost feel the boy's energy and hear Elliot's gentle, good-natured teasing. It brought a lump to Faith's throat thinking of them.

Kali had asked Faith if she should tell anyone about their meeting.

"You can tell Elliot we talked," she'd told Kali. "Say I'm fine and I miss him. But don't tell him where I am. It's better that way." Who knew what Elliot would do. He was such a romantic. Like some love-besotted knight, he'd charge off to slay her dragon.

"What about your stepfather?" Kali had asked.

After some hesitation, Faith had said she'd get in touch with him herself. There was even the smallest chance he could help her.

Lowell hadn't bargained for a daughter when he married her mother, but Faith had been part of the package and he'd treated her well. He'd been generous, too, in helping Andrew make contacts in the legal community.

What would Lowell make of Elliot, Faith wondered. And then she chastised herself for letting her mind even wander in that direction. Her life with Elliot was over.

Faith's feather duster swept over the telephone and bedside lamp, then the collection of silver-framed photographs resting on the nightstand. Family photos. She felt again the pang of missing Elliot.

Downstairs, Lolita was singing loudly over the hum of the vacuum cleaner. Before Faith knew what she was doing, she picked up the telephone and punched in Elliot's home number. He'd be at work so it was a good time to call. She only wanted to hear his voice.

"Hi, sorry to have missed your call. If you want to leave a message for Elliot or Patrick, do so after the tone. We'll get back to you as soon as we can."

Faith wasn't prepared for the rumble of longing inside her. Longing so powerful it robbed her of the ability to breathe. She bit her lip to keep from whispering his name. Slowly, she returned the phone to its cradle.

Ever alert to the possibility she was being followed, Kali kept an eye on her rearview mirror when she turned at the intersection near her house. She had begun this constant vigilance in the days immediately following Betty's murder. She'd been all nerves then, as jittery and wary as a penned colt in a storm. With every glance, she'd imagined the worst. While she was still jumpy, there was a part of her now that almost wanted the man with the serpent tattoo to show up. She had fantasies about confronting him, or maybe even capturing him. At the very least she wanted something that would help her learn his identity. The roadway behind her, however, remained empty of other cars. And there were no unfamiliar vehicles parked along her own street.

She pulled into the garage, shutting the door with the automatic control before getting out of the car. The alarm company wouldn't be able to install the security system until later in the week, but she'd devised her own plan for the interim, drawing on every clichéed gimmick she could recall. A single hair strategically placed on the computer keyboard, a dead fly just inside the back door, laundry fuzz on the telephone keypad. She entered through the garage, noting the door handle still had the imprint of hand cream she'd left that morning. No sign of disturbance in the rest of the house either, and Loretta wagged her tail with her usual good spirits.

After changing into jeans and sorting through her mail, Kali pulled out the paper on which she'd written the phone number for Blake's first wife, Jessie's mother. Former spouses were sometimes more than willing to dish out the dirt on their ex-partners. And Kali was desperate for something that would make the police take a hard look at Blake. He'd told her he didn't know Faith Foster, but that was clearly a lie.

The voice that picked up sounded young. "Mrs. Blake?" Kali asked.

"Just a minute." Then a muffled but much louder, "Mom, it's for you."

"Yes?" Mrs. Blake said, picking up.

"My name is Kali O'Brien." She used the same generalized explanation she had with Jessie, saying that she was following up on loose ends about Faith Foster's disappearance.

Her narrative met with silence.

"She was Jessie's eighth grade English teacher," Kali explained.

"I know who she was." Mrs. Blake's tone was cool.

"I'm sorry to bring up painful memories, but there's new evidence that your husband might have threatened Ms. Foster before she disappeared." Kali figured she wasn't going to get anywhere beating around the bush.

"I wouldn't know about that."

"Would it surprise you?"

"Ed was angry. That teacher put ideas into Jessie's head."

"Are you saying that your daughter was lying about what happened?"

"No, but . . ." There was a long silence. Kali waited for Mrs. Blake to continue. "It's more a matter of how one handles these things," the woman said icily. "It was a family matter and Ms. Foster turned it into a public scandal."

Kali cringed. Mrs. Blake's loss of face in the community appeared to be more important to her than the fact that her daughter had been molested. No wonder Jessie had a chip on her shoulder.

"What did you make of Ms. Foster's disappearance?" Kali asked.

"I suppose it's not very nice of me, but I remember thinking, why didn't it happen a few months earlier and save us all a lot of trouble."

That Jessie would still have been *in trouble* was seemingly lost on her. "You never suspected your husband might have had something to do with what happened to Ms. Foster?"

"Ed?" She offered a humorless laugh. "Even I wouldn't accuse him of being a murderer. I don't know what you're after. I don't have the time or inclination to—"

"One last question," Kali said, cutting her off. "Do you recall any of your husband's acquaintances who had a tattoo of a serpent or snake on his right hand?"

"Not off the top of my head. But Ed is a cosmetic dermatologist. I suppose he might have had a client who wanted to get rid of a tattoo."

Except the man Kali was interested in finding hadn't had his tattoo removed. She thanked Mrs. Blake but the line disconnected before she'd finished speaking.

Now what? Kali was antsy, but she'd about exhausted sources for getting information on Edward Blake. The kind of information she wanted, anyway. If only she could find something that might persuade the authorities to investigate.

She took Loretta for a walk, then tried calling Bryce. Maybe they could try the bodyguard thing again, and this time do it right. She wasn't able to reach him and decided not to leave a message. Finally, because she *had* to do something, she made herself a sandwich and a Thermos of coffee, then drove to Blake's house. It was a sprawling two-story pseudo-tudor surrounded by an iron picket fence. She parked in an inconspicuous spot on the street, which enabled her to see who came and went.

A black Ford with tinted windows parked at the curb halfway down the block gave her pause. It had been there before she arrived, so it couldn't have followed her. That had been her first thought. It might belong to someone in the neighborhood, though SUVs and fancy sports cars were more in line with what she'd expect to see. Was it too much to hope that the Ford belonged to someone visiting Dr. Blake? Perhaps even the man with the tattoo. It looked like something a thug might drive, at least in the movies.

The open road and black desert sky filled Sid with exhilaration. He'd always enjoyed long, solitary drives, starting with the summer he was fifteen—before he had his license—when he'd taken his old man's car for a three-day joyride halfway across the states. The adventure had been worth the beating he got on his return.

Wanderlust was in his blood. He was like the old-time trappers and cowboys who spent weeks at a stretch riding the mountains and plains with no company but their own. The open road was satisfying, no doubt about it.

But so was the knowledge that Sid was close to capping off a chapter in his life that should have been finished years earlier. *Las Vegas, here I come.*

It hadn't surprised Sid to learn Kali didn't know where Faith was staying or how to reach her. Faith had managed to elude him this long because she was careful. Of course, Kali thought she was being careful, too, having her house swept for bugs. Good thing they hadn't found the transmitter hidden inside a pen he'd left near her kitchen telephone. That was how he knew Kali didn't have the information he needed. If he wanted Faith, he had to draw her out himself.

And time was limited. Mr. D had offered Sid a way out. Maybe. Sid still wasn't sure about that. Which was another reason it was good to be out of town for a bit.

The only way for Sid to clear up the mess was to get the deed done and hope the client never found out who'd fucked up the first time.

He'd be in Las Vegas by morning. He hadn't yet decided whether to use the boy or Elliot as bait. Either one would work. He was sure Faith couldn't stay away.

His luck was changing. He could feel it in his bones. He would hit the jackpot in Las Vegas.

CHAPTER 30

There was no easy way to do what had to be done next. Kim knew that, but knowing didn't make it easier. Bauman was going to be pissed and he was going to blame her. The DA wasn't going to be any too happy either, but at least she didn't have to work with him on a daily basis. Of course, by the time all was said and done, she might not be working with Bauman, either. Or anyone in law enforcement. If word got out that she was a meddler, a pain-in-the-ass in a field where cooperation and mutual support were vitally important, she might as well kiss her career good-bye.

But what other choice did she have? She couldn't simply ignore what she'd learned from Pinkus.

Kim had wondered, at first, if Bauman was in on it. She'd wrestled with that possibility for a good part of yesterday. Though it was unlikely, she couldn't rule it out. But if there was any hope at all of saving her job, she couldn't go behind his back. She had to tell him.

When she'd reached him at home last night and announced they needed to talk, Bauman had suggested she join him for his early morning walk along the path bordering the Truckee River. So here she was at the crack of dawn pacing around a small parking lot near the river, hands pulled into the sleeves of her fleece jacket for warmth, waiting to tell her supervisor they'd arrested the wrong man.

Bauman showed up minutes later. He hadn't shaved yet and his hair tufted at odd angles on one side. His blue sweatshirt was faded, as were his jeans.

He smiled at her. "You made it. I was worried the hour might be too early for you."

"Is that why you suggested it?"

"I suggested it because you said it was important and I'll be in meetings most of the day." He bent over to tie his shoe. "Is everything okay, Kim?"

"What do you mean?"

He stood up again. "You didn't used to be so touchy."

His tone was kind. She bristled nonetheless. It was that damn Christmas party and the legacy of too many margaritas.

"Sorry," she said. "It's this case."

He raised a skeptical eyebrow. "That so?" He braced himself against a tree and stretched, then he took off at a brisk pace, his arms pumping vigorously at his sides.

Kim, who considered herself in pretty good shape, struggled to keep up. The air had a frosty bite to it. Although the temperatures were expected to reach into the seventies by the afternoon, the combination of spring and high altitude made for cool nights and mornings. Once she was moving, however, the crisp air felt good. It smelled clean and fresh. The mountain scent made her glad to be alive.

"Tell me if I'm going too fast for you," Bauman said.

"No, this is fine." She was already huffing, but she'd be damned if she let him know that.

"Tell me now, what is it that's so important it can't keep?"

"Willie Pinkus never gave Ramon Escobar's gun back."

Bauman's pace didn't falter. "I thought he said he had."

"He did say that at first." Kim panted. "But he was lying. He admitted it yesterday."

"Yesterday?"

"I went to see him. He said he lied when we first asked because one of the guards threatened him if he didn't."

"Whoa." Bauman stopped dead and looked at her. "Are you serious?"

Kim nodded, grateful for the momentary rest. She was relieved, too, that he didn't appear to know about the threat. She'd been right to trust him.

"Who's this guard?" he asked.

"His name is Kent Haskel. I checked with the warden, without saying why I was asking. Haskel's been on the job five years. He was suspended once for use of unnecessary force but there's nothing else on him. He's ex-military, served in Vietnam."

Bauman ran a hand through his hair. "Are you saying there was undue influence applied to make Escobar look guilty?"

"I guess that's the upshot of it, yes. Mostly what I'm saying is, the evidence isn't what we thought it was." They'd started walking again, but at a slower pace. "Also, I talked to Ramon's girlfriend, Nadia."

"You went to see her, too?"

"No, she called me." It sounded better that way, not as though Kim had gone out of her way to undermine a case they'd already sent to the DA. But Kim knew she'd set things in motion by talking to Nadia earlier and inviting her confidence.

"Ramon's behavior was part of what made us look at him as suspect," Kim continued. "He didn't show up for work the Friday of the murder, which was unlike him. He acted agitated all weekend, then disappeared for a few days. It all fit with a man who was guilty. But what Nadia told me casts a different light on it."

"How so?"

"Friday morning she told him she was pregnant. *That's* what Ramon was upset about. And they had a fight over the weekend because she didn't want to have the baby and he wanted her to."

Bauman frowned. "Why didn't Escobar offer that explanation when we first talked to him?"

"He wanted to protect Nadia. Her family would kill her—sorry, poor choice of words—if they found out."

Bauman continued walking in silence. Kim matched her pace to his. Around them birds began to chirp in earnest as the sun peered over the tops of the mountains.

Every now and then she stole a glance in his direction. His expression was grim. His lips were clamped together in a tight line and his eyes had narrowed to slits.

"You're telling me we arrested the wrong man?" he said at last.

"I'm afraid so."

"Jesus."

Kim fixed her eyes on the ground at her feet.

"We'll end up with egg on our face."

She nodded. There was no way to make it go away quietly.

"Proving us wrong is the job of a defense attorney, you know."

"It doesn't always happen that way though." And with what she'd been hearing about Ramon's attorney, it wasn't going to happen here. She looked at him. "Besides, holding an innocent man isn't right."

He didn't say anything.

She'd come this far, she might as well take the whole plunge. "I'd like to go to the DA," she said, then immediately corrected herself. "I *am* going to the DA." She wasn't asking his permission.

Butterflies danced in her stomach as she waited for the heat of his anger. Well, she'd just have to take it.

Bauman picked up a rock from beside the path and threw it into the rushing river. He had a good arm; the rock cleared a good two-thirds of the expanse before hitting the surface of the water. "Damn."

Kim watched him.

"What?" he said.

"You think I should?" So much for her strong stand. But his reaction was so far from the irate outburst she'd expected, she wasn't sure what to make of it.

"Of course you should. Did you think I might tell you not to?" Bauman seemed almost amused.

"It crossed my mind."

"Oh, Kim." He sat on a granite boulder by the side of the trail and pressed his fingertips to his temples. "Why do you have this image of me as such a hardass?"

"I—"

"Never mind. I probably don't want to hear it. I'm glad you came to me, though. I know that wasn't easy, especially since you thought I would fight you on it."

"Thank you." She wasn't sure what else to say.

"I think of myself as a good cop. Honest, fair, dedicated." Bauman poked at the soil with the toe of his shoe. "Why did you think I wouldn't support you?"

"Well, you seemed so eager to arrest Ramon, for one thing." Since Bauman showed no signs of getting up, Kim found herself a fallen log and straddled it.

"Eager? There was evidence pointing to him."

"But you *wanted* Ramon to be the one."

Bauman squinted at her. Kim felt a flutter in her stomach just as she had when she first met him. There was something almost magnetic about the way he looked at her.

"Yes," he said after a moment, "I suppose I did."

"Why is that, if you don't mind my asking."

Bauman crossed his arms on his knees. He looked toward the river and sighed. "Ramon and my daughter dated in high school."

"And?"

"I wasn't particularly happy about it." There was a strained quality to his voice. "My wife and I had just separated so I was already feeling . . . lonely, rejected, angry. You name it, and if it was unpleasant, I was there. Then my daughter, who I'd always been close to, started spending every waking minute with her new boyfriend. Ramon. I was no longer the most important man in her life."

Kim nodded.

"It sounds silly now, but believe me, I was crushed."

"Sounds understandable, not silly."

He turned back to look at her. "I also didn't think Ramon was good for her."

"Beneath her, you mean?"

"Yeah. I know it's not politically correct to think that way, but she was head over heels in love with him, or so she thought, and I was worried she'd throw away her whole future on the basis of hormones. She started talking about taking a job instead of going to college. She loaned him money. She'd sneak out of the house some nights to be with him. Almost overnight she went from being my cute little girl to this . . . this sexual being who didn't even try to hide the hickies on her neck."

Kim bit back a smile. She had a lot in common with his daughter. "I bet you came down hard on her."

"That I did. And all I succeeded in doing was to drive her into his arms. I guess I wanted Ramon to be guilty to vindicate myself." Bauman pressed his palms together. "It's not a story I'm proud of."

"At least you're big enough to admit it."

His eyes crinkled. "That sounded almost like a compliment."

Kim was beginning to remember what had drawn her to him initially. "A statement of fact," she said. "That's all. Where's your daughter now?"

"She's at UC San Diego."

"All that worry for nothing. Do you get along with her?"

"Splendidly." He laughed. "The checks I write for college might have helped. But she's a good kid. Excuse me, a fine young woman. I just wish she lived closer."

Bauman rose and brushed the dust from his pants. "Can I ask you something?"

"You can ask," Kim said.

"Why are things so prickly between us?"

"I don't know what—"

"Is it because of what happened the night of the Christmas party?"

Kim squared her shoulders. "I'd rather not discuss it."

"Because if it is, I'd like—"

"I said I didn't want to discuss it!" Kim couldn't bear the embarrassment of hearing what a fool she'd made of herself.

A shadow passed over his face. "That bad, huh?"

"Sir?"

"Never mind." Bauman seemed to retreat into himself for a moment.

"Shall I call the DA or do you want to do it?" she asked, eager to change the subject.

"Go ahead if you'd like. You've done a good job, Kim."

Kim left him to finish his power walk alone while she returned home and took a hot shower to warm up. Things had gone better than she'd dared hope. Not only did it look as though she'd keep her job, Bauman hadn't even been angry. Now if they could just forget that stupid incident last winter, pretend the evening simply hadn't happened. But even as Kim was wishing for a way to wipe away the memory, she was aware that part of her craved repeating it. Only sober this time.

* * *

Kim waited until nine o'clock that morning to call Kali O'Brien.

"I have a photo I'd like you to take a look at," she told Kali. That Kali would recognize Hans Vogel was something of a long shot, but Kim thought her upcoming conversation with the DA might sit better if she could offer him something positive to temper the negative.

"If you have an E-mail program that can read attached j-peg files, it's probably easiest to send it that way," Kim added.

"What's the photo?"

"It might be the man who shot you."

"Hans Vogel?"

"How'd you—"

"Detective Keating told me. I didn't get anything but the barest glimpse of the shooter. I'm sure I won't be able to recognize him."

"I'd appreciate it if you'd take a look anyway. I also have the taped greeting from his answering machine. I'd like you to call my number in about five minutes. Listen to the tape and tell me if the voice is at all familiar." While she was giving Kali her home number, Kim slipped her own greeting from the machine and plugged in the one Hans' brother had sent her.

"Where does Ramon Escobar fit in all this?" Kali asked.

"New evidence is making us rethink his involvement."

"I see." Kali was quiet a moment. "This man whose photo you're sending me doesn't have a tattoo on one hand, does he?"

"Not that anyone's mentioned. I'll check. Why?"

"Do you remember when I told you about the Faith Foster connection?"

"Right. Betty Arnold was her aunt and you thought Betty might have had information about Faith's murder."

"Only it turns out she's not dead, after all."

"What do you mean, she's not dead?"

"She was abducted by a man with a tattoo of a serpent on his hand. He tried to kill her but she got away. He's still after her, which is why she's been hiding. Faith thinks he's responsible for Betty Arnold's murder."

Kim's head was reeling. "You're losing me. How do you know all this?"

"Faith contacted me. We met and the man with the tattoo followed us."

Kim was taking notes. "You're sure it's the same man? What's he look like?"

"He was wearing a ski mask when he tried to kill Faith eight years ago. Yesterday he kept his face hidden, but Faith is sure he's the same man. He appears to be in his fifties, about five foot nine, solidly built but not fat. Faith believes he has ties to Dr. Edward Blake, a Bay Area dermatologist."

Kim continued jotting down what Kali was telling her. She'd given up trying to make sense of it for the moment. "What's Betty Arnold's connection?"

"According to Faith, Blake killed her aunt to send a message to Faith. To remind her that he was still after her."

Kim switched the phone to her other ear. "I have to be honest with you, this is sounding pretty off the wall."

"That was my reaction, too. But after meeting Faith and hearing her story, I don't know . . . It's crazy enough it just might be true."

True or not, Kim knew the information was too flimsy to use in her conversation with the D.A., and that was her big worry at the moment. "I'll keep it in mind. For right now, though, I'd like to focus on the suspect I've got. I'll send the photo right away. You'll have time to look at it?"

Kali's chair squeaked when she angled it toward the computer. She was happy to cooperate, but she knew she wasn't going to be any help. Still, if Detective Wong wanted her to look at the photo, she would. The detective had been interested enough to listen to her story about Faith and the man with the tattoo, even though Kali had nothing to offer but conjecture.

And it wasn't like Kali had any better ideas. She'd kept watch on Dr. Blake's house until the lights went out at one o'clock this morning. The Ford hadn't budged, and no one had come out of or gone into the house. Kali could tell from the bluish flicker in the upstairs window that someone in the family was watching television, but that was the extent of her information gathering. Digging up evidence against Blake was beyond the scope of what she could manage alone. The best she could hope for right now was that Detective Wong was on the right track with Hans Vogel and that there would be a way to tie him to Blake.

Maybe Hans would even roll over on the doctor if the detectives handled it right.

Kali logged on to her E-mail account and found Detective Wong's message waiting for her. She clicked on the attached file and the photo of Hans Vogel materialized on her screen. He looked to be in his late twenties. Broad shoulders, thick neck, light-colored hair cut short to his scalp. A scar ran along his jawline.

He wasn't the man who'd followed her and Irene on Sunday afternoon. That man had been older than Hans, and slighter of build. But might Hans have been the man who shot her? Kali experienced a shiver at the memory of that afternoon as she studied the face on her monitor. There was no way she could know for sure. She hadn't gotten a very good look at him to begin with, and in the weeks since the shooting, her memory had faded.

She felt the prick of disappointment even though she'd known she wouldn't be able to identify the killer. She so much wanted him caught and punished.

Kali picked up the phone and called the number Detective Wong had given her. Two rings and the answering machine kicked in. A low-pitched male voice said, "Hey, I'm out. Leave a message."

Kali pressed the phone to her ear. She felt her pulse quicken. "Let me hear it again," she said when the detective came on the line. "I'll call right back."

She dialed again. This time she listened without breathing. She wanted to concentrate on the voice. Right there near the beginning, the word "out."

You might as well come out, bitch. You can't hide.

Detective Wong picked up again. "What do you think?"

"It could be him," Kali said, hearing the excitement in her own voice. "It's the same deep, resonant tone as the shooter. And he pronounces 'out' like a Canadian. The man who shot me had the same accent."

"Hans Vogel was born in Toronto," Detective Wong said. "Why didn't you say something before, about the man's accent?"

"I wasn't aware of it until now. Have you found Hans yet?"

"Afraid not. But with what you've just told me, we'll beef up our efforts to locate him."

"And you'll remember what I told you about Dr. Blake and the man with the tattoo?"

Detective Wong hesitated. Kali knew she was skeptical. "I'll remember. You can tell Faith Foster I'd like to talk with her also."

"If I see her again, I'll do that."

Kali didn't know if Faith was still checking her E-mail. She forwarded the photo of Hans anyway, along with a message to please get in touch. Maybe, just maybe, *she* would recognize Hans Vogel.

Jared dropped a stack of papers on Kali's desk later that afternoon.

"What are these?" she asked.

"Letters requiring your signature."

"What letters?" She glanced through them. The case names were familiar but not the actual letters. "I didn't write these letters."

"I know. But they needed to be written. They're all pretty much pro forma, but you should look over them anyway."

"You did them?"

He rocked back on his heels, gave her a self-effacing shrug. "Somebody had to."

"I've been negligent, huh?"

"I don't know that I'd say negligent. But distracted, definitely."

Kali took the letters and set them on the desk. "Thanks."

"Don't mention it." Jared stopped at the door and grinned. "Though a quiet little raise would be perfectly acceptable."

Kali picked up an eraser and threw it at him. It bounced off the back of the door Jared had just closed on his way out.

He'd been mostly teasing, and Kali honestly didn't think she'd let anything important slide—she was the sort of person who finished assignments early, just in case—but her mind *had* been elsewhere these past weeks. As atonement, Kali stayed late, cleaning out her inbox and the clutter on her desk.

It wasn't yet eight when she left the office, but the combination of twilight and a cloudy sky transformed the world to shades of gray. Kali exited the building and turned in the direction of her car. Just then, her eyes caught sight of a dark Ford with tinted windows, like the one she'd seen near Dr. Blake's, parked at the curb. She reached into her purse for her car keys as she quickened her pace to a jog.

She hadn't gone more than ten feet when two men in ill-fitting business suits stepped from the car. In a flash, they each grasped one of her arms and spirited her into the backseat of the Ford.

CHAPTER 31

Fear grabbed Kali by the throat. She thrashed and bucked helplessly as the two men pinned her against the car's rear seat. Finally, as the car began to move, her lungs found air and she screamed.

The driver put his hands over his ears. "I told you this was the wrong way to go about it," he snapped.

The man on Kali's left glared in response. Then he turned to Kali. "Calm down. We're not going to hurt you." He reached into his jacket pocket and produced a leather-encased ID. "FBI. I'm Agent Monroe. He's Babcock. The wiseass driving is Hinkley."

It was too dark to see anything of the badge even though he was holding it in front of her face. She breathed a sigh of relief nonetheless. "Is there a light in here?"

Rather than turning on the car's overhead light, Monroe pulled out a penlight and illuminated the ID. It looked real, but what did she know. Quality counterfeiting was almost as good as the real thing.

"We just want to talk to you," Babcock said.

"Ever hear of office hours?"

"We wanted to keep it private."

"I don't exactly telecast my meetings."

"We're sorry," Monroe said. "Okay? But word is that your office and home were bugged not so long ago, and we're not taking any chances."

They knew about the bugging. Kali tried to decide if that made it more or less likely they were legitimate agents.

"What's your interest in Edward Blake?" Babcock asked. He

looked to be in his forties, with a narrow face and pointy nose. His ears stuck out from the side of his head like they'd been glued on.

"What's it matter to you?"

"We're the ones asking the questions here."

They were no longer gripping her arms, but she was pinned between the two men. And the third one up front kept eyeing her in the rearview mirror. What would happen if she simply refused to answer? If they were really FBI they were hardly going to beat her up. On the other hand, why shouldn't she tell them about Faith's allegations. They might already be investigating Blake's involvement in murder.

"You talked to his daughter," Monroe said. "And to his ex-wife. And you were parked outside his house the other night. We want to know why. Is he involved in a legal matter you're working on?"

"It's complicated."

"We've got time."

They also had the upper hand. "Okay," Kali said. "I'll talk to you, but only if I can call first and verify you're who you say you are."

A begrudging nod. Babcock handed her a cell phone and started to reel off the number.

"Uh-uh." Kali wasn't about to fall for that trick. If they weren't legit they'd just have a buddy pick up and say he was with the FBI. She pulled out her own cell phone, called information and got the number for the FBI in San Francisco, splurging on the quick-connect option. The call was transferred a couple of times but she finally found a woman willing to verify the identity of the agents.

"What does Babcock look like?" Kali asked.

The woman on the other end thought a moment. "A weasel with an overbite."

Kali smiled. An apt description. "And Monroe?"

"Just under six feet, blond, with a receding hairline and eyebrows that curl up in little horns at the peak. You want the other one, too? Hinkley?"

"No, I guess they're legit."

"I know, it's hard to believe sometimes. But they are."

"You're thorough," Monroe said when she got off the phone.

"Most people aren't. Hey, Hink, let's not go too far, okay? Maybe turn back and make a loop or something."

The man in the front nodded.

They'd been heading down 580 toward Pleasanton and had reached Castro Valley when they exited the freeway and turned back again. Hinkley stayed in the far right lane, not the slowest car on the road, but close.

Kali told them about Faith Foster and the man with the tattoo hired by Blake to kill her. She told them about Andrew Major and Betty Arnold, too, and how they'd likely been murdered on orders from Blake. Kali was more than happy to pass along everything she'd learned. In fact, she was grateful to have the FBI involved. They were the experts at this sort of investigation and she wasn't.

The agents listened without interrupting, though they exchanged glances occasionally. Glances Kali had trouble reading.

"I don't know about eight years ago," Monroe said when she'd finished, "but Blake's got nothing to do with the latest murder, or with the man you saw following you."

Kali bristled at his tone. "How do you know?"

"Blake's been under twenty-four-hour-a-day surveillance for the last two months."

Kali shook her head. "I'm not saying he was the actual shooter, but that he hired someone to do the job."

"I know that's what you're saying. But we're telling you it isn't so. We know every move he makes. We even know when he takes a piss and for how long. Blake is not your man."

How could that be? "You wouldn't be telling me that just to get me to back off, would you?"

Babcock actually smiled. Kali had suspected he didn't know how. "You're right, we don't want you messing up our operation, but if you think we'd actually lie about something like murder, the agency's lost a lot more credibility with the public than I thought."

"Trust me," Kali said, "it has."

Monroe growled. "Blake has nothing to do with your murders and abductions."

"Why are you watching him then?"

"It doesn't concern you."

"It *does* concern me because he's been intimidating a client of mine." Faith wasn't actually a client, but it sounded better that way. "I'm hardly going to walk away simply because you say he's not involved."

Another exchange of glances. Finally Monroe spoke. "We're just about to bust a drug ring. It's taken us forever to set this up. We've got people working on the inside, undercover. You blow this for us, and your ass will be in the sling."

Kali turned to Babcock. "See what I mean about credibility?"

"I mean it," Monroe grumbled. "This isn't a joking matter."

Neither was murder or being kidnapped by three hoods in a black Ford, but Kali decided it wasn't an argument she wanted to get into. "Do any of Blake's associates have a small serpent tattoo on their right hand?"

"Doesn't ring a bell."

"How about any of your agents?"

Monroe rolled his eyes.

"I'd be surprised," Babcock said.

Kali almost choked on her frustration. If the agents were to be believed, Blake was a dead end. At least in connection with Betty Arnold's murder.

As they dropped her off at her car, Babcock asked, "What did Nellie say when you asked her what I looked like?"

Kali looked him over. "She said you had big brown eyes and were cute as a bug's ear."

He started to grin, then caught himself. "You're pulling my leg, aren't you?"

"It's better this way." She shut the door and waved.

Sid slumped behind the wheel of his car and tried to ignore the gnawing in his stomach. The burger place next door to Elliot DeVries's clinic was hopping with customers. The food had to be either very good, or very cheap. The aroma of grilled meat and french fries wafted through the air, making Sid so hungry he almost broke down and went inside. But it was too risky. He'd come here with a job to do. It would be stupid to take a chance that someone would remember seeing him.

The radio station broke for a commercial. Sid punched the tuner, all the while keeping his eye on the clinic. After a few minutes, a man carrying a tiny powderpuff of a dog came out and drove away. Sid sneered silently. What sort of man owned a dog like that?

Finally, a woman in jeans and a blue workshirt left the clinic. The receptionist. Sid had seen her earlier when he was getting the lay of the land. She stood in the parking lot to light a cigarette, then got into a battered old VW bus and drove away. The only car left in the lot belonged to DeVries.

Perfect. The clinic closed tonight at eight. It was now five till. Since the receptionist had already left, Sid had to believe DeVries wasn't expecting more clients.

Sid had come up with this plan after carefully casing DeVries's house and the boy's school. The clinic would be easiest to get in and out of unnoticed, he'd decided. He was anxious to get the ball rolling and didn't want to waste time with a lot of elaborate planning.

A quick look around the parking lot. All the activity was at the burger place. Sid grabbed the cardboard box from the backseat, got out of his car, and pushed through the clinic's front entrance. The soft ting-a-ling of a bell announced his arrival.

Moments later, a gangly, bushy-browed man in a lab coat emerged from the back room. "We're about to close."

"The sign says you're open until eight."

"We are, only . . . Oh, never mind. What can I do for you?"

"You the doc?" Sid asked.

"Elliot DeVries." He extended a hand. Sid took it, sizing up the man's strength by his grip. It was going to be a piece of cake.

Sid gestured to the box he clutched to his chest. "It's my cat. She's been real lethargic lately. Not eating."

"Is she drinking water?"

"Not drinking, either."

"For how long?"

Sid didn't know beans about cats. "A couple of days."

"No water at all?" DeVries sounded alarmed.

"Well, maybe a few sips here and there." Sid didn't want to raise the doc's suspicions.

DeVries eyed the box in Sid's arms with a frown. "You know, in the future it would be better if you poked some airholes in that."

Ah, shit. "I was in such a hurry . . ." Sid explained. "She was looking so much worse than she had, and I was afraid—"

"She's not going to suffocate without them, but she'd be happier with more air." DeVries reached for the box. "Let's have a look."

Sid held tight. "She's real skittish. It would be better if we were in the examining room. You know, in case she tries to run."

"Sure." DeVries led him through a swinging door into the back part of the building. It consisted of a single corridor with two doors leading off on each side. They passed the first door to the left, which looked like a storage room. Sid guessed two of the others were exam rooms and one, the doctor's private office.

DeVries turned into the first room on the right. "What's her name?"

"Uh . . . Cleo." The old lady who'd lived next door when Sid was growing up had a cat named Cleo. He and his brother used to shoot at it with their BB guns.

Sid shut the door behind him. He set the box on the metal exam table, then stepped back. DeVries looked at him expectantly, then bent over the box himself and removed the lid.

"There's noth—"

Sid came down hard on the back of the doc's head with the butt of his gun.

DeVries staggered, grabbed the table, turned slightly. "What the—" Blood was already oozing from his wound.

Sid punched him hard on the side of the face, knocking DeVries across the room. He collided with a tray of supplies, and bottles and tools clattered to the floor.

DeVries was reaching for one of the sharp metal tools when Sid grabbed his arm, twisting it forcefully until it snapped. DeVries dropped to his knees and screamed out in pain.

"What is it you want?" He cradled the broken arm with his good one. His skin was pale. "There isn't much money but you can have it."

"I don't want your money."

"Drugs? This is an veterinary clinic." He winced. "We don't have—"

Sid's foot shot forward, connecting with the doctor's ribs. DeVries gasped and curled on his side on the floor. Sid kicked again. He wasn't sure how far to go. He wanted DeVries alive, not dead. Alive, but barely. It was the only way he could be sure Faith would come.

There wasn't any joy in it for Sid. The doc wasn't much of a fighter. He gave one final kick to the doc's head. Enough for a concussion, maybe. Hard to tell.

The initial wails of pain had quickly turned to whimpering, and now, even that stopped. Sid turned DeVries slightly with his foot. The doc moaned but he was otherwise inert.

Just about perfect.

Sid took out a handkerchief and was wiping his prints from the doorknob when he heard a noise outside the door.

"Dad?" A tentative knock.

Christ, it was the kid. What was he doing here?

"Dad?" More insistent this time. Another knock.

Sid yanked the door open abruptly, grabbed the boy and held a hand over his mouth.

"You cause any trouble and I'll snap your neck like a stick, you understand?"

The kid was staring at his dad with wide, frightened eyes. He didn't struggle but Sid could feel his heart racing under his sweatshirt. He was a skinny little thing. Sid tied him up easily, then gagged and blindfolded him.

Sid's first thought was to leave the boy there with his dad. Then he decided a missing kid would be added bait. He'd wavered between going for the father or the kid, anyway. Now he had the best of both worlds.

Lady Luck worked in unexpected ways, Sid thought. And she was smiling on him tonight.

CHAPTER 32

When the three agents dropped Kali off at her car, the first thing she did after locking the doors, was call Bryce. Though she was no longer frightened, she remained rattled. Her heart was going a mile a minute.

"You want to come over?" she asked when he picked up. She felt calmer already merely having reached him.

"What's up? Are you expecting trouble?"

"You think that's the only reason I'd want to see you?" His words would have hurt if she hadn't been wound so tight there was little room for new emotion. "Besides, I already had my trouble for the evening."

"What happened?"

"Come over and I'll tell you."

Bryce laughed softly. "Now there's an offer that's hard to refuse. I can't get there for an hour or so, is that okay?"

"Perfect." It would give her time to get home, walk the dog, clean up the house a bit. And freshen her makeup.

Kali checked the cars parked along her street—nothing out of the ordinary—and again worked her way through her private security checklist as she entered the house. All of the carefully placed hairs and threads and coatings of talc were untouched and just as she'd left them that morning. Not that they did much good, anyway. What if the man with the tattoo had been waiting after work instead of the FBI? Kali's stomach turned at the thought.

Despite intentions to use her time productively, Kali took Loretta for a very short walk, made only minimal improvement in the makeup department, and gave up completely on picking up around the house. She didn't let herself think about Betty Arnold, or Faith or Blake, either. She simply waited for Bryce.

He showed up carrying a brown grocery bag. "You okay?" he asked. "You sounded kind of funny on the phone."

"I'm fine."

His eyes lingered on hers. "You don't look it. Did someone get into the house again?"

Kali shook her head, tried to deflect his concern. She didn't want to get into it just yet. "What's in the bag, did you bring your pj's?"

He gave her a crooked smile. "Was I supposed to?"

Kali smiled in return. "I think we'll manage without them. So what did you bring?"

Bryce opened the bag and pulled out a bottle of champagne and a plastic carton of fresh strawberries dipped in dark chocolate. He set them on the counter. "From a specialty store near where I live."

"Wow. I'm impressed."

"Good. You're supposed to be." He kissed her cheek, his hand softly grazing the nape of her neck. "Shall I pour us some?"

Kali's flesh tingled at his touch. She felt an effervescent warmth, like bubbly liquid sunshine, spread throughout her body. Better than champagne. "Maybe later," she said.

Bryce was wearing Levis and a snug-fitting dark blue T-shirt. His skin was tanned and he smelled faintly of soap. She slid her arms around his waist and leaned into him, resting her head in the crook of his neck. This wasn't anything she'd planned—she'd moved without conscious thought at all—but it felt right.

Her hands moved across his back, down the base of his spine to his fine, firm butt. She raised her head and kissed him—a long, ever-deepening kiss that brought a groan to his throat. Then she pressed herself against him.

"Are you sure?" he whispered in her ear.

"Very sure."

They moved into the bedroom, slowly undressing each other, luxuriating in anticipation and sensation. And finally in release.

He held her afterward, and stroked her hair. "Kali?"

"Mmm."

"I'm glad you called tonight."

"Me too." She tapped his chest. "And I'm glad you were kind enough to come over."

"*Kind enough.*" He laughed softly. "I've thought of little else for months."

"You could have fooled me."

"I care about you, Kali. I didn't want our relationship to be just a, uh—"

"Another number in your little black book?"

He hesitated. "There aren't as many numbers as you might think."

She'd spent the last six months slowly learning to distinguish the man from his reputation, but she also knew that the reputation hadn't sprung from nowhere.

"I don't trust people easily," she said, rolling onto her side so she could look at him. "Men, I mean. I keep my distance in order to feel safe."

"I've noticed."

"It would really hurt to learn that I was simply another conquest."

Bryce stopped stroking her head. "That's not—"

"Okay, maybe conquest wasn't the right word. But you know what I mean."

He started to say something, then stopped and touched her lips with his fingertip. "It's not like that at all."

She snuggled against him. "Good."

"Ready for champagne?" Bryce asked after a moment.

"I could be tempted."

"Stay put, I'll be right back."

He rolled out of bed, pulled on his boxers and headed upstairs, returning minutes later with two glasses, the bottle of champagne, and a plate of the strawberries.

"Wow. Service."

"You'll have to fire your other bodyguards then."

"I don't have any—" Then she saw that he was teasing. She set her glass of champagne on the bedside table and kissed him. "Perhaps I'll do just that."

CHAPTER 33

Sid pulled off onto a deserted side road. When he was sure there wasn't anyone else around, he got out and opened the trunk. The kid startled, then stared at him dumbly. Sid had taken away his glasses so who knew what he could see.

"I'm going to remove the gag and untie your hands so you can eat," Sid told him. "But don't scream. Don't do anything but eat. Got it?"

The kid nodded uncertainly.

Sid removed the rope that bound his hands and helped him sit up. Then he handed the kid a burger and fries he'd picked up at McDonald's. Picked up specially, in fact, 'cause he thought it would be a treat.

The kid nibbled a fry tentatively, like he suspected it might be tainted.

"It's fine," Sid told him. "Maybe not the healthiest breakfast, but I guess that's the least of your worries right now, isn't it?"

The kid didn't say anything. But he didn't eat, either.

"Eat up now, we haven't got long."

How they were going to spend the day was something Sid was having trouble figuring out. He'd been hoping to find an abandoned barn or someplace where he could stash the kid, but Las Vegas was one fucking housing development and golf course after another. Wasn't anything abandoned anywhere.

If he kept the kid with him, something Sid wasn't happy about, he'd have to bring him into the car. In the trunk, he'd bake to death now that the sun was up. Baked bodies stunk.

The kid chewed a bite of french fry. "I'm thirsty," he said.

"Tough." Sid had been so intent on getting food, he hadn't even thought about something to drink.

It had been a long night. One of the longest in Sid's life. What had he been thinking anyway, grabbing the kid?

The kid was a pain. He had to eat. He had to drink. He had to pee. And he whimpered in his sleep. Sid didn't want to tote him around, but there was no place to hide him safely away, either. One night of driving around with the kid in the trunk was already one night too many.

"Where's my dad?" the kid asked. "I want to see my dad."

"Shut up! Your dad is none of your fucking business right now."

The kid threw the bag of fries and burger onto the ground. "I don't want your stupid food. You're a mean, horrible man. My dad never did anything—"

Sid slapped the boy smack across the mouth. "I told you to shut up." He jerked the boy's hands behind his back and tied them tight, then stuffed the gag back into his mouth. The kid bucked and tried to swing his feet at Sid.

Sid pushed him hard onto the trunk floor and slammed the lid. So much for trying to be nice. This wasn't going to work. He was either going to have to let the kid go or kill him. Sid didn't have time to play baby-sitter.

First thing Wednesday morning, Kali called FBI headquarters in San Francisco and again confirmed that the men she'd talked to the previous night were legitimate agents. That didn't guarantee their information was correct, she reminded herself. Nor did it rule out the possibility they were intentionally blowing smoke to keep her away from their investigation. But assuming Blake really wasn't involved, what then?

Maybe Faith was crazy. Delusional and totally wacko.

But the man with the tattoo was real. Kali had seen him with her own eyes. He'd followed them, and he'd bugged her phone and computer.

At ten, Kali headed downtown for a deposition that ate up most of her day. When she returned to the office there was a message waiting for her that Bryce had called. She called him back.

"Hi," she said.

"Hi, yourself. I've been thinking about you all morning."

"And?"

"And it's nice. Not as nice as being with you, but nice."

She smiled. Bryce sounded about sixteen. "I'm glad to hear it. I thought about you, too."

"What were you thinking?"

That up close, the rough edges and the playboy reputation seemed like nothing but smoke screen. That she needed to be careful because she could easily lose her heart to the man.

"That those were first-rate chocolate-dipped strawberries," she said with a laugh.

"You're such a romantic." He paused. "I did some checking— the FBI really does have Blake under surveillance. If he had anything to do with Betty Arnold's death, they'd know about it. Nothing about what was going on eight years ago, though."

"Thanks."

When she was off the line, she pulled the case file from the morning's deposition from her briefcase, and with it came the sheet of paper on which she'd written the phone number for Nancy Baylor, the attorney who'd been an associate of Andrew Major at the time of his death.

Kali started to put it aside, then picked up the phone instead, and punched in the number.

"Funny you should want to talk about Andrew," Nancy Baylor said when Kali had explained why she was calling. "I was just thinking about him the other day."

"Why's that?"

"I saw a vintage red Cobra. Andrew was having a replica built for himself. He was like a kid about it. He'd located a fabricator and the chassis was already under construction. Andrew would drop by my office with photos and stuff from the Web, like he was showing off his firstborn or something. I'm not much for cars but I think I was the only one at the firm who would even pretend to listen." She paused. "I always thought it was sad that he killed himself before he got a chance to drive it."

"You're convinced his death was a suicide, then?"

"There's some question it wasn't?"

"Not really." Kali slipped off her shoes and kicked them under the desk. "It's just that everyone I've talked to thinks Andrew's taking his own life was unlike him."

"It was. Totally. But he was upset by Faith's disappearance. And he'd been really on edge for a couple of weeks before that. I thought maybe they were having problems or something, which might account for why he felt so bad when she disappeared."

"I understand he took a leave of absence?"

"Not a formal leave. The partners suggested he take some time off, though I didn't think he'd do it. Work was Andrew's life. It surprised me when he didn't come into the office, but then I figured even a workaholic like Andrew had his limits. Now I keep thinking if I'd just called him or dropped by his house, it would have made a difference."

"Easy to say in hindsight."

"I know that, but I don't always *feel* it."

"When did you last talk to him?" Kali asked.

"A few days after Faith was killed. He was out of town when it happened. In Chicago with some of the partners. He was only back in the office for two days, in fact. I left early that second day for a dentist appointment. I stopped by and said something like, "You doing okay?" He said he was and I believed him. Next day though, he didn't come to work and we all just assumed he'd taken some time away. His office was kind of a mess. That should have been a red flag right there. Andrew was orderly to the point of being anal. I should have known he wasn't his usual self."

Kali's scalp prickled. "A mess how?"

"Just loose papers, drawers that looked lived in, books that weren't aligned with precision. Not a mess by most people's standards, but not typical for Andrew, either."

"Could someone have searched his office?"

Nancy Baylor was quiet a moment. "I suppose. At the time, we just assumed, with his being upset and distracted and all . . . But in light of what you're saying about his not taking his own life, and—"

"I'm not saying that," Kali corrected. "I'm merely looking into the circumstances of Faith's disappearance." And trying to come up with a name besides Blake. "There was some talk, wasn't there, that Andrew might have been involved?"

"There was, but I don't buy it. Andrew might have walked all over Faith if that's what it took to get ahead, but he'd have no reason to kill her. If anything, he needed her adoration. It was a little sickening, really, the way she looked up to him."

Kali thought she detected a note of jealousy. She hadn't even considered a lover's triangle. "Were you attracted to Andrew?" she asked after a moment.

"Attracted? I don't . . ." Nancy paused, then laughed. "You mean did I kill them both in a passionate rage?" She didn't sound offended. "I'm a lesbian in a happy, ten-plus-year relationship. Andrew was a friend. Nothing more."

CHAPTER 34

Kim Wong had a crick in her neck from talking on the telephone. She was into her seventh call of the day and all she'd learned about Hans Vogel was that he had a record for assault and burglary, which his brother had told her up front. People she'd spoken with—neighbors and coworkers—had few complaints, however. Hans had an attitude, sure, and a mind with more loose connections than most. He'd sell his own grandmother into slavery if the price was right, but all in all, he minded his own business and didn't cause trouble. No one had any idea why Hans had gone to Tahoe or where he was now. As for associates with tattoos, Kim might as well have been asking if they'd seen Hans in the company of someone with two eyes.

Kim held the phone away from her ear and rolled her shoulders, trying to loosen some of the tension. She was still smarting from her morning meeting with Danny Murphy. District attorneys did not enjoy having their case blown to bits by the very people who'd delivered it in the first place.

"What do you mean, new evidence?" Danny had scowled at her over the tops of his wire-frame glasses with eyes that bore right through her. Kim thought if she'd looked hard enough she might see steam coming from his ears. She'd been grateful for the buffer provided by his wide desk. "You guys are supposed to check the stuff like that *before* the arrest."

"We thought we had."

"You thought." He tossed his pen down in disgust. "It's not like you've got hard evidence that would lead us to someone else, either."

She'd nodded in agreement. What else could she do? "Ramon Escobar looked good for it. Arresting him was the right thing to do at the time." Not entirely true, but Kim wasn't going to start pointing the finger at Gary Bauman. "It's only in light of what we've learned since that—"

"Maybe if you'd pushed a bit," he snapped, "you'd have learned more earlier on. Instead you dump it in my lap and make me look like an idiot."

Kim knew he'd be the one to take the heat for dropping the charges. Assuming that's what he did. Sometimes it was easier to let a weak case go through the system.

"Issue a statement," she suggested. "Blame the sheriff's department if you want."

"If it were that easy, I would. No matter what I say, the public will come away with the impression the DA's office is soft on crime."

"Would you rather I hadn't told you about the gun? Let you make the discovery yourself in court?"

He sighed.

In the end, Danny Murphy had calmed down and even apologized. It was, he explained, a bad day in a particularly bad week. They'd parted on good terms.

Now Kim needed to focus on Hans Vogel. They couldn't afford to screw up again.

She'd punched in another telephone number while she was reliving her conversation with Danny. A male voice answered with anticipation. "Yeah."

Kim checked her list to remind herself which of Hans's friends she'd just called. "Mr. Triana?"

"Yeah?" Same response but different tone. Wariness in place of breezy informality.

Kim introduced herself. "I'm calling about Hans Vogel. I understand you're a friend of his."

"I know him."

"His family is worried because they haven't seen or heard from him for a while. I was hoping you might have some idea where he might be."

" 'Fraid not. His brother asked me the same thing."

"Does it seem strange to you, his disappearing like that?"

"This isn't the first time he's taken off without telling anyone."

Only this time his truck had been abandoned and he hadn't shown up for work. Kim was thinking that put a different spin on things. "Where did he go the other times?"

"I dunno. Traveling. He mighta had stuff to do."

"Stuff?"

"Yeah, like meetings or something."

Hans didn't strike Kim as the meeting type, but she let it go for the moment. "Did he ever mention a doctor by the name of Edward Blake?"

"Doctor? Is Hans sick?"

"No, Blake would be a . . . a business associate."

Triana snorted. "I don't think so. Doctors are outta his league."

"What about connections to Tahoe? He apparently went there a few days before he disappeared. Any idea why?"

"So that's where he went? He was hella secret about it. Said he had some business to attend to."

"What kind of business?"

"He didn't say."

Kim scratched Triana's name off her list and started doodling with her pencil in the margin. "Have you ever seen him with a man who has a tattoo on one hand?"

Triana hesitated. "Hand and not an arm?"

"Right."

"Funny you should mention that, because there was this dude not too long ago, an older guy."

"With a tattoo?" Kim stopped her doodling.

"Yeah. On his hand."

"What did it look like?"

"Black. Some kind of snake or something. Between his thumb and his first finger."

Excitement sparked in Kim's chest. "You have a name?"

"No. Hans and me were at the Hyatt downtown. By the Embarcadero."

"In San Francisco?"

"Yeah. We'd stopped in to use the rest room. As we were leaving Hans sees this guy he knows. He goes up to him and jokes,

'We have to stop meeting like this.' The guy looks at Hans like he's a three-headed frog. Practically mows into him trying to get away."

"That was it?"

"Pretty much." Triana paused. "I told Hans his friend was a real dickhead, and Hans said no, it was just that the guy was way too serious. And he wasn't a friend, anyway."

"Can you describe the man?"

"About five ten. Gray hair, thinning on top, cut short, kind of like a military cut. Oh, and he had a cast on one leg."

Kim remembered Kali had said the man she'd seen following her had a slight limp. And the physical description fit. She felt a surge of excitement. "Was the man staying at the Hyatt?"

"I don't know. He was dressed in a suit. There were a couple of big shindigs going on at the hotel, I got the impression he was there for one of them."

"And Hans never gave you a name or said anything about his connection with the man?"

"Nope. In fact, he seemed not to want to talk about the guy."

"Do you remember the date?"

Triana thought about it. "I'm pretty sure it was a Thursday. That's my day off. It was the last time I saw Hans, in fact, so it must have been right before he left town."

When she'd hung up, Kim rubbed her neck where it was stiff, switched the phone to the other ear and dialed the Hyatt. She was transferred several times until she reached someone who could give her the information she wanted. On the Thursday in question there'd been a funeral directors convention, a corporate retirement dinner, a private reception for something called the Mulhaney Group, and a dinner seminar on investment strategies for the new age. Of the people Kim spoke to at the desk, no one recalled seeing a guest in a leg cast.

She was about to start with the funeral directors when Gary Bauman appeared and sat in the chair next to her desk.

"I take it your meeting with Danny Murphy wasn't exactly pleasant," he said.

"Are you guessing or did he call you already?"

Bauman's mouth softened into what could pass for a smile. "He called. He was pretty reasonable, all things considered."

Kim nodded. "With me, too. After he calmed down. The good news is I think we may be on to something with Hans Vogel."

But before she could tell him about her conversation with Triana, Bauman handed her a fax.

"This just came in," he said. "Vogel isn't going to say much, I'm afraid."

Kim skimmed the fax, then read it again. A hiker with his dogs had discovered a body in the foothills outside of Sonora. Preliminary identification was that it was Hans Vogel.

CHAPTER 35

Faith felt like a junkie. She could think of nothing but calling Elliot's machine again. She needed to hear his voice, to fill the hollow deep inside her. And like a junkie, she knew what she was doing was harmful, even destructive, but the need was too great to ignore. She used a pay phone this time. It was outside the supermarket near her last cleaning job for the day. She punched the number, deposited the necessary coins, and settled in to wait four rings until the machine clicked on.

But a woman picked up after the first ring. "Hello?"

Faith was confused. Had she punched in the wrong number? "Hello? Is anyone there?"

Faith's breath caught. The woman on the other end sounded like Harriet DeVries, Elliot's mother. What would she be doing at her son's place in the middle of the day? And why was she answering his phone?

"Is it money you want?" Harriet's voice wavered. "We can pay. Just don't hurt him. Please."

Faith's scalp prickled. "Harriet?"

A beat of silence.

"Harriet, it's me. Irene. Where's Elliot? What's going on?"

"Irene! Where are you? Why did you—"

"Is Patrick sick? Why are you at Elliot's?"

"Oh, honey, I have terrible news. Elliot's in the hospital. Someone beat him up."

"Beat—"

"Badly." Harriet took an audible breath. "And Patrick is missing."

"What?" Fear sparked through Faith's body. "When did this happen?"

"Last night. At the clinic." It sounded like Harriet had to squeeze the words out. "Patrick was there with Elliot because I was going to a birthday dinner at a friend's house. If only I'd—"

Faith was impatient for facts. "They were both at the clinic?"

"Right. When the staff got there this morning they found . . ." Harriet took another gulp of air. "They found Elliot unconscious and Patrick gone."

Faith's stomach seized up. "Did you call the police?"

"Of course. It took us most of the day to convince them Patrick was kidnapped. They kept coming back to theories about a family argument."

Faith's head was pounding. She could feel the turbulence building inside her. Blake had gotten to Elliot in spite of everything! It was her fault.

Imagine losing what you love most.

"How badly is Elliot hurt?"

"He's alive, thank the Lord, but the doctors aren't sure about brain damage."

Faith gripped the phone hard. Sweet, gentle, Elliot. And Patrick. He was only nine years old, for God's sake. Anger swept over her, consumed her like a flame.

"I think I know who did this," she said.

"Who?"

"I'll explain when I get there."

"Where are you?" Harriet asked.

"On my way home."

Faith caught the last flight of the evening to Las Vegas. She'd gone to her apartment in Sacramento only long enough to gather her things, and bought a plane ticket using her credit card. So what if Blake traced her. She wanted him to.

She was tired of being on the run. Sick of death and pain and loss. And guilt.

Her car was still in the long-term lot at the Las Vegas airport where she'd left it, foolishly thinking she could cover her trail. She retrieved it and drove straight to the hospital, a sleek, modern-looking building that ignited an ember of hope in Faith's chest. The doctors who worked there would be among the best, wouldn't they?

She entered the carpeted lobby and found the visitor information desk which was, even at this late hour, staffed.

"I'm looking for Elliot DeVries," she told the gray-haired woman behind the desk. "He's in intensive care."

The woman checked the computer monitor. "Good news, honey. His condition has been upgraded. But visiting hours are over."

"I'm not visiting, I'm . . ." Tears filled Faith's eyes. Suddenly it was all too much.

The woman handed her a tissue. "He's in room four thirty-three," she said gently. "Take the elevator to your right."

"Thank you."

Faith found the room easily. The bed closest to the door was occupied by an older man who was wheezing loudly. The head of the patient in the second bed was so heavily bandaged and the face so bruised, Faith had to check the chart to assure herself it was Elliot.

She stood next to him, fighting the swell of tears. She touched his hand gently. At first he showed no reaction at all. Then one eye, purple and swollen, slowly opened.

"Irene?" It sounded as though he were talking with a mouthful of marbles.

"Yes, it's me." She pressed his hand to her face. "Oh, Elliot, I'm so sorry. About everything."

His mouth moved but the sounds that came out were unintelligible.

"Shh. Don't try to talk right now. You need to rest."

His lips moved again, this time to form a faint smile. Then his eye closed.

Faith sat in the plastic chair next to the bed. It was uncomfortable and the room was stuffy. But this was where she belonged.

She must have dozed because she woke to a lightened sky and the bustle of nurses on their morning rounds. A moment later, she heard movement in the doorway. Faith turned to find Harriet standing there.

"Irene? Is that you? You look . . . you've changed your hair."

"It's me." She hugged Harriet, then looked back at Elliot. "Is he going to be okay?" she whispered.

Harriet gestured toward the door and they moved into the hallway. "The doctors are 'cautiously optimistic,' " she said. "Whatever that means. They've got him pretty doped up right now, plus his jaw is wired shut. I guess we won't know more for at least a day or two."

"And what about Patrick? Do the police have any leads?"

"Oh, honey, God was looking out for him. They found him last night. Unharmed. He's with my daughter now."

"Did he say what happened?"

"I think whoever beat up Elliot wasn't expecting Patrick to be there. The man grabbed Patrick, shoved him in the trunk, and drove around the whole night. But he finally let Patrick go, dropped him off yesterday in an isolated spot outside of town. Luckily he was able to get to a main road and flag down a car."

"Can Patrick describe the man?"

Harriet shook her head. "The man took his glasses, and you know Patrick can't see a thing without them."

"He must have seen something, though. At least initially. Was the guy big, small? Caucasian?"

"A white guy. Older. With some kind of mark on his hand. But that's not enough to help the cops find him."

A lightness swelled behind Faith's breastbone. "Let's go have a cup of coffee, Harriet. There's a lot I have to tell you."

Sid dropped his chin to his chest as he pushed the trash cart along the hospital corridor. Avoiding contact with visitors and staff was turning out to be easier than he'd expected. No one was interested in the janitorial help.

Sid would have been happier passing as a doctor, but this was simpler to pull off and less likely to raise suspicions. Besides, he'd found a stack of janitorial greens, all freshly laundered, in the first supply closet he'd ducked into. He figured that was a sign that his luck had turned.

He'd caught a glimpse of Faith Foster earlier. She'd come running, just as he'd predicted. And much more quickly. Another sign that things were going right for a change.

She'd gone off for now with the old lady who'd been hovering around Elliot's bedside. His mother, no doubt. But Faith would be back, and he was ready for her. His plan was to wait until she left the hospital, then grab her. He had a handkerchief and a bottle of ether on hand. And his gun, of course.

All he needed was the right moment. At least he didn't have the damn kid to worry about anymore. It had been stupid to grab him. Sid should have known better. Having a hostage was nothing but a pain in the ass.

If all went well, Sid could finish off Faith today and take a late flight home. Tomorrow, he'd be back at work and his life could go on uninterrupted.

The cell phone in Sid's pocket began to vibrate. He ducked into the stairwell to answer it.

"Sid," Mr. D said. "How are you doing?"

"Just fine, sir."

"That messy little matter we talked about earlier, it's taken care of?"

Just about, Sid said to himself. Out loud he took a bolder stance. "Absolutely."

"That's good, Sid. I'd hate to see anything happen to you."

That makes two of us.

"Incidentally, the DA is letting that Mexican kid go. The one that got arrested for Betty Arnold's murder."

"They say why?"

"Insufficient evidence is what I hear. Judge McDougall got a courtesy call a little while ago since he was the victim's brother-in-law . . ." Mr. D paused. "He's in touch with some lawyer who claims to have seen Faith."

"Never trust a lawyer."

Mr. D didn't laugh. "Never trust anyone, Sid." The line went dead.

Sid heard footsteps coming up the stairway. He slid his phone back into his pocket just as one of the young interns charged past and continued up the stairs as though Sid had been invisible.

Sid wiped his brow with his sleeve. Jesus. Was it too late, already?

He worked his way back down the corridor, emptying trash as he went, always keeping an eye on Elliot's room. He heard the bing of the elevator door opening, and saw Faith and the old lady get off. They were deep in conversation and didn't even look in his direction.

Sid hoped Faith wasn't planning on spending the whole day at the hospital. He was itching to finish this job once and for all.

CHAPTER 36

The big, scar-faced guy in the exercise yard bumped against Ramon, jabbing an elbow into his ribs. Ramon flinched, stepped away, and tried to ignore what had happened. He was sure the guy had done it on purpose. This wasn't the first time.

Scar-face jostled him again. "What's the matter, you 'fraid to stand up for yourself?"

"I'm not interested in a fight," Ramon said.

He'd been leaning against the chain-link fence, enjoying his brief moment of fresh air and sun. It was funny how little things he'd taken for granted had assumed new importance. He looked longingly at the sky, turquoise blue and cloudless, and tried not to dwell on the fact that he might never see it outside the confines of a prison yard and the company of men like Scar-face.

"You a pussy?" Scar-face sprayed saliva when he talked but Ramon didn't dare wipe his face.

"Look, I don't want trouble. Just leave me alone."

The guy smiled, revealing a shiny gold front tooth. He stepped so close Ramon could feel the heat of his breath. "I like you, sugar. I'm thinking you could use some protection, know what I mean?"

Ramon felt fear thread through his veins. He glanced toward the guard, who was looking in the other direction. "I don't need protection," Ramon said, gathering the courage to look Scar-face in the eye. "Especially not from you."

"You be wrong about that, sugar." He ran a tongue over his lips. "You need me," he said slowly. "Just as bad as I need you."

Ramon swallowed. His mouth was so dry he almost choked.

Just then a voice came over the loudspeaker. "Escobar. Ramon Escobar. Report to the guard station."

Ramon stepped sideways. "That's me. I've got to go."

For a moment the guy didn't move, just continued to stare intently at Ramon. Then he relaxed. "I'll be seeing you, sugar."

His heart pounding in his chest, Ramon walked away without looking back. His stomach churned. What was he going to do next time? And the time after. The images that played before Ramon's eyes made him literally sick. He could taste the bile at the back of his throat.

"Warden wants to see you," the guard told Ramon. "Let's go."

"Why?"

His question met with silence.

News from his attorney? Or had something happened to his mother? Or Nadia? The mantle of fear drew tighter.

Inside the building, the guard cuffed Ramon's hands, then punched the security code to open the door into the main facility. Ramon followed him to an open area where a uniformed deputy met them.

"You've got a guardian angel, Escobar."

If he did, Ramon thought, she'd sure been asleep on the job. "What do you mean?"

"We're letting you go."

"I got bail?" Ramon took back all the nasty thoughts he'd had about Lamont. The guy must have been doing more than he let on.

"No bail. You're out of here. For good."

"Why? What happened?"

"You'll have to ask your attorney. I just follow orders. You're a free man." The deputy was unlocking the cuffs.

"I'm free to go? Just like that?" His head was swimming. It had to be a dream.

"Your clothing and personal items are in this plastic bag. Look through them, then sign here to show they're all accounted for. You can change in the room to your left."

So what if it was a dream, Ramon thought. He was going to enjoy it while it lasted. He changed quickly and the sheriff let him into a public lobby. His mother was there waiting. She threw her arms around him, crying loudly.

"*Hijo, estas aqui.* Let me look at you. Are you okay? My prayers have been answered."

Ramon sank into her familiar scent. "I'm really free to go? How did Lamont pull it off?"

She waved her arms, made a disparaging face. "Poo, he did nothing. It was the district attorney. He believe you now."

Ramon became aware of Helen standing behind his mother. "It's true?" he asked her.

"It's true. We'll explain on the way home."

"Where's Nadia? Does she know?"

"We tried reaching her," Helen said. "We thought she might want to come with us. But she's spending the night with a friend."

A cloud passed over Ramon's joy. A friend, or the baby-killing doctor in Reno?

Please, he prayed silently. Don't let it be too late.

When Kim leaned into Gary's Bauman's office, he was on the phone. She started to back away, but he motioned her in, then held up a finger to indicate he'd be free in a minute. He gestured to the chair and Kim sat down, using the interlude while he finished the call to watch him.

It was easy to see why she'd initially found him attractive. Why she still did, in fact. His craggy features were softened by laugh lines around his eyes and a mouth that slid easily into a sardonic smile. She'd been grateful he stood behind her on the Escobar thing, but she shouldn't have been surprised. That's the kind of man he was. Kim realized now she'd let her own personal discomfort with him color her thinking.

He hung up the phone. "Escobar's been released," he told her.

"The DA dropped the charge, then? I wasn't sure he would."

"I don't think we left him with much choice."

"That's sort of what I want to see you about," she said. "There are a couple of new developments. Maybe developments is too strong a word, but some interesting tie-ins have come to light."

Bauman leaned back, clasped his hands behind his head, and waited for her to continue.

"Remember I told you I'd talked to a friend of Hans Vogel who saw him at the Hyatt in San Francisco talking to a man with a tattoo on his hand?"

Bauman nodded.

"Betty Arnold's niece, Faith Foster, claims a man with a tattoo abducted her eight years ago and is following her still. He's apparently in Las Vegas right now, skulking around the hospital where Faith's current boyfriend was taken when he was beaten, supposedly by this same man."

Bauman dropped his arms to the desk and leaned forward. "How'd you learn that?"

"I got a call from the cops there. Also from the attorney, Kali O'Brien. She's been on this Faith Foster connection for weeks. I followed up with staff at the Hyatt, and I think there's a good chance the man was there with the Mulhaney Group."

"What's the Mulhaney Group?"

"As best I've been able to determine, it's a private foundation somehow connected with the support of Vietnam vets."

"I don't suppose you were able to get a name?"

"Sidney Mertz." Kim couldn't keep the grin from her voice.

Bauman nodded approval.

"What's more, Mertz served in the same division as Haskel, the guard at Folsom Prison who put the screws to Escobar's friend Willie Pinkus to get him to lie about the gun."

"Small world."

"Isn't it. I had Kali O'Brien listen to the answering machine tape from Hans Vogel's machine—his brother gave it to me—and she says it sounds like the voice she heard in the park when Betty Arnold was shot."

"So you're thinking Vogel was the shooter but Mertz was behind the whole thing?"

"Right. And most likely he was behind the earlier attempt on Faith Foster's life, too."

"But there's no way to pin Betty Arnold's murder on him?"

It was the entree she'd been hoping for. "I'd like permission to go to the Bay Area and follow up on a few things."

Bauman shot her a quizzical look. "How long will it take?"

"Just a day, I think. Maybe two."

He scratched his chin. "I have to tell you, getting authorization for travel is a headache these days."

"Not a problem. I can stay with a friend. Tomorrow's Friday. If I leave in the morning, I could use my own time over the weekend. That way it would only cost the department a day's absence."

His expression softened. "You're determined to break this case, aren't you?"

"I'd like to, yes."

He offered a faint smile. "I'd like to have you break it, Kim. Go ahead and take Friday. Let me know if you need more time."

"Thank you." She stood up to leave.

"Kim?"

"Yes?"

"I'm glad you're not angry at me anymore."

"I wasn't angry at you."

He raised an eyebrow. "It seemed that way."

"It was . . . is . . . complicated." Heck, she might as well get it off her chest. Clear the air. It was about time. "That night after the Christmas party when we . . . when I . . ." She looked at the floor, lowered her voice. "I drank too much, I guess. I don't remember what happened."

"You don't remember . . . any of it?"

Now she'd probably insulted him as well as making herself look foolish. "Well, I remember waking up in your . . . I remember where I woke up." Naked, she added silently. "Just not what came before that."

There was a look on his face she had trouble reading. "Really?" His voice was flat and oddly hollow. "You're not just saying that to spare my feelings?"

She gave him a puzzled look.

"What happened before isn't worth remembering," he said after a moment. His cheeks colored slightly. "I mean, there is nothing to remember. Guess maybe I drank a bit too much, myself."

She bit back a laugh but it escaped anyway.

Bauman joined in. "We're a sorry pair, aren't we?"

"Oh, dear. All this time you thought *I* was upset with *you*."

He nodded. "It hasn't been easy. I was sure you were snickering behind my back."

Yet he'd treated her fairly and professionally. In a friendly manner, in fact. Kim shook her head. "I was just embarrassed by my own behavior."

Gary Bauman met her eyes and smiled. "I'm glad we finally got that cleared up."

CHAPTER 37

From her chair at his bedside, Faith watched the rise and fall of Elliot's chest. She found the steady rhythm reassuring. He'd recognized her, she was sure he had. That, too, was a good sign. No matter that the doctors were cautious about predicting a full recovery, she wouldn't allow thoughts of anything less.

The afternoon was drawing to a close. Harriet had already gone home to be with Patrick, and Faith knew she couldn't put off the inevitable. She needed to talk to the Las Vegas cops, and to Blake. There was nothing more she could do for Elliot here anyway.

Faith stood, stretched, and ran a hand lightly over Elliot's shoulder. The man in the next bed was still wheezing loudly when she left the room. It was a godsend that Elliot was too medicated to notice.

She spoke briefly to the duty nurse, then started for the elevator, stepping around a custodian who was dry-mopping the floor. As she passed, he reached down to pick up a scrap of garbage from the floor and she caught sight of his hand. And the serpent tattoo near his thumb.

She let out an involuntary, hiccuplike yelp. Her legs turned to jelly.

Stay calm. Don't let him know you saw him.

Trying to appear natural, Faith stopped midstep, slapped her thigh as if she'd forgotten something, and turned back toward the nurses' station. Her heart was racing, her skin fiery. Terror sucked the air from her lungs. It was all she could do to keep from running.

A second nurse had joined the first. They were busy going over some sort of list on the computer.

"Please," Faith said. "Is that janitor familiar to either of you?"

"What?" It was the second, younger of the two who spoke.

"Don't be obvious, just tell me if you've seen him around before."

"I'm not sure. The custodial staff changes all the time." She turned her attention back to the computer screen.

"Call security."

The older nurse looked up, surprised.

"Call. Now."

"Ma'am, we can't—"

"It's a matter of life and death."

With a wary look at Faith, the younger nurse punched something into the telephone. Faith thought it likely the woman had called security because Faith herself seemed unstable. It didn't matter. What was important was that someone came.

She turned back. The man was gone.

Faith dashed down the hallway, peering into patient rooms. She checked the stairway landing.

An older Hispanic man in uniform appeared at the nurses' station. Faith saw the younger nurse point in her direction. Faith hurried to meet him.

"There's a man," she said breathlessly, "here at the hospital. He looks like a custodian, but he's not. He's dangerous. He's the one who beat the man in room four thirty-three."

The guard looked up and down the hallway.

"He was here," Faith explained frantically. "Just a minute ago. You can't let him get away."

"Let's not get hysterical, now."

"I'm not hysterical!" Faith's voice rose, contradicting her words.

The guard frowned. "What's the man look like?"

"There's a tattoo on his right hand." She'd been so focused on that, and not calling attention to herself, that she hadn't gotten a good look at his face. "He was about five-ten. Older but not old. Mid-fifties maybe. Caucasian. You need to post guards by the door to stop him from leaving."

He shook his head in apology. "The hospital has a lot of doors, ma'am. And a lot of fifty-year-old Caucasian visitors."

"What about the patient he beat up?"

"I can have someone look in now and then."

Now and then! This was ludicrous. "Call the police and tell them they need to come here immediately."

The guard frowned. "I can't call the police just because—"

A third nurse had joined the other two. She spoke up. "If there's any chance of trouble, we've got to take precautions."

The guard looked skeptical. Finally, he sighed and moved slowly toward the nurses' station. "Okay. Lemme use your phone."

While the guard was calling the police, Faith returned to Elliot's room. She checked his breathing. Steady still. She paced to the window and back, sat down, then jumped up again. She was agitated and scared. But inside that maelstrom of fear was a spark of something powerful and exhilarating. She'd been living too long on the run. Living like some cowering animal. No more.

She paced to the window and back. No more letting others dictate the boundaries of her life. She was a force to be reckoned with.

She picked up the bedside phone and used her calling card to call Blake's office. He'd be gone for the day but she knew he must have an answering service.

"I need to talk to the doctor," she said when the service picked up. "Immediately."

"Let me have your name and number."

"No, I need to talk to him now. It's important."

"Perhaps the advice nurse—"

"I'm not a patient," Faith explained. "This is personal. It concerns his daughter."

"His daughter?"

"Jessie."

The woman on the other end hesitated for a moment, then said, "Let me see if he's available."

Faith was put on hold to the not-so-soothing strains of a radio commercial. A few minutes later the commercial switched off and a phone picked up.

"This is Dr. Blake."

"This is Faith Foster, Dr. Blake."

"You said it was about Jessie. Has something happened?"

He apparently hadn't been listening when she said her name. She tried again. "I'm Faith Foster. Remember me?"

"Do I know y—" There was a moment of silence. "Jessie's old English teacher?"

"Right."

More silence. "It was you who caused all the ruckus. Damn near ruined me."

"It was also me you threatened."

"Threatened?"

"I bet Jessie never testified, did she?"

"Jessie is none of your business."

"Imagine losing what you love most. Remember?"

Blake let out a long breath. "I'm sorry to say I do."

"You tried to have me killed."

"Tried to have . . ." Now he sounded perplexed. "What are you talking about?"

"I escaped," she announced, triumphant.

"Escaped?"

"You sent your henchman to kill me but I got away. I got away from him the other day, too."

"What are you—" Another pause. "Jesus, I remember now. It was in the news. No wonder that attorney was asking about you. You were abducted or something, right?"

"Kidnapping and attempted murder, Blake. I know you had Andrew killed, and my aunt Betty. And you almost got Elliot. But I've called the cops. I'm going to tell them everything."

"I haven't the foggiest idea what you're talking about."

"I know you'll try to get revenge. But if you harm another person because of me, I swear, I will kill you myself."

"Look, I'm . . . I'm sorry about what happened before. I overreacted, I know that. But you practically destroyed me. I was angry."

"Attempted murder is quite an overreaction."

"Murder? I don't know where you're getting this stuff. I admit I lost my temper, said things I shouldn't have. And," he sighed, "and I tried to scare you off one evening. I totally lost it, I'll admit that. But you're nuts if you think I tried to kill you."

He was a good actor. Faith gave him credit for that. "Your friend with the tattoo is here right now. So are the police. They've got the building surrounded. He can't get away. And neither can you."

"I'm going to hang up now, Ms. Foster." Blake spoke slowly, like he was talking to a mental patient. "Any more calls like this, and I'll phone the cops myself. You understand?" The line went dead.

He was so smooth. Faith almost choked on her hatred.

She went to the door, looked into the hallway. No cops yet. The guard was there still at the desk. She caught his eye.

"They're on their way," he said. "And I alerted the front desk to keep an eye out for your custodian."

Might Blake actually get away with it? She couldn't let that happen. Faith pulled Kali's number from her purse and called. She had to talk to someone sane.

"Faith. I've been worried about you," Kali said. "I need to talk to you. Where are you?"

"Las Vegas, Sunrise Hospital. Elliot was badly beaten."

"What? How badly?"

"The doctors aren't sure. He's only semiconscious and they worry he might have some . . ." She hesitated voicing the words that so badly frightened her. "Some brain damage."

"How awful. I'm so sorry to hear that."

"I'm certain the man with the tattoo did it. I just saw him here at the hospital. I've called the cops, and Blake. The bastard pretended to know nothing about it."

"I think he might not."

"What?" Faith was sure she'd misunderstood. "He must know."

"I can't go into the details right now, but I have information that makes me think he's not involved in your aunt's murder. Maybe not in what happened before, either."

Blake *had* to be part of it. But already Faith's certainty was yielding to a fracture line of doubt.

"If not Blake," she asked, "then who?"

"That's what I wanted to ask you."

"I don't know. I'm . . ." Faith heard voices in the hallway, footsteps. "I have to go," she told Kali. "The cops are here. I'll call you back when I can."

Not Blake. Was it possible?

CHAPTER 38

It took Faith half an hour to explain the situation to the two cops who came to the hospital. Instead of letting her tell the story her way, they peppered her with questions about the man she'd seen posing as a custodian. From their reactions, she worried they wouldn't take her seriously, but in the end, they'd posted a guard outside Elliot's door and put hospital personnel on alert for suspicious behavior.

Faith had planned on returning to her own apartment for the night, but she was reluctant to leave Elliot's side, even with an officer on watch. Besides, she was safer at the hospital than she would be in her own bed. So she spent the night catnapping in an uncomfortable chair while Elliot moaned intermittently and the man in the next bed filled the room with loud, ragged snores.

Not that Faith would have slept much even in a comfortable bed. Her conversations with Blake and Kali had raised disturbing questions. And dredged up memories she'd rather have left undisturbed.

The horrifying events of her capture and escape; the grief and guilt about Andrew's murder reborn in her concern for Elliot; the mind-numbing fear of being hunted—now recast with the unsettling thought that Blake might not be behind it.

But he had to be. Dr. Blake was the only person Faith could imagine who might want her killed. She'd been a popular teacher. She had no angry ex-boyfriends and Andrew had no jealous exgirlfriends. Neither of them did drugs, owed money, or gambled beyond their means. Who else but Blake?

Maybe if the cops caught the man with the tattoo she'd have some answers.

And finally, peace of mind.

Kali lay in bed listening to the birds outside her window. They were chirping like crazy, welcoming the dawn of another day. It was only six o'clock, half an hour before her alarm was set to go off, but the dream she'd woken from had been so exhausting that wakefulness was an improvement. In the dream, she'd been back in school, madly trying to find the classroom for the final exam she'd forgotten to study for. Betty Arnold, Andrew Major, and Elliot DeVries were also in the class, and she kept thinking if only she could find one of them, she'd know she was in the right room. As she scrambled from building to building, she tried to pull together a mental outline of the course, but all she could remember was the instructor's admonishment to think outside the box. She'd woken with a racing heart and a tight chest.

Pulling the comforter around her shoulders, Kali curled into the warmth of her bed and took a moment to savor the discovery that she was truly free of the dreaded exam. The pounding in her chest subsided, but the shadow of her dream remained, tugging at the edges of her mind.

Think outside the box, indeed. She'd been listening to too many commercials.

She closed her eyes, let her mind drift, rolled onto her back. And then she sat upright.

If Blake was out of the picture, that changed everything. Faith had assumed he'd tried to have her killed because of Jessie. And that he'd killed Andrew to avenge Faith's escape. What if it wasn't about Faith at all? What if Andrew Major was the prime target?

Okay, so Kali had broken out of the box. An interesting shift in perspective, but it didn't help much. Why would the killer be after Faith as well as Andrew? Why would he *still* be hunting her down? And where did Betty Arnold fit?

Kali slipped the alarm button to off, rolled out of bed, showered, and headed for the office. She made herself a cup of coffee, then sat at the computer and ran Andrew Major's name through the legal search program, Lexus. He was the attorney of record on close to a dozen cases, but on the surface at least, none appeared to hold potential for murder. Of course he was probably involved in ten times as many matters that didn't reach adjudication. Financial matters Marsha Nix had said. Money was always a good motive for murder.

Or maybe Kali was jumping the gun. Andrew Major's death was officially a suicide.

She waited until eight before calling the hospital in Las Vegas. She wasn't sure Faith would be there but it was the only way Kali had of reaching her. Luckily, Faith picked up right away.

"You spent the night there?" Kali asked.

"I thought it was best."

"Any news?"

"Not that I've heard. I'm not sure how long they'll keep a cop posted outside the door, though." Faith sounded exhausted.

"I've been thinking," Kali said. "Maybe the killer was after Andrew, not you."

"Andrew?" She sounded confused. "Why try to kill me, then?"

"I don't know. Maybe to send a message. Or maybe you were supposed to be taken hostage."

"No, he was definitely going to kill me."

Kali reminded herself that Faith had been certain Blake was behind it, too. If she was wrong about one thing, couldn't she be wrong about the other? "Did Andrew have any enemies?"

"He was a lawyer. I guess there could be people who had it in for him. And he was . . . well, he sometimes came across as arrogant. His attitude pushed a few buttons. But I can't imagine anyone would kill him for it."

"He was the golden boy of the associates, wasn't he?"

"Ye-es." The word was drawn out, delivered with skepticism. "But again, I can't believe that would be a reason to kill him. Or me."

Kali thought the same thing but she was hoping to trigger something in Faith's mind that would offer up a clue. "What about cases he was working on? Or deals? Do you remember what he was working on at the time?"

"There was a merger, I think, and some kind of dispute over airport access. And then some estate settlement he was doing for the sister of one of the firm's big clients. Bunny Bradford was the woman's name. I remember because it sounded like it belonged to a stripper and not some seventy-year-old society matron."

"Can you recall the names of companies involved in the merger or the airport matter?"

"Andrew didn't talk much about his work. The last couple of weeks before everything happened, he was more . . . more full of himself than usual, but jumpy, too. I thought maybe he'd been told he'd make partner early. But it could have been one of his cases." She paused. "Lowell might know. Andrew sometimes conferred with him about work."

"Have you called him yet?" Kali didn't want to talk to Judge McDougall until after Faith had.

"I finally did, yesterday. I kept putting it off because I was nervous."

"What did he say?"

"He wasn't in so I left a message. I figured it was better that way. Let him get used to the idea that I'm really alive. It's going to be tough making him understand why I let everyone think I was dead all those years."

"I told him about seeing your photo," Kali offered, "so it won't be a total shock."

"Still, there's going to be lots of explaining."

"But the bottom line is, you're alive. And that's good news."

CHAPTER 39

The minute that stupid bitch Faith Foster returned to the nurses' station, Sid had known something was up. He should have taken his chances and grabbed her right then.

At least he'd managed to slip away unnoticed, sneaking out through the emergency exit just as a police cruiser pulled up to the main entrance. Sid had gone to his parked car and slouched down so that his line of vision was just above the dash. From there, he'd been able to keep an eye on both the hospital and Faith's car. Finally, at midnight, Sid had decided she wasn't leaving. He'd gotten himself a room at a nearby motel and fallen asleep immediately. Now, with his breakfast of coffee and Egg McMuffin on the seat beside him, he was back in the parking lot with a clear view of Faith's car. It still hadn't been moved.

Doing away with her wasn't going to be the tidy housekeeping detail he'd initially planned for. Too many people knew she was alive, for one thing. And she knew he was after her.

Well, all he could do was take it one step at a time.

The chirp of Sid's cell phone startled him. He answered, then immediately wished he hadn't. "Judge McDougall. Hello, sir."

"Sid, I'm glad I was able to reach you. I know you're a busy man, but I could use your help."

"Of course."

"How soon can we get together?"

"I'm tied up for the next couple of days. In fact, I'm out of town."

The judge acted like he hadn't heard. "How about this evening?"

"This evening? I'm afraid—"

"Sid, I've never asked for special favors before. I'll make it worth your while."

"I'm hundreds of miles away."

"How far from an airport?"

"It's still kind of—"

"Three thousand just for coming by the house this evening."

Three thousand. Sid saw dollar signs dancing before his eyes. The sum had a sweet sound to it. And Faith wasn't going anywhere in the next forty-eight hours. In fact, a break might be good. Give her a chance to relax a little, and let her defenses slip.

"I'll be there," Sid told him.

"Thanks, Sid. I knew I could count on you."

Every time the phone rang, Ramon hoped it was Nadia. Her mother had said she'd pass along his message as soon as her daughter came home, which should be any time now. She was only spending the night with a friend in Reno and she was expected back at work tomorrow. Ramon had tried to reach her at the friend's house, too, but there was no answer. He knew in his gut she hadn't gone to Reno to visit anyone. She'd gone for an abortion.

"You want tamales for dinner?" his mother asked. "Or maybe pot roast." Two of his all-time favorites. At the moment, they both had the appeal of sawdust.

"Don't go to any trouble, Mom."

"Trouble? My son is out of jail. What trouble is dinner?" She waved her arms. *"Vamos a festijar."*

She wanted to celebrate. Ramon flipped a mental coin. "Pot roast," he said. Now maybe she'd stop hovering.

She beamed. "With that bean casserole you like so much."

"That would be good."

"You want pie for dessert? I saw berries in the—"

The phone rang and Ramon pounced on it.

"Is it true?" Nadia said softly. "They let you go?"

"No trial, even. I guess they realized they'd made a mistake."

"Oh, Ramon. I'm so glad."

"Nadia, did you—"

"I can't talk right now. Meet me by the dock in half an hour. Okay?"

They were the longest thirty minutes of Ramon's life. He paced around the house for ten of them, then went to their spot near the dock and skipped rocks across the blue surface of the water until he saw Nadia approach. She was wearing jeans and a Cal sweatshirt. Her head scarf had slipped back and caught on her ponytail.

Ramon felt suddenly shy around her. "How are you?"

She kissed him lightly on the cheek. "Happy to see you."

He took her hand and led her to the old stump. He was unprepared for the swell of emotion in his chest. "I missed you."

"Was it terrible in jail?"

"The worst parts were in my mind. Worrying about what would happen at the trial, what it would be like to spend the rest of my life locked up, what might happen while I was there." He traced a finger over her palm. "And worrying about you. You went to Reno for an abortion, didn't you?"

She nodded.

He felt a crushing weight as though he were suddenly caught in a vise. He dropped his head to his hand.

"I couldn't go through with it, though," Nadia said. "At the last minute, I just couldn't. I . . . I needed to think about it some more."

The vise became a feather. "The baby's still alive?"

"It's not a baby yet. It's just some . . . cells or something." She started to cry.

"Then why—"

"I don't know. I'm so mixed up. I want to go to college, study to be a doctor. I want to do good. To help people and make the world a better place. I can't do that if I have a baby."

"Yes, you can. I'll take care of you. I promise. I'll work as many jobs as it takes. My mother can watch the baby. She loves babies."

"You're such a dreamer." Nadia was crying harder now. "But I love you, anyway. And this . . . these *cells* will grow into our child. How could I study to save lives and do good knowing I'd killed my own child? My whole life would be a lie."

He gathered her into his arms and held her. "Don't you see, our dreams, they're the same. We can do it, Nadia."

"There's so much to think about. I don't want to rush into it just yet."

There was still time. Ramon's heart filled with hope. Sitting in jail, he'd told himself that time was all he needed to convince her. Maybe now he could.

CHAPTER 40

McDougall had called Kali's office Thursday after she'd left for the day. She returned his call Friday morning.

"I got a phone message," he said without preamble. His voice sounded strained. "Someone claiming to be Faith. I would have written it off as a prank except that you'd already told me about that photo Betty saw." He was quiet a moment. "Do you think it might really have been Faith who called?"

Kali took a breath. "It *was* Faith. I saw her last Sunday. We talked."

"My God. She's . . ." He hesitated. "She's really alive?"

McDougall sounded like he was having trouble taking it in. Kali didn't blame him. The news had to be a shock. "What happened?" he asked. "Where's she been?"

"It's a long story. Best explained in person, I think."

"Where is she now? She didn't leave a callback number."

Faith had asked Kali not to give away her location, but that was before Faith herself had announced that she'd returned to Las Vegas. She probably no longer cared, but Kali knew she'd contact McDougall when she was ready. Better to leave it in Faith's hands.

"I don't have a number, either," Kali said. "She wanted to keep her location private for reasons of safety."

"What do you mean, safety?"

"Somebody tried to kill her eight years ago. He's still after her. She thinks he killed Andrew and Betty, as well, to get at her. She's worried about your safety as much as her own."

"Killed Betty?" His voice faltered. "But why—"

"Maybe we could discuss this in person. I'd really rather not go into it all over the phone. Besides, I have a couple of things I'd like to run by you."

"This is . . . is unbelievable. How can Faith be alive?"

"When can we meet? Any time is fine with me. My schedule is flexible."

"I'm in court all day. I've got someone coming over in the evening . . ."

A woman, Kali suspected, given the tentative thrust of his words.

"On the other hand, I'm eager to talk to you." He hesitated. "I hate to ask you to drive here again, but it would be the easiest."

"I don't mind."

"If you're sure—Around six, then? We'll have time to talk before my guest arrives."

"Fine. See you this evening."

Kim had gotten an early start Friday morning on her trip down to the Bay Area. She'd called her roommate from college who was now living in San Rafael and made arrangements to stay with her. Nancy had a husband now and a baby, and Kim was looking forward to spending time with them. But first, she had to get through a long day ferreting out what she could about Sid Mertz.

By that afternoon, without yet talking to the man, Kim had learned quite a bit about him. He was fifty-four years old, never married, and ran a security consulting firm catering to midsize companies. She knew his bank balance, credit history, educational background, and health status. Nothing remarkable about any of them. She'd spoken to a couple of his clients—the president of Coast Savings and Loan and to the operations manager of E-Z Stop—who gave him high marks for his work in overseeing their security procedures. Both confirmed that Mertz had a tattoo on his right hand. Neither had ever heard the name Hans Vogel nor did they recognize his photo.

Kim checked the address of the next name on her list. Otis Meyer Advertising on the twelfth floor of the Embarcadero Tower. She made sure she'd found the correct bank of elevators, then pressed the button. Given the late hour, this would probably be the last of the business contacts for today. Tomorrow she'd talk to Mertz's neighbors and to members of the Mulhaney Group.

The receptionist looked up when Kim pushed through the wide plate-glass office door.

"May I help you?" the woman asked. She was young, with a wide, toothy smile.

"I'm with the Placer County sheriff's department. I'd like to speak to whoever is in charge."

"Uh, there's really no one here right now. Except me, that is."

Kim raised an eyebrow. "No one?"

The receptionist made a show of crossing her heart. "Honest. They're all at an off-site strategy session. Can I help?"

"I'm interested in the security consultant your company works with, Sid Mertz."

"Yeah, I know him. He was here just last week."

"What kind of security service does he provide?"

"For us, it's mostly computer stuff. We can't have our competitors knowing what we're up to." She grinned. "It's a cutthroat business. Or so everyone seems to think. And last year when one of the secretaries was getting divorced, we had some problems with her husband. Mr. Mertz took care of that, too."

"Took care of?"

"Assigned a guard to our reception area. He also talked to the husband, made it clear the guy needed to stay away. I know he does private parties and such, too. That's how Mr. Meyer . . ." She curled her fingers in the air like quote marks. ". . . as in Otis Meyer Advertising, first connected with him. His friend, the judge, uses Mr. Mertz."

Kim pulled out her notebook. It might be worth talking to one of Mertz's private clients as well as his business clients. "Do you know the name of this friend?"

"McDougall is the last name. I don't know his first name. Mr. Meyer always calls him Judge."

Kim jotted down the name. There was something familiar about it. She struggled to make the connection—a case she'd worked on? A newspaper article?

Then it hit her. Judge McDougall was Faith Foster's stepfather.

Now there was an interesting coincidence. One definitely worth looking into further.

Sid poured the serving-size bottle of Jack Daniel's into his plastic airline glass. He'd planned on sticking to soda water, but when he discovered the seat next to him was occupied by—make that overflowing with—a woman so large she'd had to request a seat-belt extender, he knew the only way he'd get through the flight was to temper his nerves with whiskey. Even then, it was going to be a challenge. He'd bumped his elbow into her fleshy midsection more than once just opening his bottle.

He'd been looking forward to peanuts but found his foil packet contained tropical trail mix instead. Coconut and dried papaya. Not his idea of an edible snack under any circumstances. Sid was hungry but he'd have to wait until he got into San Francisco and pick up a bite to eat there.

As the flight leveled out at cruising altitude, Sid slipped on his headphones, leaned back, and tried to imagine how he'd spend the three grand McDougall had offered simply for meeting. Only fleetingly did he wonder what the job entailed. Something out of the ordinary, given the urgency of the request. Sid's previous work for the judge had been fairly mundane. Parties, private events, an occasional stint as a bodyguard.

With the notable exception of that one other matter, of course.

CHAPTER 41

Friday afternoon traffic was worse than Kali expected and she arrived at McDougall's house almost half an hour late.

She apologized profusely when he greeted her at the door. "I thought I'd allowed plenty of time."

"You can never tell what the roads are going to be like." He stood back. "Come in. Can I get you something to drink?" He was holding what looked like scotch on the rocks.

"Do you have wine already open?"

"Both red and white. Which would you prefer?"

"White, thanks." She usually drank red, but McDougall's light beige carpet made her nervous about spilling.

He went to the bar at the far end of the room and poured her a generous glass. She took it and sat in the same chair where she'd sat the last time she'd visited. McDougall sat across from her on the couch.

"Now tell me what's going on," he said. "I have so many questions I don't know where to begin."

"I'm sure you do. I have to warn you, though, I don't have all the answers." Kali sipped her wine. It was cold and smooth. Some kind of pinot grigio if she had to guess.

She told him how Faith had been abducted and had escaped. How Blake had threatened her and how she'd held him responsible for Andrew's death and then Betty's.

"Betty's murder?" McDougall frowned.

"That was Faith's assumption. I have information now that makes me think Blake wasn't involved. Maybe not in what happened eight years ago, either."

"And you say this man, whoever he is, is still after Faith?" McDougall had grown pale, like a ghost of himself.

Kali nodded. "He followed us on Sunday, after planting listening devices in my house and office. And he apparently beat up the man Faith's been seeing recently. Put him in the hospital."

McDougall brushed a hand across his forehead, then he rose, went to the bar and poured himself another drink. He stood with his back to Kali for a few moments while he took a hearty swallow.

"Have you talked to Faith recently?" he asked, returning to his seat.

"Not since I spoke to you the other day. She mentioned that Andrew Major sometimes talked to you about the cases he was working on. I'm wondering if any of them might be pertinent."

"Pertinent?"

"To what happened. I know it's a stretch, but except for Blake, Faith can't think of anyone who would want her dead. Andrew, on the other hand . . ."

McDougall sat forward. "Did Faith suggest that?"

"No, it came to me the other night. According to Faith, he was working on a merger, something involving airport access, and the settlement of an estate. Bunny Bradford, the widow, was the sister of one of the firm's clients."

McDougall shook his head. "If he mentioned anything about them, I've forgotten. Certainly there was nothing that stood out at the time."

The doorbell rang and McDougall got out of his chair. "Excuse me for a moment."

Kali saw him open the door and say a few words to the man standing there before ushering him into the foyer. McDougall returned to the living room to pour a glass of tonic water from the bar. "I'll be right back," he told her. "Just let me get my guest settled in the den."

While McDougall was at the bar, Kali studied the man in the foyer. He looked familiar. Then her eyes caught the dark markings on his hand. A shiver snaked down her spine.

The man with the tattoo.

Kali's lungs closed down. What was he doing at Judge McDougall's? Had *he* recognized *her*?

She turned her head quickly away, forced herself to breathe. As soon as McDougall showed his visitor to the den, Kali was out of her chair. When McDougall returned, she was waiting.

"Who is that man?" she demanded.

"Sid? He's someone who does security work for me occasionally. Why?"

"It's him, the man who tried to kill Faith. The one who is still after her."

"What? Are you sure?" McDougall looked as if he'd been hit with a jolt of electricity.

"It's him," Kali said. "We have to call the police."

"I don't know . . ." McDougall said uneasily. "I mean, let's think about this."

"There's nothing to think about. Call them."

"And say what? I really think—"

Just then the man appeared in the doorway, the glint of metal in his hand.

A gun. Fear grabbed Kali, sucking the air from her lungs. She felt again the searing heat of the bullet that had slammed into her in the Tahoe parking lot.

"Sorry, Judge," the man said, "but you know you can't make that call."

"Put that thing down, Sid. Let me handle it."

A whimper was working its way up Kali's throat. She fought it back.

"No way," Sid said. "You'd turn me in."

McDougall ran a hand through his hair. His face was pinched. "It's true?" he said finally. "It was you?"

Kali tried to catch McDougall's gaze. They were two against one. If they acted in concert they might be able to overtake this guy Sid. But McDougall never looked her way.

"Let's focus on the present," Sid said.

"Okay, the present."

Kali's legs felt wobbly. Her heart was pounding. "Don't make matters worse," she said, addressing the man with the gun. "If you kill us—"

"Shut up." He turned to McDougall. "What are we going to do about her?"

"About Kali?"

"Seems like the only choice we got is to put her away for good."

The man's words echoed in Kali's ears. They weren't right. And his tone was wrong. "What did he mean, *we*?"

"I never knew it was you," McDougall said quietly.

"You weren't supposed to know. Does it matter?"

McDougall rubbed his jaw. He had the bewildered look of a man who'd just been struck by a punch he hadn't seen coming. "Faith's been alive all this time. She wasn't killed, she—"

"She got away from me."

"Got away?"

"She never caused any problem though, right? Dead or alive, you got what you wanted."

"What I—"

Sid waved the gun at McDougall. "Don't try to pull any holier-than-me shit. You asked me here tonight because you had a job for me. It was Faith, right? You'd learned she was alive and you wanted it taken care of."

"I—"

"You're hardly one to point the finger, McDougall. I've known all along it was you who ordered the hits. Faith and her fiancé, right?"

Kali's blood turned to ice. McDougall was part of it? She turned to look at him. His eyebrow twitched rhythmically.

"How did you know? I thought—"

"That Mr. D would keep it quiet?" Sid smiled. "That's the beauty of the system, isn't it? But sometimes there are slip-ups."

Kali looked quickly around the room. No place to hide. No easy escape. She inched closer to the fireplace. There was a poker there. It would be useless against a gun but what other choice did she have?

"Does Mr. D know she's alive?" McDougall asked at last.

"He didn't until you told him. It was just a minor housekeeping detail until Ms. Bigmouth here"—he gestured toward Kali—"got herself involved. So I repeat, what do you want to do about her?"

"Not my problem, Sid. You're the one who fucked up."

"With all due respect, sir, it *is* your problem."

"You've got no proof of anything."

"My word against yours, you mean?" Sid snickered. "Not only do we have our witness here"—another gesture toward Kali—"though we can take care of her easy enough. But there's also the tape Major stumbled across. You talking with Wex Bradford, right-hand man to the mob."

McDougall's face blanched. "I thought . . . Mr. D said it had been destroyed."

"The original, yeah." Sid's lips curled. "But not the copy I made."

"You *what*?" McDougall's eyes narrowed. "Where is it?"

"It's safe. One last time, what do you want to do about this lawyer bitch? Way I see it is, we need to get her away from your place before we kill her. That's added protection for you."

"You're so thoughtful, Sid." McDougall's words were encrusted with sarcasm.

The two men were talking as though Kali weren't there, but they were both watching her closely. She'd never make it to the fireplace poker. Better to wait until they tried to take her away and then make a run for it.

"I know a couple of places we could dump her. First thing, though, we got to get her out of here without anyone seeing."

"Let me think a moment," McDougall said. He ran his hands through his hair. "You want a drink?"

"No thanks."

"I'm going to freshen mine if you don't mind."

"Go ahead."

McDougall moved slowly to the bar as though he were sleepwalking. Sid stepped back to keep them both in his line of vision, but the gun stayed aimed at Kali.

"Who else knows about the tape?" McDougall asked.

"Relax, nobody knows but me. I don't suppose you have any ether in the house? Or heavy-duty tranquilizers?"

McDougall plunked ice cubes into his glass. "Not that I can think of. What about the tape? If it falls into the wrong hands . . ."

"It won't. Trust me. You do have duct tape, don't you?"

McDougall opened the cabinet door and reached for the bottle of scotch. He bent low, then straightened and spun around suddenly, darting behind Sid. In place of a cocktail glass, his hand held a gun. He pressed it against Sid's back.

"Drop it, Sid."

Kali couldn't breathe. Sid's gun was still pointed squarely at her. She wasn't sure who was going to shoot first. Any way it went down, she was likely to be hit.

Sid angled his head. "What are you doing, Judge? We're on the same side here."

"I didn't fuck up, Sid. And I didn't try to double-cross anyone either."

"You mean the tape? That was no double-cross. *I* never tried to blackmail you with it, did I? Don't go putting me in the same category as Major."

"Just drop the gun, Sid. Then we'll talk."

"What's to talk about? You wanted Major stopped before he exposed you. Seems to me you got no complaints."

"Get rid of the gun. Now."

Sid hesitated. He lowered his arm. The minute his eyes left Kali, she knew what was coming.

Sid jerked to the left and spiraled to face McDougall.

Gunfire exploded.

Kali jumped. She ducked behind a large club chair, her heart hammering in the echoing silence that filled the room. The acrid smell of gunpowder burned her nostrils.

She heard a groan, then raspy breathing. Carefully, she peeked from behind her hiding place.

Sid lay on the floor, twitching. A pool of blood was forming on the hardwood floor. McDougall was slumped against the wall, his face ashen white.

But the gun was still clutched in his hand.

Friend or foe? Kali wondered. Should she risk making a dash for the phone? Did she dare risk even giving away her location? She crouched there, still as a mouse. Her muscles cramped. She fought the tickle in her throat, terrified that if she moved or made a sound, McDougall would shoot her.

She heard a shuffling sound, like he was attempting to stand. More racked gasping for air.

A charley horse clamped Kali's calf. She shifted slightly but audibly.

McDougall fired. Once and then again. The shots skimmed the back of the chair, barely missing the top of her scalp.

Kali's heart thumped against her ribs. She could hear the

pounding in her ears. The pounding grew louder and she real-ized it wasn't entirely in her head. There was someone knocking loudly at the door.

Kim had debated the wisdom of arriving at Judge McDougall's home unannounced, but he'd left his chambers at the courthouse by the time she tried to reach him there and she had to head north anyway to get to Nancy's. When she'd pulled up to his house, she'd been relieved to find lights on and signs of movement in-side. For all she'd known, he might have stayed in the city after work.

She approached the front door and knocked. No response. She was about to knock again when she heard a sharp burst of what sounded like gunshots.

Kim felt a rush of adrenaline. She cursed her luck at being out of her own district, where a simple push of a button would bring backup. She grabbed her cell phone and quickly punched in 9-1-1.

Then she drew her gun and listened. The house was abnor-mally quiet. Part of her wanted to wait for the local cops to arrive, but she knew someone inside might be in danger.

Standing off to the side, out of direct gunfire range, she knocked again, harder. "Police, open up."

A woman's voice yelled, "He's got a gun." Another clap of gun-fire followed.

Kim's decision was made. She tried the door. Locked. With sharpened senses, she moved silently up the side of the house in search of a window. What she found were French doors offering a clear view of the living room.

She was struck first by the blood. There were spatters on the back wall, a puddle spreading out from under a fallen male body, and more blood covering a second male—who was still clutching a gun.

And then she saw the woman crouched behind a chair. It took a moment before Kim recognized her as the attorney in the Arnold shooting, Kali O'Brien. Odds were, one of the men was Judge McDougall but Kim hadn't a clue which one.

Another shot. One which came precariously close to hitting Kali. Kim crept around the corner of the house and found an open window. She popped the screen and climbed through. Not as quietly as she would have liked. She hoped she hadn't announced her presence to the man holding the gun.

Kim slipped down the hallway, thankful for the massive oriental runner that muffled her footsteps. She entered the room by a doorway to the right of the injured man.

"Police. Drop the gun," she shouted.

At first the man with the gun didn't respond. Then he turned slightly and awkwardly attempted to raise his arm.

"Drop it!" In all her years as a cop, Kim had drawn her gun only twice, and she'd never shot anyone. Her throat burned at the thought she might be forced to pull the trigger.

The man's arm wavered, then fell to the floor. He released his grip on the gun.

"Push it away from your body," Kim said.

He made a small motion with his arm, nudging the gun a few feet to the side.

"You'll have to do better than that."

"I can't. My arm won't move any farther."

Kim had role-played this very scene at the academy. Only then she'd been the injured victim planning an ambush. "Keep your hands right where they are. You move even a fraction of an inch and I'll kill you. You got that?"

"I understand."

"Are you okay?" she yelled to Kali.

"I'm not hurt."

"Is there anyone else here?"

"Not that I'm aware of."

"Stay back until I get his gun." Perspiration gathered on the back of Kim's neck. She held her weapon so tight she was half afraid she'd set it off accidentally. But she managed to get close enough to kick the injured man's gun out of his reach.

Kali stood from behind the chair. "The man who talked to you is Lowell McDougall. The other man is Sid something. He's the one who tried to kill Faith Foster."

"Sid Mertz," Kim said. Her words were drowned out by the screech of approaching sirens.

CHAPTER 42

Faith gripped the phone. She was still reeling from the impact of Kali's words. It hadn't been Blake who wanted her killed. It was Lowell. She'd been wrong all along.

And now it was over. Faith was too much in shock to feel any relief.

She finally found her voice. "Lowell was taking bribes?" She'd never have imagined such a thing. "Why?"

"The slippery slope of wrongdoing," Kali replied. "To listen to him, anyway. The first time it was just a little thing, but then they had him. He had to continue doing their bidding or risk exposure."

"And he actually confessed?"

"I think he realized he didn't have much choice. He's trying to work out a deal. Cooperate with the authorities. But from what I understand, he doesn't know a lot. Everything was handled very arm's length. They want names and Lowell can't supply them."

"The man with the tattoo," Faith said. "Lowell knew him."

"Knew him, yes. But only as someone who worked security. He didn't know Mertz was the one who'd been sent to kill you. That was handled through an anonymous Mr. D. And Mertz is dead so he's not any help."

"But Lowell must . . . I mean, how did he contact this Mr. D? How did he get his bribe money? He must know something."

"Like I said, it was all handled at a distance. Calls to pay phones, anonymous drops for the money. Lowell would occasionally meet a courier, but he doesn't have any names."

Faith's stomach felt sour. She'd always felt genuine affection for her stepfather. "You're saying all Lowell had to do to have me killed was make a phone call? This Mr. D handled the rest?"

"In a nutshell, yes. Andrew found out Lowell was taking bribes, and threatened to blackmail him. Lowell told Mr. D, who was the person who'd contacted him in the past about needing inside information or favors."

"What kind of information?" Faith was still trying to reconcile the Lowell McDougall she'd always respected with this new information.

"Details of a grand jury investigation," Kali said. "A favorable ruling. That sort of thing. Lowell claims it didn't happen often."

"How did Andrew know that Lowell was being bought?"

"The estate he was handling when he was killed. Bunny Bradford. You told me about her, remember?"

Faith was confused. "What does that have to do with anything?"

"Mrs. Bradford's late husband was one of Lowell's contacts when he was handing over information. Bradford got Lowell on tape talking about the bribes. The tape ended up in his estate among the boxes of stuff Mrs. Bradford dumped on Andrew." Kali made a hoarse sound, almost like a bark. "What's crazy is, here's this guy Bradford who's like an assistant to the mob, and he keeps evidence like that in a shoebox in his bedroom closet."

"And rather than turn it over to the authorities, Andrew tried to blackmail Lowell."

"Right."

Faith sucked in a breath. "That's why Andrew was so full of himself in those last weeks. He thought he'd found a gold mine."

"Probably. The really unfortunate part is that he told Lowell you were part of it."

"What! I didn't know anything about his dirty scheme." Faith felt doubly betrayed. Her stepfather had tried to have her killed and her fiancé had set it in motion by implicating her. All this time, she'd been feeling guilty for what happened to Andrew when it was really the other way around.

"I figured you didn't," Kali said, "or you wouldn't have been so sure it was Blake who was after you."

"So he's completely . . . innocent?"

"Of trying to have you killed, yes. The FBI has arrested him on drug charges and Jessie is going to turn state's evidence."

"On the abuse charge?"

"On the drug charges. She was helping him, though at a very peripheral level."

"Oh, God." Faith had a flash image of the defenseless girl who'd been in such pain eight years ago. "I was hoping that she would be okay."

"She may be someday. She's young yet and she's doing the right thing now. How is Elliot?"

"It's going to be a long road to recovery, but the doctors are feeling more hopeful he'll make it." Looking at him, Faith sometimes had doubts. But then he'd squeeze her hand or follow her with his eyes, and she'd sense that he was right there, whole again in every way but for the broken bones.

"And Patrick?"

"Shaken, but more by what happened to Elliot than the kidnapping. Or maybe he's still just in shock."

"I'll be rooting for both of them."

"Thanks, Kali. For everything."

Kali hung up the phone feeling oddly drained. So many lives turned upside down for so little. McDougall hadn't needed the money. Hadn't even wanted it in the end, if he was to be believed. He claimed he hadn't wanted Faith and Andrew killed either, that he'd simply told Mr. D that Andrew had a tape. Kali didn't believe it. Everything the man had done or said was self-serving. Whatever deal he cut, she hoped he ended up behind bars for a long time.

She massaged her injured shoulder as she leaned back in her most comfortable living room chair and stared out at the fog blowing through the Golden Gate. Her own life had been among those affected. She was angry about the toll it had taken. And she was saddened by Betty's senseless death. But mostly what she felt was a shadow of vulnerability that had changed her personal landscape forever.

The phone rang. Kali picked it up, half expecting it would be Faith with some question she'd forgotten to ask.

Instead, it was Bryce, who'd stayed with her last night, holding her until she fell asleep, and then gotten up early to bring her breakfast in bed.

"Hi," he said, managing to convey a lot of affection in one short syllable. "How are you doing?"

"Pretty good. Did I thank you for taking such good care of me?"

"I don't know," he said, teasing. "But you certainly showed your appreciation."

"Deeds speak louder than words."

"Yeah, my mom used to say that. I thought you'd want to know pieces are coming together on Sid Mertz and Hans Vogel. The guard who put the heat on Willie Pinkus to get him to lie about the gun is spilling his gut, trying to save his neck."

"Does he know much?"

"Enough. Turns out Sid Mertz was hoping to use Betty Arnold to locate Faith. He hired Vogel because he had a bum leg and couldn't do the job himself, but Vogel got trigger happy and started shooting instead of getting the information."

"A stupid hit man hires a stupider assistant."

"Looks that way."

"So the only reason I wasn't killed too was—"

"Pure luck. You ducked at the right time."

Kali felt a rush of vertigo. She'd come so close. Death had found Betty, but it had only brushed her shoulder and passed on.

"You're quiet." Bryce said.

"Counting my blessings."

"How about we take that weekend in Napa I canceled out of not so long ago."

If he hadn't canceled, she wouldn't have gone antique shopping with Margot and she might never have discovered the photograph of Faith. Taking the trip now seemed a fitting end to that chapter. And, perhaps, the beginning of a new and much more pleasant one. "I'd love to. When?"

"Half an hour?"

She laughed. "You mean, just pick up and go?"

"Right. I managed to get reservations at Auberge du Soleil for dinner and at a very private B&B nearby."

"Aren't you efficient."

"That, and a whole lot more." He paused and his voice grew softer. "I think we've finally turned the corner, Kali."

Her skin tingled as though he'd touched her at the base of the neck. "I hope so."